KT-104-241

THE PURSUIT OF WILLIAM ABBEY

CLAIRE NORTH

orbit

www.orbitbooks.net

ORBIT

First published in Great Britain in 2019 by Orbit
This paperback edition published in 2020 by Orbit

1 3 5 7 9 10 8 6 4 2

Typeset in Bembo and Melior by M Rules
Printed and bound in Great Britain by Clays Ltd, Elcograf S.p.A.

Papers used by Orbit are from well-managed forests
and other responsible sources.

Orbit
An imprint of
Little, Brown Book Group
Carmelite House
50 Victoria Embankment
London EC4Y 0DZ

An Hachette UK Company
www.hachette.co.uk

www.orbitbooks.net

Chapter 1

France, 1917

The truth-speaker was tall as a stretcher, thin as a rifle. He wore a black coat that stopped just above his knees, a tie the colour of drying blood, a black felt Derby hat and a pair of horn-rimmed spectacles on a string. He carried a brown doctor's bag in one hand, and a military-issue shoulder sack. Behind him the sky popped with cannon, the sound rolling in half a minute later like the wash of the sea. His curse can't have been too near then, because he looked me in the eye and lied.

"My name is Dr Abbey," he said. "I've been sent by HQ."

I never asked to check his papers. Matron was so relieved, she babbled.

Sister Beatrice had to move from her room. A doctor needed better quarters than a nurse. She, being senior to me and Helene, immediately claimed ours. The window was small and let in the winter air, but it was in a good position on the south side of the building and there had been no rats seen for nearly three months.

Me and Helene was pushed into a tiny, lime-washed, spider-scuttling den in the eastern corner of the house. We dragged my bed on its side through the corridors, shuffling in socks, trying to keep the scraping of metal on wood from waking the patients below. In whispers we grumbled about this new intruder on our routines, and Helene wrote a letter to her Ma saying it were all terrible and she wanted to come home, but she never sent it, and I put my head down on my pillow with resentment in my heart,

1

and slept badly, and woke for a moment frightened, and was surprised I could still be scared.

When I went down for the afternoon shift, I found Dr Abbey about his rounds, drifting from bed to bed with the same expression on his face for every patient, whether they were hopeful of recovery or waiting for death. He did not smile, did not frown, but with every man he stopped, looked into their eyes as if he were staring down the barrel of a gun, asked a few questions, nodded at a couple of replies, then moved on without a word.

In this way – cold, almost bored – he was just another typical bloody doctor. On the battlefield the surgeons only saw flesh, never the men they cut open. We were all getting good at not seeing eyes. It were the sisters who carried the bodies to the carts, stripped the beds, put the unfinished letters to family in a bag, trimmed off the corners that were stained with blood. We picked up the limbs the surgeons cut and put them in a box: an arm without a hand; a leg hanging together by a stitch of muscle at the knee. We cleaned brain off the knife and picked out bone from between the teeth of the saw, held the boys down when the ether ran low.

When I first came to the battlefield, I would listen to the cannon and think I heard the end of the world.

There was one other doctor at the house. Dr Nicolson had been sent to us at the Jardin du Pansée, six miles back from the line, after being caught inhaling ether. Matron kept the cupboards locked tight when Dr Nicolson did his rounds. The arrival of Dr Abbey at last let Nicolson indulge in his love of Indian gin, shipped to him by his mother every six weeks via a small Portuguese man who he called "cousin" and who had not a word of English. When the gin came late, he would stand vigil by the garden gate; if it came early, he might share the smallest of drams, and then look immediately regretful as we drank it down, and hide the bottles after.

If Abbey cared, it didn't show. He arrived in shadow, and in shadow he stayed, and in silence we performed our duties, numb to neither cannon or the cries of men to pull us from our thoughts.

Chapter 2

On his second night in the Jardin, Lieutenant Charlwood came down with a fever. We sisters took turns by his bed, waiting. I had been trained by the Nightingale sisters, and back in Manchester I could tie bandages, staunch bleeding, prepare saline and spoon-feed a mother and her freshly born babe; but here only God chose which man with his face burnt to a plum or what soldier with his gut ripped out might by a miracle live or die. We were powerless before pus and poison, and when the blind men came off the field, faces burst with mustard gas, blisters the size of apples popping from their skin, what could we do? The Jardin was a place for men to die, or if they did not, they would be sent back to England, no longer fit to fight.

I knew there was little I could do except pray for Charlwood as he clawed at his sheets, bloody eyes bulging, tongue pushing in and out of snapping yellow teeth as he groaned at the night. I knelt by his side and prayed, and knew I didn't believe no more, and that there weren't no God listening, but felt as how I should try. We all liked Charlwood. Like many men, he neither looked at nor spoke about his injuries, but laughed and smiled and joked that he was in a bit of a pickle, and wondered if the ladies would mind – all the usual talk of brave boys who didn't know that we had heard this bravery from a thousand other broken ones before.

That night, the truth-speaker came, no knock at the door. In socks, his black coat pulled over striped red flannel pyjamas, right arm wrapped tight across his body against the cold, left carrying an oil lamp by its curved brass handle. His dark brown hair was combed back from his face, turning up long streaks of grey from beneath the surface. His beard was trimmed and flecked with the same pallor – was he old before his time, a man in his forties marked by war? Or was he a slow ager, already into his sixties and hiding beneath hat and hair? He had eyes the colour of my grand-dad's dining table, all polished and gleaming in the light, which vanished beneath thick eyebrows when he looked down, then popped wide like an egg when he raised his head. Like all of us, he had no real meat on him, and the skin hung loose beneath his jaw, and there was nothing – not hook nose nor protruding ear – that gave him any feature that was remarkable. If the men who drew the caricatures of native peoples of the world had wanted to draw an average Englishman, they could have drawn him.

I stood when he entered the room, but he gestured me down with a finger to his lips. Putting his lamp on the nightstand by Charlwood's head, he examined his eyes, felt for his pulse, the temperature of his skin, smelt his breath and his sweat, rolled back his gown, examined the edges of the bandages around his hips, sniffed at stumps, nodded, returned the gown and pulled the blankets back up again, pushing the edges in around his torso like a parent tucking in a child.

Then he sat.

And watched.

And waited.

I didn't know what to make of this. The silence of the lonely night was a ritual for every sister who kept vigil, and we did not share it. We waited alone with the dying men; the doctors never came, and only the women watched.

Yet now he sat there, and in his silence it seemed that he was admitting the thing that the nurses all knew, and the doctors never said – that we were powerless.

The cannon were quiet that night. Sometimes they were quiet because they were out of shells, or the generals had lost interest, or there were other battles somewhere further down the writhing line from sea to mountain where the bigger guns were blasting. Sometimes they were quiet because the men were climbing into

4

the dark, crawling towards the machine guns. You never could tell, unless the wind blew right to carry the sound of the dying.

We sat by lamplight watching the soldier groaning in his bed, and neither me nor Abbey said a word, until after an hour, or perhaps two, he left as quietly as he had come, and closed the door behind him.

Chapter 3

When this war began and I were in the field hospital, I would gossip with the sisters about the latest pretty young doctor come to the tents, though Lord knows I couldn't have cared less for them. It was a ritual we performed for every young man who arrived with his bones intact and light in his eyes. We giggled like we were home in England, laughing at private jokes and fantasies, forgetting for a little time where we were.

There was none of that in the Jardin. Those of us sent to this place were just performing functions, without feigning life, without noting death. It were meant as a kind of respite. In the Jardin, Matron said, there was no struggle. There was no terror, no expectation, no story to be told. There was just the day passing, and the morning truck to deliver the living and the evening truck to take away the dead.

Once, it had been a stately home, a place where French maidens had picnicked in the summer sun while artists in berets and white smocks painted the lilies on the water. In spring the garden was a quilt of pale violet and lavender, pinks and pockets of creamy yellow. In summer the shrubs broke out into wine red and royal blue, and we would sit and watch the evening primroses open on the quietest nights, when you could imagine the war was some other place.

It was winter now, felt like it had been winter for ever.

On the next night I sat with Charlwood, waiting for him to die, Abbey came again. I was holding the soldier's right hand, squeezing it tight at the moments of the worst pain. Then Abbey took his left, and I nearly let go. There was something inappropriate about the thing, like through the injured man we were sharing an unclean, intimate touch.

We waited.

I wanted to ask questions, but they all seemed inane.

I thought I might cry, and hadn't realised how much harder it were to sit with someone else than to sit alone.

I held on to Charlwood's hand, and found that I wanted him to live, and didn't know as how I had that sort of feeling in me no more.

And after a few hours, he seemed a little quieter, and the doctor went back to bed.

On the third day, the fever broke, and on the fourth, as Abbey made his rounds, Charlwood opened his eyes and looked up into the doctor's face and said, "I know you, don't I?"

Abbey simply shook his head, and walked on.

Chapter 4

We were having dinner when Captain Fairchild died. It happened so fast; Helene ran in on the verge of tears, and though Matron insisted that a sister never run, Abbey was already out of his chair and sprinting down the hall before Helene had finished rattling her words. Fairchild was gasping, his lips turning blue, eyes rolling from side to side in search of remedy. Even Nicholson was roused at the fuss, and stood in the door watching as we tried raising him up to breathe better, Matron wheeling in the heavy gas mask and gas cylinder. But Abbey just shook his head as Matron moved to fix the mask over Fairchild's face, and the Captain saw it, and he like everyone else knew he was going to die. I don't know if that made the next three minutes in which he gasped for life easier; perhaps it did. He passed out before his heart stopped, and we laid him back down. He had been due for discharge back to England the next day.

That night, I stood in the garden beneath the great-leafed fig tree as the rains came. The cannon were a half-hearted rumble, grunting without order or meaning. The rain, when it burst, pushed all other sound away, filling the night with water on stone, water on soil, water on furry leaf, water dripping off needle and spine, on metal pipe and tapping on dirty glass. I put my hands out beneath the reach of the tree and listened to water on skin, and wondered who I would be when I went home.

I don't know how long he'd been there, or if he'd even arrived before me and I hadn't seen him in the shadows, but I heard his feet on wet leaves and thick black soil, and jumped, pulling my shawl around me to see him half caught against the light of far-off cannon and slithered moon.

"Apologies, Sister," he mumbled. "I didn't mean to intrude."

"No." A half-mutter, pulling my shawl so tight it bent my shoulders forward, stepping a little further from him, back to the house, head brushing a low-hanging leaf. "Of course."

By now, I was almost used to his strangeness. We had kept vigil over Charlwood, and he had watched as we prepared the body of Fairchild for the undertaker's cart, saying nothing. I felt no need to show him the usual deference due a doctor. Now, we were two people watching the rain.

When I spoke, therefore, I were surprised to hear myself, and even more at how clearly my voice pushed through the gloom. "Fairchild wasn't phosgene."

"No. If it was the gas, he would have been hit sooner. It was a pulmonary embolism. There was nothing to be done." Then, an afterthought, a flicker of something human through the doctor's mask: "It wasn't anyone's fault."

"It was the enemy's fault," I replied flatly. "It was the war."

We watched the rain.

His eyes were somewhere else, his voice talking to a different place. "The woman I love is alive and well. The children lived. The shadow will not come." These words sounded almost like prayer, a ritual of speech. Being spoken, he shook his head, as if working out a fuzzy notion, and declared a little louder, "Sister Ellis. You know that she is waiting for you, that she forgives you. But in its way, her forgiveness makes it harder for you to go home."

My heart is marble in my chest. My skin is stone, cleansed with rain. The cannon are thundering at the skies but haven't made a dent yet.

Abbey nodded once, satisfied with his pronouncement, and walked into the house, and didn't look back.

Chapter 5

Matilda always accepted who she was, and how she wanted to live. Her conviction, defying all other certainties, made her more beautiful. I never had that confidence, but despite it she still seemed to love me, until I ran away.

I didn't sleep that night, nearly fell asleep at dinner, and jerked back to attention terrified of Matron catching me napping. There was blood in the sergeant's piss when we pulled the bedpan away, and Charlwood cried out with pain when he tried to have a shit, and kept on apologising for not being strong, for not being better, so sorry, Sister, so sorry. He were scared of eating, because of how much it would hurt. We cut away some of the bandages where they were stained with shit.

Felt good to whisper these words under my breath when no one was looking. Piss. Shit. Nightingale nurses are Christian women with excellent values. They pray three times a day, are clean in word and deed, read the Bible to their patients and tell the men to think of their country and their wives.

I thought about writing to Matilda. Thought about sneaking into Abbey's room, going through his things, but got to his door and just kept on walking like I had somewhere else to be.

Charlwood lay in his bed and declared, "Bit of rotten luck, really. And just before the push; I feel so awful about it, awful about leaving the men."

Once, a major with very similar injuries to these had made a very similar speech, and I had blurted, "Don't you think you've given enough? Don't you think it's time to be honest?"

He had blustered something behind his great grey moustache, and muttered that at least he'd had the Boer War, and the next day hadn't met my eye, and complained that the pain was getting worse, and when we sent him home, I didn't know if I had done a terrible thing or a great good. I still don't know, and kept my mouth shut after.

"I feel so sure we've met, Dr Abbey," mused Charlwood. "I feel certain of it."

And Abbey smiled, and said nothing, and sniffed at Charlwood's bandages, and eased back the sheets to check for pus seeping between the plaster wedges at his groin, and Charlwood lay on his back and stared at the ceiling and proclaimed, fingers clawing at the sheet and smile locked like a bayonet, "Maybe in London, or at HQ perhaps? Or maybe I'm just confused, very likely, you know, very likely."

Slowly Abbey straightened up, pulled sheet and blanket back over the lieutenant's hips, looked him in the eye and said, "Given your paperwork, Lieutenant, do you think acquaintance advantageous at this time?"

I saw it then in Charlwood; like he'd seen a spider in the corner of his room. He was frozen for a moment, then gave a single, short laugh and blurted, "Ah well, you know how it is with faces!" and looked away, and held a little tighter to the sheets bunched in his fists, to stop himself scratching at the places where limbs should be.

At night, I sat on a bench of gently blooming yellow lichen and green weeds, and smelt the trenches' stink on the breeze, piss and rubber and wet khaki and smoke and acid and shit. Before the War Department started shifting gas masks – so slow, everything so slow – men wrapped socks soaked in their own urine around their noses and mouths. It made a bit of a difference, the survivors said. The only other thing to do was stand as high as they could, away from the trenches and tunnels where the gas pooled, and hope that no one shot you as you made yourself a welcoming target.

Abbey sat down next to me without a word, no socks or shoes, bare feet pressing on cold stones. The moon was fat and brilliant, drowning out the stars; a good killing moon. First time we'd seen a plane fly towards the battlefield, all the sisters had waved and screamed, before we realised it was German, not one of our own. An owl screeched, exasperated at disturbances. A sister dropped her pan in the pantry, and I hoped it were empty before it hit the floor.

Finally I said, "HQ didn't send you." He swung bare feet back and forth, a child kicking at an imaginary stream, and didn't answer. "You here for Charlwood?"

His feet kept kicking, and now his bottom lip curled in, chewing on a reply. A single nod. The kicking slowed and stopped, then he nodded again.

"Are you going to hurt him?"

He shook his head, paused, as if wondering whether that flat denial conveyed the nuance of his response, then shook his head again.

I let my head roll back to watch the moon, until I found even its light too dazzling. "I saw this lady speak once in Manchester; suffrage, socialism, freedom – all that. My da worked in the mill; Ma was a maid. She taught me to speak properly, like the Nightingale sisters, said a proper maid with a proper voice would go further than a factory girl. Got me my job, working in the house where Matilda lived. But when we ... after we realised that there was ... I had to go away. Matilda arranged for me to be a nurse, brushed my hair like I'd brushed hers and said she'd be waiting for me, that she was proud.

"I know liars: my da lied his whole life, to Ma, to his boss, to me. Matilda weren't lying, but that didn't mean I could stay. Ps and Qs. Proper manners. Our father, which art in heaven, hallowed be thy name. Matron thinks I come from a nice house, respectable. If she found out, she wouldn't say a word, because I'm good at what I do and they always need more sisters. But she wouldn't let the new girls sit with me at dinner neither. I went to join the suffragettes but they said I weren't quite what they

12

were looking for. I went to join the suffragists and they said I was clearly good with my hands so could make the bunting. Now the girls work in the munitions factories and the boys die walking in a straight line towards a machine gun cos men in a big room back home decide that's how it's gotta be. And that's it. That's me. That's my story. What's yours?"

The owl screeched and fled from the moonlight.

The cannon fired, then stopped, then fired again, as if the gunner couldn't quite work out what he was aiming at.

In the pantry, Sister Louise cursed and muttered and mopped up a stinking mess from the floor.

In the house, the men slept, or lay awake and stared at the darkness, or pretended to sleep, and fluttered their eyelids open only when the lamplight had passed by.

In the garden, Dr Abbey stretched his arms and legs, rolled his neck up to the sky, his eyes down to the earth, and began to tell me his story.

Chapter 6

I am a truth-speaker, he said, and where I go the shadow follows.

I was cursed in Natal, in 1884. I stood by as a boy was beaten to death by a mob. I was the local doctor. I did not try to heal his wounds. His mother cursed us all by truth and by blood, but the shadow took to me and we have been together since.

I was born in London at the height of Queen Victoria's reign. Then it was almost impossible to imagine that the sun could set on the Empire, or that white men might ever have to meet the consequences of their barbarism. We were the chosen people, leaders of the world, destined to carry the white man's burden.

I was nearly the youngest of seven children, and as such I was permitted to choose my profession, to a degree. I chose doctor. This was not as acceptable as banker, lawyer or politician, but at least it had a certain moral probity about it. Younger sons should be vicars, dispensing wholesome wisdom to women of middling income; a doctor struck my father as a modern interpretation of this traditional path.

I studied at University College, and was a terrible physician. Our family doctor had not studied at any college at all, but had been apprenticed to an apothecary and believed there was almost nothing in this world that, if one were male, could not be cured by brisk walking with plenty of well-fed dogs for company, or if one were female by the inhalation of scented lavender and massages to the pelvic area that if illustrated in a textbook would result in said text being banned.

The reality – of stinking corpses three days out of the ground, of intestines and the crack crack crack of breaking bones, of the shark-tooth saw, of weeping cysts and black-bursting ulcers – had me vomiting on the laboratory floor and on the verge of quitting within a week. Only fear of my father's terrible judgement kept me learning, and I was somewhat reconciled by the fact that my fellow pupils were as nauseated as I.

In time, we grew used to putrefaction, and were able to regard the corpses on our slabs and the organs beneath our scalpels as scientific exercises, to be cut, considered and cured through the brilliance of our own intellects. It was a dazzling time to be a physician, and a jubilant time to be young in a city at the centre of the world. My dearest friend Plender introduced me to alcohol, the music hall and women. Women were a revelation, which blinded me outright, and through this I was introduced to debt, which compelled me to get through my exams despite the inherent mediocrity of my character.

"Whatever we are, we are better than the alternative!" Plender would repeat, as we swung, drunk as midnight rum, through the back entrance to the morgue. "Even if we cannot cure it, we can at least cut it out!"

This was medicine's approach to most things, and Plender at least was highly skilled with the knife and saw, merrily hacking off a leg in four minutes, determined to beat Lister at his own game and get the record down to two. His patients died regularly, of course, but everyone was still hugely impressed at the speed of the thing.

I was not that talented, so to the London Hospital I was sent to offer up a regular cascade of bad news to the desperate crawling through our door. Too poor to pay for treatment, our patients would wait until their chests were distended with the black body of the tumour, or their eyes could no longer open beneath the weight of sagging, ulcerated flesh, or they could hardly breathe from the fluid in their lungs, before finally yielding to their desperation and coming to my ward. By then there was very little I could do, and what small compassion I had in me at nine a.m. was by close of business little more than a brisk: "You've come too late, now you must see to the provision of your children."

But the dying will tell their stories. Prostitutes who could not feed themselves, let alone their children, torn from the ward to another night's work not hours after birthing a child. Mangled limbs crushed on factory floors; women with faces ripped in two by flesh-gnawing sulphur. Children coughing tar from the chimney stacks; bursts of pestilence that swept through eight-to-a-room tenements faster than a man could sneeze. Faced with this, I longed to escape my patients entirely and the reality of their suffering. When I had money to spend, I spent it on bad drink with Plender and flowers for beautiful, unobtainable women, and it was my pursuit of the latter that banished me from England.

I was twenty-five years old, and wildly and inappropriately in love. Her name was Isabella, and her father was a general who owned most of Wiltshire, her mother a secret reformer who owned most of Suffolk. Consequently, it was decided that Isabella should marry a man who owned most of some other place, a destiny that had been made very clear to her almost from the moment of her birth. Who this man would be was still unclear when we met, I steeped in perfume of ammonia, she seventeen years old and determined to flirt with every man she could before her final imprisonment in marriage. When she deigned to flirt with me, I was at once smitten, and understood that our love was the single most magnificent thing that had ever blazed in scarlet. She encouraged me along with the many other suitors who brought fresh flowers and rotten poetry to her door, but it all fell apart when in a moment of madness her aunt discovered us with my hand upon Isabella's modestly garbed thigh. When I leapt to my feet with the declaration that I was ready to propose and that a doctor's life was as noble as it was poor, the older woman screamed, the younger fainted, and I found myself being packed off to Plymouth faster than you could say "eternal devotion".

"I'm being banished!" I wailed at Plender, who tutted and

said, "Do you have the money to support yourself? If you can support yourself then of course you're not being banished. Just write back to your father and say you're your own man and can woo where you will."

"I have debts! And I need to buy a ring for Isabella otherwise she'll never believe in my love!"

"Well," he mused. "That does rather muddy the waters, old thing."

Naturally, my father won, as he always did. The calling-in of my debts and subsequent penury, the best part of my income having already been spent on Isabella, settled the case. He offered me only one way out: a position, secured I knew not how, as doctor to some pestilential backwater in Natal. Take it, he said, and you will still be my son.

"Old thing, you know I'd love to help, but I just don't see it doing any good," Plender sighed, as I lamented the brutality of this cruel, harsh world on his parlour floor. "Perhaps getting away will be good for you? An opportunity? Make your fortune, strike gold, do well, then come back and sweep her off her feet, that's the ticket! Besides, I hear that since the whole Zulu thing was settled, Natal is just charming in winter!"

It was the best part of a month at sea.

Sometimes we pulled in to restock with coal from sweating, buzzing stations off the Oil Coast, and I sank into a horizon of black trees, limbs slithering into the muddy mouth of the sea like rotting claws, and heard the shrieking of the jungle, and thought of the stories I'd read of Livingstone, and the exploits of the great adventurers. Livingstone had died in the interior, too wretched to move, and was buried in Westminster Abbey; his mission of Christianity, Commerce, Civilisation was bashed into the brain of every British schoolboy with chalk and cane.

When we rounded the Cape, forcing our way past black rocks and through howling winds sent by the gods to prevent our mooring, Cape Colony was not what I expected. Not blackened swamp; neither blazing desert. Rather a warmer version of

17

English summer, a place where fruits were beginning to grow where once green-grey shrubs had clung to the mountainside; where native men wore striped suits and straw hats and said "God bless you, sir." Men about their evening repose read Engels, Dickens, Nietzsche, Eliot, Reid, Hardy, James, Gaskell and all the plethora of penny dreadfuls that were washed in, a little dog-eared, from far-flung shores. Beneath a silver sky and over an azure sea came Germans, French, Dutch, American, Spanish and Portuguese, drawn to the tip of Africa by promise of vast land, good cattle, and diamonds. No one mentioned that these lands were already occupied; true occupation meant a flag, a brick wall and a gun, not the rights of those people who'd lived there since before the time of Jesus. There were also bearded, glowering Boers, descendants of those trekkers who had first set out into the wilds when the English came, fleeing one tyranny to create their own.

In Durban, there were more peoples again. Now to the mix were added Malays, Ceylonese and Indians, brought over in their thousands to work the docks, factories and fields. They weren't kept as slaves; that would have been illegal. Merely they would not receive a penny of their pay until they had earned back the cost of their passage. On to which cost would then be added that of their rooms and food, the matter of payment never quite settled.

Nor was the condition of the Bantu peoples within Natal or the neighbouring Boer states slavery, for lo – if a white man killed a black man, beat a black child to death, assaulted a black woman or burnt their property, they would duly be taken before the court of law. There, guarded by white men, they would be judged by their white peers, their plea considered by a white judge, and there might even upon some occasion be a fine passed down, if the case was considered severe. If matters got that far.

Of course, should a black man kill a white man, it was unlikely that the wandering lawmen of the wild grasslands would have anything to say on the matter. The white men would come with rifle and rope, and before all his family they would most likely torture that same black man to death, leaving his mutilated body for crows. And if, incensed by this, his black neighbours turned against the white and drove the farmers from the land, impaling hand and head with spears hoarded in the secret places of the kraal, those bruised survivors of Boer or English stock would flee to Pretoria, Durban, Kimberley or the Cape and report on the feared uprising of the natives, and there would come marching with drum and Maxim gun all the queen's horses and all the queen's men, and the vultures would flock in from mountain and far-off withered perch to feast royally on a spread of flesh.

Thus all men were free, under God and the law.

I did not stay in Durban long, but headed inland over the forested, monkey-shaking, mist-soaked Drakensberg. You did not have to travel more than a day before the white-timbered houses, civic stone monuments and military men's brick barracks gave way to the abyss. Rivers of sluggish summer mud where the fish gasped and died beneath the endless blaze; cragged hills crowned with burnt-out kraals of men and women who had fled before Shaka's Zulus before being turned and turned again to flee before the Boers who had fled before the British, each new migration bringing more ways to kill, more blood between men.

In some places the grassland was a maze of biting spines as tall as a horse, hiding spitting black snakes, a million bugs that sucked, leeched, sapped and poisoned with their bites, great beasts and growling predators that circled the camp at night. In others it was a barren plain where the dust bit bone shards into blinking eyes, and the only company was the vultures circling overhead. In some places we passed cattle grown to huge, sagged-belly slaughter as they prowled at the river, guarded by boys with sticks and bare feet; in others the creatures of the earth were as the men that watched them, ribs mottled with grey, as if they were turning to chalk from the inside out.

By this road I came to Kimberley, which in 1884 had a

marvel I hadn't seen even in London — electric street lights, threaded down the main street like a festive dance. The rush for diamonds had brought every kind to this place. Men gestured and hollered in their jabber-tongue for a shovel and a map; wealthy potentates in stovepipe hats bickered about the route of the railway line that would connect Cape Colony to Kimberley to the world, little caring whose territory they needed to travel through for their dream of money. Redcoats eyed Boers with their rifles slung across the saddle, faces turned yellow from the kicked-up dust of their travels; Boers glared at every Bantu they passed, be they wrapped in wax band and animal cloth or dressed in the finest three-piece suit of the Cape, dapper gentlemen with scars on their faces and money in their pockets.

If Kimberley was a haven of roaring business and booming change, the town where I was to doctor was not. Baker, some thirty miles from Kimberley's bright lights, was a frontier nowhere for smugglers, miners and thieves. It had been founded not fifteen years since by a man called Baker, and was run now by himself and his three sons, who pillaged cattle from black men and white with absolute impunity, and had built a church because it was pious to pray, and a brothel next door because to err was human.

Once a month riders of the Natal Native Horse came through, but they were mostly black men of the amaNgwane, hated by Zulu and Boer alike. The back room of the church could serve as lock-up for any criminals lucky enough to survive capture, and the magistrate could pass sentence from Kimberley on local matters, or order the criminal sent to the Cape for more serious crimes, but by and large Baker policed itself, and it was policed by Baker.

The town had been built to mine for diamonds, and in fifteen years had found nothing. But men having given up everything to come scrabbled with what little they had left to remain, and Baker had been one of the few places to do well from the recent war, the locals robbing anyone who appeared at the time to be losing and selling their goods to the next most likely victor, with as little respect for national or religious loyalties as a scorpion had to a snake.

It was, in short, a den of inequity bathed in the chanting of righteous prayers. I loathed it on sight, and seeing no easy way to return at once to England and my beloved, fell head-first into corruption, apathy and damnation.

Chapter 7

I was at the brothel when they came to lynch the boy.

Alas, that night I was not partaking. Like every Englishman raised in the age of Queen Victoria, I had come to Natal with only one idea of African women in my mind – the Hottentot. Be she from Sahara desert or Congo river, from the grassland where the Masai hunted or the long-necked Xhosa of the south, I had condensed every woman in the great sweep of Africa down to a single obscene notion: enormous buttock and gigantic breast, childlike in her mind and savage in her witchcraft. I expected dolts and dullards, and for a little while was convinced that this was what I saw, for the women of Baker were very careful indeed not to catch a white man's eye, or to be seen to laugh too particularly, or weep where they might be caught showing their weakness. Such flickers of life were dangerous, for the white man's wrath might ignite at the tiniest spark, from the cheeky smile of a delighted child through to the muttered sedition of an old man too tired to feign ignorance any more.

And why?

As I am a truth-speaker, let me proclaim the hearts of men: that every white master knew there were more Bantu than Boers or Englishmen, and that should he ever permit the spark of life to grow in the soul of his black neighbour, it could destroy the privilege that the white man held so dear. So he beat the smiles from the children, and starved the men who grumbled, and lay awake at night with a gun under his bed, knowing retribution would slip through the open window in the form of a black man clothed in blood, and in his terror for crimes committed committed more crimes to keep the terror at bay.

This was Natal in 1884, where the circle of violence was too deeply burnt to be broken.

In the midst of this, I grudgingly plied my trade, oblivious to it all. Every girl in the brothel had some disease or another. It was a spawning hellhole for the pox, dysentery and a dozen diseases of the sexual organs, and every time I thought enough bedding had been burnt and enough powder administered, another convoy of travellers would sweep in from the grasslands bringing lice, crabs and plagues to undo all my efforts.

Worst were the children. Nearly nine offspring ran around the place, the palest nearly as blonde as his long-since-vanished father, scrubbing, stealing and working in the kitchen. At least two had the symptoms of diseases they had inherited from their parents, and that night I was called to tend to one boy, no more than four years old, who had come down with another bout of the fever that would see him buried in a half-sized coffin within a few months of my departure. His teeth were sharp, pointed, not growing flat and even as a normal child's might; his eyes were shot with red, and he was already remarked to be especially dull. Our science then couldn't name the congenital syphilis that would damn him, and no one would pay for the mercury to treat him, nor the exorbitant costs of fetching more from Durban; nor was I even sure that mercury could be ingested by one so young, or what the dosage might be.

All this I said, in so many words, as his anxious mother held him and refused to show weakness, to sob or express any sentiment before a white man; and when I left, I did not linger by her door to hear her cry.

I had been in Baker for five months, and knew where the boundaries lay.

There were no street lights in Baker. The town was a splat

of materials daubed together by men who weren't sure if they would remain. Some effort had been made to create what the Americans would have called Main Street, a ridiculously wide avenue of pressed yellow dust around which the general store, church, farrier and brothel lay, along with the four high houses of the four Baker men and their mistresses, thrown down like stakes in the ground to proclaim that here they had come, and here they would remain.

At first I had been frightened by the size of the sky and the depth of the darkness, a far cry from the green gaslight hues of Whitechapel and spilling yellow lamps of the midnight wards. Now I swaggered through the night towards my little room without second thought for the rustlings of the dark, knowing that Englishmen needed me, Boers had no interest in me and all black men feared me, for the shadow of the gun was at every Englishman's back.

Then there was fire.

Rounding the corner where the Knofius stable sat, lost in my own thoughts, I looked up to see torchlight and hear the braying of voices. A parade of around forty men and women approached, led by some ten initiates to whom the rest had been drawn like iron to a magnet. They barked commands and instructions, yapped noises at each other and their growing audience, as much I think to keep themselves moving as to convey anything of matter, since silence would perhaps have exposed the viciousness of their purpose.

For there, dragged between the leading men by rope and halter, was a boy. I vaguely recognised him, a Zulu child from the edge of the town whose mother kept house for the Holdstock family and whose father worked the wagons in Kimberley. Now there was blood across his face and bare skinny chest, and one arm was broken so that the white of the bone popped up through his torn and weeping flesh. This obvious rupture to his body did not stop his captors, who had tied a rope to his wrist and hauled him forward despite his groans of pain. Behind him men with sun-bleached beards nodded

24

in wise appreciation at this punishment, and women walked stately with shawls across their shoulders and backs, faces set as though to say they were too kind or Christian to wish this cruelty upon a child, but understood that justice must be done.

I, too dumb to speak or act, stood mutely on the corner of the street, the perpetual smell of manure pushed back by the smoke of torch and lamp, as the procession marched solemnly by. They moved at the stately pace of a religious parade, as though they bore the image of some saint upon their shoulders, or were lost in confessional thoughts. Only the boy staggered and swayed like a living thing, awake to his surroundings and the world, howling sometimes in pain, and sometimes falling with lip bitten and tears flooding his eyes. As the procession passed, my curiosity overwhelmed the flat stupidity of my soul, and seeing Mrs Smid at the rear of the crowd, who sometimes served as midwife to these parts, I approached.

"What's this?" I mumbled, not sure how to classify what I was seeing, not daring to give it a name. To name it made it obscene, and for me to stand by while obscenity happened was clearly impossible, for I knew myself a good man. Better to continue in a state of ignorance than challenge that self-deception.

"Boy violated the Baker girl. Caught him red-handed. Shouldn't be done, shouldn't be done."

This is the truth of Mrs Smid's heart:

Her father was Boer, her mother was French, and they married in secret when they were seventeen years old. She was born one year later, but her father was often away with the cattle. Her mother taught her that true love conquered all, and told stories of Eleanor of Aquitaine and the old court of the Sun King. But her father slept with another woman, and little by little his absences grew until he never came home. Still her mother wouldn't speak a bad word against him, would hit her children for repeating the jibes of their bullying friends. Love was everything, she said, as they begged for bread at the chapel door. Love will bring us together, when he has found himself again.

Mrs Smid married Mr Smid when she was eighteen, after he promised her a reliable but unflashy income, good Christian standards and a decent pumpkin patch. They slept in separate beds, were cordial in the morning, closest during prayers, and that was it, thank you kindly.

Sometimes she recalled that she had a housegirl by the name of Esther, who slept on a pallet by the fire; or that the men who brought in the harvest were all Zulus, who sang until they caught her listening. Sometimes she even found herself staring at the men with black wax around their heads and leopard skin at their groins and wondering what manner of place created men so ... she was not sure of the word to use here, but knew it could only be a sin, hot and soft and burning inside — and then she looked away.

This was the truth of Mrs Smid's heart. She was one of the first whose souls I knew, when the shadow came.

So went the crowd, and I followed.

I followed them to the white boab tree, where they set to tying the boy with ridiculous quantities of rope to the bulging, swollen trunk, his body smothered like a bee in a hive by the sheer weight of cordage. Above the sprout of crooked branches that crowned the tree like greasy hair, the moon was rising, nearly full, and its light beat against the torchlight as the men passed their judgement.

I saw the eldest Baker, once a Scottish sailor who had taken a liking to the shores of Africa, and two of his sons, their father's accents eroded down to something respectable in merchants' halls and bankers' clubs across the Empire. I saw the pastor exchange a few words with the youngest of this clan, who shook his head in gentle reproach, as if chiding the priest for his foolery. Then the assembled crowd stretched and thinned, forming a wide circle around the tree, and I saw the faces of black men and women, their eyes open and lips sealed, clustered together as if for warmth among the icy pools of white men, watching.

I watched too.

It would be comforting to say that I thought of intervening. That fantasies of myself as a hero, leaping between the mob and its victim, crossed my mind.

They did not.

It never even occurred to me.

I was spectator to something that seemed so natural to this place that to intervene would have been as to ask the stars to stop spinning in the sky, or to beg the waters to flow away from the sea. At no moment did it cross my mind that I was a human, watching another – a child – about to be put to death with no recourse to justice, truth or law. No, not even when his mother pushed through her friends and fell to her knees before Baker, begging sometimes in English, sometimes in broken half-Dutch, sometimes in her native tongue for the life of her boy, washing the feet of the old man with her tears – even then, I stood by as one might watch a puppy that needs to be trained, wondering at the strangeness of it all.

Was I in shock?

Was I such a good man that my whole soul froze?

These are pleasant lies that I would tell myself in later months, as I sought to find anything to excuse my complete and utter cowardice, my inhumanity.

Here is the truth of my soul: that I looked at this black child and saw only the savage, and the rule of law. Perhaps one day all men would be equal; but for now, white men knew best.

They doused him in paraffin oil.

I thought at first it was water, until the stench of it and the logic of the situation hit me.

There were no big speeches, no grand words. Her family pulled his mother back, eyeing the revolver on the hip of one of the Bakers, the rifles held in their men's arms, and without ceremony the father of the girl who was said to have been violated set the boy on fire.

In the stories of these things, we always try to make it easier than it was.

He screamed a while, a stench of burning, popping flesh, bits

27

of him dripping off in bubbles of fat, until he didn't have lips to scream through, air to inhale. It would have been enough for him to die then, but he lived, for a little while. They cut him down from the tree and let him fall to the ground. For a while people watched, and some whites returned to their houses, and some blacks shuffled in, releasing his mother from their grasp to hold her son's melted body.

He breathed.

He still breathed.

There was almost no skin left on him, but it wasn't the fire that was going to kill him. Either the pain would be too much, or the infections would turn what was left of his flesh into liquid, oozing pus. If he was lucky, his heart would go, or his lungs would be too burnt for him to inhale for very much longer. If not, it could take days.

I knew all of this, and perhaps it was the knowing that kept me standing there, staring at this scene. Perhaps I waited to see if there was anything more, if this lingering demise was also a part of this strange ritual I had witnessed. Or perhaps some part of me was still a doctor, despite myself, and when all his skin was burnt away I at last saw a child, dying.

To this day, I don't know. Truth-speakers see the truths of other people's hearts, never their own.

His mother held him, and screamed and clawed the earth, seeking with the movement of her arms beneath his shredded back some way to hold him that didn't hurt him more, something to be done. Some of the men poured cold water over him from flasks or skins; others whispered comfort to the mother, having nothing that could be said to the boy.

I prayed that he was unconscious, and that the slight fluttering of his eyes came from a mind too far gone in pain to register it any more. I prayed that he would die, and saw his chest move again, and for the very first time, closed my eyes.

When I opened them again, someone had given his mother a knife.

She turned her head from him so that the saltiness of her

tears wouldn't hurt him, and in doing so, seemed for the very first time to see me.

I do not think there was any place in her heart for hate that night. Hate comes after, when the grieving is done.

She looked at me as one might behold the wolf on the edge of the forest, its muzzle still stained with blood, and in that moment I understood that I was the animal. Civilised man with my civilised ways, had I truly not spoken? Had I not raised my voice, called out in my judicious, cultivated way for the law, for a little thought, a moment of examination? Where was my education, my learning, the gifts of ingenuity and culture that I was meant to have brought with me to the dark continent? Where was my oath to do no harm? Where was that fine young man I believed myself to be? Perhaps he had never lived. Perhaps we were all just savages, in the moonlight through the blackened boab tree.

Her brother helped her drive the point of the knife through her son's heart.

I heard ribcage crack as she twisted the blade.

She eased his body to the earth as the blood turned dust to crimson mud, and with the scarlet tips of her fingers skimmed his eyelids shut, brushed the white grin of his teeth, exposed beneath dissolved lips, pulled the knife free with a jerk that swung it high up over her head, where it paused as if it might fall again, and then she rose to her feet, and now gave me the full force of her attention.

Like one caught in the gaze of a lion, I was frozen.

She spoke isiZulu, or at least I thought she did. She did not move as she spoke, nor do I think she blinked. She did not drop the knife wet with her son's blood, or point, or howl, or catch the moonlight in her fingers. She did not laugh, or fall down in a fit, or foam at the mouth. She looked me in the eye, and with her gift she put the curse upon me, and I knew it, and could not name it, felt the cold of it crawl up from my feet to my ankles, ankles to my knees, all the way up my body as if the earth had grown fingers of icy bone that now pushed with will alone into knuckle-deep hollows of my flesh.

Then it was done, and both her stare and the ice let me go, and I realised that my whole life I had known nothing of anything, and that the only truth I had in my heart was ignorance.

And for a second, something more.

For an instant, I thought I knew myself. The limit of my soul, the shape my shadow threw on the earth, the dreams I had not yet dreamt, the fears and the stories that kept me at bay, the path of the lines on my hands and the truth of the questions in my heart I had never dared ask.

And then it passed. And like a penitent who has seen God for only a second, I was pulled back into darkness.

Men came and lifted up the boy's body, carrying it away to some place of their own. I thought, as they lifted it, it seemed like nothing. A burnt carcass of flesh and bone that flopped and jangled loose in their arms.

Then I thought something else: that as they carried the boy's body, his shadow remained still upon the earth. And as I watched, the black, half-hollowed-out imprint of darkness that the body had left behind seemed to move.

Only then, with just me, the darkness and the blood drying in the earth, did some semblance of sense come back to me, and I turned and ran.

Chapter 8

At night, alone in my bed, I dreamt the dreams of the sleeping town.

Of Mr Knofius, the stable master, who when the war broke out wanted to fight for Pretoria, but kept on inventing excuses to stay at home until it was too late and the Boers had won, and he was left without glory or pride, the man who would have, would have, would have, if only he ever had.

Of Mrs Smid, who permitted her husband to copulate with her once every two weeks until her seventh child was born, at which point she considered her duty done and informed him of this, and who dreams of the men with feathers in their hair and cowtails on their shins, two spears and a shield, marching through the sun. The black man is a terrible, terrible thing, savage in his lusts, brutal in his desires, but once she saw a Xhosa man laughing with a woman with ochre on her hands and they seemed almost human, skin brushing skin, lips sharing in secrets and desires, our father, deliver us from evil, deliver us from temptation ...

Of Esther, her housegirl, whose mother was cruel and whose father was never very interested, but who will build a house far from this place as soon as she can, and raise children who are loved, and do better than her elders did, and find that spot of earth where every footprint is sacred, somewhere beyond the river.

Of Baker Senior – spears, spears, spears, coming for him,

31

coming for him, coming in the dark, and he can neither fight nor run away.

Of Mpilo, his houseman, who was called a runt when he lived in the kraal and rejoices now in ratting on his fellow Zulu men, in the little slivers of power his position gives him, man-made god by drip-fed cruelty.

Of Fanyana, who works in the fields, and who secretly fought at Isandlwana and gutted three redcoats and a man in a funny hat; but who, when retribution came, hid in the caves and pretended he'd never held a spear in his life, and resented the world that had given him so much honour when he was young, because now that honour was lost for ever and the only way to bear the grief was to pretend it had never mattered in the first place.

Of Baker Junior, who dreams of going to England one day, and being considered a gentleman.

Of his daughter, who dreams of Langa. Langa was his name, the boy who burnt – Langa with the laughing smile. For a little while they had been children together, in the earliest days of Baker. No one had told them that she was white and he was black, and that this law surpassed all others. When she had finally come to understand this, she had at first cast him away, haughty in her new-found greatness, but he had refused to hate her. Then she had been kind to him, as you might to a mewling kitten, but he had refused to accept her scraps. Then she had been wicked and brutal, but he'd simply walked away without looking back. Then she had been lonely, and when at last they had outgrown all the childish notions that their parents told them were grown-up truths, they had been friends together again, and kissed a little, and not really got into the mood of it, and been caught with him fumbling with her bonnet.

Her father has locked her indoors now, and soon she shall be sent to a cousin in the Cape. When they took Langa away, she told him that they wouldn't hurt him, that her family were good people; kind people. They haven't yet told her what happened at the boab tree, but it won't be a surprise.

Sometimes she'll wish that she died in the fire, and then she won't, because she wasn't prepared to die then and doesn't want to die now. Sometimes she is ashamed of her own will to live, but the veld leaves little place for sentimentality of this kind.

When she gets older, she will try to bring some sort of understanding between the Bantu peoples and the whites, and will be assaulted once by a white man, once by a white woman, and eventually stabbed to death for her purse by a wandering black man too hungry to talk about the harmony of mankind.

That is her future, but for now she dreams of Langa, and the life they will live together, in another place.

Then I opened my eyes, and Langa was at the end of my bed.

He was barely perceptible against the thin dawn washing through the cracks in my wall. His face was an obscure medley of contours and depressions, washed away by flame, no colour to his eyes, nor lips, nor blood; merely shadow, shaped. His right arm was still broken, bone protruding, and when he moved it was not as if he stepped, but rather as if he were propelled forward across the earth upon a haze, left arm reaching out for me, fingers of popped bone and blistered flesh uncoiling for my eyes.

I didn't scream. Fear and the half-thought of dreaming held me prisoner, and perhaps I reasoned that if this was a nightmare, a guilt-induced fantasy, it was one I deserved. His shadow should come for me and claim its prize, and if I could do nothing for his life, at least in his death I could confess my sins to him.

So I didn't move, and his fingers closed around my face with the same frozen touch as his mother's voice in my mind, and then passed inside me, so that greyness and ice filled my sight, and then he folded into me, becoming one with my body, and the darkness consumed me whole.

When I woke again, he was gone.

*

33

Eleven days later, I received the telegram informing me of my sister's death.

She had died instantly of an unknown condition, assumed to be her heart, at the precise moment that the shadow of Langa had entered my body.

Chapter 9

Abbey stopped speaking, and for a while stared into the fire-scalded sky. The rain had died down as he spoke, and I waited, not daring to move, thinking that the slightest tremor might break this moment. Inside, my sisters were sleeping, dead as the grave. I wondered what time it was, and how long he had been talking, but decided in the same moment that it didn't matter.

At last, with a sigh and a shifting of his weight, he creaked to his feet and said, "Tea, Sister?"

I rose at once, feeling now how cold I was within my bundled shawl, and the dampness at my cuffs and feet. "Tea would be pleasant," I replied, as prim and proper as Matron might ever have wished.

We went into the house, and in the dining room I set some logs into the fireplace and a few handfuls of shattered kindling, and squatted, huffing and puffing over their infant glows as Abbey pumped water into the iron kettle and, grumbling a little, rifled through our cupboards in search of a proper brew.

"Matron hides the good stuff," I murmured, coming into the kitchen to find him sniffing jars and tins with an expression of distaste. "She hides the good tea, whisky, brandy, rubbing alcohol, and the good ink and paper. She shares them in the end, but waits until we're all so pent up that the smallest kindness will make us love her. That way she can always be a hero when things are bad, having let them get bad in the first place. You fetch the cups; I'll find the drink."

I felt both incredibly calm and strangely light as I burrowed into Matron's secret supplies. I could drink Matron dry and she'd never be able to complain; not about someone stealing goods she herself stole. As I scrambled back to the dining room, clutching my prize, I wondered why I'd never done this before.

Abbey was waiting by the fire, sitting on the floor with legs curled up beneath him, hands out to the flame. The kettle was on its rod above the blazing logs, not yet singing. Four metal mugs sat between us, one for tea, one for booze. I poured us each a finger of whisky, and, fetching a bundle of itchy cushion from the wooden bench by the door, made myself a little den of wool and fluff that I could curl into as sometimes I had with Matilda, in those days before.

I wondered how long he'd waited to tell this story, if it had brought him to the Jardin. All of us here were just waiting: to live or die, powerless. Sisters waiting for another bed, another patient, another coffin, another fond farewell. Matron waiting for it all to end, every day building another wall between herself and tomorrow, in case she woke one day and discovered that it would never end at all. Abbey watching Charlwood, a story on the tip of his tongue, unspoken.

Matilda waiting for me on the other side of the ocean.

This was the grey place where the world was suspended, lost in rain.

I waited, and he watched the fire, and for a while that was enough.

Chapter 10

I have six brothers and sisters, he said. The eldest, Carmine, died on 8 July 1884 at 11.23 p.m. She was a nurse, as you are, and I suppose the person I loved more than any other. That's why the shadow killed her, of course. Her husband saw it slither from her body at the instant of her death, drag itself up by broken arm and blistered limb. He said it lurched, feet still buried in the heart of her, and looked around their parlour in Houndsditch for a moment as if trying to orientate itself, then put its gaze to the south and shuffled out of the room, right through the wall. It was fading from his sight before it left his house. You have to have the curse, or be present at the moment of dying, to ever see the shadow clearly.

Langa. His name was Langa.

I knew none of this until the telegram came. The message was delivered by a Xhosa man in a blue uniform on a dusty horse.

> Carmine dead STOP Died suddenly 8th this
> month STOP Buried St Saviour's STOP

That was all.

Forty-three days after that, the letter from her husband arrived, outlining the further details of my sister's end, but by then I had already begun to suspect that it wasn't a random act that had killed her, but me myself, and my shadow.

*

I should tell you something of the place I grew up.

I was raised on the outskirts of London, in Highgate. I say the outskirts – when I was born, it was still a leafy hill looking down to the city, but now these things are almost indistinguishable, city from town from village from field. My father, Clifton Abbey, was a banker with aspirations to being accepted among men too rich to ever have need of common sense. My mother, Eugenia, was a hypochondriac. These were their two defining characteristics.

There was a time when my parents loved each other.

I have sat with my mother when the shadow is near, and looked her in the eye and known the truth of it. She was not sure she would love him when they married, but resolved to love him nonetheless with such a strength of passion, duty and determination that his every fault vanished before her eyes, and his nobler qualities were built up to a tower of strength. Can it therefore be said that she didn't love him, having shaped him to such a creature?

Maybe the worst that can be said is that she loved the idea of her husband, and for a while that was enough. She aspired to be a good wife, but their mutual sense of what this meant was unconducive. A good wife is quiet in company. A good wife is dutiful in the bedroom but does not enjoy sex, because for a woman to enjoy copulation is to be in some profound way unclean. A good wife manages the household so that the man need not, without complaint and without question. A good wife ensures that the children's governess is strict and honourable, and that the baby does not cry while the husband works. She has only a few female friends, who are as good as she, and no male ones whatsoever. She predicts her husband's needs, and is grateful for the financial support he provides. All these things my mother aspired to be, above and beyond all else, and for a while it worked, until being all these things and nothing else, she became lonely, disturbed and a little mad.

When her first child was born, Carmine, my father reported that she was a very beautiful baby, and that when she had a brother she would make the perfect companion for the little boy. And ten months later, my mother gave birth to Edward, and my father cried with joy – actually cried – and I would not have believed he was capable of such feelings if I had not heard my mother speak of it when the knowing was on me.

But children often die when they are young, and the next child was born stillborn, and eleven months after that my brother Andrew came along, and a year and a half after that there was Ernestine, then a child whose name was never spoken who died three days into life, then Gregory, then me, and finally my youngest sister Anne. After Anne, there was one more child born prematurely and too weak to live. But by then it was clear that both Edward and Andrew were going to grow to be strong, healthy boys, and my parents did not attempt to have children again, and my mother retreated to her rooms upstairs, her duty done.

My father, being a good husband, did not take a mistress.

My mother, being a good wife, did not complain. She did not complain of loneliness, or of the hole in her body torn by childbirth that meant she was plagued by painful, persistent urinary incontinence. She did not complain that her children were all raised by other women, or that she had nothing to say, nothing to do, no learning or occupation. Instead, she acquired an endless succession of medical complications, which she also handled without complaint. Her belly swelled hugely, then contracted in a single night. Her skin broke out in violent red spots, and then faded to sallow grey. She lost her hair, then it re-grew, curly like fresh ferns. She lost her appetite, then gorged on nothing but potatoes for almost a month. She ballooned. She shrank. Her feet became purple, humongous, then her hands, then they reverted again to normal. The doctors announced that she had a woman's hysteria. I would say that this war has given us enough men struck blind without ever bleeding, and more soldiers become cripples without a single blow being inflicted, that perhaps the time has come to alter the language of such things.

39

By the time Carmine was fifteen, she was already running much of the house, as my mother waxed and waned in her upstairs room. My father's prophecy had been made truth – my eldest sister was nurse, teacher, sometimes even maid to my brothers, charged with constantly watching over them and ensuring that they did not bump their knees or eat boiled sweets. At the end of the day she would present herself with the whole clan in my father's study and deliver a report on our well-being. Edward and Andrew are doing well with letters. Ernestine has been attending to her singing. Gregory continues to improve his handwriting. William and Anne have been diligent in their prayers.

When Edward and Andrew were shipped off to boarding school, with Gregory and me put under the more formal supervision of a tutor for most of the day – a butcher of Latin, bleeder of pious proverbs – it was naturally assumed that Carmine would marry. She had been such a dutiful child that there could be no question of her refusing a suitable match if one were found, so when she was discovered kissing Ivor, the watchmaker's boy, the shock was so great that my mother went blind for two days.

The whole business was hushed up, and Carmine sent to live with my uncle in Kettering. If anything could purge a girl of reckless ideas, it was Kettering.

Unfortunately, my uncle had a wife with some distinctly modern notions. Despite having declared sympathies for Chartists, suffragists and other agitators, no one really paid her much attention, and she was tolerated as a good Christian woman, visiting the sick, poor and needy on a regular basis and generally showing a vigour that induced in my mother one of the few scowls of hatred she ever showed in all her long years of confinement. Had my parents realised that my aunt actually went so far as to *tend* the sick and *talk* to the needy, they might have forbid Carmine from going north at all.

As it was, they didn't. They assumed my aunt's goodness was nothing more than the standard once-monthly disposing of meagre charity to the grateful unwashed. So when Carmine wrote home saying that she had been visiting the infirmary, they thought nothing of it, and were frankly astonished when she declared her intention to abandon Kettering, marriage and conventional wisdom and enrol with the Nightingale School for Nurses.

Furious letters and telegrams flew, but by the time my father realised how earnest Carmine was and got on a train to put things straight, he was too late. She was already on her way, and the mistress of the school declared in a letter written in a tiny, stiff hand that Carmine demonstrated precisely the kind of character the Nightingale sisters looked for.

My father abandoned the chase, his pride and his daughter.

Though not ostracised in the way Gregory would later be, she was rarely spoken of, almost never welcomed at family functions, and her picture was removed from the staircase wall.

I was twelve when my sister qualified as a nurse, and she was invited to the house of Florence Nightingale herself to be blessed by the lady of the lamp. My brothers were all off at boarding school, and my father had long since lost interest in his younger offspring. I was an underfoot annoyance, left in the care of governesses and tutors who cared as little for me as I did for them. I read alone, played alone, and dreamt of breaking free and exploring the world. And Carmine, my rebellious, dangerous oldest sister was my hero.

When I was finally sent to boarding school, I was informed I should regularly write to my family; any boy who didn't fulfil this ritual requirement would go without supper, or receive a few swipes of the cane for repeated offences. I naturally wished to eat and avoid pain, so would write to my father and mother, who almost never replied, or to Edward or Andrew, who absolutely never replied. As other boys received correspondence from home and I did not, I became even more isolated in my eccentric little world, and in this way and without any particular fanfare, I wrote one day to Carmine. She was, after all, family, and my teachers had no knowledge of the shame that

41

was attached to her name. It wasn't a very good letter: a general well-wishing upon her birthday, which I got wrong by several days, and a hope that she was enjoying being a nurse – something of that sort.

Four days later, what a reply I received! As warm and lively a rush of words as I had ever dreamt of, a cascade of affection and enquiry for my well-being, my hopes and my education; exhortations to look after myself and, of course, take more walks and breathe more fresh air (nursing felt much as physicians did on this topic – if walking and fresh air couldn't cure your malady, you were in considerable difficulty) – and to write regularly.

So began a correspondence. In Carmine I found all the warmth and joy I had lacked at home, and in me I think Carmine found a connection with the family that had forsaken her, however feeble it might be through the pen of a fourteen-year-old boy.

Sometimes, when I returned to London, I would sneak away to see her, and we would have tea and cake and I would feel marvellously mature and responsible, and she would tell me about nursing and her secret fiancé, who felt that more votes for men, and eventually even votes for women, was both a social necessity and an inevitability, and my head swam and my heart soared and I loved her.

I loved her, and it is testimony to her excellence that growing up did not diminish my affection, but if anything made it stronger. When boyish illusions were swept away and I began to perceive the real Carmine beneath the sisterly care, I saw that she was more herself, more whole in her heart and her stories, than anyone else I had ever known. I was a spider's web of humanity, blown and torn in the slightest of breezes, and longed to be as solid and majestic as she.

When I declared my intention to become a doctor, my father never suspected that it was Carmine's voice that had pushed me down this path, and, my older brothers having already fulfilled their purpose by entering finance, law and government,

I was given apathetic permission to follow this less than ideal career.

Carmine kept me going through my years of inadequacy and doubt at university. She had raised me where my mother had not, then carried me to manhood while my father fussed with his papers and ink.

I loved her more than I ever loved the woman I thought I had fancied and for whose affections I had been banished to Natal.

And whatever you love the most is the thing the shadow kills. That is the first lesson of the curse that was laid upon me.

Chapter 11

How does the mind begin to approach the impossible?

For the days after Langa was murdered at the boab tree, I looked upon the memory of his shadow as a tormented dream, a sign that my own conscience was at last, too late, stirred to action. I went to church and managed to pray a little. I was diligent in the care of my patients, and spoke long and earnestly with the pastor, a malarial man by the name of Kent, as to how a good man might make a difference.

He knew what I was truly asking, and where my conscience lay, but was disinclined to offer the forgiveness I desired, and instead spoke of kindness to our neighbours and Christianity towards all men. He clearly intended that I should go into the places where the black men lived and try to practise some sort of evangelism, but all I saw in my dreams were the eyes of Langa's mother upon me, and waking I would immediately find something more important to do among the cowering, barking, killing whites of the town.

Then my father's telegram came, and of course I connected Carmine's death to the moment of my dream; and at once dismissed it as self-pitying foolery. I went through sheets of paper trying to compose a reply, and in the end could only manage something as brisk as he himself had achieved.

```
Message received STOP God rest STOP
```

Nothing else I could say to the old man seemed to have any meaning.

For a while I mourned, and found that I didn't think about Isabella, the woman I had tried to love in London. I would never have compared Carmine and Isabella before; it would never have occurred to me to line up their qualities side by side, but now that Carmine was so high in my thoughts, I could not help but notice how profoundly more whole she was in my recollection than Isabella, who flitted from one thing to another, never quite pinned down to anything more than a half-fantasy of a woman I had half aspired to love.

And so the time passed.

Sometimes it passed in isolation. My own people were murderers, that much was clear even to me; yet it seemed impossible that the Bantu people might ever forgive us for our cruelties and oppression, and so I soon slipped into the habits of nearly all white men in that place, and in my shame and insecurity shunned black men.

Sometimes I found company. Whenever Kent's malarial fever brought him low, I would sit by his bedside and read him psalms until I discovered that he found them as boring as I did, at which point I'd read the newspaper, four or five days out of date but still full of salacious tittle-tattle of cattle thefts, indiscretions, rows in the Cape, fabled impis sighted, riches discovered and constant rumblings along the border.

At the brothel, I was called to a woman who had hidden her pregnancy for months beneath tight bandages, and who now was in labour weeks before she should have been. The white midwife would not come, and the sangoma was too far away to reach in haste, so as a final, depressing last resort they summoned me, and the child came out, tiny, silent, a sparrow of weight in my hands. I scrubbed and cleaned it and rubbed its chest and waved smelling salts beneath its nose and was ready to pronounce the tiny thing dead when at last it screamed. It screamed, and for the first time in I knew not how long there were tears in my eyes and I knew perfectly well that it was nothing I had done that had saved this creature's life, and it was still most likely to die, and I handed the child to his mother, who, exhausted and bleeding, was too tired to pretend that she was anything less than human, and whose world burst apart in that moment with a love supreme.

A few moments later the sangoma arrived, breathless from his summons, and at once I was bundled from the room, covered in fluids and the stink of childbirth, so that he might perform those prayers and rituals for the child's well-being that were most necessary. My eyes met the mother's for only a moment, and I thought she mouthed something at me between her tears, and I didn't know what it was, and had never learnt her name, for why should she share it with me, and why would I ever ask?

It was at this moment perhaps, standing stinking and sodden in the dark, flies lapping at the drying blood and fluids that coated my sleeves and waistcoat, that I began to think about visiting the witch doctors of the veld.

It was Thozoma, the Knofiuses' housekeeper, who set me on the path.

Every day she and her husband, Khwezi, were silent presences around the Knofius house and stables. In his starched white shirt and stiffly creased brown trousers, Khwezi was the epitome of the stern, dedicated hand, tender to his horses and iron to all others; while in her blue frock and little white apron, Thozoma cooked, scrubbed and prayed like a Christian woman of Kensington.

But at night, when the lamps were turned down, they sometimes stood together before the stars, and once a month they would leave for a day to go even Mrs Knofius wasn't sure where, and when they returned they were quieter still, and there was that which glowed within their eyes that whispered of secrets untold.

When Thozoma came down with a fever, she was put to bed and Mrs Knofius served her disgusting soups with vile mashed

46

vegetables in them, a terrible falling-off from Thozoma's own excellent cooking. When the disease worsened, and pus began to seep from her red eyes, I presented myself with my medical wisdom, and was indeed able to announce that yes, she had an eye infection, and to wash her eyes regularly with lightly salted water. This was the limit of my medical prowess: superb diagnosis, with very little in the way of remedy. Many is the doctor who takes great satisfaction in proclaiming, "Why yes, you have yellow fever and are like to die!" before turning away, incredibly pleased at their science for having diagnosed the disease, and utterly powerless before it.

When, after a week, Thozoma's condition was barely improving, her husband took her to the sangoma. I was so outraged by this that I asked the Knofiuses to keep their servant at home; but they would not interfere, save, at my insistence, to permit me to travel with them. Khwezi was dismayed, but what could he do against his master's command? Nothing that would not endanger him; nothing but agree.

The first sangoma I met that day covered Thozoma in pigments and fats, chanted and danced, drummed, burnt something that stung my eyes, and sent her home with a slap on her shoulder, and lo, when two weeks later she was recovering well, as is often the course of any disease that does not kill you, she smiled meekly and murmured, "It was the sangoma."

I blustered and flustered and said that was an outrageous suggestion, and, determined in some manner to prove the point, demanded to meet more of these quacks and vagrants to truly show how meagre their craft was next to mine. Reluctantly, ordered to it, Thozoma became my chaperone.

One woman, sitting on a reed mat with legs folded, barely interested in glancing at the mewling, diseased baby laid before her, threw a handful of bones upon the floor, poked and muttered at their alignment and finally, with a wave of her hand, dismissed the babe without having done anything more, and the family bobbed in tearful gratitude and swept their child away to whatever fate awaited it.

Another, a man with scars popping across his face, arms and hands, pranced and swung around a boy held in chains, chanting and screaming, dealing the boy such whacks across his back, buttocks and legs that I feared he'd break him. The child writhed and foamed and howled on the ground, but did not resist the treatment.

An old fellow with hair painted in white coils exclaimed briskly, "Bend over!" and before the crowd of six or seven onlookers applied an enema with the care of a riveter hammering home a bolt.

I saw men and women cut with knives on which there were poisonous and curative concoctions; an old man drink a bucket, and then another, of some stinking herbal sort, and then retch and shudder as he puked it all up again before declaring that he was better, cured!

I saw a mother crying, sobbing into the sangoma's arms as she held her and whispered that it would be all right.

I heard spells intoned in a language I didn't understand, clicks and clatters of rattling speech, and I will confess there were times when I saw the sangoma do little more than I might have done, suggesting heat for a pain, cool water for a burn, and one who popped a dislocated patella back over the knee with a single swing of a wooden club, which, though there had been some preamble about said club's sacred history, nevertheless did the job as well as any London doctor could.

"What did she say at the end?" I asked Thozoma as we rattled on the cart down the dusty road to home.

"She said to walk regularly, and breathe clean air."

I found Ndiliwisa the day she was initiated. My presence was fretfully tolerated at the ceremony as it had been at all the huts I had attended, but here more than elsewhere I found myself pressed back by a cordon of men, who, though they never threatened me, would not permit me to go too close to the dancing woman.

Tall and thin, with a round face descending to a sharp point and wide eyes framing a short nose, she had been called to heal

48

after a period of long illness in which she had experienced many convulsions and visions. These were seen as a sign of her destiny, and to refuse it was to anger the spirits; so on a spring evening in August, the stifling heat of the day beginning to blow away in the wind off the mountains, Ndiliwisa danced and drummed her way to enlightenment, bare feet pounding the baked dust, arms encased in beads of white and red, a collar of leopard skin at her throat. She lay on her back and her knees kicked at the sky, her feet tore and stretched at the ground, her fingers clawed, her eyes boggled and her tongue lolled as she had a seizure of such force and duration that, had we been in London, I would have ordered her dosed with bromine on the spot.

At last, panting, soaked in sweat, spit on her face and urine between her legs, she slowed, drew down, succumbed, head turned to one side on the dusty earth. Her wide eyes looked without seeing, spun across the assembled viewers, once, twice, closed, opened, looked again and at last fell on me.

Here they stayed, and though the whites of her eyes were so wide that surely her face must hurt with the force of it, and though her tongue still lolled loosely between her panting lips, I knew she saw me, and saw through me, and saw the truth of me.

She began to speak, a language I didn't know. As she did, people stirred uneasily, glanced at me. A few men moved a little away from me as her voice rose; a muttering began, tutting, shaking of heads. I was in danger, I knew this now, heard the threats of the Englishman at once start to my lips in their usual terror – the guns, the fire, the retribution that would fall if any harm came to me. Some thin morsel of common sense held me back, for surely this little patch of earth would burn if I vanished in it, but I would still be dead, my body dismembered to be fed to laughing hyenas or the vultures that swooped down from the mountain.

Now some people were shoving, pushing me back, and still Ndiliwisa shrieked her accusations at my face, one shaking finger rising from the earth, her body buckling up as if pulled by strings threaded through belly and hips, a puppet tortured by her maker. Someone spat at my feet; another shoved me hard enough that I lost my balance, falling onto my backside, and now scrambling back in the dust, I felt tiny beneath a wall of openly hostile, angry faces. I rolled onto my hands and knees, then ran. Englishmen didn't run from black men, from cowed children grateful for our civilisation. They only ran from cannibals and savages.

I ran, and knew in my heart that I was wrong about everything that could possibly matter.

It took me a week to muster the courage to go back.

I enlisted Thozoma as my translator, and secretly packed a gun borrowed from Mr Smid in my doctor's bag. Together we wove through the mud streets on the edge of town, open sewers down the middle and men huddled in the shadows turning to stare as we passed, bare chests and bare feet, laughter from a place where a fire burnt; a voice raised in anger; an old woman dressed in folds of endless brown cloth despite the blazing summer heat, children running by a tiny grey stream.

We found Ndiliwisa in her mother's hut, grinding some sort of reddish root in a hollow stone bowl. She glanced up as we approached, and seemed to recognise me, and wasn't surprised.

Thozoma rattled off polite greetings, respect, a hope that we didn't intrude, an offer to pay for her services.

The sangoma replied briskly, not looking up from her grinding, and a short conversation ensued between the women. Speaking her own tongue, Thozoma had nothing of the breathy softness I associated with her English. She was a matron, bartering with an intransigent who would be cowed before her. She was master of her own home, her own world. These truths were all apparent in her native voice, and vanished immediately when she slipped back to English to translate for me.

"The sangoma says she will not take your money. She says you are cursed, Dr Abbey."

"What does she mean, cursed?"

Another conversation. Now Ndiliwisa talked more, still not looking in my direction, and Thozoma nodded and occasionally cut in with another question, and I waited, the sweat running down my back and sides, aware of eyes all around and the gun in my bag.

At last, with a meek bowing of her head: "Dr Abbey, the sangoma says that you have the truth-speaker's curse on you. She says that there is a ldozl that follows you, and it will not rest until it has killed those you love."

A rush of blood in my head, a sudden swell of darkness before my eyes. I leant against the hard wall of the hut, and breathed deeply of its strange odours, of the foul herbs and roots that Ndiliwisa ground, her rhythm never breaking. The ice of it hit me as hard as if the shadow had been on top of me, as if I could see it in the corner of my eye. Thozoma watched me, and did not move to help me as I swayed, but asked softly, cautious, "Are you well, Dr Abbey?"

"How do I get rid of it? How do I get rid of the curse?"

Question: answer. Conversation, enquiry. I was an alien in a strange land, unable to speak these people's language. I was a mute, helpless child. I should not have come here.

"She says that there are some who know how to lift the curse. She says with some it is given as a blessing." A clarification from Ndiliwisa, a hasty addendum lest Thozoma miss a vital point. "But with you," she added, "it is a curse."

"If she can see it, can she get rid of it?"

More conversation. Now when Thozoma answered she would not meet my eye.

"Dr Abbey, she says that even if she could, she would not. If you are followed by the shadow of one who died, it is because you have called to the darkness. It is not her place to interfere in such things. It would not be pleasing to the spirits."

Desperation now, overwhelming all else.

51

Can she do it?

Will she do it?

I can pay, I can pay anything.

Damn you I can pay I'm a doctor I'm British I can do this you *will* do this, you must do this, are you listening to me you bitch, are you listening to me?

She was not.

She ground her herbs, and Thozoma stood quietly by and did not look me in the eye as she intoned my words, and when I bent down low to strike the witch, one hand raised, I heard Thozoma catch her breath, and Ndiliwisa did not look up at me, though my shadow hunched over her, and I knew I was a monster, and I knew I was damned.

We rode home in silence, Thozoma and I, sitting together at the front of the Knofiuses' small horse and cart.

Only once did Thozoma speak, as we drew close to the house.

"Dr Abbey," she murmured, "you should leave this place soon, before you fall in love."

I didn't ask for an explanation, and she never again looked me in the eye.

Chapter 12

He comes. He comes, he comes, he comes.

Langa always comes back to me.

He travels at an injured boy's shuffle, limping across the earth. He walks through walls, climbs a mountain at the same pace as he descends, does not slow for sea or desert.

He comes.

Once, when the years had rolled by, I returned to the Cape to try and find his mother. Her name was Sibongile, and she had borne four children and lost three, two to disease, one to the fire. I rode for weeks in a widening spiral around Kimberley, through a land torn by conflict. The British and the Boers had gone back to war, as had been inevitable, and in the camps, the starved faces of the white women and children peered out from between wire fences; while in the veld, the black men and women died without marker for their graves or counting of their blood, lost to the white men who would later write the histories. I found a woman who thought she knew Sibongile, but she lied. Then I found a man who said he was her brother, and the truth was on me and I knew he believed that of which he spoke, but he also believed he was a king, and that the moon watched him, and he had seen some sights that broke his seeing for ever, and people laughed at him and he dared not dream when he closed his eyes.

At last I found Sibongile's surviving daughter, Mbalenhle. She lived in a kraal far from the fighting, the third wife of a man who puffed himself up as great, and beat his children to prove that he was, because he was not. She was safe, and knew me at once upon my coming to her hearth, and fed me as was the correct way of things, and spoke some English, and sat knees drawn to her chest and listened patiently as I tried to explain myself.

In the town of Baker ... there was a night when a child was burnt ... his mother ... there was a thing ... a shadow ... I ... have you ... does she ... did you ... ?

I ran out of words. Saying truth is even harder than knowing it.

For a long time she was quiet, thinking about all that I had muttered. Then:

"You want to forgive. To be ... forgive. But you kill my brother. You start fire. All you. All you kill him. You make this world. Men. British. You make this. And you say it is good, because you, for you, it is good. You do well. And when I say it is bad, you say no, because you feel good. You make this world, where it is good to kill Langa. You kill him. You in making. You kill him. Then you think, maybe this thing was bad. So you come here. Ask me to tell you that you are good. To forgive. My English is not – I speak three, but English is not. I speak language was spoken here thousands years. Before you made this world. Now you come here, say, make me good again.

"Langa follows me. He follows. You know nothing of him. You do not know who he loved. You do not know why he laughed. You do not know his story. His way of walking. His way of being. You just know black woman put shadow on you, black boy follow you, black woman forgive you. We – in your story. You do not know our story. You do not hear our story of when white men came and killed my brother. You do not see. Want everything to serve you. I will not. I will not serve you. You will never know Langa. It is not him that follows you. It is shadow. Only shadow. Langa died and I do not forgive. Do not need to tell you why. Do not need you. Go away, white man. Come back when you speak my language."

54

She would say nothing more to me. I could not persuade her. Truth was, I had no right to try.

At 11.23 p.m. on 8 July 1884, the shadow of Langa was observed crawling out of the body of my sister in her home in Houndsditch, turning south and beginning its slow walk.

One hundred and fifty days later, I began to dream the dreams of my neighbours.

Three days after that, I began to know the truth of my neighbours' hearts.

Six days after that, the truth that was maddening me was a compulsion upon my lips, a desperate babble of unwished-for realities that no one wanted to hear and that drove me, like a man caught in a dream, to stagger around the town from man to woman howling the deepest secrets of their hearts.

He moves without resting, at a set speed, always towards me. These things may be plotted, understood, mapped and named.

I did not know that then, and so the shadow came again to Baker.

Here are some of the truths of the people of Baker, screamed out into the bloody setting sun.

Baker Senior was never first mate upon his vessel as he claimed, but robbed a man in port and fled for Blood River with scarlet on his skin and a gun upon his back. He has made his children into monsters who no one will ever love, but it was the only way he could think to do right by them, in this land of dust.

Thozoma does not understand why the men of her tribe do not rise up as Cetshwayo kaMpande did, standing for honour, justice and the rights of his people against a foreign plague, and thinks they all are cowards, and wishes she had been born a man.

Khwezi loves his wife even more than he loves the horses, and every time he tries to say so he gets it wrong, so he declares his affection to the beasts rather than the human, since they are so much easier to talk to.

Ndiliwisa has epilepsy, and knows that's her disease because her mother had it too, and once met a Xhosa man with the same condition who had assisted a surgeon in Cape Colony who was frequently too drunk to work, and who didn't know that his servant loved to read. And Ndiliwisa knows that in time, it will take her mind as it is taking her mother's, and that if she is not a sangoma then she is a cursed half-child, but this way she is blessed, and her mother knows secrets that are as true as the darkness itself.

Mr Smid knows that his wife looks at black men with lust in her eyes, and understands that he is small, and weak, and ugly, and hates the world without understanding how that hatred grew. Sometimes – very, very occasionally – he catches himself in acts of meaningless cruelty, and repents his habit, then forgets.

Kent fell to malaria trying to bring Jesus to the people of the Congo basin. They were perfectly polite, listened patiently, spoke French, Italian and a dozen other native tongues, and sent him on his way with a present of ripe nuts and a flagon of Plymouth rum, which they had traded with the merchants who came up the river. He had gone into the jungle looking for the savage, but the merchants had got there first, and so he found men and women dressed half in animal skins and strings of woven leaves, and half in cheap Chinese silks and French lace, American hats and English frock coats. "Thank you, thank you," they murmured. "Thank you for your Jesus. We will definitely keep it in mind."

He had not seen any signs of cannibalism, except once when a woman ate a monkey's arm, and he had come away bitterly disappointed and with a permanent itch in his right eye, which was steadily going blind.

These are the truths I screamed to anyone who dared to look at me on that hot sunset night in the town of Baker. In the end, Kent suggested they take me to Kimberley, that I was clearly sick and needed help. Baker Senior replied that I was a rabid dog and needed a bullet more than a needle, and blustered away before I could blather any more secrets to his face.

And as people wondered what to do about me – without daring to get too close for fear of the truths I might utter – there was the shadow. He shuffled down the middle of Main Street, swaying a little against the setting crimson sun. As he approached, his broken arm lifted towards me, a greeting of open fingers and upraised palm. His face was as I had seen it before, a thing of contours without colour, a form through which I could still half make out the houses and people. His lips were still melted, his hair burnt to a sizzling scalp. Langa came, as he had come before, and I wept and begged anyone, anyone at all, to say they could see him, and they could not, so in the end I climbed to my feet, and turned, and ran away.

Chapter 13

I run, and the shadow follows.

This is the way of things.

I fled Baker with just the clothes I wore and the money in my pocket. I ran without direction for a little while, into the dusty places of orange soil and faded leaves, broken here and there by patches of tiny yellow and purple flowers that cling on to water that only they can find. The boab offered no shade, and the earth peeled like onion beneath my feet. In the distance, white bones of stone pushed upwards like tumours from the flesh of the earth, and once I nearly stepped on a snake, which didn't even hiss its contempt as it slithered away into the spiky brown grass.

After an hour or two, I couldn't see Langa behind me, and stopped, hands on my knees, gasping for breath, wondering what madness had overtaken me. Here, away from men, the pounding of their truths in my heart was faded to nothing, and there was only the thin, cold wind and an afterthought of setting sun, silky greys and forest blues across the star-speckled sky. I realised that I was almost certainly lost, and thought of lions and scorpions, and was immediately a whole new flavour of afraid. I tried to retrace my steps, to turn back towards Baker, but in the starlight all I could see were different layers of darkness against the soil, a curve of black that rolled down towards a flat, infinite horizon. I laughed, and shouted, "Help!" and the world around me was far too big for the sound to make any difference at all.

In the end, I picked a direction, and walked as loudly as I

could to frighten any animals that might be lurking, thumping against the earth, kicking at scrub and thorny grass, until I came to an outcrop of stone above a thin, sluggish river. Scrambling to the top, I sat down to catch my breath, and told myself that it would be all right not to sleep, but simply to watch the stars and think about what had happened to me and how to remedy it, since I was clearly ill. A lunatic asylum wouldn't do, of course – I had seen the chains that held the insane, and had no desire to be dunked in icy baths or beaten with birch to effect my cure.

And yet, how sane I felt, now that I was away from people! Clearly my malady was so potent it had deceived me into believing that I was cured when obviously I was not; how terrible it was to be unable to trust in my own thoughts. Self-pity would wait; my condition needed diagnosis. I had witnessed a trauma, experienced some guilt, and been affected by the sun. Fresh air and hearty walks! If all else failed, that prescription would still be my salvation.

Such was my thinking, and a wild loop of conclusion and rejection, enquiry and dismissal it was, so that I could not imagine I would sleep, until, of course, I did.

I woke to the dawn light, and thought for an instant that it was still the sunset glow by which I'd fled, and I had spun, spun and spun again. A beetle was sitting upon my cheek; my neck, hands and ankles were flecked with a hundred bites from tiny flies, but other than that I seemed fairly untouched by nature, save that my whole body hurt from my uncomfortable bed. Crawling upright in a creaking of bones and groans, I looked back along the broken path I'd carved across the dusty land, and there he was, no more than a hundred yards behind, coming towards me. Langa, a bare half-shadow against the cold morning light, a thing that might be illusion, if there was any choice other than to think he was real.

He came; I ran.

*

I have witnessed sunrise in the frozen steppes of Asia: symphonies of azures and silvers, punched through with snowy whiteness as if the sun was sending sharpened heralds to announce its progress. I have watched dawn on the China Sea, the water a mirror of slippery gold that burns the sky to puffy white. I have stood on the shores of Japan and heard the temple bell; watched the shadows chased out of the canyons of North America like dogs before the wolf. But that morning in the grasslands, I ran with the shadow at my back, and the sky was the purple of an emperor's robes, shredded with blood, and the land seemed to swallow the crimson whole and bleed with the day.

Sometimes I outran him, and he vanished from my sight.

Then I would climb an outcropping of chalky grey rock, and look back, and there he was, shimmering in the morning heat, following, and I ran.

Sometimes I would stop to catch my breath, or pause by a pool of stagnant blue-green water to gulp and gasp, and when I looked up it was as if an hour had passed, and maybe it had, and there he was, and I howled like an injured cat and scrambled on.

Soon I could only walk, feet swollen in my shoes, jacket discarded, buttons undone to the midday heat. By evening, our pace was more or less the same. He shuffled his burnt-out gait, never lifting his feet, and I limped on, like two ships in the same wind; never closing, never retreating, caught just on the edge of sight.

The pain in my feet and legs, the dizzy nausea of too long walking unprotected in the sun, kept me from thinking about hunger. As the sun dipped back towards the horizon, one sensation at a time surfaced and fell within the cauldron of my soul. At this instant: my mouth was leather and surely I would die. And then at the next: my legs were stone and surely I would fall. And now: my feet were fire and surely I would never walk again. In this way, my maladies almost helped me on, for I had so little time to invest in the extremity of one before the extremity of the next distracted me. And so on we went, as the stars blossomed overhead. We walked together through the desert, as the dreamers did in Australia before the fences came, and I thought for a while I knew the names of every star and the secrets of every scuttling living thing that fled before me, and saw behind me the spreading wake of life that I had disturbed, and before me the narrow path I must still walk. And then I looked again, and saw only Langa in the pale moonlight, and he did not stop, and he did not rest, and so on we went.

I fell, and didn't get up again.

I laughed, and Langa came.

I thought that if he touched me, maybe I would die, and that wasn't so bad.

Just like Carmine had died.

Closer, closer, a little closer now.

The laughter died on pastry lips.

I got back to my feet, and scrambled a little faster, a little further, then stopped to breathe for a few seconds, then scampered, then stopped, then scampered again, like the wounded springbok runs before the lioness.

A little before dawn I heard the hyena laughing in the scrub. That gave me enough fear to run, for a while.

The boys were tending cattle when they found me. The youngest was nine, the oldest twelve. Two stayed behind, and one helped me up, too small to carry me, but giving me enough of a push by his presence that I made it to the kraal. Langa drifted behind, not half a mile away, oblivious to the rising sun.

In the woven dome, adults, watching, communicating in actions and forced, hard smiles. They gave me water, dry meat, madumbe. One went to remove my shoes, but I shook my head. If my shoes came off, I didn't know if they'd ever go back on again.

None of the children and only one of the women had ever seen a white man before. The father and his oldest son had, and didn't think us so fierce. There were nearer, more important fish to fry, for listen, listen, this was the truth of the hearts of those who tended the kraal. I babbled it constantly in a broken whisper as they pushed water between my lips, but thankfully they spoke no English and I had no words of isiZulu.

A mother looks on me in dread and wonders what others will come, if this is the beginning of the end. She fears fire and does not know who she would be if the family fled.

Another, a junior wife, married when she was twelve to this man of forty, has fixed her gaze upon the earth lest anyone see that she has caught the eye of her husband's son by another wife, a boy of her age. Run away, say his eyes, run away with me and together we shall find our own place . . .

A boy seethes with resentment that the impis of Cetshwayo no longer muster at Ulundi, and that the promises made to him in the crib of spear and shield were lies; he paints his face and arms with ochre in secret, and prays to the ancestors for a chance to prove his worth, and hopes one day his father will look on him and say something kind, and call him a man.

A brother wonders if I have any money.

His first wife still carries the soul of the child that died in her, and knows she must accept that her failure to bring life is why he has so many other women who do their duty by him, and is grateful to be allowed to remain, and wishes someone else would howl grief with her in the secret hours of the night.

A child laughs, because something strange and new and exciting and wonderful is sitting before it, a creature with burnt red skin and alien, loose hair, and in its heart is joy, and at its lips is a language not yet formed, and full of hope.

They give me food, because you need not like a stranger to know that hospitality is everything.

They give me a skin of water, and gesture no, no, keep it, because hospitality is sacred, but it is also wise to fear someone who comes from nowhere, is going nowhere in the midday sun.

They point in a direction where other white men are.

They smile.

They are eager that I am gone, but would not raise a word against me if I asked to stay, as long as I did not violate the unspoken rules of the guest.

The oldest man heard the hyenas laugh in the night. They will not hunt me during the day, his smile says, but when the sun goes down, be careful that they do not catch you limping.

I look back over my shoulder, and Langa is there, a few hundred yards out.

I try to thank them profusely between my tumbling words, and their hearts understand even if their ears do not, and I stagger on.

Chapter 14

In the dry place, where the hyenas laugh ...

I met, or thought I met, a man digging by a muddy pool.

What are you doing? I asked, although perhaps I didn't, because my voice was gone and my skin was as broken as the earth.

"Nothing," he replied.

Looking for gold, his heart said. Looking for gold in a place where there is no gold to be found.

"There is no gold," I rasped, echoing his soul, questioning, confused by the truth of it. "There is no gold."

"No. Absolutely. Why would you think that? I'm not digging for gold. I'm just digging."

He came from Lyme Regis, spent everything he had to get to the Cape. The first time he begged, he swore it would be the last, and when he stole the money to get himself to Kimberley, he knew he'd pay it back. All he needed to do was strike lucky.

He has lost everything now. His pride, his home, his money and his dreams.

The last thing that goes will be hope, and then he will lie down in this place to die. Until then, he keeps on digging, though there is no gold.

Langa followed, so I fled, and left him there, if he was ever there at all.

Someone had raised a crucifix in this place.

There was no road, no shrine, no mound of rocks.

There were no houses, people or cattle.

No pools of water, no running streams.

Only a cross, set upright in the scarlet earth.

I looked for a little while, and kept on walking.

A place where the land turned green. A few shoots of brilliance poking through beneath my feet, thickening, thickening into a carpet of grass. Springbok pecked at grey shrubs, glanced up as I approached, sauntered away, disturbed perhaps less by me than by the predators at my back.

I paused beneath the camel thorn tree, and decided that this was it.

This was where it ended.

If I died, then perhaps the shadow would leave my sisters alone.

Perhaps that was its purpose: to drive a man to this. It seemed just, all things considered.

The first Boer on his yellow-powdered horse spoke Afrikaans when he saw me, and I didn't understand.

So the second, a boy with the beginning of a man's beard, said in English, "Are you lost, traveller?"

A hundred yards behind, Langa reached for me as a mother for its child. I laughed, opened my mouth to tell them the hidden truths of their hearts, and someone caught me when I fell.

Chapter 15

I know that they put me on the back of a horse, slung like an old blanket across its rump.

I do not remember the experience, but I woke with the certain knowledge that this was what they had done.

The Boers travelled fast. Their speed on horseback was one of many ways in which they beat the British.

I woke for a little while, and blathered the truths of men's hearts.

Then I slept again.

When I woke, it was in a white room with a crucifix on the wall, and the compulsion to speak was gone.

I was in a room behind a church. The church was timber and dirt. The priest, Vinke, had come to his calling when he was eight years old. Peeping through the cracks in the wall one insect-chittering night in summer, he had caught the slightest glimpse of his mother, naked, reaching out to his father, who took her in his arms and ...

Well, there Vinke had looked away, but from that day forth the fire of the sermons in the church had beaten against his conscience, and though he had finally had sexual experiences aged twenty-six and come to reassess quite how he viewed his parents' depravity in the light of older age, that early commitment to the gospel of purity had left far too deep a mark upon him to ever be scrubbed away.

All this I knew, but felt no compulsion to say it.

"We worried we would lose you," he mused, sitting by the side of my bed. "For a while they thought you were dead."

"Where is this?"

"We are outside Bloemfontein. You are English?"

"Yes."

"I think you are lost."

I looked at this man, square face on square shoulders, square beard cut beneath square greying hair; nose like a castle buttress, hands you could lose a football in, made soft with the touch of sacred things, and I knew the truth of his heart.

And in that moment, finally, I knew I was not mad.

I was not mad.

"I need to leave," I said. "I need to keep moving, before it's too late."

"You've been very ill. You've suffered from the sun, from—"

"I have to move."

"It's not as simple as—"

"Have you spoken to the sangomas? Do you know about the magic they do?"

Vinke's lips thinned. He knows that the sangomas are charlatans and heathens. He also knows that he came with the word of Jesus, but these charlatans and heathens have, thus far, proven too much even for the Lord. He doesn't know what this means, and assumes that his failure is a result of his sin, and fears in the deepest, most secret part of his heart that it is not.

When he hesitated, I said all of this out loud, rasping out the truth of his heart as he sat in prey-frozen stillness.

The truth can be a wonderful motivator. They put me on the back of the post wagon to Durban that night, shoved between boxes of letters and freshly harvested asparagus. The driver of my vehicle was Ndebele, and partially deaf; he wouldn't mind my talking, they said.

A horse and wagon weaving through the hills of Natal does not travel significantly faster than the shadow of a boy. We stick

67

to the road; he travels in straight lines, and though he is slow, he does not rest. Plot the course that we take to Durban, and you will find him constantly adjusting his route to edge a little nearer, a little nearer.

The post, however, was a sacred sign of civilisation, and the driver pushed his horses hard, sleeping only four hours when we rested and bullying me in a mixture of Afrikaans and isiNdebele to watch the road as he slumbered for twenty minutes at a time during the day. His name was Zenzo, and in the five and a half days it took us to reach Pietermaritzburg, I came to love him. The compulsion to speak the truth faded a little at the end of the first day, but never in that time was I free of the knowledge of his heart, and as the time rolled out across the rising hills of the Drakensberg, I sat and silently communed with the essence of his soul.

By the time we crested the forest road that led down to the sea, I could feel the touch of his wife's hand in mine as she died for the stillborn child; I tasted the salt in his mouth, felt the beating of his heart when roused to anger, the laughter he secretly shared at childish things. I knew that he respected his boss, who was fair where others were merely tyrants, and loathed many of his colleagues on the old post road, who he considered vulgar, lazy and crude. He feared the railway that was gnawing one iron bar at a time from Cape Colony to Pietermaritzburg, knew that when the first train came his world would end; and hated crossing the Transvaal, where neither white nor black men would look at him, as if the pride of the Boers had infected their beaten servants too, who learnt to look on other black men as though to say "See this poverty I have? It is a better poverty than yours."

He had no interest in me. Strays often hitched a ride on his wagon, and the Boers had been eager to see me gone, paid a little extra for the service.

When I left him in Durban, I wished I spoke his language to express how grateful I was for the size of the heart that beat within him, but didn't know how to say it, so held his hand

and hoped he understood what I meant, and knew he didn't as he trotted away.

Durban gave me a little respite, a day at most; but the shadow was coming, and though I could keep my lips sealed, I could not help but see the truth of everyone I passed as I struggled my way to the docks.

Chapter 16

I had no money, no way of buying passage out of Africa. I had one set of clothes, which I had worn since I left Baker, a week's worth of travel between Bloemfontein and the sea on my face and in my fingers, no medical supplies and nothing to barter except my skills. I approached eleven captains in the port, and all but one laughed in my face.

"A medical man," mused the last. "Well, yes, sometimes they're useful."

But in his heart he was wondering what kind of debt I might be in, and whether that debt made me desperate, malleable. I thought of committing myself to him anyway, just to escape these shores before Langa came; but I could not trust his soul, so I repented and went looking for help elsewhere.

I went to government offices, and they had no time for me. They told me to go to the poorhouse or the chapel. So I went to the priest, feeling with every word that fell from my lips the urge to speak truth coming a little nearer as Langa approached, struggling to hold back the words that grew within my belly. And one man gave me broth, and another man gave me a cup of small ale, and a third suggested a place where the vagrants slept, and none could give me a way to escape my shadow.

I had no money to telegram my father for help, and wasn't sure he'd care even if I did.

I sat on the edge of the Indian Ocean and wondered if I should fill my pockets with stones and walk into it, and laughed at how sandy and warm the beach was beneath my fingers, and how you could never find good English shingle when you needed it.

In the end, I tried picking the pocket of a man dressed for a first-class voyage to a first-class destination, and failed, and was caught instantly, beaten around the ears and thrown into gaol.

I sometimes wish I had faith.

I have known what it is to believe, for a little while. A guru in India who knew without a doubt that the cycle was ending. A rabbi who felt the spirit move through him. A medium in Yangshi who cut herself so that the spirits might enter; a miner in Argentina who heard the voice of Jesus in the stones themselves. I have known revelation in the call to prayers, and felt the presence of all manner of higher powers in the dancing of the incense, but it has never been *my* truth. Never been *my* conviction. Only when the shadow is close do I know what it is to have divinity in your heart.

And also, I have sat with the mother whose child is dying from influenza, and watched the girl's lips turn blue.

Talked with lovers betrayed for a whim.

Sat with soldiers in the ruins of war, seen the places where the Communards fell in Paris, the soldiers marching forward in a stiff straight line, and known with a ringing in my heart: there is no God.

There is no God.

All these things I have known as absolutely as I know the sun will rise.

And then the shadow passes, and I know nothing any more. Conviction fades, and I'm left behind, wondering what I believe, when everyone else is gone.

In the cells in Durban, twenty to a stinking room, beaten and with the truth flowing freely now from my lips, I knew the heart of every thief, beggar, killer and broken man pushed

71

within the prison walls, and knew nothing of myself, save that I had failed.

In the night, the shadow came. It stretched out its broken arm as I screamed and clawed at stone, and one man hit me, smashed my head into the wall to keep me quiet, and that still wasn't enough, and Langa reached into my soul with blackened hands, and all was darkness.

Chapter 17

The second person the shadow killed was Huw Plender. My old university friend, who I had shared lodgings with and who had given me the gift of friendship, and the somewhat more dubious gift of a taste for strong drink and pretty women. When I had decided that I loved Isabella above all other women, he had proclaimed, "Well, better to do this while you're young, and have time to get over it."

He was my colleague, my friend, a devastatingly fast surgeon, a somewhat unethical doctor.

On 29 December 1884, he dropped dead mid-sentence on ward round in Whitechapel, and the four people who stood by swore that something black crawled from his body, a living, reaching creature that vanished into the gloom.

I never knew where his mother lived, and never found the words I would say to her, had I really tried to make amends.

Chapter 18

I came before the magistrate, who lamented at seeing a medical man brought low, and was minded to give me a second chance. Thus my sentence was only thirty days' imprisonment, and a fine, to be paid as soon as I had secured proper medical employment.

I took all this in silence. I had no more words to say. I didn't know who the shadow had killed, and wasn't to find out that it was Plender until nearly two years later. I assumed that it had killed Isabella, the woman for whom I had been flung to the far side of the world. I resolved to find some means to have myself murdered by the inmates of the prison, as soon as I was able, and thus spare the life of anyone else I loved.

Fate, however, had another hand to play.

Kalberloh was tall as a pike, broad as a barrel. Like the Boers, he had taken to wearing clothes indistinguishable from the pale dust through which he galloped, with thick skin trousers and boots up his calves, scuffed at toe and heel. He wore a pistol on his hip, a hat on his faded sandy hair, and sported a beard that starlings could have nested in. He spoke Dutch, German, English, French, Portuguese, isiZulu, isiXhosa and a smattering of Cantonese. People took him for an idiot, for when he did speak, it was slowly, each word as precise as a bullet fired into a crowd, seeking just one target. Then they listened for a while, and changed their minds.

He met me at the prison gate. No one said why I was being

released. They just picked me up, walked me to the door, pushed me into the grey dawn light and slammed the gate behind me. The dawn chorus of Durban was a shrieking, hooting affair. The morning birds, feathers of blood red and sapphire blue, emerald eyes and plumes of saffron, looked spectacular, but the noises from their throats were as ugly as a rutting fox.

Kalberloh came up to me and said, "Dr William Abbey?"

"Who are you?"

"My name is Kalberloh. I have been sent to take you to the hotel."

"What hotel? What? Sent by whom? *Who are you?*" Questions passed my lips faster than I could reason, creating a tumble of confusion.

He put one steak-slab hand on my shoulder, gently, and replied, "Would you like some breakfast?"

The hotel was by the sea, a new establishment of high white walls and ornate metal balconies. I sat in the breakfast room and was served toast and jam, apricots and figs, papaya, Indian tea and slices of cold meat, and had no idea what was going on. The place in my soul where the truth had been as the shadow came was now a deafening silence, and for a moment I almost missed my madness, the malady of certainty that had afflicted me since Baker. Kalberloh read the newspaper while I ate, then invited me to join him for a constitutional. This involved walking down the pinkish-grey sands of the beach to the warm, lapping edge of the sea, where he stripped off into a bathing suit that hooked over his shoulders and clung to his thighs, leaving a hollow U shape across his back and hairy chest, before running into the waves. I took off my socks and shoes, not knowing what else I should do, and paddled lamely on the shore as he proceeded to breaststroke up and down like a frog hunting its mate.

When he was done, he shuffled back to shore, emerging from the depths like the Ancient Mariner. Lying back in the now high, blistering sun, he crinkled his eyes in the first signs of delight I had seen, and exclaimed, "I love the sea!"

I sat awkwardly next to him, silent now, having given up on getting anything from him before he was ready to speak.

This meek quiet was perhaps the invitation he was waiting for, having broken me to his way of things through toast and exercise. He sat up a little on his elbows, and looking out over the curving, gentle ocean asked, "Have you spoken to the sangomas?"

"What? I . . . No. Yes. A couple."

"What did they say?"

Mouth hanging open, I stared at this strange man, looking, hoping for anything else from him, some sign of his intent. He just sat there, sandy, salty, waiting. I closed my mouth, looked at my bare feet, at the whitewashed summer sky, and said, "They say I'm cursed."

"Do you believe them?"

"Yes. I do."

To my surprise, he smiled, and patted me on the back. "You are absolutely correct, Dr Abbey. It is marvellous."

He sprang back to his feet as if propelled by a catapult, slung his jacket over one arm and his shoes round his neck, and gave his fiercest battle cry: "Now we drink iced beverages and celebrate!"

The next hour was a sun-soaked blur. Now we walked, now we sat beneath the pale green shade of the palm tree. Now we drank strange concoctions of crushed ice and stirred fruit that cost more than I earned in a week; now we strode on triumphantly. "Of course there have been many like you," he exclaimed brightly, the floodgates of his speech opened by invigoration. "My employers have studied numerous primitive peoples for this purpose. We think the Russians have one, and maybe the Ottoman sultan, but the rumours come, rumours go. There's definitely one in Hunan, but she keeps on moving. Of course you people keep on moving, of course. I was sent to find sangomas with the condition, thought there might be one up at Angra Pequena but then the German gunboats came and I had to turn back, frustrating! Then you! An Englishman, no less. You should have contacted us in Kimberley. We could have saved you a great difficulty."

"Who are *we*? Who are you?"

He looked up from his contemplation of iced beverages and tales half told, and smiled. "Dr Abbey," he replied, "is it not obvious? I am a spy."

I do not know the truth of Kalberloh's soul. Like most of my masters, he went to some efforts to ensure I never would. On the one hand, he is trusted by the Xhosa of the southern Cape, who call him brother, friend, and have shown him how to honour the dead, and the old drumming dances for healing and for war; and he says that they can find divinity in the stars and the wind, in the water and in the earth, and that justice spoken in quiet counsel between all men – though never the women – is wiser than our arbitrary scribbled laws.

And then again, when the Nineteen say "go find us a sangoma", out he rides into the veld, and kills any man, British, Boer or Bantu, who stands in his way without a thought, for he has a job to do and is good at doing it, and back to Cape Colony he drags the screaming sangoma with a rope around her neck, knowing what fate awaits her at the truth station, and caring not a jot. Lo, he deposits his charge; lo, he rides away; lo, he returns to the Xhosa that he calls brother, sister, lover, friend.

Of all men, I wish I had met him with the shadow at my back, and known the truth of his heart.

Instead, I tumbled into his grasp that day in Durban, too numb and dumb to think.

Chapter 19

He gave me a night to think about it.

A night was never to be long enough, and at the time I was grateful. The Nineteen are supremely skilled at making you grateful for your cages.

He paid for my hotel room, fresh new clothes, food, drink.

He had me followed, though I didn't know it then, by a Malay of questionable character, as I prowled along the shore of the ocean.

He never threatened me. He never said, "We lock you up and let the shadow come until everyone you love is dead."

He simply looked at me when I asked, "What if I say no?" and shrugged and replied, "It's your road."

Just me and my shadow, walking together. I sat by the sea as the moon rose against a southern sky, and had no idea how to find Polaris, and not a penny in my pocket, and wondered for a moment where he was now, the boy who had burnt at the boab tree. I thought of finding a sangoma, of falling at their feet and begging, begging, look how repentant I am, look how far I've come, set me free, please, set me free. I wondered if Langa was truly dead, or if some part of his soul was enslaved to his shadow, yearning to be free. The sea washed at my feet, salted the rolled-up hems of my trousers.

In the years to come, I'd find a woman who knew the secret ways of the thing, and like Mbalenhle she would shake her head at my story, and tut, and eventually say, "She that cursed you – she has my love."

She had never met Sibongile, of course. Nor did she need to. A mother's love for a child carries on unchanged, no matter how long the road is.

I tried bartering, when dawn came.

"Can I quit?"

A shrug, slow and mighty as an earthquake through shallow, dusty earth. "Whenever you feel you wish to."

"Will I be paid?"

"Of course. Generously."

"These people ... these spies you work for – who do they answer to?"

"Britain. The Empire. What is best."

"You make that sound simple."

"For them it is."

"How much do they know? About my condition, about this ... How much do they know?"

"More than you, I think."

"Is there a cure?"

Another mighty shrug. Kalberloh knew this battle was won long before I shuffled sleepless and sweating down to the breakfast table. All this talk is wasting his time; time that could be spent on a hearty constitutional, or eating beef. "Ask them."

"I'm ... I'm just a doctor. I'm not a spy."

His eyebrows rose and fell like the gates of a bridge, and I looked away, shame and sweat mixing on my skin. A little sigh; a little patience. He leant forward and patted me on the shoulder like a puppy. "What do you want, Dr Abbey? What do you want?"

"To make this right."

"Is that the same as a cure?"

I opened my mouth to blurt some obvious reply, to snap at him, to bat his hand away from my skin like a fly, to rage and bark like the white men of Baker, you dolt, you idiot, you ...

I said nothing at all, and he smiled again, leant back in his chair, folded his fingers in his lap, stared up at the ceiling and mused, "Something to think about on your way home."

I sailed for England on the next day's tide.

Chapter 20

Weeks at sea, and a man may get to a little thinking.

Somewhere off the tip of Gibraltar, I fancied I tasted the burnt truth of Langa, marching stoically towards me even as I headed home. Like a comet, his course bent towards me as if pulled by the gravity of the sun, curling across the world unerringly to find my heart.

During the first few days at sea: sickness, the universal malady of the boat from the top deck to the lowest bilges, every class of passenger united in groaning despair.

On the fourth and fifth days: pure lethargy, which only the stink of my cabin and the churning stench of the tiny wooden bathroom I shared with the compartment next door could drive me from.

On the sixth day: pacing the deck, watching the ocean, face pressed away from the sun, back of my neck burning red and raw.

On the seventh: excessive drinking, followed by another solid day of nausea.

On the ninth, my next-door neighbour, Ms Colette Maury, finally burst into my cabin through the shared bathroom door with a cry of "Are you dead?!"

For several days, she, as bored of the voyage as anyone else for whom a deck of cards held limited appeal, had entertained herself by observing her fellow passengers, and, observing me, had been struck by my pallor, melancholy and finally hermetic, if alcoholic, retreat. The combination of boredom, heat and a reasonably excitable Christian spirit had finally convinced her that I was, if not dead, then probably well on the path.

Finding me not dead, she tutted and flapped and bullied me into shoes and exclaimed, "Fresh air and—"

"A healthy walk around deck," I groaned, licking acid off my teeth. "Just what the doctor ordered."

Colette Maury was a preacher's daughter. Her father was white, her mother was black; she had inherited her mother's skin and her father's nose, but society didn't care about the details of the thing. She spoke French, Afrikaans, Greek, English and German, discoursed at great length on Darwin ("could have kept his argument more succinct") and Faraday ("apt to make significant leaps without filling in the details"), and in the Cape had been told that the best she could hope for was to be a housekeeper. In Paris she had been offered employment at a grocer's run by her aunt, keeping books and selling cabbages.

She made me walk back and forth along the second-class deck, and on finding I was a doctor demanded that I talk to her about Koch, Bernard, Virchow, Galton, Lister and Behring, before pronouncing, "Who would have thought so much could be achieved just by washing one's hands?"

In the evening, we listened to out-of-tune singing and the plink-plonk of a storm-tuned piano in the lounge, and at night we closed the door between us with a cordial "good night". The next day I took my constitutional on the deck and so did she, and I didn't bother to pretend I wasn't pleased to see her.

"I'm going to go to America," she confided as we sat beneath the stars, huddled close against the Atlantic wind. "My family doesn't know, but I'll save everything I have, then go to America and meet a man who'll marry me."

"I'm going to be a spy," I replied. "I have no idea what this means, but I couldn't see any other way. I tried. I tried to find something that was different, a way out, but there was nothing. Nothing I could see. Nothing except ... So I said yes. I think

82

I may have made a terrible mistake. I don't think I could have done anything else."

"You will be," she announced after a judicious silence, "a terrible spy."

"That's what I think."

"Who are you going to spy for?"

"The British."

"Are you a patriot?"

"I don't think so. My brothers are."

"Older brothers?"

"Yes."

"Ah – then you definitely can't be; that's how siblings work. Will you have to hurt people?"

"I don't know. Maybe. I think ... what I have seen of the Empire, all we do is hurt people. I think you can't be part of something like that without ripping something else apart."

"Why did you agree to do it?"

I closed my eyes, pressed a little closer to her. Too close, and she didn't pull away. "I'm afraid," I replied. "I thought I was someone I'm not. I thought my life was big enough to fill a world. Now all I know is that I am tiny, and the world is vast, and full of things I do not understand, and I am very, very afraid."

She was silent a long while, staring into the sea. Then she asked, curious only, "Would you marry me?"

"Would it help?" I asked.

"I am brave, and clever. You are white. In America, we could make something with that. What do you think?"

I thought, for a moment, of saying yes. I had no idea of the truth of her heart, and that was fine. I was not yet an addict to the knowing. Her conviction was the inverse of my broken, flailing soul, a lighthouse shining above raging seas. I could picture the two of us, in a house in some far-flung land: the respectable doctor and his clever, confident wife. The sky is blue, the path to our door is neat and tended, and along it, Langa comes.

He comes, even to an American dream he comes.

I squeezed her tight, pressed my cheek against her head. "It sounds like a nice idea. You will do much, much better than me."

She sighed, and a little too high and a little too easy: "I know. In time."

The next day, we walked our separate ways along the deck, and in Liverpool she paused only for a moment to turn when she reached the gangplank, and wave goodbye.

Chapter 21

I came to Liverpool at the beginning of February 1885, and was met by Mrs Nellie Parr. Five foot two, made a little less diminutive by her absurd lavender bonnet and heavy, clumping heels on brown leather shoes, she bobbed up and down by the medical officer at the arrivals shed, waving earnestly a piece of paper on which she'd written my name, hollering for my attention to the outrage of all assembled.

Weary, my legs wobbling from the strange stability of land after weeks at sea, I approached, and she, recognising my intent if not my face, at once hollered, "Dr Abbey! Dr Abbey, here, I say!" People blushed the blushes that she seemed too oblivious to shed, horrified at her lack of deportment. I, summoned like a puppy, wondered whether this was the kind of red-faced nanny who always fed the children sweeties, or who secretly whipped her charges when the parents were away, and promised another beating if they ever confessed.

"Dr Abbey, good, yes, well come quickly, do you have any more baggage than this – doesn't matter, we can get it sent on. Now, at once!"

So I returned to the country of my birth. Grey-black snow had frozen around the manure and filth of the dockers' yards, a cold I was entirely unprepared for after the blazing summer of the Cape. Red-brick chimneys belched into the sky above the tight, curling streets that ran away from the sea, and everywhere there was noise, noise, noise. Crates and iron and coal and steel, the clanker-clatter of the world's goods coming into port, the barks of the dock men, the belch of the furnace, arguments about the loading of cotton and the handling of pepper, clusters of Indian men and beaten Malays pressed to sea, curled up into the darkest places where fires burnt in low black stoves, cowering from the bitter wind; a surge of hats and caps, a thump thump thump of the piston and clang clang clang of the master's bell.

I had found the chittering of the African plains frightening when I first lay down to sleep on the road to Kimberley, but now, this! This teeth-jangling, sense-shuddering shock, the air turned to tar, every man's face and hands blackened by being, the press of people crowding into the streets, the shoving hollering of the costermongers plying their wares at the edges of the alleys that ran down to the tenements where the workers slept, five to a room, nine to a privy; I had not thought it might overwhelm me, and yet I was overwhelmed. As a man struck dumb, lifted here and there like a seed never allowed to grow to a shrub, I permitted myself to be swept along by Parr as she constantly checked a great silver fob watch and muttered, "Leaving it tight, well yes, hum ... "

Her destination, I belatedly realised, was the railway station. An expansive half-moon of glass and steel set above open pillars of yellow brick turned ashen by the city's belching, it was no less loud and even more smoky than the docks. I had only a few seconds to glance at the black-tiled spires and dirty windows of the more expansive buildings that had sprung up around it before, whoosh, I was grabbed by the arm and pulled towards a platform, and smack, the door was shut behind us as we piled into a second-class carriage, and with a high whistle and a jerk we were off, heading south, towards London.

"So," exhaled Parr, reaching into a bag the size and texture of a small sofa for a folded map that turned out to be of the world at large. "Welcome to Her Majesty's service."

My induction into the world of espionage was, to say the least, erratic.

Mrs Parr said almost nothing from Liverpool to London, unless prodded by questions, when her answers were professionally bland remarks concerning the Whigs' latest arguments on Irish Home Rule, how unimpressed she was with the recent serialisations in the *Times*, the problem with Pinkerton's and their ongoing rivalries with the officers of Scotland Yard, and how little she liked the latest trends in ladies' hats, which were, she felt, entirely over the top if mildly pleasing on a plum-faced girl of the brighter sort.

I mumbled some half-words somewhere in between the rattle, but in truth I felt now as little accustomed to my home country as I had felt in the Cape, where no self-respecting Boer would be caught dead pronouncing any sort of views on women's hats, unless perhaps to denounce them to the Devil. In the end I gave up asking, which was precisely what she wished to achieve, and for a few minutes I may even have slept.

Then it was rattling and shouting and the whistle and the station, the roaring heart of Empire, straight into a cab at Euston to a small office at the less fashionable end of Westminster. There was no plaque on the door to declare the purpose of the red-brick building into which I was propelled, and the one man who guarded a small counter within seemed more interested in warming his hands at a tiny iron stove than in checking on our identities. But up up up, up to the topmost floor, where the roof sloped in tight beneath soot-smeared tiles, where in a small office it was sign sign sign the paperwork and here, a travel allowance of some twenty pounds and a new passport that looked fairly indistinguishable from my old and which was handed over to me as if I had received the Crown Jewels.

"Keep it safe; we have such a problem with paperwork these days."

"I don't have lodgings for the night," I blathered incoherently as Parr rolled out more papers, more maps across the table between us. "My family are in Highgate, but I ... "

Here my words died, for what could I possibly say to my family? Good evening, Father, I am unexpectedly returned having gone mad in the exile to which you confined me, sorry to hear that my sister is dead, even more so that I killed her.

Mrs Parr had no time to care for this social nicety. "We will put you in the Strand tonight and you will breakfast with the colonel and the professor in the morning, and then it is to the tailor for a suit, bustle bustle bustle, yes indeed, more haste less speed!"

A night alone in a hotel off the Strand. This city is at once strange and familiar to me. The noise, the smoke, the boys sweeping horse dung from the cobbled streets, the girls selling flowers and watercress on the corners, the women selling something more. Not two streets back from my hotel window, the rookery of St Giles, black as a raven's eye, where the thieves scamper between rooms of cloth and the bodies of the dead are flung into the necropolis train without name or merit. If a medical man may know a place by its diseases, then it is cholera, tuberculosis, smallpox, dysentery and the eroded, flesh-eaten, jaw-bright smile of the matchstick girls, or the cotton man's flaking cough.

Towards the river, lights – some beginning to turn electric as the revolution came, orange filaments strung inside dirty, soot-smeared globes. Theatres, top hats, stiff canes, white shirts, and women laughing at unexpressed understandings. The diseases here are gout, syphilis, arthritis among the elderly and hysteria among the locked-up wives tended to by men who have heard of the female orgasm and know it to be a kind of plague.

I wrote a letter to Plender, my old medical friend, and didn't know that he was dead, and it would never reach him.

I started a letter to my father, and never finished it.

I started a letter Isabella, and never finished that either.

I fell asleep in my clothes, and was woken the next morning by a thirteen-year-old boy in a red flat hat who was too well trained to hold out his hand for an extra shilling for his diligence, and invited downstairs.

Colonel Ferrall met me first. He had already eaten breakfast, insisting that it was important for a man to be up by six a.m. and have taken a constitutional by seven. He was a doctor's dream patient, for before anyone could even suggest that fresh air was the solution to all the world's medical ills, he would book himself an ice bath, a hearty rubbing, and shooting in the New Forest, where he would kill more than his fair share of game and make himself by his skill highly unpopular at parties.

He was everything I could have expected or hoped for from a spymaster. Born to a military family, he had been sent to Cambridge before joining the army in time to serve in the Crimea, in China with General Gordon, in India after the mutiny, in Canada against the Fenian raids and in the Cape against the Boers, by which time his genius for calling out nonsense when he saw it had pushed him into military intelligence.

"That's all it is, really," he declaimed as I tucked into a softboiled egg and cold, salty ham. "If a thing seems too good to be true, it probably is. Two hundred buggers just waiting to be ambushed? I'll believe it when I see it. King ready to capitulate? Doesn't mean anything until the ink is dry, and even then what's that worth? Just paper; paper is cheap these days."

Among the many, many things he didn't believe in, I suspected, was me.

"Truth-speakers; they're real. Met one in China, woman in a Daoist temple. Tried to have her nabbed, shipped off to Hong Kong, but the second she saw me she knew what I was about and fled before I could get the people in. Americans had one, for a while. Indian fellow, grabbed him from the Chickasaw just before they marched the bastards out west. But they wasted him, as Americans will. Got him shot during the Civil War, dissected his brain after, couldn't see anything special about it. We think the Russians have one, maybe the Turks too. Had Kalberloh out

89

in the Cape trying to pick up someone from the sangomas, and then he telegrams saying he's found a British man, a *white* man, all shadowed up and, well, I can tell you. I can tell you."

What can he tell me?

Very little, it seems.

He has come to watch me, to judge, and to be unimpressed. Things that are too good to be true always are. Perhaps my brain will end up being dissected too. Maybe when the British cut open my skull, they'll do a better job than the Americans would.

His eyes are the green of summer algae on a still pond, his face is as long as his spaniel's. His whiskers are already going grey; he has a bald patch that he hides beneath an array of increasingly severe hats and caps. He likes to wear a high Chinese collar as a reminder of his service in far-flung places, and carries a lucky glass eye given to him by a man in Nepal who died three days later in a mudslide.

"We'll be sending you to Berlin first. Ever since Bismarck put a Prussian on the German throne, everyone's been spoiling for a fight. The French can't forgive the Germans for ransacking Paris. The Austrians can't forgive the Russians for antagonising the Serbs, the Russians can't forgive the French and the British for supporting the Turks. The Belgians think the French want the Congo, the Germans think we want Uganda, we suspect the Italians are eyeing up Abyssinia, the French hate us for putting troops into Egypt, everyone's waiting for the Sudan to explode again, and now there are German warships on the west coast of Africa. You'll have a wonderful time. Berlin is a model of fine leadership. Mrs Parr will handle the logistics of the thing. Her husband used to run Burma, you know? Just do whatever you do, and we'll see how it goes."

"Wait, I have—"

"Glad to have you on board, Dr Abbey. Follow instructions and all will be fine."

"I have questions . . . "

"Mrs Parr will answer all that; must dash!"

No sooner was the colonel gone than Mrs Parr had appeared like a rash at my side. "A tailor next, yes indeed!"

She did not have the bearing of a woman to whom you could object.

Over the following days, the rudimentaries of spycraft.

An American thief – he claimed to have quit his profession for a heady life of gambling and high society – taught me how to lift a wallet from a pocket, the quietest way to break a window or force a lock, and when drunk whispered that he knew who had stolen the portrait of the Duchess of Devonshire, and I thought perhaps he believed it too, but Langa was far behind and it was not considered of huge importance that I get to the bottom of that matter.

A Scotland Yard detective by the name of Curry taught me the landscape of rookeries, the tattoos of the dockyard gangs and the haircuts of the Liverpool bully boys. He made me practise fisticuffs in a wooden ring, and announced that I was one of the most feeble fighters he had ever seen. The next day he took me into an alley behind the station house and instead made me practise pushing my opponent's head into a brick wall, kicking men in the groin and sticking two fingers in my assailant's eyes.

"Queensberry rules are for men who can fight," he explained. "That will never be you."

Mrs Parr drilled me on languages, of which it turned out she had a remarkably broad grasp. "*Wieder!*" she barked, as I stammered through German grammar, Russian nouns, French verbs. "*Otra vez!*"

The colonel took it upon himself to teach me how to fire a revolver. It was almost the closest we came to a human connection. "Rum sort of ticket, aren't you, Abbey?" he muttered at my fumbling aim. "Not the straightest sort of wicket!"

Most people in the colonel's world, from empresses to mudlarks, could be defined by their relationship with cricket.

At the end of it all, there was Albert.

*

I met him in a tea room in St James's, head spinning and fingers stained with chemicals – those for revealing secrets, those for hiding them, a few dozen nitrates in between. He strode in, tailcoat and bowler hat, his small brown beard trimmed to a sharp point, greeted the proprietor by the door with a gloved handshake and a cry of "How is the tea today?", laughed at some unheard answer, pivoted on his heels, saw me and seemed to know me at once.

He burst across the floor with far too much energy for a man who'd earned his heady academic title, grabbed one of my hands in both of his own, shook and squeezed and exclaimed, "Such a privilege, such a fortunate privilege!" and ordered scones.

"You must forgive the colonel," he explained, hunching in over porcelain plates, crumbs clinging to his beard as his busy, wriggling fingers danced in the air. "He has no imagination, no sense of wonder or purpose. Everyone is in such a tizzy. If the Berlin Conference doesn't go well, there'll be war, the war to end all wars – pish, say I. Pish! There is such important work to be done, so much to be learnt, but I am overruled, of course. Always they overrule me."

His accent was a clipped thing that I had sometimes heard in the nurses at the hospital, women from the west who'd had the Somerset barked out of them by the Nightingale sisters; or in the men of aspiration who had frequented my father's circle, desperate to buy with words an acceptance in society that even wealth could not.

Later – much later – he would tell me that his father was Jewish, from Bavaria, and his mother had worked in a hotel in Newcastle, and they'd made a great deal of money through wise investment, and a bit more through less upright means, and sworn that their son would be accepted even if they were not. Thus, when he was born, they called him Albert, in honour of the Prince Consort, and never really let him understand what it meant to be Jewish; and sent him to a school in Surrey for the children of great men, and told him when the other boys beat him that it would toughen him up, and they were wrong.

You will not see any sign of Albert's origins in his children. One generation was enough to scrub clean all that they were.

"You must be feeling . . . well, how do I even know what you are feeling? Tell me what you're feeling, I want to know."

My mouth bobbed open and shut like a suffocating fish. In the days since I had arrived back in England, in all the lessons and drilling and secret signings of contracts and deeds, no one had stopped long enough to answer a single one of my questions, let alone ask for my sentiment on the subject. Yet now he sat before me, staring with open, curious eyes, fingers steepled, leaning so far forward that he might topple off his seat into the clotted cream at any moment.

I mumbled, "I feel . . . incredibly tired. And confused. And not a little afraid."

His smile didn't flicker. "Of course. Very sensible."

"I feel . . . that I have no idea what I've got myself into, and that the promises that were made to me in the Cape – especially concerning understanding my condition – have thus far been entirely unfulfilled."

If anything, his smile widened. He opened up his palms expansively, eyes crinkling tight, and declared, "Here I am, dear fellow. Here I am!"

"Who are you, precisely?"

"Professor Albert Wilson, of the Nineteen Committee. We are specialists in areas of security international and domestic, including some of the more unusual threats against and opportunities arising for the Empire. Government, of course, but with somewhat more flexible oversight than your normal army rot. Sometimes, to serve Parliament, it's best to keep MPs out of it. My area of expertise is, shall we say, the study of eccentric phenomena. Do you understand?"

"No. Not really."

A little huff, a little nod; he was used to this not making sense, it was nothing personal. Few things bored him as much as a paper that proved a theorem; it was disproving the world that set him whirling with imagination, fingers dancing as if he could spin a tapestry of the universe. He was a connoisseur of strange happenings, and swore blind that he had once met a man who he then immediately and entirely forgot (I could not see how he could be so convinced of this), and a woman who claimed that she knew the future because she had lived it a hundred times already. In France there was one who had gambled the love of her child on a secret game, another who moved between the mortal bodies of men like air, and one who swore that cities generated a power that the wise could manipulate to achieve miracles. Such possibilities! Such marvels! Think of the truths now held dear that such things might disprove; think of the new questions we might learn to ask!

"What of my condition?" I mumbled, not a little baffled by his spinning delight in all this. "What of the shadow?"

"We've encountered it before, of course. There are many cultures where you see its emergence. It is possible that there have been practitioners on the British Isles in the past who have understood its secrets and put the thing on people here; but they are long since dead, I fear. Our ancestors were perhaps a little too zealous in the imposition of their beliefs."

"Is there a cure?" I asked slowly, and found my hands shaking, recognised with a start all the mannerisms of every patient I had seen at the London Hospital who, knowing already that the hand of death was upon them, still gazed up at the physician for the words of comfort that could never be.

This being so, I knew Albert's answer before he gave it. The little leaning-back. The shifting of weight, the smile now that sat only on his lips, not in his eyes. Generous sympathy, a tilt of his head, the truth blanketed in words. "Not that we know of, yet."

I have done this. I have told the dying that no, right now we do not have a treatment, but perhaps in time? And I have seen in their eyes the last vestige of light go out, the last glimmer of hope, for they do not hear the caveat, only the truth that matters. There is no cure.

Langa comes, and there is no cure.

"I ... I was told ... " I stammered.

"We know a great deal."

"I was told, in London, that you knew ... "

"We know how fast your shadow moves, we know how its behaviour manifests, its effects ... "

"But not a cure."

"No. Not that."

"How am I meant to live like this? How am I meant to be alive?"

"We will help; we can keep you moving, keep you safe. There is no one better than the Nineteen."

"He doesn't stop. He doesn't sleep. He will never not find me."

"We are scientists. We study, we learn ... "

"He'll kill everyone I love." And it's my fault. "He'll kill them one at a time." And there will be a kind of justice to it.

Albert's face was kind, his words slow, gaze steady. Plender did a similar thing, when he lived: a gentle declaration of yes, now, now I will cut your leg off, yes; yes, now, now it is most likely you will die, and I will perhaps kill you, and it is needful, and I am sorry for it, and there is nothing else to be done. I knew it well, and Albert performed it as if he had been working in the hospital his whole life.

"You'll need to take trains," he murmured, "if you want to stay ahead of him. He travels slower than an old man's walk, but as you say, he never sleeps. He will never stop. If you get injured; if you are stuck in the desert; if you lose your compass – he will come. Be careful of getting caught in a Russian winter. Only take the steamer ship, never anything with rigged sails – you don't want to risk getting caught in port. If you have to climb a mountain, you will be slower than him, but if you can get down the other side, you'll outpace him in an hour. He won't change how fast he moves for snow or sea. Don't get into trouble with the law. A prison sentence will kill them for sure. What do you know about Nepal? There is a place on the summit of a mountain where there are some carvings that may be of relevance to you. If you can get to it, there are also some caves on the Yellow River I've been trying to reach for years. Please don't kill yourself. Please don't. I know you don't know me, but I would be … it would be a great shame. And I do not know what would happen to your shadow, if you die. Perhaps that will be enough to end the curse. Perhaps not. Perhaps not; the evidence is unclear. But I would urge you to run, if you can. Run, and be very, very careful who you love."

I stared at my shoes, he at the end of his long, pressed fingers. Finally I said, "If I walk away now, will you let me go?"

"I will, of course. Of course."

"And the Nineteen?"

"I cannot speak for them. I am just a scientist."

I smiled, nodded at the floor. "What should I do?"

He drew back into his chair, lips thin, unblinking. "The Nineteen will open doors. The monasteries of Nepal, the caves of China … There is no cure now, but think what we can learn."

"And all I have to do is be your spy?"

"Is that so bad? This way, you have a chance."

He held out his hand, and it took me a dumb moment to realise that I should shake it. I did, aware of my clammy palm, the strength of his grip, which held a moment longer than it should, and squeezed tight once, before it released.

The Nineteen never forced me to join.

No one beat me, imprisoned me, threatened me or my family.

There was never any other choice.

96

Chapter 22

My first assignment as a spy for Her Majesty's Government was remarkably dull.

The Berlin Conference shredded the world like an old curtain, selling the lives of millions without bothering to inform the peoples it bartered away. They said it brought peace, and to Europe it did. Of course, in Africa, it brought only the gun.

The logic of it was inescapable. Even if France had little interest in the mud mosques of Djenné, it had to plant its flag in Mali before the Belgians could. Though the British were hardly concerned with Sudan, they needed to stake a claim before the Germans, to protect Egypt. What was Morocco, save a territory at threat from the Italians? What were Madagascar, Nigeria, Guinea, Portuguese East Africa, Libya, Eritrea – why, they were all countries that another Great Power might claim if you didn't claim them first. Peace in Europe hung by a thread, no power ready to move against its neighbour for fear of losing the fight. Conquest, the butchery of the world beyond Europe's mountains, kept the peace – at least for a little while.

The peoples of these places were just a footnote, a logistical problem barely worth mentioning. Christianity was an excuse; one devoutly believed by many, but still, a nice sentiment to ease any quibbles of doubt about the massacres that would come. You understand this, I think, Sister Ellis. You understand how quickly truth can become greater than compassion. To the generals our lives are nothing more than lead men moved across a tabletop map, ten thousand, twenty thousand men picked away in a night, for a truth that matters more than their lives.

It has taken us nearly thirty years to conquer the world, and when there was nothing left to take, it sounded a starting gun whose shot echoed from Verdun to the Somme. That is the truth of it.

On the ferry from Dover, Mrs Parr spread a map of the world across the table between us. Laying a round, rosy finger down on the Alps she barked, "We think it's about here. Hard to tell, of course, lacking all the data, but it's our best guess. It will have started deviating in its course when you hit the west African coast ... " her finger traced a loose swing across the sea towards the tip of Spain, "before reverting to a northwards direction as you passed Portugal and headed for Liverpool. If our assumptions are correct, by the time you reach Berlin the shadow should be approximately twenty days behind you. That gives us ten days to settle, then ten days of productive activity. We will rendezvous with the baron in Berlin. Now: you will practise German."

"I will practise German," I intoned.

"*In German!*" Sarcasm was as the needle to the castle wall, in the world of Mrs Nellie Parr.

We arrived in Berlin just as the conference was coming to an end, to pick and gnaw at the last pieces of Europe's triumph. The city was roaring with new life and power, raised up from the squalid, typhus-swilling slum it had been just ten years ago. Now every part rattled and rumbled with growing strength: the brand-new Reichstag, the wide avenues and electric lights. Every other building was encased in scaffolding as fresh timber and stone were laid; theatres and operas were rushing to this suddenly booming heart of empire, while scientists and philosophers competed to design the most perfect city to capture the Kaiser's new model state.

Between black-stone church and whitewashed fresh new

mansion, I was dragged from engagement to engagement by Parr, constantly testing me on this new invention or that man's latest mistress or the rumours concerning his financial affairs.

Then we met the baron.

"Terrible place, Berlin!" he roared as we rattled towards yet another ambassadorial affair. "Another St Petersburg – looks very well and good but is still just a man's ego in a swamp!"

Baron Cresswood, the fourteenth of that name, was my gateway to those circles within which a mere doctor could not move. Ostensibly a roaming diplomat, whose brief from the British government changed as rapidly as his mood, he had sat in on, as he put it, "Every goddam matter of goddam importance since the goddam Chinese tried to sink the *Arrow*!"

He had witnessed Prince Gong, brother of the Qing emperor, sign the Convention of Peking, and felt damn proud to see good British ships sail into Chinese ports with casks of opium, and leave with bales of silver and silk. He had watched the Prussians march towards Paris, and fled from the pestilential Commune that followed before the mob could pluck out his beard. He had been in Alexandria when the Egyptians went mad and chose to renege on their due and needful reparations to British bankers, choosing instead rebellion and absurd independence; and had stood by as the khedive took back his throne with a council of sensible British soldiers, bankers and civil servants at his back to see that right was done. He had even been, if you believed him, in Washington the day Abraham Lincoln was shot, and while he hadn't personally witnessed that gentleman's demise, he had sat by the bedside of his injured Secretary of State, Seward, and read the newspaper to him until he was fully recovered from his wounds.

The truth, of course, was something in between. He had, through the contriving of his government and a strange fortune, indeed been at or in proximity to nearly all of these events. Even if he hadn't personally sat by Seward's bed, he had been careful to deliver letters of news and good wishes, and to enquire politely after his health, which had in his mind become much the same thing. Likewise, he hadn't seen Prince Gong from the front, but had definitely seen the plaited back of his head – or what he assumed was his head, though it might just have been some other official – and in his mind this glance had grown to absolute certainty. Absolute certainty was the baron's stock in trade. It was what made him so brilliantly qualified for his position, especially now that I was in Her Majesty's employ.

"Some sort of mystic chappie, are you?" he tutted, flicking through the briefing papers that Parr had given him and downing Portuguese port like it was lemon tea. "Yes, well, can't say I approve of such things, but if the other side will play funny games – mesmers and mediums and whatnot – I suppose we must do our part. Do you do that thing with ecotoplasm, or bend spoons?"

"No, sir."

"Well, no, probably for the best."

At my failure to manipulate cutlery with my mind, he largely lost interest. He had a job to do, and would do it, and if in the process he gained a private physician who didn't smell too bad and could carry his luggage whenever he decided he was feeling his age, all the better! "You don't mind, Abbey?" he'd tut whenever I heaved under his bear's-weight of bags. "Did something rotten to my back in Russia, pulled it I think the day they assassinated the tsar!"

The vast majority of the baron's luggage was tobacco and port; having been stranded in Singapore once during a cholera outbreak, he'd sworn never to be caught short again. For actual clothes, I rarely saw him out of the same burgundy waistcoat and slightly tattered black jacket, nor would he wear any hat apart from a silk opera hat he'd had made in Savile Row, nor any coat save a silver sable fur he'd purchased in St Petersburg and which he wore from September to April, regardless of the weather, and would not touch from May to August even if we had crossed the equator and were shivering our toes off on the southern lip of the world. If the baron had decided it was summer, summer it would be, geography be damned!

Everyone knew him; many found him amusing, especially the ageing ladies who lurked in the cafés around Unter den Linden and loved to watch men made uneasy by his casual rudeness. Many more found him an obnoxious bore, but good manners and some lingering suspicion that he might have connections he could spitefully use against those who displeased him opened every door with a cry of "Ah, Herr Baron! How ... nice."

And indeed, as promised, some ten days after I came to Berlin, I started to dream the dreams of my neighbours. Then to know the truth of men's hearts, including the baron's, for I shared his apartments by the Lustgarten.

"You have never doubted yourself at all, have you, sir?" I mused, as the truth settled upon my soul.

"Absolutely not! I was taught from infancy what it is to be right, and what it means to do right. Live your life righteously, William, it is the only happiness!"

In this way, we spied on the final days of the Berlin Conference.

I suppose some of what we gathered was useful. The questions my handlers wanted answered – the strength of the growing German navy, the ambitions of the French, the intricacies of the Austrian court, the business dealings of the Belgians – were so specific that I struggled to answer them. I could not, by simply willing it, know these things. Those truths that came to me were directly proportional to how strongly a person felt it, as thus:

A colonel of the oldest Prussian guard, who doubtless knew many a secret my government desired, stood before me as Langa approached, and at once I knew not his military stratagems, but that he loathed his wife. He *loathed* her, ye gods he loathed her, for she had discovered long ago that she could sleep with the man she truly loved (a midget! A veritable shrivelled thing, and worse, a poet! A *bad* poet!) and her colonel husband was so paralysed by shame and horror at her liberty that he did precisely nothing. He who had stood before the line of fire and risked his life to rise in an air balloon above the roaring field, who had been shot twice, once in the chest and once in a part he would rather not disclose – but which absolutely did not diminish his manly prowess! – was cowed by a woman. They never spoke of it, of course. They ate breakfast and made small talk about the weather, and she sometimes attended the parades, and they went to lectures together, a mutual interest in ornithology being one of their few shared traits. But he *knew*, and it burnt within his soul with such brightness that he had worn down two of his front teeth with silent, endless gnashing, and would soon need to be fitted with dentures.

This was the truth of his heart.

Or she, whose mother had been dead some thirty years but was still cursed every morning and every night, and held accountable for the fears, failures and bitter loneliness of the daughter who hated her as much as she hated that she had not done any better with her own child.

He who knows that he will die soon from the lump growing between his legs, and hasn't told anyone, and has left it so long now that he doubts he ever will.

She who has not asked her husband what the matter is, because she knows it will not be good, and does not think she can bear having to care.

The nearer the shadow came, the more I could deduce – more than deduce; the more the hearts of men filled my own, their sentiments drowning out my own. Did I feel hungry, or did he? Did I shake with rage, or was it the magnetic pull of another's fury? Now Langa comes, and now I know more and more, and here the baron was most useful, for with his casual rudeness he could demand, "And how are the naval plans going, Admiral?" with a wink in the corner of his eye, and as the admiral laughed and lied, I would listen to the truth in his heart, surging like the stormy sea. Damned if I knew what any of it meant for international politics, but I transcribed it all anyway, every petty lie and grandiose scheme, and Parr dispatched it to London and seemed, generally speaking, pleased.

In this way we traversed Berlin, wandering between old fountains and new monuments; taking champagne with the great, beer with the moderately empowered and coffee with the disreputable.

And every day my shadow came, and the truths of men's hearts grew that little bit louder on my lips. That man who served us tea by the Tiergarten barely glanced our way, so much did his heart blaze with a freshly felt rebuke from his master. This woman with her child wonders at her daughter growing up so fast, and wishes she had not made so many mistakes when she was young. The couple who sit opposite us laugh and flirt and secretly touch ankles beneath the table, but she has had sexual relations before and knows that he is not nearly as wonderful beneath the sheets as he thinks he is; and he is delighted that she let him take her virginity, and is relieved that she is so innocent and he so worldly, since he has nothing much more to give than his experience.

The maid who steals from work, and damn right she does, stingy bastards.

The socialist who meets with a Russian who knows someone who knows someone who is cousins with someone who helped assassinate the tsar! She doesn't believe in violence, of course, but think of it! To kill a king!

The anarchist who isn't sure what anarchy is, but saw his sister sold to a man for a mark and a lump of beef, and never saw her again, and hasn't read Engels or Marx but heard from a man in a tavern about the People's Society, fighting for the just, and thought it sounded like his kind of heroism.

The baron put extra sugar into his coffee, and remembered a time when that was a ridiculous, luxurious thing, and added another spoonful with a grin even though he didn't really enjoy the taste.

103

Langa comes, shuffling beneath the full moon across muddy plains.

"I need to leave," I told Parr, pacing round our apartment on a cold night in February. "I can feel him, I can feel him coming, ask me to lie ask me anything did I ever love Isabella I don't think so, my brothers were cruel and so was I, please, I need to go, I need to ..."

Mrs Parr watches me, arms folded, and the baron pretends to read his newspaper.

"You love the game," I snapped at her implacable crocodile stare. "You love the dance, the sweep of pieces on the board; you don't see people, only duty and success, but because you are a woman no one takes you seriously. You will never be permitted to do what a man might, you will never be treated with the respect you are due, the Nineteen never tell you their real plans; they rely on you to be ignorant. Ignorant, foolish Nellie Parr, that's what they say, as long as she knows nothing then Abbey will know nothing too, it's the perfect way to use the old woman. You know it, you hate it, but at least it is something. At least it is something. And you will show them by God how good you are at it too."

I slapped my hands over my mouth, trying to swallow back the babbled truth of her heart, but the knowing was strong on me then and I tasted blood as I bit my lip, closing my eyes against her unflinching gaze.

A moment of silence in the room, in which even the baron deigned to glance up, eyebrow raised, from his study of the newspaper. Then a rustle of fabric, a great unfolding of petticoat and tweaking of perfect cuff.

"Yes," Mrs Parr declared. "That is about the truth of it. Come, gentlemen. Let us find a train."

On the day I left Berlin, Langa could not have been more than eight hours behind.

"Well," mused the baron as I dug my nails into my skin,

swallowing down the truths that threatened to burst from my chest. "Looking a little peaky, what?"

With every mile we put between ourselves and the city, the desperate knowing, the desire to holler the truth of every man I met, receded, until at last, a little calmer, we dismounted and shuffled towards a snowy guest house, to sleep and speak without the burden of truth between us.

"Whisky, perhaps a little," was Parr's conclusion, upon cautiously asking me if I felt any especial compulsion towards honesty.

"I love my work," I grunted. "I am happy and fulfilled and always imagined that my life would come to this." Then, ashamed: "I'm sorry. For ... in Berlin, for ... "

"Never be sorry for the truth!" she barked, and that was the end of that.

At night, I wrote my reports. I wrote of generals and kings, princes and ministers who knew above all other truths that they were *right*. Man's heart is an inconsistent, flailing thing. We doubt ourselves in every moment, constantly quest for some sort of absolute meaning in which we are immortal heroes, rather than organic matter shuffling towards the grave, unremarkable, forgotten in a week. To live in a state of truth, to truly *know* the world as it is, rather than as you wish to perceive it, is frightening. Terrifying. A wonder. It is easier to believe in yourself, to spin a thousand fantastic lies and construct a palace in which you are king, than to look with eyes open and truly *see*. The bricks and mortars of our lives are built on a story in which we are right, which no cannon of truth can ever blast down. So it was that the hearts of the men who divided up the world were stripped of all confusion. They believed in their nation, whichever it might be, and that it was superior. Superior in moral fibre. In consciousness, in leadership, in good Christian judgement, in power of arms. Superior because of the character of the men who led it – men bred to lead.

No one could back down.

No one could concede of the rightness of anyone else's cause. To concede of someone else's rightness was to perhaps admit that the very heart of you, the very essence of who you were, was wrong. Not merely your doctrine, but you, yourself – wrong.

And that was impossible.

The Great War has been coming for such a long time. It was born in the hearts of our ruling men the day they were held up in the crib and told that they were blessed with a greatness that others could not share. It was nurtured when they saw their greatness challenged, and sought some way to prove their strength. Now it eats us whole. Though it does not yet eat the men who created it.

This is the truth. I pronounce it now, as a truth-speaker must. And in my own way, I helped create it.

Chapter 23

Here, the doctor stopped.

The distant cannon had snored themselves to sleep somewhere in the night, and now a lone magpie greeted the coming dawn. The fire was shivering, shimmering embers in the hearth, and when I turned my face away from the stove, my breath puffed and huffed in the air.

"Enough for now," he exclaimed briskly, lurching to his feet. "Matron will want us both in a few hours. Enough."

I wanted to argue with him, to tell him to sit back down and tell his damn story; but almost immediately I opened my mouth, I realised how tired I was.

I tiptoed into my room, and Helene stirred when I came in, but didn't wake. I must have been asleep the moment my head touched the hard pillow, but it wasn't two seconds later that Helene was shaking me awake, ordering me to get dressed quickly, quickly, before Matron realised we were late!

Habit got me into my hat and dress, smoothed down my apron, buckled my shoes. Habit kept me quiet at breakfast, and quiet as I went about the wards. Once I passed Abbey in a corridor, but he showed no sign of even seeing me. I wondered how close his shadow was now. If he was to be believed, was the need to speak truth coming upon him? What would he do if Langa came and he could not keep silent? Would he point at Matron and denounce her for the hidden secrets of her heart? Would he call me a coward?

Immediately after supper, when usually we had some few

hours to ourselves to write and pray, I went straight to nap, ordering Helene to wake me on the stroke of nine.

"That's ridiculous!" she exclaimed. "Just sleep!"

"At nine!" I commanded, and she grunted and woke me at ten past without apology. For a moment I wondered what the truth of her heart was, what she made of this place, this endless war, and our odd, forced friendship. I were almost tempted to ask Abbey, but stopped myself. Even if he told the truth, what would I do? Truth wouldn't make our sharing a room above dying men easier.

This time, we met in the dining room a little after ten without saying this was what we would do. If he was a truth-speaker, he should simply know. I put fresh logs on the fire and a kettle to brew, and like the steam from the spout were a captain's whistle, he was there.

Matron had moved her whisky bottle without saying a word about its sudden decrease, so we made do with weaker stuff. Folding himself by the flames, Abbey muttered, "I really enjoy Wagner. I never betrayed my friends. Saira forgave me."

Did the words come a little harder tonight? Maybe. Maybe I just imagined it. The important thing, I decided, was that William Abbey could still lie.

At last he said, "There were others, of course. Other truth-speakers. There had to be, for the Nineteen Committee to know so much about them. Kalberloh had hunted them for years. At the time, I imagined that they'd never caught anyone, but of course ... I imagined a great deal then, and my masters were always very careful to have Parr handle me. That way I would only ever know the truth in her heart, and never the secrets that they kept from her. I never considered how deep the deceptions went."

Chapter 24

Without family, he said, it can be hard to stop and think.

I had been swept off my feet from the Cape, flung up the African coast to Liverpool without really knowing what I was doing. By the time I realised just what a bargain I'd made, the papers were signed and I was in Mrs Parr's care. There was no time to stop or make demands. There was simply the job that had to be done, and then the next job, and the job after that, so that very quickly the absurdity of the situation, the shock of suddenly being a spy where not six months ago I had been a doctor, became purely habit. I didn't ask questions. The Nineteen were relying on that too.

We travelled east, the baron, Parr and I. Our trick was to always travel just fast enough that the shadow could never catch me, but never too fast that I lost my value. So we went from Berlin to Prague, visited all the great men of Bohemia, and as soon as the shadow was a little too close for comfort, we hopped onto the next train south, to Vienna. There we repeated our trick of wait – visit – flee. Vienna, Budapest, Istanbul, then around the Black Sea, Moscow, St Petersburg, Krakow, back to Berlin. I became quite the connoisseur of the railways. Russian trains were either calamitous dives of appalling squalor and delay, which several times risked my sanity as Langa shuffled towards our paralysed engine; or luxurious machines with a samovar and two porters to every coach who scrambled up and down to fulfil your every need. Turkish trains, such as they were, were built by the French from their half-used rolling stock, while the trains in America were great roaring beasts that stopped for neither snow, sand nor buffalo.

Sometimes the necessities of geography put us under greater pressures. Visiting the shah in Persia could only be accomplished by laborious journeys on dusty roads. Under such circumstances I would not stay more than a few days in one place, dreading my shadow's approach, and Parr never forced me to remain in a town where a speedy exit might prove difficult.

In this way our strange little band travelled. The baron who was not sick, the woman in a great lavender bonnet who knew all things, myself, and my shadow. Always my shadow. They indulged me sometimes, of course. A man drinking black sludge coffee in Samarkand hummed and hawed and tugged his beard and finally said no, no, he had never heard of my curse, though he was an expert in such things. A naked fellow surrounded by shaven-headed brides in India pronounced on a great many things that were sometimes true, frequently unintelligible, and never once glimmered towards my case. A woman in Egypt took one look at me and ran away, and she probably knew more than all of them about my case; but she ran fast, and I couldn't catch her in the black alleys of the city.

These things take time, Albert explained, his letters tucked into diplomatic bags and padded with rumours of another mystic to investigate, another mystery to explore. *How do you feel about a trip to Sinai?*

I felt pretty depressed about a trip to Sinai, but if there were answers to be found among its wandering peoples or in the tumbled towers where once the hermits waited for God, into Sinai I would go – and out I would emerge three weeks later, dusty, tired and none the wiser.

Maybe not Sinai, replied Albert to my despairing missives. *Maybe my sources meant the Sahara.*

Soon I had travelled half the globe, and was ensnared in this ritual, too drained by travel and truth to question it, when in 1887 we were unexpectedly summoned home.

*

Her name was Margot Halloran, and she never really knew who she loved.

We met in Dublin, in the rain. Ireland was a mess of Britain's making. In the north, the Unionists celebrated Queen and Church; in the south, the Catholics cried conspiracy, mayhem, rebellion. Every time Westminster failed to pass another Home Rule Bill put another stick of dynamite under the foundations of the state. Yet for all that the fires were simmering, Dublin felt as drab a place as any I had seen. Away from the tumble and belch of the port, its wide streets were illustrated by brick terraces attended by horse and carriage, butler and maid. Its buildings of state, from the pillared portico of Trinity College to the state rooms of the castle, were well appointed, without pomp or frippery, its theatres were polite, its music halls no more or no less rowdy than any in London. The churches rang with song, and though there were the usual winds of alleys and factory paths down which respectable men might not go, what rebellion was brewing felt still a thing of cigars and sherry, not blood and brimstone.

In Trinity College, I listened to a man thunder against admitting Catholics to the classrooms, but no one really cared for his speech, and most of the Catholics present thought it was a mite old-fashioned.

In the pubs clinging to the sluggish, stinking waters of the Liffey, men grumbled at the tyranny of the British and the failures of their parties; but their mouths were washed with ale and their stomachs yearned for bread, and their hearts beat out a drumbeat not of flaming revolution, but of better wages and the luxuries they saw their neighbours had, which if they could not get by damned hard working on the docks must surely be an injustice that society and law must settle.

Langa was then some seven days behind. The truth was not a deep, burning secret of the soul, but rather the pedestrian realities of day-to-day. I did my usual rounds, sometimes with the baron, sometimes without. A Fenian said to have taken a shot at Gladstone's cousin was beaten in Dublin Castle, his mouth too swollen to speak a confession, and in his heart he was proud that he would die without talking, and hoped his family would know and no longer think he was useless and needed to get a job. He was terrified of the rope, and prayed that he would be shot. He had not, in fact, pulled the trigger, but considered it good to die for Ireland.

"Let him go," I said. "And pay for the infirmary."

A missionary fresh from Africa was said to have slaughtered, or permitted to die, or in some other way enacted barbaric acts upon his native servants as he wandered along the Niger delta, and this was a source of some embarrassment. We shared tea in an establishment hung heavy with the stench of cigars, curtains gummy and yellow, windows clouded from the puffing habits of the clientele, and he told me with fire in his eyes of Jesus and salvation, of a new faith born in the heart of the continent, and of the mouth of hell. He had raped one black woman who did not speak his language but who he thought had something of the Jezebel about her, and afterwards given her his Bible that she might find peace, though she did not read. Her family told her to go with him, being no longer worth keeping, and he found her presence awkward for a while, until at last he managed to sell her to a man from Angola, and that settled that.

It had all been terribly educational, and he was humbled by the experience, and had for sure come closer to Jesus. He had not learned the woman's name.

He was also oozing a thin yellow discharge laced with blood from his penis, and sometimes the head of a living white worm appeared from the bottom of his left foot, but no matter how many times he pulled, sliced, burnt or cut at it, still it would poke its head out of his ravaged limb, as he wasted thinner and thinner away.

I reported his crimes to my employers, who judged that it was fitter that he die a hero than become even more of an embarrassment, and lo, he was dead three months later and the mourners lined the streets for him.

And then there was Margot.

We met in the house of an Irish Conservative by the name of Hutton, whose cosy position as undisputed master of local parliamentary politics had been grievously disturbed by the rise of Parnell and the Irish Home Rulers, and who had found safety in an alliance with racketeers who beat heads in his name, and with his blessing. Those beaten heads then beat back, and the beaters beat harder, and so it went on, spinning towards destruction. That was all very fine and well; the money he was embezzling from the exchequer was less so.

In the hall of his house there were dried flowers in white bowls to smother the stink of the coal-soaked, rain-slithered city outside. Women laid aside fur mufflers and extravagant blue capes to reveal beneath demure high-collared white necks; tittered in corners to discuss terrible secrets in the politest of ways. Portuguese wine, American tobacco, a man from Scotland who had once shot a bear; another from Cornwall whose father had taken eleven years to die, and he had resented every minute of it. Two journalists, three soldiers, four lawyers, five bankers and six men of land and governance made up the potentates of note, along with the usual muddle of lesser cousins, hangers-on and earnest fresh-faced boys who yes sir, no sir, how droll sir as they quested for a living from older, richer men.

The baron offered up his assessment: "Terrible place, Ireland! Can't see what Cromwell saw in it!"

There was music, and a little dancing of the tight four-step kind that allowed the women who fancied themselves beautiful to flutter their eyelids in promise of unnamed temptations restrained beneath social courtesies, and every girl who had been told she was plain and could only hope for a middling kind of man, maybe a doctor or someone of that sort, to look down at the floor without reproach.

I stood by the baron, as I often did, his personal physician, and let the men swirl round him in smoke and alcohol, their spirits roused by his regular, merry provocation.

"Parnell, Parnell ... isn't he the fella who's topping that Essex girl?"

Scandal! Outrage! Where even to begin on the baron's crudeness? And there was something terribly liberating, was there not, in being able to say out loud all the terrible things you loved to whisper in the privacy of quieter places?

No one was much interested in me, and that was fine, and as the night turned and the music played, Langa came, he came, he came, and so did the truth of Hutton's heart.

And it was righteous, as most men are.

He was righteous when he ordered men beaten, and he was righteous in his victory.

He was righteous in his friends, his purpose, his politics and his God.

He was righteous in his enemies, broken, and his motives and his deeds.

He was righteous, too, in the mistress he kept across town, and in the blackmail money he had been paying, stolen from the government, to keep that secret from his wife, his family and the press. He was a man who had very carefully made himself righteous, because when he was not righteous, he was tiny, frightened and ashamed.

Blackmail. What a depressingly predictable outcome.

I headed for the garden, soft drizzle and wet leaves, and as I did, I caught in the corner of my eye the look that Hutton threw to a woman in a yellow dress, and a bare second later, a glimpse of her heart that froze me in my place.

She laughed, a practised thing that had within it a secret that amused only her. Brick-brown hair curled high above a long, skinny neck, black silk gloves, a bird's plumage of taffeta at the rear of her gown, a copper band around her wrist, eyes that danced to Hutton in every other moment, and from whose gaze he turned away.

Now, there she was.

There she was.

Brown eyes laughing at her prey.

Laughing at Hutton.

His blackmailer had come to the ball.

And she was like me.

She was like me.

She was like me, and her curse was coming, and her shadow was Doireann, child of her blood, whose body was buried in an unmarked grave in Clonakilty, and she would never tell the father where to find her girl, no matter what he took from her.

All this I knew, as surely as I knew that I stood feet upon the earth and blood within my veins. I knew as surely as you may know the ending of a final breath.

And then she turned, feeling perhaps a stare upon her cheek, a silence from the dark.

And looked at me.

And saw the truth of my heart with the same potency with which I saw hers.

And for a moment there were just the two of us, she and I, hanging in that frozen moment when the heart beats its last, when the rivers of the body cease their motion.

She knew me, as I cannot. And I knew her.

Of the two of us, she was always faster.

She met my eye, and saw my soul, and putting one hand on the arm of her colleague, she murmured an apology, and turned, and ran.

Chapter 25

Other truth-speakers I have met:

Hideo, who should have died long before I killed him.

Saira, who said, "There are some things you cannot cure."

Polina, kept in a cage.

Patigul, who caught religion to save her life, and was accounted sacred to Muslim, Buddhist, Daoist, Shinto, Christian and Hindu, depending on where she wandered and what she wanted for dinner that day.

Nashja, hunted from one ocean to another.

Khanyiswa, who swore blind that there was no one she loved, and who lied.

Taavi, who was lucky in that he met me after I had learnt the truth, so lived, and wandered in the desert, and said he had an allergy to rain.

Jarli, following the songlines beneath a crimson sun.

Margot, who liked to blackmail great men, and who on that wet night in Dublin looked me in the eye, and ran.

I had no doubt about my course. I followed.

It was not a very long chase. Her dress was impractical, her shoes absurd, slipping on wet stone and catching in cobbled streets. She hitched her skirts up to scamper, but there was such a mass of daffodil to hoick that the weight of it all between her fists made her sway from side to side like a conker on a string. She kept her eyes fixed firmly to the gaslit ground, the sickly green of the street lamps turning everything into a diseased pall, flaring dull around each sconce and muted by the rain. I came level with her easily, and half hopped, half skipped by her side as she struggled to get any kind of speed, demanding to know who she was, begging her to stop, blurting out, I'm like you, I'm like you, listen! *I'm like you!*

Having caught up with her, I wasn't entirely sure how I was meant to stop her short of grappling her to the floor. I caught her arm and she whipped it at once away, pulling it back as if she might strike me. My hand slipped on silk and the truth of her heart was that she hated this dress and these shoes, which she had told herself she loved for the character they helped her play; well, all things contrary, all things change, we make our certainties, we make our truths. This was the beating mantra of her soul.

"Wait," I implored. "Surely you can see that I don't mean you any harm?"

She sees it, of course.

Why then does she run?

Ah, here it is, here is the answer as we swing sharply round the side of a low white church, here it is. She sees that I am a spy, and that I am therefore her enemy, as men so often are.

This understanding came a few seconds too late to be of much service. She'd carried the knife for so long it was not important to her, and so I only saw it too late.

She shoved me back against the wall in this tight little space away from the eyes of men, and I was easily shoved, so desperate not to be a threat to her that it took a moment for me to recognise in the dark that the new sensation itching for attention at my throat was the little folded blade she had removed from her boot, resting against my trachea.

I was so surprised I didn't even cry out, or start begging for my life. Sixty seconds ago I had been drinking bad wine; my mind was not as fast as my feet in racing from that moment to this.

And yet even here, what I felt more than fear was curiosity. Would she really kill me?

Could she?

I looked into eyes like marble, and she looked into mine, and I nearly laughed to see that she did not know if she could kill me either, and she saw me understand this, and pushed the blade a little closer to my throat, testing whether in fact she could, and that silenced me, because ultimately, she hated people doubting her abilities and would fight a lion to prove a point. This too she saw, and as the sickly thought that perhaps I would die right here, right now, as the details of how it would be, the medical precision of my death, ran across my mind, so it ran across hers.

And the blade relaxed, just a little, and I thought I might laugh again, and thought I might cry, and for a moment had no idea where my heart ended or hers began. Drunk on fear, intoxicated on it, was the beating in my ears my pulse, or hers? She didn't know either, wondered in a moment of fancy if our shadows were now meeting on the road, squaring up to each other as we did now in this slithering corner of the tar-black city.

There was no point speaking. No need to beg for my life. She would look, and she would choose, as only God can do on judgement day. I nearly thanked her for it, asked in silence if she could tell me what she saw there, in the twisted knot of my heart. Did she see anyone worth forgiving? And if she could forgive me for what I had done, and who I had become, did that mean I could forgive myself? Was I a man worth sparing? I caught her arm, not fighting her, not trying to wrench the knife away, but steadying it, asking, what did she see? Who did she see? Who was I, and did she, who knew the truth that I did not, think my life worth living? .

For a moment then she pitied me, and I nearly howled with disappointment and rage. I wanted forgiveness and truth, not pity; to be a man, responsible for all I did, rather than fortune's pet.

She saw that too, and for a second smiled, and understood perfectly, and in that moment she cracked my soul in two, and I asked, "Is there a cure?"

And she shook her head.

Like Albert, she didn't know.

But neither did she seek to find the answer. A truth that baffled me; a shock written large across my soul. I had a thousand questions, but now the men came running; her bully boys set to watch over her from the shadows. I hadn't noticed them there, nor seen them in her heart. They were irrelevant to her, an exasperating adjunct to her work – men sent to do her business because no one ever took a woman seriously, and who had in the course of this mistaken their role for something serious. One called her name, and she rolled her eyes at the stupidity of it all, and stepped away, folding the knife into its wooden handle, and didn't take her eyes off me, and smiled again, and nodded, just once.

I smiled back despite myself, and touched the fingers of my right hand to my heart in thanks. Then her men were on me, and they were ignorant, and frightened, and bored, and hadn't got a clue what they were doing or why they did it, but at least it was something that seemed important. This sense of self-worth only increased in them as the first punched me in gut, the second across the jaw. I dropped to the street, not because I felt they were doing a good job at beating me, but because it seemed to be what they wanted and expected, men who could indeed throw a mighty punch, and there they set about kicking my back, my ribs and my arms where they barrelled around my head. They didn't think about whether they would kill me, or what the consequences might be. Their condition had been, a few moments ago, one of absolute boredom as they waited for Margot to return. This boredom, settling colder and deeper upon the soul with every drop of rain, had exploded apart as they realised that she was being pursued by one such as I. Thought had not really manifested in the few seconds between deathly dullness and the dealing of blows. Kicking me to a jelly was something exciting, interesting and therefore most essential. Killing me would mean that their work mattered, and therefore they did too. Any engagement with the question of my humanity was secondary to this fluttering pride, and so they kicked, and kicked, and kicked, until Margot barked:

"Enough!"

At which point they stopped, a little disappointed perhaps, but obedient.

She knelt down beside me, eased my bloodied face out from beneath the wrapping of my hands, brushed sodden hair back from my forehead, then leant down, and kissed me softly above my left eye, where it peered up from the street. Her lips came away with blood as she did it, and she smiled, and touched two fingers to her heart, and nodded, and rose, and turned away.

"Come!" she snapped, and reluctantly, the men followed her into the dark.

Chapter 26

Injury is one of my greatest fears.

We may flatter ourselves that we have come a very long way in our science, but in truth we have come as far as being able to pronounce "Ah yes, you have this disease, and this is how it shall kill you, goodbye!"

Yet my very specific, very personal fear is this: being confined to a bed. Unable to walk, or run. Not able to reach a train, or catch a ferry, or sit upon the back of a horse should it come to that. Why then, I will lie, and wait, and bleed, and heal, and Langa will come.

He will come.

So you see, lying at the side of a church in Dublin, every part of me in pain, it occurred to me that I must not lose consciousness, or fall apart too spectacularly, or let some well-meaning individual get me to an infirmary from which I might not be able to discharge myself. Calling out for help was unfashionably needy, and every breath I took into my lungs was a new kind of agony, but I gave it my best and was disappointed for nearly five minutes by the singular failure of help to arrive.

When it did come, it came in the form of a stranger in flannel trousers, and I nearly wept to see his round, glistening face peering through the street-lamp gloom. Seeing me, he opened with a barrage of "Dear Lord!" and "Holy Mary!" and other such unhelpful imprecations. "What should I do, shall I get the police – the infirmary, we must get you to the infirmary, can I move you should I touch you are you stabbed what should I do?!"

I grunted an address, and more came running, and finally the baron too, who barked, "A cab! Someone fetch a cab!" with much the same urgency he used to pronounce on matters of polo.

A hansom was hailed. A little crowd formed as I was slung, groaning, into its musty recesses. The baron tutted loudly for the pleasure of his audience about the inconvenience of hiring a doctor who needed medical attention, and kept up his performance until the door slammed and the horses neighed.

"Are you shot, boy?" he barked, the moment the blinds were down. "Are you stabbed?"

"Not shot. Not shot."

The baron's concern, a strangely brilliant thing, crumpled into relief, the force of which astounded me. "We'll have to call a doctor!"

He found this notion very funny, and with Langa near, in a way so did I.

They put me to bed in our little suite of rooms to the north of Ha'penny Bridge. A doctor came, and examined the floral display of bruises blossoming across my ribs, hips, legs, arms and chest. "Bed rest, fresh air!"

Bed rest was easier to achieve than fresh air, and for three or four days I lay, half muttering the dreams of our next-door neighbours, of

... lust, why doesn't he understand, why can't he see that she is also a sexual creature – he has his pleasures and then stops and she moans and groans beneath him and hopes that he will get the message, but it's been six years now and the time passed five years and nine months ago to raise the question of his minimal prowess ...

... again and again the foreman points and laughs, again and again naked before all his peers who see at last that he is tiny, meaningless ...

Dreams of fire, bastard, bastard, *bastard*! Bastard how could you how could you how could you do it to me do it to me do it to me bastard want to punch punch punch but in my dreams my fist freezes in the air powerless powerless powerless *bastard*!

Every night she dreams that he is dead, and she wakes weeping, and wonders if she is going mad.

On the fourth day, I grabbed Mrs Parr by the arm, the truth a blather on my lips. "We have to leave Dublin."

"I hardly think—"

"You don't like your brother," I growled. "You love him, dutifully, because you have to. You enjoy his company, some of the time. You respect what he achieves and are occasionally proud of him, and his odd flashes of humanity. But you don't *like* him. In your heart, you know that he is not a good man, and lacks enough compassion to ever be bothered by that fact. *He's coming*. Get me out of here!"

That afternoon, four men carried me on a stretcher to the back of a cart, and hoped that I was insane and did not know of what I spoke. And the cart rattled us to the docks, and at the docks I was carried onto the steamer to Liverpool, and they put me in a cabin with a window that looked towards the departing shore, and I thought I saw the shadow of the boy who died by the boab tree following me through the crowd, one arm reaching up, as if he would hold my hand.

Chapter 27

So much of my life is spent in maps.

The journey to Liverpool took a little under fourteen hours, and as we sailed, the need to babble the truth faded. One hundred and thirty-five miles in less than a day was enough speed to buy us time, and at Liverpool we were straight to the station, and onwards, to London. One hundred and eighty miles in four hours. At Langa's unchanging speed across land or water, calculated from months of observations, that distance should buy us a little over a hundred hours before the truth returned to my tongue. Four days to heal; four days of silence.

At Euston station, Parr asked if I wanted to go home.

For a moment, I didn't know what she meant. It didn't occur to me that she could be asking about family; my family.

"No," I said, not sure why. "Not . . . right now."

She didn't ask any questions.

They put me in that same hotel off the Strand where I had first met the colonel. I think the housekeeper was a spy, but without the shadow close upon me, I couldn't be sure, and that was wonderful.

I lied about Margot.

I couldn't lie about all of it. Hutton was being blackmailed; that was unavoidable. I had chased a woman in yellow and received a split lip for my troubles. These things were a matter of mere observation.

But sitting at the colonel's desk, as he asked me who she was and what she did, I lied.

"I didn't catch her name. She is a blackmailer. I don't know how she knew I was an agent. I don't think she's with the Fenians. Or the socialists. I don't know how she got her information."

I lied for one who was like me, for the shadow and the bond I imagined that gave us. It was a foolish reason to make myself a traitor, but having committed to it, I could hardly change my mind.

They interviewed me for two days before I began to dream my neighbours' dreams again.

Waking in the middle of the night, it occurred to me that this would be a good time to rock madly on the end of my bed.

To howl.

To march through the London streets looking for a fight.

To get immensely drunk, find a brothel, visit old friends, write offensive letters to ancient, half-forgotten adversaries.

Smash glass.

Pray.

Langa comes.

He comes.

He comes.

I just lay there, wide awake, and understood that I was a prisoner in a gilded cage, and that my life would be spent running, and violating the hearts of men, and I did nothing until the morning came.

Then they sent me on my way again.

Chapter 28

The British government were not the only ones with a truth-speaker.

"They have orders to shoot me, of course," mused Polina as we walked together through Budapest. "I know the truth of their hearts too."

Polina had worked for the Russians for nearly twenty years, ever since they'd torn her from her village by the banks of the Ob. We crossed paths in 1899 at a particularly tedious party held by an especially pompous minor lordling who had once married someone who was distantly related to a cousin of a king, and we were both working, and we knew the truth of each other's hearts.

She would not betray another of her kind, and saw in my eyes that neither would I, and smiled, and made her way over to me like a petal blown in the summer breeze, and shook my hand, and asked my name, and pretended to find my answers surprising.

"This man is an English doctor," she informed her escort, who trailed perpetually behind. "We shall now discuss irregular women's bleeding."

This statement, made loudly enough for ladies nearby to blush crimson, brought us a little privacy. She looped her arm through mine, and the truths of each other's hearts swept upon us both, and she seemed more amused than disappointed in whatever she saw in me, and whispered, "Say something medical. My keeper rubs himself in his private places with stinging nettles to keep away impure thoughts."

"Have you tried electrical stimulation to the genital region?" I intoned, voice carrying clear across the room as she turned me towards the door. "I also can recommend some innovative uses for salt."

We walked together between the white walls of Budapest, gas lamp and scratching violin, the Danube running high and children scuttling away into the alleys where the great men never went, and we were not disturbed.

Polina walked with her shadow barely ten hours behind, and seemed to have no fear of it, words controlled carefully on her tongue, and noted the truth of my heart without regret, as I noted hers. She had been violated by a man in her village. The only way to redress the crime was for her to marry him, which she had done, and sobbed through the wedding, and sobbed in the night when he violated her again. Then the man's father, proclaiming that clearly his son hadn't done a good enough job in restraining his wife, joined in. In the end, her misery annoyed her husband and he tried to strangle her with his bare hands. She killed him with a sickle, and his mother, in rage, cursed her with the shadow that had followed her ever since. She had been fourteen years old. "If a woman cries," she explained, watching as the horror of her truth rippled through my bones, "it is because the man has not hurt her enough to silence her."

As a spy for the Russians, she lived well enough. She had clean clothes, a good allowance, had travelled far and wide and was treated with a stand-offish respect. Her guards followed at a hundred yards' remove, and had orders to kill her if she was ever in danger of capture. She told them that I was a foolish British doctor with interesting views on a woman's bodily functions, and when I asked her, already knowing the answer, if she wanted to defect, she simply shrugged and smiled.

"Your side will kill you too," she tutted, "if they ever think you know too much. Cut our your brains first to see how you work; then kill you. I don't know why, but I find it comforting to think I will be murdered by people who speak my own language. Of the two men who guard me, one already knows he does not have it in his heart to execute me, but he will look the other way if the order comes to Nikolai. Looking the other way is the least he can do, for his duty."

"I'm no threat to anyone," I replied. "I'm far too much of a coward." Then, as always: "Is there a cure?"

"I think so," she concluded. "But it is in no one's interest for us to know it, save the ones we love. And who would be foolish enough to be loved by us?"

We shook hands, and in our hearts swore not to tell the other's secrets, and saw the truth of that pledge in each other, and she vanished in 1905 during the failed Russian Revolution, and was never seen again.

Chapter 29

Spinning round the world.

In America, a gangster buys the mayorship of a city not because it will give him anything he doesn't already have, but because he wants it as a child wants an expensive new toy, so why the hell not?

In Mexico, the general swears that he works day and night for the good of his country, and believes it. It is the truth of his heart – the work is killing him! That is why his family is paid so much and eats so well, because if he dies from overwork and neglect, he will be useless to Mexico. Then what will the peasants do without him?

A Spanish nobleman sighs in the gardens of Madrid. "We used to be something," he muses. "We used to be people of principle."

He has mortgaged his estates to three different lenders – one French, one British, one Italian – and lives in dread of the day they discover his duplicity. His wife complains that the other women laugh at her scuffed shoes; he doesn't know what to say.

In Ireland, a man is imprisoned for writing incendiary literature, and while in prison he is tortured, and when he leaves he kills a man, seeing no other way, and having no other dignity. That man's son grows up to hate the idea that killed his father, and so he kills another whose child will one day grow up to kill, and all things considered, the constabulary's policy of beating men bloody to clean up the blood is somewhat flawed.

Socialism; communism; anarchism; nationalism. They

are the new words of the day. Long before the death of an Austrian archduke plunged this continent into war, Spanish, Russian and Italian kings all met their end by violence and an American president was gunned down by an anarchist at a New York music hall.

In Rome, I was sent to learn the truth of the revolutionaries who gathered in the shadow of the old Aurelian Walls. They huddled around fires and broke bread together and whispered of rebellion and freedom and justice and truth, and their bellies were empty and their deaths rang like the factory bell before their eyes, and among them was one man – barely more than a boy – who had made a bomb from stolen dynamite and tin cans filled with nails. He listened to the whispered talk of rebellion and liberty, resolved that day that he would kill the king, but must have seen me staring at him. He saw me, and though he had no shadow, he knew the truth of my heart as surely as I knew his. He knew I was a spy, who would tell all of his people's secrets to my masters. And perhaps my masters would share some names with the Italians in exchange for favours of finance and signatures on pieces of paper, and some men would be arrested, and others killed; or perhaps they'd let them run riot, because it was of benefit to the British if Italy could not so easily sell its wares across the Alps. Either way, these men with their gutted lives would be sacrificed as pieces in our bigger game, just as they always had been, as they always would be.

He saw this, and knew it, and ran away. He didn't get very far. The dynamite he'd stolen was more than a year old, nitro-glycerin weeping in thick little globules from the clay. He, being unable to read or write his own name, orphaned by hardship and accident, nothing more, was not well versed in the rules of explosives. In his haste to escape my gaze, he stumbled and tripped on a red stone protruding from the tufts of shadowy grass, and fell, and the shock of that was enough. The bomb, when it blew, killed no one of importance. Of the six people who died instantly – including him – one was a child, one a mother, two were fathers and two were men of uncertain origin, their faces too mangled to be identified, no one coming forward to claim them. I was not injured, being too far from the blast. My ears sang for a week and my hands shook; there was dirt and other people's blood on my skin and in my hair. For a few minutes, I was a doctor again, tearing up coat and jacket to press into the wounds of those whose bleeding was heavy enough to merit attention, but slow enough that they were not already lost causes. I was astonished to discover that this was still within me; that the old profession still lingered in my heart, so focused and fixed on its objective that for a little while even the pain of my patients, amplified by Langa's encroaching presence, was numbed behind the necessity of the task I performed.

I worked for six hours, as the stretchers and carts came to carry off the wounded and the dead in dribs and drabs. It was dawn by the time I looked up, every part of me shredded to a rag, and saw the perfect image of the young man's face, the would-be bomber with his unstable explosives, frescoed on the wall just behind where he'd fallen, plucked from his skull and pasted to stone at the moment of detonation, a ghoulish flaying. I sat beneath it for a while, shaking, until I realised that I was whispering the truth of men's hearts, the muttered exclamations of this man's infidelity, that woman's true and burning love; the depth of her grief, her fury in the murder of the one she loved, a story she tells about herself, in which she, the living, is the true victim – not he, the dead. I put my hand over my mouth, and still the truth came, unstoppable, and somehow it didn't occur to me to run. Running from that place seemed so entirely insignificant, so thoroughly pointless, that for a moment I thought, maybe even believed, that this time when Langa came he'd take mercy, and just kill me, not the ones I loved. If love was even in my heart any more.

People turned away from me as I sank to my knees and tried to bury the sound of the truth in my chest, curling into the words, burying them. One man who had no fear, had refused

131

to be afraid ever since the day he ran away; and a woman who believed herself kind in all things and had frequently beaten children for not respecting her compassion, and who was yet here, yet kind, bent over me and whispered that all would be well. But they spoke Italian, and I spoke English, and my garbled, babbling gratitude spat beneath the torrent of their spoken souls fell on deaf ears, and for that I was almost grateful.

And there he was.

Langa, coming towards me across the bloody field, caught against the grey light of rising day. A flock of pigeons burst and wheeled away from the cracked rooftop of the house behind him, as if startled by a pouncing cat. The insects wittering in the crooked trees fell silent, stayed silent, shuffled away into the nooks and cracks of the branches. The fat-bodied, gleaming flies that had gathered to feast on the blood buzzed and spun into the sky, gorged and eager to be gone. The tip of the sun peaked over the lip of an ancient wall built from a thousand years of different stones, monuments defaced and mortared back together again to make a kitchen, or a room for lovers to lounge in, and Langa came.

He came, one hand raised towards me, a shuffle without movement, a shimmer in the air, reaching, inviting. I blurted the truths of all whom my eyes settled on, shrieked that once her uncle had touched her when she was young and told her it was fine, it was good, it was just a nice game they were playing, and now the sight of physical intimacy fascinated her, terrified her, she had no name for the torrent she experienced inside, there was no one to whom she could scream the thoughts that she did not know in her head, here he comes, here he comes, here comes my shadow ...

And I screamed the truth of the man who hated all Jews because he had lost his job, lost his money, lost his place, lost his family, lost his self-respect, and while he had never actually met a Jew or seen one as far as he knew, to be where he was without reason, to be merely a victim of life's stormy currents, was an injustice, an indignity too great to bear, and so there must be, *there must be* someone to blame, there must be a reason, must be order, must be . . .

"William!" Mrs Parr, overdressed and over-bustled for an Italian spring, running towards me. "Dr Abbey!"

And in her way, she loves me too. It is a maternal love, because she never had a son. Just a series of early miscarriages, and one girl, nearly fully formed, who kicked within her belly until the day she kicked no more, and was born dead, her eyes closed and perfect fingers curled across her chest, forming, Mrs Parr felt, the sign of the crucifix, the sign of the angels, it had to mean something, there must be something, there must be . . .

The angle of her scamper towards me took her directly into Langa's path. I howled a warning, but it was lost somewhere in the babble of souls pushing their way from between my lips. For a moment, woman and shadow were the same, Mrs Parr scurrying up behind Langa and then passing straight through him without slowing, oblivious to his presence, calling out my name. I gasped so deeply it hurt, then doubled forward again, wrapping my arms over my mouth, pushing my head against the wet grass.

"William!"

She caught me under the arm, pulled me to my feet. "You have to move! We have to go!"

"She would have been called Caroline," I whimpered. "You never told him that was her name, you never told him because he would never have understood . . . "

"Can you see it? Can you see the shadow?"

I nodded, pointed at Langa as he pointed at me, two poles steady in a spinning world. "There! He's *there*!"

"Run. Don't stand there, man! *Run!*"

Somehow, it hadn't occurred to me to do this until she said it. She wanted me to live. So desperately, with all her heart, she wanted me to live, and in that moment, her desire was strong enough to fill the empty place where I imagine my desire should have been too. I grasped at her arm for support, and ran.

133

On a star-spilling night in Rome, beneath the broken frescoes of past, lurid dreams, I knew the terrors that paralyse men in the trenches, felt the frozen, broken horror of all that was and all that had to be, and my skin began to pock and pucker with a sweeping purple rash, which I could not medically explain. You and I, Sister Ellis, have seen this before – and far, far worse. But we have both, I think, discharged men back to the fight in this condition, arguing that only by facing their terrors and conquering – or dying – will they be cured. This was the attitude of my masters then, as it is the attitude of our masters now, and many a man has died, shot between the eyes, gun at his side, because his mind could no longer bring his hand to grasp, lift and pull the trigger. This is also the truth that must be spoken: that men have gone to die simply because we did not have time to think of something better to do with them. We did not have time.

Anxiety and terror are no use to my government. Mrs Parr berated me into standing up straight and pulling myself together. The baron told me to put a stiff upper lip on, and think of Britain – and both of them, of course, meant it. They always meant it; that was why they were my companions.

And Langa came, and I spoke the truth, and turned my face towards the light, and in this manner we trudged round the world, outrunning my shadow a few days at a time, looking for a cure that no one else wanted me to find.

For Margot's sake, I had already lied to the Nineteen; but it was around this time, soaked in blood and chased by shadow, that I finally resolved to betray absolutely my friends, my masters and my country.

Chapter 30

There was, the doctor said, a moment when I realised I was a traitor. It took me a while to reach this conclusion, but being reached, the revelation was unavoidable. It was the very nature of my condition that brought about the certainty, for here was I, a man who every day in every way defined myself as good, just and upright, doing my best for my fellow men, and who was useful in my work only by the spirit of the African boy who had been lynched by the very system that I swore to serve. Even in death, I remained a tyrant, a cowardly, frightened butcher of Langa's soul, transforming his life into nothing more than a tool to be used and discarded by powerful men.

How to reconcile the truth of my heart with the truth of all that I did?

How to serve and yet be redeemed?

It was, I concluded, simply impossible. To serve the Empire that killed the child was to kill him again. Our Empire made its peoples nothing more than puppets and shadows to the white man's story; and here I was doing the same. That was the truth of it, to this very day.

Margot gave me the means to turn against my masters, when we found each other again. But it was in India where Saira who showed me the truth of myself and sealed my fate.

Chapter 31

In the small mountain kingdom of Vaniyali, hugging the lower hills of the Himalayas, a queen and her sons were plotting treason.

This was 1891, and technically she was well within her rights to do so. She was within her rights to set her own taxes, to command her own armies, to protect her people from the exploitation of the plantation owners and rich white men come to profit off her lands. She was rani, after all. The British was merely there to ... advise. Advice was so much cheaper than the gun.

Usually, such flutters of independent will from one of the hundreds of rajas still ostensibly in charge of their Indian domains were bought off by the British with pretty diamonds and florid titles; with scholarships to Oxford for the children of the great and a six-gun salute whenever the raja was summoned – no, not summoned – *humbly invited* by the British government to attend in Delhi, should it be convenient. When those failed, another raja or rani with some distant claim to ownership over the land could usually be found to stage a quiet internal coup, supported by redcoats only too happy to see that right was done, and that the taxes flowed to London from a more willing puppet.

Not so with Rani Darabai, for in her ambition she had done something unforgivable: she had been seen talking with the Russians.

"Terrible place, India!" concluded the baron. "And if the Russians ever do stick their finger in, well!"

Well, what a war it would be, he mused, and if he were a younger man, oh yes indeed, he might even be game for a bit of the old swash and bother, setting things right with one big brouhaha, that's how to do it, what.

Talking to the Russians meant that no mercy would be shown when the British came. The Great Game could not permit St Petersburg to put a finger in India. But first, the government had a question they needed asked . . .

"Does she believe that the Russians will aid any rebellion, or possess knowledge of any Russian plans to invade?"

This was why I had been sent halfway round the world, to know the truth of this moment, a thing so important that only a truth-speaker would do. In the palace of the Rani of Vaniyali, incense burnt beneath portraits of spaniels purchased from a dealer in London. Candles in bowls of water spluttered in the corners to drive back the shadows. A phonograph was silent on top of a pile of books, and mounds of cushions had been stacked by past occupants who had spilled their bodies this way and that across the cold stone floor. A monkey sat on the balcony, nibbling its way through an apricot, its vanilla face framed with peanut hair. And behind a folded four-panel divider of carved wood that had been set by the rani's chair, I thought I saw a swish of red as a foot was withdrawn, and thought I felt something more besides, but couldn't be sure.

"Dr Abbey – does she believe that the Russians will invade?"

The man asking the question was one Major Mudeford, a man promoted entirely for his skill in discrete, unrecorded destruction meted out against those foolish enough not to be grateful for the British and their ways. He did not believe in witchery, but trusted his commanders absolutely. If they said I knew the truth of things, why then, that was absolute. I knew what my answer would mean, and hung my head and replied:

"No. She tried to convince them, but knows they won't. They can't make it past Kabul; everyone who tries dies. She's bluffing." An intake of breath; a tightening of muscles in fingers and chest. Rani Darabai was twenty years younger than her ancient, ailing husband. He had seen the Indian Mutiny, and gone from being a great king to a man who merely nodded and smiled and waved at the latest laws of the British. She would see her sons rule in greatness again, and one stood to her left, a fine player of polo, able to recite from beginning to end a bowdlerised *Hamlet* in which everyone lived happily ever after. Through the open balcony doors, a paradise on earth rolled up into the mountains, streams of crystal water and purple petals thick and wide as my hand, courtyards of carved stone where once the ancient gods had been worshipped and named, and where now tennis courts had been carved for the latest fashion, the newest way. I had expected a woman bristling with gold, adorned with every mark of status, pins in her hair and chains around her fingers, wrists and arms. Instead, the lady of the kingdom wore a pale green sari and leather thong sandals and carried a fan of white lace. Her skin was a paler almond than her son's, and her long hair was pulled back so tightly from her forehead that her eyebrows rose in permanent surprise from the strain, and as she looked at me I thought I heard another woman whisper from behind the wooden divider, and the shadows moved strangely upon the floor and it seemed to me . . .

Then she looked me in the eye and snapped, "Are you willing to trust one man's word on this? Will you risk war across India?"

Mudeford hesitated. If it was he making the decisions, he absolutely would not. But then, he had been in Afghanistan during the disastrous, bloody invasion of the British, and had primarily learned that few forces would be as effective at keeping Russia from India than the men of the Hindu Kush. That truth made this process somewhat more academic for him, but he had a job to do and so asked the second question for which I had been sent halfway round the world. "Will other rajas rise if she does, and who are they?"

I looked into the truth of the Rani's heart, and in that moment condemned her kingdom to burn. "None will rise,"

I replied. "She went to them and told them that the people of their lands were suffering, that they lived in chains, and the rajas replied that be that as it may, they personally were doing very well out of the British thank you, and would mind her not to trouble her little lady's head."

Whisper, whisper, whisper – a figure moving to her side, a face unseen, and I have a feeling that I know something of who hides there, that I hear the beating of a stranger's heart, catch a taste of their truth on my tongue, and it is ...

"She hopes that when your soldiers attack, and she knows they will," I sighed, "the tales of atrocity she spreads will spark a second mutiny."

"I see," mused Mudeford. "How keen. What a pity that the telegram that could spark this rebellion will be sent by British equipment on British cables by British men. Not even history will remember this, because real history, ma'am, is written in English. We are not unreasonable people. It is Her Majesty's Government's sincere wish to maintain cordial relationships with all her ... fellow kings. Yet your actions have demonstrated a shocking disrespect for the civilised way of things ... "

Whisper whisper whisper from behind the wooden wall, and the rani's eyes are on me, though Mudeford is speaking, and it occurs to me that she knows the truth of my heart as surely as I know hers, and sees the shape of my shadow, however far behind he may be.

"And so," Mudeford rattled on, "to make reparations as quick and as effective as possible, and to ensure that there are no more misunderstandings of this sort again, we are proposing a strengthening of the British mission, including the provision of a military attaché ... "

The rani rose. Her oldest son caught her arm, as if to steady her, but she brushed it off in an instant, and finally now turned her attention on Mudeford. "Sir," she proclaimed, "two hundred years before the Romans invaded Britain, Asoka was proclaiming the laws of his empire in stone across the entire

139

continent of India, founding libraries and temples that still stand today. When Hadrian built his wall, the Gupta empire was making astronomical and medical discoveries that you would not see in your lands for over a thousand years. The British have no genius for conquest. Your weapon is greed, fatting a few powerful pigs for the slaughter. But, sir, you have misunderstood our character if you think we will dine on British beef alone."

A hand shot out from behind the wooden divider. It was a woman's hand, the colour of cinnamon, unadorned with bangles or rings. It caught the rani by the wrist, and she froze as if spiked with curare. The monkey on the balcony bounded away. Her son stood rooted to the spot, straight as a spire, face locked tighter than the Bank of England.

I stared at that hand, and in the moment of certainty knew the truth of its owner's heart. Perhaps she already knew mine. I wondered if I could apologise, if there was anything I could possibly say that would make my role anything other than filthy.

Slowly the rani sank back into her seat, and the hand let go.

Mudeford looked round the room, like a new buyer considering a fresh lick of paint. "You should not have talked with the Russians, ma'am," he said at last. "You shouldn't have tried to play games with powers bigger than yourself."

She stared at nothing, and it was only because she did not know herself what she would do that I missed it, until a moment too late.

"Mudeford!" I called out, and a woman's voice also called out, words I didn't understand from behind the divide, but the rani grabbed her son's ceremonial sword from the sheath at his hip, rose to her feet without a word and was charging across the room. I fell over backwards, legs up and stool down as I tumbled out of her way, but she had no interest in me, and caught Mudeford as he was half turning away. The blade split the soft flesh of his abdomen on a slanting angle through his intestines, liver and out the other side. She let go of the handle, but the blade stayed in, sliding down under its own weight. There wasn't yet much blood, but as Mudeford dropped and I scrambled back, ready to beg for mercy with all the garbled sincerity I could muster, the rani fell to her knees, hands over her eyes.

Everything over.

Everything gone.

That is the truth of her heart.

And how much worse that truth is when you know you have tried to do what is right, and ended up the villain of your own story.

Mudeford fell, and it was a very awkward falling, the angle of the sword sticking through his back making it impossible to land gracefully, his own weight just adding to the slow driving of the blade through his flesh.

The rani, if she had it in her to kill again, seemed to have no interest in me. Her son was already grabbing her, pulling her to her feet, snapping, "Mother, come!" – a man with a plan. He would grab all the gold he could carry, dress in suit and tie, and run away. The moment the Russian had come to the palace gates, sparking rebellion in his mother's eyes, he'd been preparing for this, and his only regret was that he'd stood by and let it happen. He thought about having me killed, calling for the guards as had been his mother's plan, but it all seemed very pointless now, and I was a no one, a drop of blood in the ocean that must be spilt. In that moment there was, I suppose, a kind of mercy in him, as he dragged his mother away.

I knelt by Mudeford's side, and he knew was going to die. I didn't particularly like the man – he was too pleased with his own truth, with the rightness of the butchery he commanded – but then I could have asked him any question, any secret of his heart, and all I would know was the absolute certainty of his death. He had been raised a Christian, and until the exact moment he'd been run through had believed completely in a heaven, and that he was destined for it. The second steel parted skin, that belief had parted too, torn open and bleeding. He had never doubted; never questioned. Death changed all that.

I pulled the sword free in a puckered kiss of flesh, rolled him onto his side, pressed fine silken pillows to the wound at his front and back, tied them off with tears of curtain fabric ripped from the wall, thought of calling for help, wondered who'd answer, kept my mouth shut. Mudeford was lucky, in a way. The rani's blade had sliced the abdominal aorta. He bled to death in six minutes. I stayed with him, kneeling in a pool of crimson cushions. He didn't say anything profound. He didn't have any messages for his family. Everything up to that point seemed much less important, now that he looked back on it. If it hadn't hurt, he might have laughed.

Instead, he died.

I felt for a pulse, and there wasn't one.

I looked into his eyes, which did not move, listened for his breath. I laid his head back down, and turned to the one person left in the room.

The other truth-speaker.

She had emerged from behind the partition screen, and stood and watched in silence, as immersed perhaps in the truth of Mudeford's death as I had been. She wore a red sari with frayed hem and no adornment. Her head was shaved to a thin black shadow across an uneven scalp. Her hands were dry and closed one on top of the other above her stomach, as if digesting a bad meal. Her eyes were close to the thin bridge of her nose, the colour of roast cumin. Her chin was tiny beneath a long, drawn mouth; there were pinpoint scars in the lobes of her ears from jewellery, which she had not worn for a very long time. She was half a foot shorter than me, with square wrists sunk to hungry bones and a scar above her left elbow where her mother-in-law had tried to kill her the day her husband died, and her name was Saira, and the truth was that she had never seen so much blood before in her life, no, not even when the mob came to drive her from her home, and she was astonished that it affected her so little.

And the truth of her heart was that she had not known a man could walk with the shadow at his back, and such a notion was heresy, and yet here was the reality of it before her eyes, as inescapable as night.

And the truth of her heart was that she had thought the white men were going to kill her, and had in a single moment come to terms with that fact, and now looking at me didn't quite know what to think.

She watched me with busy, soul-tearing interest as I rose, blood soaked into my skin and clothes, and knew the truth of my heart as surely as I knew the truth of hers.

And she was a truth-speaker, who walked alone down a dusty road; and she was blessed and cursed as I was.

For a moment, we balanced, she and I, with blood spreading between us, and read the secrets of each other's hearts.

Then, without a word, she held out her hand.

I took it.

Together we ran.

Chapter 32

Saira led me from the palace by the quiet ways that only the servants and unwashed ones knew as Vaniyali burnt. It did not do to let a truth-speaker like herself be too much seen. People said they brought bad luck.

When the redcoats came, their main interest was in destroying the palace. Destroy the palace, destroy the history, change the story of everything that happened. Pillaging was of secondary concern, and in no one's particular interest. But as word spread of the changing of the guard, eager neighbours quickly rushed to inform on *he* who had whispered sedition, or *she* who had been in league with the rani, or *he* who had behaved suspiciously, or of the wealthy neighbour who was caught looking in a most peculiar way at a sedan chair. By midday, neither British soldiers nor local residents were asking permission to act on their instincts, but rather were happy to investigate the private quarters and locked boxes of every man who had ever said something rude about their personal hygiene, or looked funny at their wife.

Within hours, queues of local dignitaries were besieging the British consulate, ready to reiterate their loyalty in exchange for protection for their and their brother's homes; or to name a long-time rival as a likely loyalist to the rani and her court. The old raja had been freshly enthroned on a pile of cushions at the back of the consulate, guarded for his protection and fed on iced tea, seemingly perfectly content with the distant sounds of screaming and tearing-up of floors as the soldiers went to work.

By the early afternoon, a militia of local men had organised to reinforce the British efforts, all in the name of the raja. The rani had gone mad, they said; there was treason in the palace. By cooperating with the British, order would be quickly restored, and if that wasn't good enough reason to pick up an ancient gun and your best feathered cap, the instant the militia received endorsement for its work with a puffed "yes yes, whatever!" from a newly promoted major, they too could join in the time-honoured orderly practice of ransacking the homes of people they disliked, or who might have a nice pocket watch they could steal.

In this way, in the name of law, order and the good of the people, Vaniyali fell into total bloody chaos.

I hid beneath a copse of trees threaded with hanging moss outside the palace, Saira by my side, watching the city burn. She had no real interest in being near me, but at that moment the colour of my skin was the only protection I could offer, and it would do. I was not looking for the truth of her shadow, but it came upon me as soft as a hand brushing my cheek, and I said, "Your shadow is near."

She glanced my way, and nodded once, and now her silence had a different weight to it, for she was terrified that if she opened her mouth and spoke, the truth would come tumbling out in a cascade.

I nodded again, the smoke from the flames of the city drifting in between the hanging leaves, pinching at my eyes and charring my lips. Held out my hand; she took it without a word.

Chapter 33

They say the foothills of the Himalayas are the Garden of Eden rediscovered, but that day Vaniyali was a hell on earth. Who started the fire, no one knew, but no one in a position to put it out cared. It swayed like a living beast through the city, seeming now to sit hunkered like a prowling cat at the end of the road, only to close its jaws and blot out the sun, pushing people into tighter and tighter spaces as they ran any way that wasn't into the flames. And yet now, turn a corner and some streets were silent, shuttered down, as if the inhabitants had single-mindedly concurred at the same instant that no one existed and nothing moved, even the chickens and the children hushed behind blocked doors. Others were total mayhem, groups of militia and redcoats bursting into homes that had already been three times burst through to pick over the skeletons of households judged insurrectionist by whatever criteria was most profitable for this minute, while above the flames still climbed and climbed, reflecting scarlet off the smoky mirror of the sky.

Twice we ran into armed native men: one group with ancient flintlock muskets that looked like they couldn't fire a shot, but that would have been more than enough to batter us to death; and one with a mix of scythes and sticks transformed into weapons by the addition of nails or wrapped weights. To them both Saira blurted that I was an American journalist, and she was guiding me to safety that I might report on the terrible British injustices and bring the truth to the world.

The absolute confidence with which she said this astonished me; the truth of men's hearts flowed through her fingers like silk through the loom, and she responded to every beat of every soul in every chest while I still reeled from the battery of truths that came upon me from each eye I met.

When we at last stumbled on British soldiers, I hollered that I was with Mudeford, and that Saira was my translator, and that we needed escort immediately to the consulate and transport out of town. The desperation in my voice must have carried some effect, because four men were immediately assigned to escort us to the consul's encircled home, and the truth of their hearts was that this was just another job, and they'd have liked to get a bit more booty from it, and it sickened them to see these damn coolies making a profit while they had to stand by waiting for permission to take what should have been rightfully theirs, and that was about all they felt on the situation. Not the crying of children nor the weeping of mothers thrown to the dust annoyed them half as much as not getting their fair share.

By the time we reached the consulate, Saira was beginning to mutter under her breath. I didn't know the language she spoke, but could recognise the potency of it, the power of the shadow as it came near, the pressure of truth erupting from her lips. Sometimes, in between the gibbered noises, she grabbed my sleeve and blurted, "I need ... need to ... he's coming!" and the truth of her heart was that she didn't know who she loved, but the face of her son still terrified her more than the truth-speaker's tongue could say.

I found Mrs Parr upstairs, looking down on the chaos below and the fires above. "Where have you been?" she demanded as I burst through the door. "What the hell even happened? What's this about the rani?"

"Shadow, here now!" I snapped. "Need to go now! *Now!*"

Mrs Parr, for all that she had been appointed to be ignored, was good in a crisis. "Horses!" she bellowed. "This man needs horses!"

We had horses saddled and ready in four minutes, and an

escort of seven riders in red to see us out of town. Saira now had her hands pressed over her mouth, even as I tried to boost her up into a saddle.

"She all right, sir?" asked one of our escorts.

"Just hysterical!" I replied, briefly grateful to the generations of physicians who had used this as an excuse for almost anything a woman did since the dawn of time. "I'm a doctor. We have to go now!"

We galloped away from Vaniyali, and Saira didn't look back.

I did, and thought for an instant that I saw the shadow of Langa – or no, not of Langa. This boy was younger, smaller, with wild hair grown around his head and little fingers that reached out to be held. He moved at the same relentless, endless pace of my shadow, following for ever, but it was Saira that he reached for, not me, and he was lost to the dust thrown from our horse's hooves as we raced away from the fires and the mountain.

Chapter 34

This is the truth of Saira's heart:

When she was a young mother, little more than a girl, her husband and son had both died within a few days of each other, taken by the same fever, and she had lived. It had been politely expected that she would either kill herself or cut herself off entirely from society, as widows brought terrible bad luck. She had done neither of these things, the one being entirely distasteful to both her and her deceased love – and the other being untenable for a woman who still, despite her grief, craved water and bread. So the village shunned her. Her name was whispered as a curse through the valley, and wherever she went it seemed that this knowledge travelled faster than her feet could carry her, until at last she fell at the foot of a shaven-headed widow in muddy green, who picked her up and said, "How long is it since your son died?"

It was three weeks, and the woman in green tutted and said it might be too long, but they could but try. So together they went back to the place where her son and husband were buried beneath the apricot tree, and the woman whispered certain words over the parched, cracking soil, and spilt a little blood, and the shadow of Saira's son rose up to follow her into eternity.

And the woman in green said, "We have a sacred duty. We bring the truth wherever it is needed. We will walk until the day we die, and we must never be tempted to take our own lives, lest our shadows divide and multiply, but wait for our natural end when everyone we could ever have loved will be dead. We do this because as widows it impossible that we could ever love again, and thus the people will let us speak the truth of men's hearts. Do not love. Your love will kill the one you put it on. And do not expect people to listen to the truth they do not want to hear. It is your duty to tell it, but they will never thank you for it. This too is our curse, as well as the shadow."

This was Saira's truth. She spoke the truth that people needed and paid to hear, sometimes to the fathers of anxious brides, assuring them that the dowry would be paid as promised, or that no, the boy was as reprobate as he appeared; and sometimes to great kings and princes, who knew how to hire a truth-speaker and were wiser than to share this knowledge with the British. After all, what awkward and embarrassing truths might the white man have learnt about Indian hearts, had he ever bothered to look?

Thus she had come into the rani's service, and whispered truths in her ear, and known at the same instant I had of the queen's murderous intentions, and the weight of death in Mudeford's soul, and a moment later she had looked on me and known the truth of my heart too.

My heart was hardly an impressive thing. A cowardly, shrivelled little organ, barely fluttering in the confusion of all things; but still, the heart of a truth-speaker, cursed as she was.

She had taken my hand, out of courtesy, if nothing else.

The least I could do was repay that kindness.

By nightfall, a long, hard ride from the palace, our horses flecked with sweat and foam, we took lodging in an inn that was little more than a series of wooden pallets raised above a cockroach floor. Our escort slept in one room, and we were the first to bring news of Vaniyali from the mountain, riding ahead of the stories of blood that would soon follow. There was much gasping and gathering of worried eyes around the hearth, which interested Saira not a jot. Instead, she sat outside beneath a drooping tree where green-feathered birds shrieked their indignation, and drew in slow, steady breaths, and watched the sun go down, and did not look back to the mountains.

A British man who is not explicitly asked to join a woman who is alone will always hesitate. I watched Saira for the best part of five minutes before, without turning her head, she barked, "It's just so ridiculous!"

I was ridiculous. Langa was close enough that this was obvious to the both of us, not just her; my heart, her heart, the lines were a little thin.

I sat down on a rough wooden stool by her side, a few inches lower than her, knees pressed up like a huddled child, waiting for beneficence. She glanced at me through half-veiled lids as I shuffled into some manner of merely mild discomfort, and seeming unimpressed at what she saw, huffed again and said, "When I was initiated to my order, it was explained to me that obvious things are always best said out loud. If you do not speak them, they are still not true – that was my teacher's command. People can imagine that they merely felt something in the whiff of a moment, and it did not matter, and it passed."

Her English was good, learnt during her service to the great kings, aspiring bankers, would-be lawyers and civil servants who scrubbed with carbolic soap to look a little paler to the white man. "If you make a thing real with saying it, it is harder to dismiss when the truth no longer serves you. The truth does not serve man, you see. I believe that. Man must serve truth. There is something higher."

She said all of this, and in an instant I concluded I didn't believe a word of it, and she tutted and clicked her tongue and snapped, "And where is your vaunted reason now, Englishman? Burning in the rani's palace, I would say."

"Since you know the truth of my heart, I'm not sure what I can contribute to this conversation," I muttered. Was this how others felt when I spoke truth to them? Crushed beneath its weight, looking for something to say and finding nothing but

151

hollow, feeble protestations and self-delusion. Truth, I thought, should be kind.

"We can say truths out loud. That way they will become real."

She declared this with the certainty of a prophet, and turning a little in her seat, angled her knees towards me and announced, "I am Saira."

"William. As we are so ... thoroughly connected ... my name is William."

She shook my hand stiffly, and at her touch my soul shivered with the tension in her body, the ridged determination that was threaded through her like the strings of a violin, on the edge of snapping. It had not occurred to me until that moment how hard it was for her to look at my face, or see in me anything other than an enemy.

"You serve wicked men, William."

There it was. As simple a truth as any that had ever been spoken in my life. I looked down at my feet, and the desire to retaliate came easily to my lips, bursting up through the web of denials and half-baked justifications in which I had woven my life. "And you do not believe your order to be sacred, blessed or noble at all. Just angry old women trying to stay alive however they can."

Her lips thinned, then curled into a smile. "Quite so."

"Why did you go to the rani's palace?"

"Because she paid me. If I do not have money, I cannot eat. If I stay too long in one place, I am driven away. Travel is expensive. I have slept too many nights on dust, and wanted to sleep on silk. I knew it was a risk. The rani is ambitious, her husband is a dolt, her sons are foolish. I was greedy. That is all. Why did you?"

"Because I was ordered to. I obey those orders because if I stay still, someone will die, and I am too weak to find my own way through this world."

She nodded, seemingly satisfied with this answer. "So," she mused. "We have both outrun our curses for now, but must keep on moving. Your company is of use. Your money is better. You are consumed with curiosity, and that is why you will help me. Yes?"

"Sounds about right."

"Good. You will give me money. I will answer your questions. That is the correct way of it."

She was right.

Of course – Saira was always right.

Chapter 35

The three days that followed were some of the strangest of my life.

We ditched our escort at a two-horse town, and bought both horses.

Mine was stubborn, stinky and too small for my legs. Saira's was a dullard, too tired to cause much in the way of trouble. Half the time it was faster to lead the creatures by the bridle than to ride them, but neither of us complained. Neither midnight cold nor midday sun scared us half as much as our shadows, which followed, followed, followed, eating away every inch of ground we had gained whenever we lay down to rest.

We rested rarely.

Instead we walked, we talked, truth-speaker to truth-speaker, and the lies of our lives fell away.

"I tell myself that I don't hate the British," mused Saira. "I have yet to meet a single man or woman who has not founded some corner of their soul on having power over another, whether money, mind, heart, child, possession, loss – a single point where they may say, 'but here I have something a little more', however pitiful that thing may be. A little more rice. A little more suffering. It is not important. And the white man in India has so much more power that I sometimes forget that the truth of each man's soul lies in this measuring. Then I hate him. A truth-speaker should not hate any living thing."

"Perhaps you don't hate the British," I mused. "Perhaps it is simply injustice."

"Of course!" she tutted, not turning her head from her examination of the road before us. "Of course it is injustice! But when injustice wears the same pasty face, you make connections, no? It is not truth. It is simply how the heart works."

"I have spent a lot of time watching men's hearts, and the common feature I have observed in the most brutal of men is that they are terrified of the day their slaves realise that the master bleeds."

She clicked her tongue in the roof of her mouth and kept on walking. The roads were quiet, surrounded on all sides by laughing forest of unseen sharp-toothed cats and giddy, playing creatures. I feared bandits, and my fear was palpable enough that she barked, "Only the foolish would attack you, and only the profane would attack me."

At night, we camped beneath mossy rocks by a rushing river, and I gathered timber and twigs, and she lit a fire with stone, and puffed until the kindling smoked, and told me that there had been a time when other people had lit fires for her, and then looked immediately away, and the pain at things that were lost was too deep even for me to speak of, and she was grateful that on this matter at least I could keep my mouth shut.

We moved on before dawn, travelling in a sleepless shuffle, testing our tongues for unwanted truths and finding that we both had a degree of control, talked of nothing much. "I don't know if the shadow can be lifted," she mused as the birds wheeled in the sky. "I have dedicated myself to believing that it is sacred, in order to find contentment. Asking if there is a cure means that all this is meaningless. Therefore I do not ask. So I am able to believe."

"That sounds ... fantastically dangerous."

The words came out far too easily, and she stopped dead in her tracks. "The Rani of Vaniyali managed to believe that she served her people, because that justified cruelties. Your Mudeford believed that he was making the world a better place, and that was why he needed soldiers to enforce his will on ignorant people."

155

"I ... I didn't mean ... I apologise. When I was a doctor, patients would swear to me that a dish of radishes or pills of antimony blasted with mother's milk could save their lives, even though there was nothing but hope to make them believe it. Hope was always far more convincing than truth. I know that. It's just that I ... have never really believed much of anything at all."

Her face softened a little, and nodding once, she resumed walking. For a moment she had thought of something else, of a thing that was almost comforting. Then it had passed, because widows did not comfort, and they did not bring kindness, and people feared their kindness because a truth-speaker's love was poison, and this more than anything else she had taken to her heart.

So in this way we continued, heading towards the railway.

And then she said, to make it true, "There is no cure."

She said it to make it real. To take away the hope.

And then, because she was still human beneath her pain, and the stone bottom of her shuffling feet: "That is the truth I believe. That does not mean it is true. I met a woman once who had walked and the shadow had followed, but when I passed her on the road, she was free. I thought I had made a mistake, thought it was just the lying of men's hearts, the lying they do to themselves, that truth within – but I know it, as surely as I know that my path will never end. She was free. They say that there are people in the mountains, that they curse their children when they turn thirteen, and send them walking, that they might know truth, and when they come back they are adults, but they too are free. I wanted to find them, but never could. So I believe that there is no cure. That is my happiness."

"And are you happy?"

She didn't answer.

We kept on walking.

At the railway station, Saira drew her robe over her head to hide her baldness, and I paid for a pair of first-class tickets,

156

and the man in the compartment who traded in timber and ballast was horrified to see an unwashed Indian woman in his space, but rather than argue with another white man, he huffed and puffed and moved carriages, so we had the space entirely to ourselves.

Heading south, away from the mountains, away from our shadows, the truth receded with the fires of Vaniyali. Barely an hour of iron rattling, and the ever-present certainty of Saira's spirit next to mine had receded to a gentle glow of instinct. Two hours later, and when I closed my eyes against the glare of the sun, the only light I saw behind my eyes was my own, and the only certainty I felt in my heart was the old familiar dullness where a better man might have held belief, conviction or love.

Now, for the first time, Saira and I spoke without knowing each other's hearts, and it was as if a pillar to which she had been chained had been pulled away, and she could collapse, limp as a tissue, onto the floor.

"I had forgotten," she breathed, "what it was to know myself."

I didn't answer, and she glanced my way quickly, surprised by my new-found reticence. "Do you not find it wonderful? To have only your own thoughts in your head, to feel only what you want to feel inside?"

"No," I replied flatly. "I find it lonely."

A smile, softer now. She lay sideways across the carriage seats, giggled at her own impropriety, stretched her hands overhead, tangling her fingers in the flickering sunlight through rushing trees. Without the truth on her, she was suddenly younger, a living woman rather than a walking curse. "One day," she proclaimed, "you will find something worth caring for. You will probably have to abandon your cowardly, wretched and corrupt way of life to achieve it, but I think you can do it, perhaps."

"That's a ringing vote of confidence."

"You can't tell if I'm lying," she replied with a hoot of merriment. "For all you know, I might think you're just as much a coward as you think yourself to be."

My frozen, cracking heart stopped in my chest, and I slumped back into my seat like a man punched. She glanced over at me, and though the shadow was far behind, the truth was still obvious in my eyes. Swinging her legs rapidly round and sitting bolt upright, she leant across the gap between us, putting her hands in mine, her face only a few inches away. "Foolish man," she whispered. "Scared boy. I do believe. I do believe. You can be free. One day. You will be. I know it."

"I don't know it. I don't know anything of the sort."

"Of course not. But the only truth the shadow never shows us is our own. So believe me." She squeezed my fingers tighter in hers. "I know you better than you know yourself, and I didn't even make you pay." For a moment I thought there was something there, a look in her eye that could have been more, something new. Then she looked away, and the moment passed.

Later, I would wonder what more might have been in that moment. But without the certainty of my shadow, I had not asked, not dared to act. In our travels together, we would both sometimes consider sexual relations, not so much because we found each other especially attractive, but in that the intimacy our shadows brought seemed to make physical intercourse faintly inevitable. Thankfully, no sooner had we considered the notion than the other knew of it, and we both at once understood that should our lips meet or our flesh touch, there would be no hiding any awkwardness or unsatisfactory experiences from each other. Oh, perhaps it could have been ecstasy – perhaps it could have been something that the poets describe with shooting stars or volcanoes or some such rot. But the truth could equally have been very, very embarrassing for us both.

Damned this way, or damned the other, I concluded.

"I have to go back to the British," I said, as we stood outside the station door. "They will hunt me to the ends of the earth if I do not."

"I will go back to the road," she replied with a shrug. "It is my duty." Then: "William. There are ... they say there are caves in

158

the north, where the widows go to die. When we cannot walk any further, we go there to purge the last of any love from our hearts, to die angry and alone. It is the safest way, to die lonely, and without friends. They say there are ... mysteries there. Questions and answers. If I ever find my way there, and find my way back, I will think of you, and your cure."

"Thank you."

"The men you serve: do you trust them? Do you think they are sincere in their promises to you?"

I shook my head. "I don't know. They never meet me when the truth is near."

She smiled, tiny teeth in a crooked mouth. "Well," she mused. "That might tell you something too."

We did not shake hands, and she did not look back, though I watched her until she was out of sight.

Chapter 36

My employers, when I finally reported in, were furious.

"Where the hell," Mrs Parr fumed, pacing across the floor of the Delhi hotel the Nineteen shoved me in, "did you go? You left with some ... some woman ... in the middle of all of that! Mudeford dead, the city on fire, the rani fled, where the hell were you?"

In Burma, her husband had shaken all the hands, walked the walk, smiled the smile and generally been considered a damn fine naval man who'd make a damn fine colonies man. But it had been Mrs Parr who wrote letters to the local businessmen and would-be barons of industry. It had been Mrs Parr who stayed up to three a.m. drafting the proclamation that would hang three revolutionaries and a would-be bomber, who wrote her husband's reports to London while he lay in a happy opium haze, sacked the judges and hired the sensible men, thank you very much.

I let her shout, and offered a few feeble excuses. The fire, the fighting, the death of Mudeford, Langa had been coming, he was coming ...

"You should have telegrammed the moment you were out of danger! Not five days later – *five days*! We've had half the constabulary of India out looking for you! So much for discretion; it's been chaos, absolute chaos! I want a full report, everywhere you went, everyone you talked to! I can't believe you were so irresponsible!"

"Yes, Mrs Parr."

"*Irresponsible!*"

The baron, huddled up in his chair, watched all of this without a word, hands folded and skin grey. Then, when it was done and Mrs Parr had stormed from the room to shout at the next fool stupid enough to cross her line of sight, he leant in and whispered, "I'm no truth-speaker, boy, but I know when a man's lying. Be careful she doesn't."

With that, he sat back, gave a little nod, and fell asleep.

Vaniyali doesn't exist any more.

The rani and her children were caught within days, and packed off to an extended vacation in Canada. Lovely rural living to be had in Canada, the British said. When the raja died, the succession passed to a cousin in Mysore, who turned out to have been educated at Eton and had a summer house in Bournemouth and was, all things considered, a very good egg. The kingdom was formally absorbed into its neighbours three years after he came to the throne, and the cousin was able to retire back to Bournemouth with a nice pension and an invitation to tea with the First Lord of the Admiralty, who confirmed the government's position that everything had turned out really rather splendidly.

And so it goes.

And so it goes.

And so it goes.

Chapter 37

I must have dozed, and woke with a start. Abbey was gone, a blanket over me where I slept, and the Jardin was beginning to stir for another day.

I barely had time to wash my face and straighten out my uniform – Matron couldn't stand girls what didn't look perfect – before the day turned insane. Two trucks came down, three stretchers in each and another six men on crutches or carried in the orderlies' arms. One was a conscientious objector, given a choice between the ambulance and the prison who helped another whose teeth clattered though he weren't cold. The soldier he carried had his guts pressed up in sheets of parchment paper, and was just holding them – swaddling them like a child – from where they'd fallen out of his belly. He should have been dead. He would be dead in nine hours, but the surgeons had sent him here to die, cos they didn't have the space up front. I felt angry at that, making it our problem, but Matron spotted him and helped him to lie down and was so kind, just so kind that I felt embarrassed. There was some sort of push going on in the German lines, they said. No one thought it would be here, where the trenches were quiet, and there was a smell on the air, something that burnt.

We didn't have enough proper beds, so put them what were most likely to survive on sheets and laid the rest out on the floor. I didn't see Abbey for nearly the best part of the day, except for once when he emerged, coated in blood, to throw his thick rubber gloves to the ground and snap at Helene to stop snivelling.

Then he saw me, and looked away, and nearly muttered an apology, and stormed back into the ward. When dinner was called, I ate like I'd never eaten before, and carried my plate with me, still shovelling potato into my mouth – Matron would have been furious if she'd seen it – when they told me that the boy with his gut hanging out were in his last moments.

He didn't cry when he died. He were too gone for that. He drifted in and out for a little while, and sometimes looked like he'd speak, and then didn't, as if he couldn't work out any words. I held the ether mask over his mouth, but we didn't have much left and weren't supposed to spend it on the no-hope cases, but we'd all seen this sort of death before and it was easier to die quiet, than to struggle on. Sometimes it were just easier.

I didn't look for the doctor that night. I was too tired. The moment my shift was done, I went straight upstairs to bed, and lay flat on my face in my filthy uniform. Helene didn't come to bed immediately, which I were grateful for. I knew she'd be working extra long, extra hard, as I should have been, making sure the ones who died weren't gonna die alone, hushing them that cried before they could disturb the rest of the boys. I didn't care. That night, God forgive me, I didn't care, and I woke with a shock at 4.15 to finally smell myself, see myself, see the sheets I'd stained with all these soldiers' blood where I'd just collapsed, like an animal, dirty and ashamed.

I tiptoed to the bathroom and washed in frozen water, enjoying the pain of it, and bundled my uniform into the laundry and scrubbed with soap until my hands were red and peeling. Then in my nightgown and socks, my way lit by a storm lamp that creaked with every step like an alarm, I began to head back upstairs to my room, flinching at every glow of light or whisper of voice that I passed by.

That was when I saw Abbey again, heading away from the laundry towards the soldiers' beds, that same walk I'd seen every doctor use a hundred times, too fast to stop, too fast to think, no place for dead men in his mind. I knew at once, with a strange kind of certainty, where he was going, but I weren't no truth-speaker. I followed him quietly and peeked round the corner to the officers' rooms, and sure as eggs, there he was, striding into Lieutenant Charlwood's room.

Three nights ago, I would have just gone to bed. Matron had lashed discipline into us all, beaten us with her paddle tongue. But I had already broken so many rules, was still breaking them now, and the telling of the doctor's story had convinced me of only one thing: that a darkness followed him, wherever he went.

I put my lantern down at the end of the corridor, and crept along the walls, tasting something sharp on my tongue, feeling a trembling from my lips to my legs. No one came running, of course, and how much more stupid would I have looked trying to explain myself by creeping than if I had just walked where I had every right to be, but something childish in my soul took hold of me, and I sneaked like a naughty six-year-old to the door of Charlwood's room.

Abbey had closed it behind him, but these old doors never shut proper unless you put your shoulder into them, letting out the groans of the dying as surely as the secrets of the living. I pushed it back another centimetre, and it was the bravest thing I'd ever done, and could see through the gap the sleeping Charlwood, looking more peaceful now, a strange, shortened lump beneath the sheets, lying on his back, snoring a little, from drugs or nature I didn't know.

Abbey was watching him.

Just watching him.

Like I watched Abbey.

Once, for a moment, he bent down as if he might smell the sleeping soldier, then pulled back.

And once he put his head in his hands like he couldn't bear to see what were in front of him.

But mostly he just stood, arms folded, staring.

Then he pulled out the knife.

It was an ordinary pocket knife, with a wooden handle and dark steel blade. It looked like it had travelled a very long way. He held it folded in his hand for a moment, then opened it up, resting the blade against his palm as if he might cut himself with it, then turning the point towards the soldier like he might cut him.

Turns out I'm not a coward. I thought that maybe I was too; after everything Abbey had said, I thought perhaps everyone in this stupid bloody war was a coward.

Not me, it turns out. Something in the dying of men's eyes made me brave; Matilda, you should have seen it.

I pushed the door open, glaring at Abbey.

He looked briefly ashamed, lowering the blade to his side as if he could undo whatever it was he had been about to do by pretending it weren't so.

For the longest time, I just glared at him, daring him to say a word, arms folded, feeling ten times bigger than I was.

He stared back, and I wondered what truths he was seeing in my heart, and hardened my face and bunched my fingers into fists and hoped he saw something frightening, solid and real.

He looked away, and I didn't need no shadow to know that he was ashamed. Folding the knife up, he put it back in his pocket and said, "I really ... hate ... Wagner. I did not kill ... I did not ... I did not kill the ... "

The words wouldn't come.

He tried to lie, and he couldn't.

How much of what he'd said to me before was a fib?

How much more would he dare say to me, now that he couldn't pretend?

"What do you want with Charlwood?" I demanded, face flushed, revelling in this sudden power, in the curl of his shoulders and the hanging of his head. "Tell me now."

"I want to ... I need to ... " Trying to find some form of words that he could speak, he was pushing so hard to get something past his curse, and the curse wouldn't let him. He looked down, and was suddenly small, and old, and I couldn't believe that my whole life I'd been scared of men like him. "I'm here to kill his father," he explained. "And if I can't kill the father, I'll kill the son. I haven't yet worked out which one has the greater justice in it."

165

I didn't find this half as surprising as I thought I should. "Who's his father?" I barked, and then, an afterthought: "Who's his mother?"

He looked up quickly, trying to piece out something from my soul, from the thoughts in my eyes, then shook his head. "No, not that. You're wrong. He's not . . . it's not that . . . I'm trying to . . ."

This time, the words gave way in a snarl of frustration. They had come easy in previous nights, but now the truth was bending him this way and that. I waited, whole body shimmering with the moment, cold forgotten in the blood running through me, exhilarating in his terror, my bravery. Outside I thought I heard an engine shudder, a cry of voices, quickly hushed. I could hear rifles in the night, cracking out loud; that wasn't right, shouldn't be able to hear them in this place.

Then Abbey met my eyes, and there was not a shred of kindness in his gaze, not an inch of the healer, the physician that should have been in this place of death. And he said, "His father is Professor Albert Wilson. I wrote to him four days ago, informing him that his son, who enlisted aged fifteen years and ten months under the name of Richard Charlwood, is here. Albert will come. If he doesn't, I am going to summon the shadows of the ones the boy left behind in the trenches, and curse Charlwood. The darkness will follow him wherever he goes; everyone he loves will die. Given his condition, I can't imagine killing his loved ones will take very long at all. That's why I'm here, Sister Ellis. That's why I came to the Jardin. Please don't try to stop me."

"I will," I blurted, astonished by how quickly the words came, and knowing in my heart that perhaps, suddenly, I didn't mean them. I had pushed open the door to this room believing myself invincible; now the conviction in Abbey's eyes made me less sure of my own safety. But I'd come this far, and this braver woman than me, wearing my skin, declared, "I will stop you."

His head turned to one side, and with it went the last shreds of my confidence, flying off me like warmth in a blizzard. He knew my heart. He knew my sudden fear. He saw it with perfect conviction, and straightening up said, "Maybe you will. Maybe you won't. You won't know until the moment comes. Come; Charlwood is drugged and won't wake for hours. Fetch the whisky – no, I'll fetch the whisky, so you don't have to worry what I might do in your absence. I'll fetch the whisky and some blankets and we can finish this merry little tale, yes?"

I nodded, dumb and cold, and without a word he pushed past me into the corridor, while I waited by the sleeping child in a white, half-used bed.

Chapter 38

There are things, Dr Abbey said, which I have perhaps told out of order. Or which, by omission, have been given a little less weight than perhaps they should. I was to meet Saira many more times, and learn certain truths from her that are now ... pertinent. Together we would look for answers that were to her heresy, and to me my only hope of freedom. But first, there was Margot.

There's always Margot.

The workers' strikes of the 1890s weren't as spectacular as the newspapers claimed, though the fact that there was any attempt to coordinate them at all, from the mines of Maine to the factories of the Rhine, sent a shudder through the halls of power. All the oratory of the socialists and unionists was only air against the hired Pinkerton's and strike-breakers sent to batter the pickets into submission. But the air hummed with revolution, from the palaces of India to the collieries of Wales. And in the middle of all of it, the People's Society dropped its blackmail like a grenade.

The articles started in salacious local rags. The mainstream press wouldn't print such garbage, but the farthing gazettes had no such concerns.

Coming to the house on Tuesday last upon the recommendation of a trusted informant, our correspondent was astonished to discover Mr P. B. in a grasp of passion with two girls and one boy of some fifteen years of age. Both Mr P. B. and the boy were attired in corset, silk stockings, women's shoes and lockets bearing the visage of Her Majesty the Queen ...

Everyone knew Mr P. B. Everyone knew his sexual inclinations. No one talked about it, and two days after the papers exposed him, Mr P. B. went to take the water cure in the Swiss mountains, and did not set foot in Britain again.

Lord P., having returned to London for the season, brought with him a young Miss A. L. Introducing her to everyone as his niece, it is of course behoven upon this reporter to wonder how his niece came to be, given that Lord P. is an only child; and whether it is suitable for the said niece to be fitted up with private lodgings at which, our correspondent observes, Lord P. is a regular nocturnal visitor.

Lord P. was far too important and self-assured to leave London. Only after he had paid out nearly four thousand pounds in blackmail money to the unknown informant was he quietly demoted, and put in charge of the arsenal at Woolwich.

When I was summoned to see the colonel, I expressed some mild amusement at such things, and was astonished by his thundering roar of "For a man who knows the truth, you know nothing!"

He was angry; more so than I'd seen him when faced with French spies or Austrian betrayals. Something profoundly true and personal in his understanding of the ordered way of things was under threat; and woe betide he who threatened the ordered way of things.

"Blackmail," he snarled, tossing a small sheaf of carefully type-written letters in front of me. "What you see in the papers is the very tip of it. Someone is running a vendetta against our best men!"

My shadow was five days behind, otherwise I might have questioned what made these men our "best". Given that our prime minister was fond of going into the East End with his britches sewn up to save the fallen women of Wapping, followed by some brisk self-flagellation, one had to wonder quite how to measure these things.

"What do these blackmailers want?" I asked, fingering the paper edge of the letters.

"Money, usually. Sometimes they tell a man to resign his post, or try to influence policy – *policy*! They call themselves 'the People's Society' – utter rot. The Nineteen fear it's cover for a foreign power, but to me this feels domestic, anarchists or some such. We shall root it out!"

"You mean *I* shall root it out?"

"Blackmail is the crudest, most criminal tool of revolution, showing just how little honour, how little respect our enemy has. The country must be run by educated men ... "

The truth of his heart, not that I need Langa near to know this, is that the colonel believes every word he says. The system has been very good to him and his friends. He has never seen a poor man or woman in the street who was not indolent before they were destitute. And if the system is broken, it is men like the colonel who shall fix it.

(And Langa is coming, he's coming ...)

"What do you want me to do?"

"A certain gentleman received a letter two days ago demanding two thousand pounds. He is to hand it over at Paddington station. You will go in his place."

"Of course I will," I intoned. "I've never seen two thousand pounds before."

Two thousand pounds in five-pound banknotes turned out to be remarkably heavy. Leather bag clasped in both hands, I cursed and struggled into the smoking, belching, rumbling interior of the soot-black station, coughing on coal. I wore an absurd red ascot tie, the kind of adornment that my father would have derided as the neckpiece of a weak-livered middle man with foolish aspirations. My father, having once been a middle man with aspirations, knew of what he spoke.

Under one arm, constantly on the verge of slipping, I carried a copy of *Huckleberry Finn*. English society had heard the tome was crude and vulgar, and thus didn't need to read it.

My being forced to carry it for identification, along with the tie, felt like mockery.

Under the pretence of getting the money together, my employers had delayed this encounter for two days, so now my third inconvenience, the shadow at my back, was also starting to pick at my good mood. Shoving my way through the crowds beneath the great smoke-smothered arch of the station, spun by porters

who think on Sunday, Sunday at the ache in my hand that has not faded not faded now for five weeks too long something wrong something . . .

buffeted by ladies with puffed-up mutton sleeves and scarred faces,

she had freckles and as a child another child told her that freckles meant her mama had slept with a black man, that she wasn't pure, wasn't white, so she took the carbolic acid and scrubbed scrubbed scrubbed to hide her shame

and young men in three-piece suits whose hearts yearn upon

the great philosophers – the great philosophers! – one day he too will be a great philosopher if only he could think of something interesting to say!

The bench where I was to wait was already occupied. A family – mother, father, two daughters, three sons – crowded over portmanteau and shoe box. The adults drooped as the five youngsters rushed and screamed and howled and clawed at each other's hair and were, all things considered, utterly repulsive snots. I hovered, trying to find an excuse to usher them away. The baron would have a lie ready in an instant, but all I could think of was "Did you see them remove the leper's corpse last night?"

I stood silently a little to the left, and nudged the bag at my feet to make sure it was still there and someone hadn't managed to whisk a small fortune in banknotes from under my running nose, and squinted through the smoke at the shadows of men and women about their business. The place was near the great black engine of the train. They would come, I

171

realised, at the moment of its departure, when the coal furnace would be stoked to the height and billows of smoke would obscure even the eyes of the keenest watchers. It was a good time to stab me in the back and rob me blind; I wondered if I'd even feel the knife.

I thought of running, and knew I wouldn't. The Nineteen had trained me like a dancing bear. Langa would come, and I would stand my ground. Death would come, and mute and dumb I would look it in the eye and at the final moment shrug and say, "I couldn't think of anything better."

I closed my eyes, and waited. Let the knowing of other people's hearts wash over me, let their truths be my truths, drowning my thoughts. Easier to live in other people than be myself; thank you, Langa, for that gift.

He knows he's let his father down should have been someone but isn't not really just an average man with an average job a betrayal of his education ...

Married too young. Married too young. Thought she knew what love was, but married too young.

She said, "Is that my money?"

Two truth-speakers meet, in the smoke of Paddington station, and there is rarely need for words. She wore blue and white stripes, a bonnet that bloomed around her head like a cotton bud, tight black leather shoes that pinched her feet, and a smile. Behind her, a man, half recognised from a midnight alley in Dublin, all curly mahogany hair, eyes sunk low beneath rolling brows, chin a little too broad for his tight-pursed mouth, thin neck above stooping shoulders. He hated me instinctively, had arrived ready to hate me, the agent of imperialism. She had little time for hate; she knew too much of men's hearts.

Margot, smiling as if we were the oldest friends.

Her soul is warm amber, hard as time. She loves the colour yellow. The painters of Europe have only just discovered the cheapest way to make this brightest pigment shine, and now it is the colour of life, danger, a new way of seeing the sun.

She learnt French to sound sophisticated, and speaks it terribly.

Her shadow is near enough for her to know the truth of my heart, but far enough that she can smile as she lies.

And she sees me.

She sees me.

Langa comes, and she sees me, and smiles.

And to my surprise, I smile back. Smiling to see my enemy; delighting in the delight of her heart, unsure where her joy at this encounter ended and mine began. The man beside her twitched, moved forward, one hand heading into the pocket of his cord waistcoat, but she put a hand on his arm, holding him back. She could stand here all day watching herself being watched in my heart, but there is business to be done.

Briskly: "Followed?"

I nodded.

"He'll take the money and run. Will they go after him?"

"Yes. It will be embarrassing for me on a professional level if you get away with two thousand of Her Majesty's dirtiest pounds. Margot ..."

"We can't have you embarrassed on a professional level, can we?"

"I didn't think it would be you."

"I've been waiting for you. My colleague will take the money now."

"If you wouldn't mind bungling your escape ...?" I suggested, lifting the case higher, fingering the catches. "Within reason, of course. Two thousand pounds is a lot to lose on the job."

Her eyes didn't leave mine as she addressed the man by her side. "Coman," she murmured. "Be a dear and take William's money."

"William?"

"This gentleman is William Abbey, agent of Her Majesty's most secret, most potent intelligence service. You may recall striking him repeatedly in Dublin. Take the money, run, and when the police draw a little too near, open the case and spill its contents in the street. That will slow down even the most dedicated enforcers, feed a few poor and allow you to escape with ease."

"This is—"

"Peadar, please."

For a moment, he thought of refusing her order. Any other man would have. But the man called Peadar Coman had seen Margot perform miracles. He knew her to be blessed, not cursed; to have a wisdom that exceeded that of all men and all women. And even then, in his own way, his trust was beginning to bloom into something more, so his hesitation passed, and he stepped forward, unsure if he should stab or thank me.

"With the whistle," mused Margot, and for a moment longer the three of us stood there, smothered in the bustle of the station, until the whistle of the great train blew, belching smoke, shrouding us in a blackening, choking cloud of hot dust. Coman grabbed the case from my hands and was running down the platform in a moment. Margot hooked her arm in mine at the same instant, spun me the other way, marching for the gate to the porters' bay, into the mass of cargo boxes and trunks, of stacked cases and lost property waiting for transfer to the cart, the canal or the warehouse. I heard a police whistle cut through the chugging of the train as it began to pull away, glanced back but was immediately pulled along by Margot, who had walked this way before, mapped out every turn of the station before coming here, prepared as I should have done, if I were a proper spy.

In a forest of crates and portmanteaus, of suitcases lashed together with leather straps and trolleys buckling under their load, we scampered from the shadow of one tower of trunkage to another, sometimes stopping for Margot to listen, to glance to the left, to the right, then grab me by the hand and pull me quickly on. A pair of porters rattled behind us, an old man with a stinking pipe, and a boy little more than thirteen years old dressed in trousers too big for him that he would never grow into, hauling post sacks on their backs. Margot waited for them to pass, then broke into a half-trot, half-run, barrelled up a ramp towards a man in a flat black cap and exclaimed, "Afternoon!" as if we were the most common, natural sight in the world, shouldering the gate open beside him with a delighted smile and pulling me into the shadowed road beyond. At the top, where light broke through the domed, soot-black arch that shielded us from the sun, carriages and omnibuses clattered and clacked, old nags and broken bays shuddering, heads down through the day. Around us, post wagons and cargo carts waited in a straw-chewed, shit-slewed mess of cobble and bustling men, through which Margot marched as if she were queen of them all. A single carriage waited at the top of the mass, a heavy dent on one side, the wood splintered and not yet sanded back, the driver shrouded in hat and cloak. She knocked twice on the door as if for good luck, heaved it back and pushed me inside.

Once within, the carriage pulled away in an instant, blinds down and doors locked, the whole affair perhaps less than twenty seconds from the blowing of the whistle to what I supposed I would have to tell my employers was a terrible kidnapping.

She fussed to arrange a great volume of skirt in a small den of seating, the shuttered space smelling of leather and other people's sweat, our knees pressed tight to the bench, and then, with the light of day obscured down to a fabricked orange glow, she let out a breath, beamed, pulled the bonnet from her head, rattled her fingers through her hair, sat back and exclaimed, "So, William, how have you been?"

Chapter 39

This is the story of Margot Halloran, gleaned from the deepest recesses of her heart.

She was born by the sea, on a night of storms. There were more women than men in the village where she was born, and more empty houses than full. The men had all left in the famine, and promised to send to their sisters and their wives from America, and never been heard of again.

Her mother swore that they were of Romani blood, but the last four generations or more of Hallorans had gone to church, and sworn on the Bible, and thanked Jesus for what little they had, and even though their women were strong, clever and wise, these days they were hardly ever called witches.

Margot should have been raised a romantic, but her father died at sea and her mother died bringing her youngest brother into the world, and so, as Carmine had been to me, so Margot became to her nine younger siblings – a mother they didn't have.

To live, the youngest were set to stealing, but that wasn't enough, and the law cared nothing for the age of children. Her ten-year-old brother was sentenced to hard labour for larceny; her fourteen-year-old sister was put to unpaid service with the Sisters of Mercy after the pregnancy started to show, the child taken for who knew what destination. Boredom was as much a burden as poverty, and it was, she felt sure, boredom that made her brother take to hitting her the moment he was bigger than she.

She met Eyre when bringing laundry to the big house on the

cliff. He was nineteen; she was eighteen. He was beautiful, in his way; she was beautiful by all the measures of the time. He didn't promise her money, or freedom, or marriage. He didn't need to promise any such things. He took an interest in her, and laughed when she laughed, and smiled when she smiled, and this was the greatest human connection she had experienced in ... she didn't know how long.

She didn't ask him to pay for sex. It didn't occur to her that this was the nature of their transaction. He enjoyed her for a while, then went back to college without a word, and never thought of her again.

When the baby showed, she lost her job.

The nuns told her she was a sinful little witch.

The priests urged her to confess.

Her siblings could not support her, and were already going their different ways, torn apart by money and law.

In the end, she went to her aunt, who she had always been told was a wicked woman, and who fed crows and wore men's boots and fished from black rocks and never sang the songs the women were meant to sing. And her aunt was not, in fact, a wicked woman, but tutted and sighed and told Margot to sit by the fire and demanded, "What skills do you have?" and Margot snapped, leaning back against the weight of her own belly, "Cooking, cleaning, stealing and whoring."

"I hope you're a better cook than whore," was the reply.

It was only the two of them there when Doireann was born. The girl looked too much like her father, but Margot found that she loved her all the same, and had no idea where such a foolish sentiment had come from.

By day she helped her aunt plant and harvest the vegetables from the patch behind the cottage, and fish and set snares for rabbits, Doireann on her back. And on a Friday her aunt would take the child from her, bid Margot brush her hair and put on her brightest whoring smile, and go into town to sell whatever surplus they had, proclaiming, "They know I'm a witch, but don't yet know what you are."

177

When she came home, and Doireann was fed, Margot would sit by her aunt's side as the old woman told her of secret remedies and herbs, of the old ways of healing and the powers of certain stones. Sometimes women would come to her for help, always at night, always with faces shrouded from the sight of men, and she would slap tinctures on their warts and unguents on their blisters and exclaim, "Apply this for three days, say your prayers to the Virgin Mary, do not look east more than is necessary . . . and get plenty of fresh air and walking."

Even witches of the Irish Sea have certain commonalities with modern medicine.

Some secrets that Margot learnt were not so savoury. Most were nonsense. At least one was not.

When the end came, there was no warning. No one had told the Halloran family that the land they lived on was anyone's but their own. No one invited them to court to state their claim, or establish ownership of that which had been theirs since birth. No one was interested in hearing their appeal. The bailiffs simply came to their door, already armed with hook and truncheon, and told them that they were trespassers on a great gentleman's property, and had to leave at once.

"I have lived here all my life, this is my land!" hollered the aunt.

"Then you have trespassed all your life," was the reply.

Still the old woman refused, standing in the door, fingers dug into the frame, back straight, glaring at all who came near her. So fearful was her reputation and so ferocious her gaze that no one wanted to be the first to strike, but in the end the oldest, most senior of the men, sensing perhaps that his authority was waning a little, stepped forward and smashed the old woman around the head with his cudgel. Then they marched over her crumpled form and proceeded to burn her house to the ground.

The initial blow didn't kill her outright. Margot's aunt lingered on for eight more days, as the slow, untreated bleed in her brain stole first her hearing, then her speech, then her sight, then her ability to chew, and finally her breath. She had been taken to the workhouse, but Margot was not allowed to sit with her as she died, for she had to pay her and her daughter's way in that place, and slackers were sinners in the eyes of Jesus.

Doireann died three weeks later, from workhouse typhus. This time, Margot was with her, holding her tiny body close as the child faded in her arms. And this time, with the gaze of mighty men looking down upon her as stone from the high balcony where the masters ate, with the women walking silently by, too broken down to lift their gazes to a mother's grief, this time Margot put her fingers on her child's lips and spoke the secret knowledge her aunt had given her, and from the body of her dead daughter brought forth the shadow of the only one she could ever love, the bringer of truth, blood of her blood, so that they might be together for ever more.

Her daughter was not her curse. The shadow that followed Margot from that place was her beloved, her blessing, a spirit of truth come to bring down powerful men from their great places. Doireann was her freedom, her redemption and her forgiveness, and with her at her back, no one would ever make Margot grieve, or love, ever again.

Chapter 40

In a carriage stuck in traffic in the streets of London, Margot and I listen to the truths of each other's souls and are, perhaps, surprised by what we find there.

"Well," she muses at last.

"Quite," I concur.

"You are a terrible spy, Dr Abbey."

"I'm not convinced that you are the world's greatest blackmailer."

A half-shrug. "I've fallen in with some people. They have ideas."

"What sort of ideas?"

"Oh, social justice, revolution, votes for all – well, all men. Sometimes I remind them about women too, but they say we shouldn't be unrealistic with our ambitions. Some of them are rich boys playing at being poor because it makes them feel moral. Some are poor men who found Engels when God stopped answering their prayers. A few are thieves and crooks. One is an agent of the Russians, sent to sow discord; another is French, sent to do much the same but far less effectively, and isn't sure if promoting anarchy is going to be helpful for anyone in the long run. Many are just looking for something to believe in, and hear in the words of the People's Society whatever it is they need to have hope again."

"They sound ... thoroughly frustrating."

Her face flickered with a smile, smaller yet perhaps truer than the glimmer of delight I associated with her features.

"They can be. They'll be excited to know that the British have sent their very own pet truth-speaker to glean the truths of their hearts."

"I think my masters will be less thrilled to hear that their rivals have a truth-speaker of their own."

Her eyes flickered for a moment, then she looked away, as if she could stare straight through the blinds of the coach and into the outside world. "Will you tell them?"

"I don't know. I have to tell them something. They sent me to learn the truth."

"What do you want?"

"I . . . honestly don't know. To be free of it all."

"Why?"

"Because my shadow makes me the villain," I replied simply, and was surprised to discover that it was the truth. "What I do and who I am makes me ashamed, and I would be done with the whole thing."

Her head turned back slowly, as if taking in some scenic view, and I wondered how much closer her shadow was than mine, and whether the truth was on the tip of her tongue, waiting to spill. "William," she chided. "If you were not this, then I do not think you would be anyone at all. What you have is a gift. One you did not earn well, but still a gift. A kindness in revelation. *Truth*. How much is this world bettered by truth, by honest knowing? How many people have perished in pain, for the simple want of that?"

Somewhere in Ireland is her daughter's grave, and she knows that the child's father is doing very well for himself, thank you, and thinks that one day she will remedy this fact.

"You are blessed," she declared, eyes focused now somewhere past my head, on a distant place in her heart, not mine. "You walk the songlines."

A little piece of another world, a snatch of someone else's stories. She too had travelled, and listened to the call to prayers from the highest towers, sought out the wise men of the sands, imbibed far too much rum with the medicine women by the

181

low dawn fires, and perhaps in doing so she had come to believe, with all her heart, in the truth of what she said. It is good for a truth-speaker to believe in something, I think. I've never quite mastered the trick of it.

"I could join you," I blurted. "Run from the Nineteen. Even revolutionaries need a doctor."

Her smile twisted down, an immediate no, a kind rejection. "And how long do you think it would take the Nineteen to find you? You are a precious gift to them – a polite white man they can put in rooms with other white men. No woman or sage whose skin is even a shimmer darker than old milk can do the same. They'd hunt you down, and they'd destroy my people in the process. No, William. You can run, but not to me."

"Then what do we do now?" I stammered, trying to hide the hurt even as she saw it ripple through my soul. "What now?"

"How would you feel about betraying your government, your queen and your country?" she mused.

I thought about it for barely a moment, then replied, "Will you help me find a cure?"

"Why would you want one?" An honest answer. I put my head on one side, let her read the truth of it from my heart. She sighed, shook her head, did not approve, then held out her hand. "If you will be our inside man in the secret halls of power, William Abbey, then as the daughter of witches I swear I will help you find your cure, foolish though it be."

I shook her hand, and let the truth of her soul run through me as I did. "Socialism, liberty and votes for all, you say?"

This time, her smile was sunlight at the parting of clouds.

Chapter 41

Margot and I, we spent years chasing each other's shadow.

In 1893, after nearly a decade of trying to find a little piece of redemption, I turned traitor, and it was the greatest thing I had ever done.

Later, I would fully appreciate just how little Margot trusted me.

She revealed nothing of her intentions, her hopes or her truth. With laughter in her voice she patted me on the shoulder and told me it would all be fine, and asked what did I know about secret inks. I knew more about secret inks than I'd expected, and so she gave me the addresses of three reputable-sounding people around the world to whom I could write, by which I might betray my country.

"What would you like to know?" I asked earnestly.

"Anything at all! It's all of great interest to the People's Society."

Sometimes I wrote nonsense; rambling missives regarding my travels and exploits. Sometimes I handed over precise, detailed intelligence: names of people to be arrested, the shape of investigations, new warrants or counter-intelligence operations against the revolutionaries of the world.

Only occasionally did I feel a flicker of guilt, as in handing over the name of an undercover policeman set to spy on a circle of socialists, but no no, she assured me, fear not. None of these people will come to harm. They just won't come to truth either. I never knew if she lied. The question was never important to her heart, and I never asked.

I very rarely got a reply, left in dead drops in libraries and little corners of obscure social clubs. When I did, it ranged from the blunt "thank you for your work" through to more detailed requests for information on my colleagues, masters and ministers.

It was a weak system, at first. I could go months without making contact. Gradually, we refined it. In Berlin, I frequented a certain café where I was to accidentally leave a letter for Tante Hilde by the potted fir tree. In Paris, a lecture hall where I sometimes attended talks on vaccinations and infectious disease offered a diabolically uncomfortable set of benches, beneath which missives to one "Dr Giles" could go astray.

In New York, I found a reproachful note waiting for me in Central Park, chiding me for having talked too long and too personally in my last missive, and to keep things to business, lest someone catch wind of what we were about.

In Hong Kong, a girl with bare feet and strange, wide grey eyes came begging whenever we were passing through, and usually I gave her a few coins, and sometimes I gave her a tiny, folded slip of paper with my latest news, and sometimes received a tiny scrap of paper in reply.

In this way, a little at a time, haphazard and chaotic, I betrayed my nation, and felt for the first time in a very long while free.

First, I had to face my employers.

"A woman? Kidnapped you?" demanded the colonel.

"Yes. With a gun."

"A woman with a gun?!" Truly, what had civilisation come to?

"What did you learn of her heart?" asked Albert, always the more level-headed of my masters.

"She's a suffragette, and a socialist. She believes passionately in rights for all, in political freedom, and doesn't think it will be granted without turning to crime, maybe even violence."

"Her name?"

"Mary. I didn't get the rest."

"And why did she kidnap you?"

"To send you a message. She wants you to know that revolution is coming. She wants the government to take the People's Society seriously; to respect and fear the power of the masses. She's a believer. I've rarely met someone who believes so much."

Believers – could anything cause more outrage? The colonel huffed and puffed and hummed and hawed, and Albert said nothing and smiled politely, and on my way I was sent, round and round, leaving the truth far behind.

Chapter 42

Back round the world.

The indiscretions of generals in Bavaria, the corruption of Hungarian princelings, the ambitions of fresh-minted Italian politicians and the secret dealings of French traders out to make a packet. We spun from truth to truth, mining the shallow, pathetic vanities of men's hearts, picking apart ego and pompous self-deceit, the fragile, futile pillars on which the so-called "happiness" of the great and the good was constructed. Lies, threaded so deeply into the veins of men. Here, the husband who was never so happy as when he beat his wife, because in work he was a maggot, a mouse, looked down on by all, but at home, when he clenched his fist, he was glory, he was fire, he was the master of his tiny, bloody universe.

Here, the sexual conqueror; the more they screamed the better he felt, because he was in charge, he liked the way other people were disgusted by his fluids, his bodily fluids, he liked the way they tried to clean him off, knowing he went deep.

The missionary, who whipped himself for finding African women beautiful; the slave-seller from Mali who couldn't believe how well men paid for children; the soldier who knew he had to shoot first, because war was inevitable, and if he shot first it was because the other side were evil and were about to shoot first themselves. Someone always had to shoot first. That didn't make them wrong. From the tiniest grudge to the great sweep of armies across the field, no one is ever wrong, until enough blood has been spilt and enough voices raised in

186

pain that the pillars of their deceit crack, and all that is left is brutal, arctic truth.

The truth that they all know in their hearts, deep below the surface.

That they lie to themselves.

That they deceive in order to pretend that they are right, and they are happy.

That the values they use to say that they are good and great are nothing but a laugh twinkling in God's eye, and all their vaulting, self-important noise will blow to dusty silence in the end.

Everyone lies, Sister.

Sometimes they lie to others, but mostly they lie to themselves. Even the best of men – sometimes, I think, especially the best of men – lie.

It is how they get through the day. It is the gift that makes beauty possible. It is why we are in this godforsaken war. It is the truth of men's hearts. It is the truth of my heart too.

I also lied. Perhaps I've always been a traitor, in some way or another.

And so the years passed.

Albert was, in his way, sometimes honest. He never gave up looking for a cure.

Visiting him in London – never with my shadow near – he and I would visit mesmers, hoodwinkers, card readers and scholars of magnetism to see if any of them might have something to say about my condition.

"I see that you are often afraid," offered a woman in Enfield who claimed descent from an Aztec priestess. She smoked constantly from a clay pipe, hacking up yellow and black spittle that ran from the corner of her mouth in between her pronouncements.

"Have you ever lost someone close to you?" mused a man in Tonbridge who had studied galvanism and the anatomy of the toad and had concluded through his labours that the

187

"other side" could be reached through the vibrations of certain crystals.

"You are cursed!" pronounced a woman from Chelmsford, whose words stirred the briefest tingle of excitement in myself and Albert until, sending in Mrs Parr a few days later to double-check the powers of this wonder, she too was informed that she was cursed, and the matter could only be remedied with large sums of cash.

"I don't know whether to be relieved that so much is bunk," mused Albert as we returned from yet another of our jaunts, "or to wonder what it was that England has lost through all that it has gained." At my raised eyebrow, he threw his hands up, an unopened newspaper in his lap and hat forgotten on the rack above us. "I am not saying I yearn after any sort of naïve, romantic vision of a *mystical* England, or that I would be surprised to find that Merlin was skilled at open-ended questions or had a certain knack for predicting the weather; yet here you are, living proof that there is something our science hasn't yet penetrated. It is so unspeakably frustrating to be able to see the symptoms, know the nature of the disease, and yet to lack the tools to say that *this* is what it is, that it was born of such and such or can be measured in such and such a way."

"I worked in a hospital," I chided. "I know precisely how frustrating it is."

At this, a slightly sad smile tugged the corners of his lips. "You know," he murmured, "I do sometimes envy you. 'Knowing' and 'truth'. They are the two cornerstones of man's existence. Philosophers have picked at their meaning for millennia, of course, but when you strip away the airy-fairy rot about existence or the soul, you have to return to this simplest truth: that mankind loves to be *sure*. To *know*. We cling to the most irrational *truths* like cornerstones in the houses of our lives. My father, for example, claimed until the day he died that you could cure a fever by rubbing fresh baby's urine into your skull. Naturally I could present him with all sorts of arguments and evidence to prove him wrong. I could convince him of the validity of hypothesis, method, elimination. But he had spent so much of his life insisting that he was right that to admit he was wrong then would have been to raise the terrible shadow of what else he was wrong about. A strong man can't be wrong. A father can't be wrong. It is against what he needs to be; what he thinks his children need him to be. And so he was right; he had his truth. Stinking of pee, but happy.

"Now I often believe that the excitement of my profession – of yours perhaps too, as a medical man – is how much I don't know. How much there is to know. I have very few truths in my heart, other than that I think, and I believe the methods I work by are the clearest and most effective ways to achieve clarity, and that I strive to be a good man. I may not always achieve this, but I try, within the moral framework by which I currently define 'good'. Yet even these have about them a certain emotional ... power. Emotional truth, if you will, a thing that stands entirely separate from the function of test and calculation, and that gives me a warm and contented feeling inside. I am pleased with who I am. I hold up some image of myself to the light and, as I see it, I find it satisfactory. And this satisfaction is, if we look at it too closely, built of no more firm stuff than my father's conviction in the power of piss. Yet if you should take it away from me, remove my truth ... how brutal would this world then seem. To serve a flag, a piece of tattered cloth, rather than an idea of Britain. To strive to find answers to questions that may never be solved, my life's work just shouting into the storm. To make money for no better reason than to eat, sleep, die. To see in the sky only endless emptiness that will survive humanity by a million years, to feel in earth only dirt, to be deprived of those ideas that we swathe ourselves in to make of reality something better, something ... *true*. That we *know*. As sure as we know that tomorrow the sun will rise and in the evening it will set. A thing we do not know at all, save that there is some experiential evidence to this effect; but not a truth at all. Not in the strictest sense of the thing. Without knowing, without this conviction, we are thoroughly damned."

I listened to all this very carefully, and managed throughout not to shout, or laugh, or let the shaking of my soul manifest in my hands or mouth. Then, when he seemed to have nothing more to say and I thought I could speak without mangling every word on my tongue, I said, "I know the truth of men's hearts, and what I know is that they are right, every single one of them. They live within the power of their own rightness, and anyone who disagrees with them can only be wrong, and being wrong, they are therefore less. That is what I know, and it terrifies me."

We sat in the compartment in silence for a while. The stations along the route were hung with summer flowering baskets, and children stood on the bridges above the track to wave at the driver as we chugged below. It was a little cutting of England to put on a postcard, as far removed from the crippled wounds of Whitechapel or the docks of Liverpool as a desert from the river.

Finally Albert said, "When did you last see your family?"

The question surprised me, made my fingers clench into fists before I even noticed it, and perhaps I had spent too long with Langa's company, for I was not used to being surprised.

I blurted: "A long time ago. Why?"

"A man should have a home. A man should have ... certain truths. I think that is most essential. It offers a certain conviction."

"My family hasn't been home for a very long time."

"No. No. Of course not. It would be ... I know it is frightening for you to feel ... affection. Sentiment. By loving someone, you naturally endanger them. But I believe that you and I have a professional respect, a courtesy perhaps ... " Here he stopped, and I had never before seen him struggle with an idea, let alone expressing it. "I am, of course, frightened of you – naturally I am. Oh, not of *you*. But of your affliction. If the colonel appears ... it is because he too is terrified of you having any sort of sentiment. I tell him the notion is laughable; neither he nor I is worth your affection. And yet, humans have always wanted friendship. You are no different, and I ... have put a great deal of my value, my self-truth, upon the notion of being a good man. If that endangers me, then ... "

Again he stopped, stumbling over the words.

What would I have seen if the shadow had been upon me?

As well as the truth of his heart, perhaps I would have seen a genuine kindness. These things are never absolute.

"We all take risks," he concluded. "For one reason or another."

It was the closest he ever came to admitting that we were friends, and at the time I thought it was the bravest thing I had ever heard.

I did see my family again — or at least, parts of it.

The Nineteen informed me that my father was ill, and to his bed I went, and he blinked at me suspiciously and muttered, "Oh ... you. Didn't think I'd see you. Well; tell me about your affairs."

I lied, and told him I was rich. I didn't say how, or what possible relevance my wealth had to my profession, and he didn't much care. He was satisfied, and summed the experience up with a brisk "That will do," and was dead a week later.

He died angry, in his brother's house in Kettering. Edward and Andrew had plucked the business from him, and in a sense he admired them for that. They were every bit as ruthless and determined as he had bred them to be, and though he was the final victim of their ambition, at least he knew the business would be in good hands. Yet from being a great potentate in a little world, he was overnight a doddering, boring old man. No one who mattered at all, and that was what really killed him.

I would like to say that the truth of his heart was that he loved me.

Regrettably, he loved only the idea of sons. Sons were correct, worthy, and it was his duty to love them. The reality of humans, whole and true, was far more messy than he was willing to engage with.

191

My mother outlived my father, and on his death made a remarkably swift recovery from her endless maladies, aided no doubt by a move to a town in Norfolk, where she took up work for the local council and discovered, in doing so, that she was in fact capable of more than childbirth. We wrote occasionally, and I lied to her by omission, and visited when I could, and she secretly wrote mildly erotic letters to the vicar, who wrote letters of such poorly imagined sexual depravity in reply that it would put a rabbit off mating in spring, and they never kissed, and were remarkably happy.

Edward is still alive, running Father's business in London. He had two sons, who died within days of each other in the first weeks of the war, and he doesn't understand the idea of leaving a man's affairs in the hands of his surviving daughter. It'll be broken up when he dies, and I will not regret its end.

I suppose it was easy for Albert to become family; my true family. His wife, Flora, eleven years younger than he, dressed in the garb of a woman some fifteen years older - voluminous skirts and yellow hair beneath a starched white bonnet. She held out a gloved hand to welcome me to their home and served cold meats and over-boiled vegetables, talked about the rights of Catholics and the latest fashions on the London stage, and said she was proud to have married a scientist. Then Albert would hold forth on the difficulty of preserving bodies and the science of the brain, and when I suggested that we had plenty of brains, plenty of scalpels, plenty of microscopes and still not a damn jot of science, he pursed his lips and hummed and hawed and pretended he wasn't annoyed by this particular truth.

He was no baron; he could not abide to see me when Langa was near. Yet every time I visited London with my shadow far behind, they invited me to visit in their small, neat home in Richmond, and we would eat bad food kindly made and I would practise French with Flora and pontificating with Albert, and feel, for a little while, like I had a home.

I was there when in 1900 Flora finally gave birth to the child she so desperately wanted. Little Richard Wilson, born late and ridiculously large, given to bawling unless he was fed or rocked constantly; the apple of his mother's eye, a creature to love and dote on while her husband continued to politely kiss her on the cheek and marvel at how strong a baby's hand could be.

Richard Wilson, son of the professor and his wife.

He was fourteen years old when this war broke out, and wanted to enlist immediately. When he turned fifteen, he tried to sign up again, and was caught, and his father sent him to the countryside to work on his uncle's farm, in the hope that the lad would feel he was at least doing some sort of honest labour. Two months before he turned sixteen, he finally made it into the ranks under a false name – Richard Charlwood – and was shipped to France within the month. His mother is probably proud, even though she is terribly, terribly afraid.

I don't know whether I will curse the son and kill the father, or curse the father and let him watch his son die. I am still weighing my options in that regard.

Chapter 43

I was not the only one spinning round the world.

A year after Margot vanished from Paddington station, the People's Society were implicated in riots in Paris; but then the working people of Paris had always been inclined to radical ideas, tutted the colonel, and the French had never known how to keep these things in order.

Six months after that, the Society was blamed for a spate of resignations and sudden departures for prolonged yachting trips among the gentry of northern Italy; three weeks after that, Pinkerton informed Scotland Yard that they suspected the Society of having swayed a senator in New Jersey over a matter of certain improprieties, inappropriately learnt.

Margot was up to her old tricks, peeking above the parapet again, and I followed her every move with fascination from afar, and kept her always one step ahead of the law, and wondered if I would see her again for more than the briefest exchange of coded messages, and was bitterly disappointed when I did not.

Then there was Vienna.

We came to Vienna in the winter of 1895. Few courts of Europe had the bombast of the Austrians; even the Russians had more savour in their pomposity, relishing the grandeur of their pageants, whereas the Austrians claimed to have been performing their pronouncements and endless, tedious duties since the age of Charlemagne. I had no time for it, but the baron was in his element, for he loved nothing more than a duel of grandiloquence.

He was also dying. There was no escaping the truth of it by then, and though we should have written to the Nineteen weeks ago and requested his transfer home, Mrs Parr and I had concluded mutually that the only thing more likely to kill him than time and pneumonia would be enforced retirement.

I had spent so much time with the truth of his heart, and had no doubt of it. There had been a moment, aged twenty-three, when he had been discharged from his commission with the cavalry after having a seizure on the parade grounds. He'd only ever had one seizure in his life preceding, when as a three-year-old boy he nearly died from the measles; he'd only ever have one after, when aged forty-eight he was taken with a parasitical worm that crawled into his feet through the bare sand of Siam. But even one seizure was one too far, and announcing briskly in his papers that he was "crippled – beyond medical use", he found himself stuck in St James's Park in the pouring rain, shaking with rage and indignity, and swore never to leave the parade ground ever again. Since then, his every moment had been spent carving a podium for himself from which not infirmity, general, minister or God himself might dislodge the baron's essential, inescapable value. Death was kinder than to take away the truth he had made of himself.

"Just a sniffle," he would mutter as his eyes sank deeper into his skull and every breath came in a rattle. "Just a bit peaky!"

And in his heart, he was terrified, and he hoped he would die alone, no one to see his end, and couldn't bear for us to leave him behind.

Yet the Nineteen still had orders, which must be obeyed. I waited for Langa to draw near, ready to write reports on princes and princelings with as much interest as if I were a fishmonger scraping scales, and at night I sat with the baron and read him the newspapers, and wondered if he would die tonight, or tomorrow, or next month, or next year, and didn't know the answer, merely that the only thing left to do for how-ever long he had left to do in it was die.

When the woman in the blue skirt and white shawl knocked on my door, it was both a terrible imposition and a dreadful relief.

"You doctor?" she demanded, lips blue from the cold. "English doctor?"

"Um, I suppose ... "

"Doir-e-ann very ill. You must come now!"

She struggled to say "Doireann", sounds unfamiliar on her tongue. Margot's child, buried beneath a crooked beech tree somewhere in southern Ireland. My heart stuck in my throat. "I'll come at once."

Snow was falling heavily from a bruised purple sky, muffling all sound and life in the city save for the jingling of horses' bells. The baron was sleeping, wheezing and swaddled in his bed. Mrs Parr sat dozing by the fire. I woke neither as I slipped into the dark. Shuffling through ankle-deep fresh fallen snow, slipping over frozen horse piss and cobbles turned to blackened sheet ice, I followed the woman in the shawl through lung-locking cold, not sure if I'd ever be able to find my way back. The grandeur of the centre of the city rolled down to ever shorter houses, the parade of Habsburg monuments to this emperor or that triumph breaking down now to scratchy crucifixes and low, bolted black doors. Sometimes a carriage emerged, slipping and sliding, through the falling ice. Sometimes a man tripped and cursed, far, far away, and probably right next to where I walked. My trousers began to seep through, damp and frozen, frost crawling up towards my knees. I shivered and panted, lips turning blue, and still the woman tutted, "Come, come come!"

The street she led me to was perfectly polite, in its way. In summer, boxes of flowers might have bloomed in the win-dowsills, and the neighbours all kept a servant upstairs and a clean pantry below. Through one, the woman took me to a room adorned with cross-stitched figures of mortified saints, withered purple posies in dusty white-blue vases, and there, swathed in blankets and furs, head towards the fire: Margot.

"Hello, William," she said, as the door closed behind me. "Take your shoes off; dry those socks by the fire."

Since London, we had almost never met, and I had wondered about her, dreamt about her, not even known what to call the tumult of my thoughts and fantasies. Now there she was, huddling against an orange glow, consumed beneath the weight of blankets, smiling, eyes bright, laughing at my fluster as I struggled, undignified, into the great armchair opposite hers.

"For God's sake," she barked, when I fidgeted and fumbled at the bag in my lap, "Just take your socks off and get comfortable. Do you think I care if you have hairy feet?"

I took my shoes and socks off, wiggled my toes by the fire, and even that was a stranger intimacy with a woman than I was used to.

"How have you been, in yourself, William?" she asked at last, watching me.

I shrugged. "It all continues as it always does."

"Langa?"

The awareness that for the first time we were meeting and my shadow was nowhere to be found made me shuffle a little lower in my chair as I mumbled, "Ten days away, at least. There's talk of revolts in the Balkans, and unrest in Russia. The Austrians are hoping the tsar has enough problems at home to keep him occupied, and the tsar is hoping the Austrians have enough problems in Serbia and Bulgaria to keep them busy."

"I imagine it makes them feel like big men, to have such big problems to worry about. Why do the British care, or does it just make them feel sizeable in the trouser region to swagger around?"

To my surprise, I blushed. I have spent a large part of my life dusting the nether regions of infected individuals with an array of powders and poultices, but to hear the sweep of global politics reduced to pissing up the wall was briskly unsettling for me. My answer was a pink-cheeked mumble delivered to the flames. "We want the Russians weak, but we don't want the Austrians too strong. We need the Ottoman sultanate to remain stable enough to keep on paying its debts and legitimising our occupation of Suez, so that the trade routes remain open. An Austrian resurgence might threaten that status quo, or worse, allow the Germans to move in and ..." She laughed, high and sharp, and I stopped, strangely embarrassed. "I'm ... sorry. This is my job."

"No, no! I didn't mean to laugh. Peadar, the Society – they see everything as a struggle for the working man to be free. Everything the great men of Vienna do is seen as a personal assault on the freedoms of ordinary men, but I try to tell them – it has nothing to do with you, or me, or anyone you'd meet in the street. We don't even register. If they go to war, it is not men that are going to be fighting. It is Austria. It is this idea that is Austria. There is nothing about *man* or *woman* within that, at all. We are not in the calculations of great men."

"When you say 'we', does that include you?"

A dismissive wave of the hand. "I have drunk the cup of revolution too long now to drink anything else, even if I sometimes just want a shandy. There are arrest warrants for me in every country of the civilised world, as far as I can tell. Peadar says that's a sign we must be doing something right."

"Peadar ... the overprotective gentleman with the fists?"

A brief nod, a slightly apologetic smile. "He thinks I'm magic."

"Magic? Literally or metaphorically?"

"A bit of both; can't it be a bit of both, William? He's a believer. Sometimes he believes so hard that I forget what I think. The lines, when the truth is on me, the gap between his heart and mine – it can be difficult, you know?"

"I ... have some familiarity with it."

"I sometimes think it would have been easier to meet a dashing rogue, or a wealthy libertine. I could have believed in doing nothing at all then, except travel and wine. Would have been much easier."

"Don't you believe anything for yourself?"

"Do you?" she retorted, eyebrow flicking. "I find knowing how strongly and how deeply people believe in their own personal little truths, their deep certainties and fantastical lies makes it hard for me to give much credence to anything at all these days." I looked down at my soggy socks, wiggled my toes towards the fire, said nothing. Her face softened a little, and leaning out she brushed my knee with her hand, a strange intimacy entirely alien to any women I'd known. "Thank you for your letters."

"I hope they've been useful."

"Very. And I appreciate the danger you put yourself in."

"Sometimes, believing nothing . . . is harder than believing in even a flawed idea."

"You think the People's Society is flawed?" She laughed before I could reply, backpedal over my words. "You're right. Of course you are. But if truth-speaking is good for anything, it should be good for giving the silent truths a voice, no?"

"That's . . . probably what I'd like written on my tombstone."

"A terrible epitaph for a spy."

"As you say: I am a terrible spy."

Another laugh, and now I wished Langa were near, yearned for him with every fibre of my being, longed to know what was in her heart. Now she talked, chatted away as if we were the oldest of friends, above revolutions and pamphlets, bickering among the committees – how could even revolutions have bickering committees? – about blackmail and funds, how she hated a wet winter and would rather have snow, and whether this absurd "zipper" thing would really catch on in clothing.

I made some feeble noises as she talked, and all the time watched her watching me, and wondered how far Doireann was, and what she saw in my heart.

And abruptly as she had started, she stopped talking, as if she had walked straight into the wall of my curiosity, and staring past me as if I were suddenly no more than a piece of furniture said, "Near enough, William. She's near enough."

I nodded, found I had nothing more to add.

Head on one side, she examined me a little while more, then blurted, "I've married him, you know?"

"Married . . . ?"

"Peadar. Don't look like that. He's loved me as long as he's known me, and if you spend enough time in the presence of someone who loves you so much, and if you are a woman, travelling – you make a choice, don't you? He's a good man. He is absolutely sincere in his intention to take a bullet for me, and understands that I have my own ideas about what marriage means. He's very intelligent, in his way. He appreciates the game."

"Congratulations, I suppose."

"You suppose nothing of the sort. It's an arrangement. I'll probably leave him, in a few years, once I've saved enough. You can't fund a revolution on blackmail alone; sooner or later I'll want to retire and leave them to it, and I'm thinking sooner. I've worked it all out; with the railway lines between San Francisco, Chicago and New York I can reside at one address for almost three months before I need to run. Three houses and a train ticket – that's what I need. That's long enough to build something, to make something real."

"I . . . don't know what to say to that. I don't know what I'm meant to say."

"You've spent too much time on the road; you've forgotten how to say anything for yourself."

"You know the truth of my heart. I don't know yours."

"You've seen it before."

"Only twice, and one of those I ended up bleeding."

"But you saw enough to betray your masters."

"Yes. I did. But that . . . that doesn't mean I did it for you."

The words stuck as soon as they came from my mouth, and again, I looked away, suddenly ashamed. What would Langa say, if he could speak now? What would Sibongile make of the use to which I had put the ghost of her son?

"And is all this . . . " I gestured limply round the room, low ceiling and wood panels, reflected firelight and smothering snow through the glass, "a test? Neither of us is good at trust. Not when we could simply know."

She half shrugged, practised, meaningless, watching me in reflected firelight. "I suppose you could call it a test, if you like. Peadar has been itching for me to sit down with you, pick at your soul when your shadow is too far away to pick at mine. He thinks you're double-crossing us. He can't work out how, though. He can't see what your angle is, is still trying to find a reason to put a bomb in your carriage. Does that upset you? Bombings – that upsets you. I see. Why?"

"I'm a doctor."

"You think that sounds more righteous than saying you are a victim? Of course it does. A man of science must defend the truth of his method, rather than admit to a life lived, and the man it made him. The boy who died in Italy when the nitroglycerin blew; he didn't die for you. Neither did Langa. They would have died anyway. The world killed them; all you did was play your part."

"That's all anyone ever does," I snapped, harder than I meant. "That's all the butchers say."

Firelight in her eyes, something more in the turn of her head. "Do you think it will change? Your masters, this system they've built for their own benefit; do you think they will ever stop playing their great games, and look to their own streets? They are fantastically skilled in keeping us from rising up in our own name, making every beggar grateful for a scrap of bread, every poor man angry to see a beggar eat. They set raja on raja, union on union, brother on brother, and like the white men who killed a black boy at the boab tree, the only thing they fear is the moment the persecuted stop persecuting each other, and see. See the truth of where this oppression was truly born. Truth-speakers should be honest with each other. Do you ever think it will change?" I felt sick, and her shadow was near. "You don't. Do you think we can make them change with blackmail and pamphlets? Honestly? You don't. Well then, when all else is gone . . . "

201

I stood quickly. "This isn't fair. This isn't ... I have interrogated plenty of men, and pulled their secrets from their souls without their permission. It was not ... ethical, it was not kind or righteous. Tear me apart if you want to; I won't run. I understand how hard trust can be. Just don't think you get to wrap yourself in a mantle of decency while you do it."

For a moment, she stared up, watching, wondering, balancing choices on an edge. Then she raised her hands, placating, gestured back towards the chair. "You're right. I apologise. It is easy to forget sometimes that I ... that we are more than the things other people use us for. The Society – there is a list. Of names, great men who do terrible things. They think they're untouchable, and maybe they are, but the Society has its little black book too, of the ones they think need to die before the revolution comes. Does that shock you?"

"No."

"Good. I think it's ridiculous, but one day, they say – one day violence may be all that is left, watering the tree of liberty and all that nonsense. One day. Perhaps one day they'll be right. Who knows who we will become? Please stay. I'll say no more. I'm sorry. I ... would like you to stay."

Slowly I sank back down into my seat, pressed hard to the back, legs crossed, arms folded, chin down, contemplating my own lap. Finally: "You know everything about me, and I know little about you. It is pure hypocrisy to ask you not to say it out loud. Much of what we are is hypocrisy, I understand that. The incredible contradictions that we must, need to hold in our hearts to be who we are, without going mad. It is a necessary game. Thank you for ... for saying nothing more. For now."

She shrugged, drifted back into her seat, shuffled her furs a little tighter around her shoulders, watched me for a while. Then: "Who do you love, William Abbey?"

I closed my eyes. "I have no idea."

"Then why do you run from Langa?"

"I ... care for people. Is that enough? Is that true?" Her lips thinned, and she didn't answer, and I didn't know. "Albert spends so much of his time researching, researching, today another legend, tomorrow a new sample, it's a miracle he hasn't cut open my skull to test the grey matter of my brain. And I ask him, 'What if there is no one left who I love?' and neither he nor I has an answer. Who will Langa kill if I no longer care? But there are people ... Mrs Parr, the baron, even Albert, I suppose ... a woman in India, there are ... but I suppose at the end of the day I run because I cannot imagine a life without some sort of human connection, and if I ever stopped running it would be because there's nothing worth living for any more. Does that answer your question?"

"Yes. It does."

Something in the way she answered, an age in her voice I had not heard before, made me open my eyes, to find her leaning forward now, elbows on her knees, chin down and gaze up, on the edge of her seat. I licked my lips, mumbled, "Why do you run?"

"I love Peadar," she replied simply, and then in the same breath: "Actually, I don't think I do. But he loves me and Doireann is near so often, and there are habits, always habits you see, you get into ... but like you, it seems that standing still would be admitting something I'm not ready for. Not yet. Peadar doesn't listen to me. Not really. All the black-mail, the truths, the knowing – of course that, yes. But that doesn't matter, not really. The People's Society don't listen to a woman with an opinion. And then I tell him that I love him and he knows that's a lie, but if he knows then I must know, and he doesn't understand how I could possibly say it, not something so important. So I must love him after all. Otherwise I'd never be able to say it. He doesn't understand why some lies come easy to some people and hard to others. He doesn't know how to think any way other than the way he thinks. When I tell him that you won't betray us, he doesn't believe it. You're going to be followed until the day you die, William Abbey."

"That's hardly news."

"He means well. It's useful for me to have a man to say the things I want said to other men. Makes things easier."

"I think Mrs Parr would agree with you there."

"The legendary Mrs Parr! How I would love to spend an hour sitting in her shadow."

"You would find her precisely as she seems to be."

"No one is ever that."

"I think perhaps she is. I think she has shaped herself to be exactly what she appears to be, even if once she was something else."

"A good trick, if you can do it."

"If you can."

We sat for a while in silence, as the logs spat and the snow fell. Then at last she said, "Your shadow is far away now, but you've spent time in my company while he was near. What did you see?"

"Why do you ask?"

"I'm curious. The people I am surrounded by shroud me in a near-mystical devotion. Cursed with ancient magic, coming good for the working man, as if the very nice clothes and very pretty jewels I buy for myself are just a necessary tithe, or I don't enjoy ripping apart bombast. The men I rob see me as either a woman or a wallet; the Society see me as a frightening tool. Peadar is very brave, to try and make me love him. But you are the only other one of my kind I've met. What did you see?"

"I saw your daughter. Doireann."

She nodded, slow and stiff. "That makes sense. What else?"

"I saw how much you love the game. How much you love being adored, and important; tearing down great men is your greatest pleasure."

"I'd say that was fair. What else?"

"I saw the men who wronged you; how easy it is to have everything taken away."

"You only have to have eyes to see that, not a shadow. What about the ones I love?"

"What of them?"

"Did you see them?"

"No."

"Strange."

"Is it?"

"Saira is strong in your heart."

"I ... she is ... please let's not talk of her."

"But you saw no one in me?"

"No."

She nodded again, leant back into her chair as if the strings that held her had been cut. "Would you sleep with me, William Abbey?"

"I beg your pardon?"

"I know you find me attractive."

"That ... is an unfair use of ... that is hardly kind."

"Don't be ridiculous; sometimes eyes are enough. Peadar knows. I pick up men here or there, just ... because I can. Peadar *knows*. He has convinced himself that I do it so that we can never love each other fully. That way he might not die, when Doireann catches me. Therefore I love him more than if I hadn't tried to hurt him. His truths are very complicated."

"Are yours?"

A puff of air, a half-closing of her eyes, and suddenly she seemed tired. "I don't know. Doireann never lets me see myself. I met a woman once who loved her husband with every fibre of her being, who blazed with pleasure at the sight of his face, the brush of his skin against hers. I thought I loved her for a while, behaved a little erratically in her presence, I will admit, but it was just her love I loved. The rare power of it. It was the most beautiful thing I'd ever seen, and I nearly let Doireann catch me just to be close to it. But it wasn't for me, not loving *me*. I kept on moving, and there have been some boys who have lusted after me, and I enjoy that, but they assume a connection, assume it's something more, and I have to stop myself from saying, no, sweet thing. It's just the situation we're in. It's not love. Perhaps Peadar would drop dead, and be very gratified at his dying, if Doireann caught me. The curse always finds a connection. I would have liked to know if anyone stood out to you."

"Only Doireann; only the dead."

She nodded into the fire, irises dark in reflected light, then puffed out a breath like a weary whale and grinned, false and brittle as cut glass. "Well. Hasn't this been a delight?"

I met her eyes, and wanted to look away, and found I couldn't. Her head drifted to one side, contemplating.

"Shall we be honest with each other, William Abbey?"

"I don't see that we have much of a choice."

"Nonsense. Everyone knows the truth, always. They know it with a great and fiery intensity, and keep on knowing it even when they have been proven wrong. To choose to be honest, really honest ... that is a rare privilege. One of a few rare privileges we might share."

"I have no shadow, I don't know if ... "

"You know precisely; please don't be a fool. People know all the time, without being cursed."

"I do not consider this wise."

"And yet you have not left. Have you?"

I managed to break her gaze, stare down at the floor. A sighing and a shifting of furs pulled my eyes back up, as, like a bear shaking itself free of a deep slumber, she sloughed off her layers of blanket, pushing them to the floor, and half rising to her feet, half leaning forward, put one hand on my knee, and the other on my chin.

"Just one honest thing," she whispered, as our lips met.

That night we became lovers, and never spoke on the subject again.

Chapter 44

"You love her," sighed Dr Abbey, and it took me a moment to realise that he was not addressing a memory or telling a story, but speaking to me. "You hated yourself for loving her. Your mother would be ashamed of you. You are disgusting, there is something wrong with you. That's why you never talked to anyone about Matilda's love, because you already knew what they would say, that you were broken on the inside. You hate that you are too weak to fix yourself – but it's a lie. How can it possibly be weak to love someone? So here you are, Sister Ellis, stuck between love and death, unable to believe Matilda when she tells you that you are beautiful, because you know inside that you are hideous. They put that inside you. The whole world put that inside you, and now you can't get it out of your head, you can't—"

"Stop," I barked, louder than I'd meant. Then, quieter, fearful of the sleeping house: "Please. Stop now."

He stopped, and it was hard, a grunting, a half-turning-away. He pinched the soft flesh of his palm hard enough for the skin to turn red, then white, and closed his eyes around the pain, and managed to let out a shuddering breath before saying, "I'm sorry. He's close now. That was ... he's getting close."

In the bed between us, drugged and broken, the half-man slept, nostrils flaring, a damp grumbling at the back of his throat sometimes rumbling up, then falling silent for so long I wondered if Richard Charlwood had stopped breathing. If he had, I would not move. There was nothing to be done.

For a moment, glancing at the window, I thought the dawn was coming, but it was only the light of the battlefield. The wind had turned, carrying the sound of the cannon away from us, but if I closed my eyes and listened for the place between Charlwood's breathing, there it was. Perhaps I would hear its echo until the day I died.

"I'm going back to her," I announced, and was surprised to hear myself saying it. "If she'll have me. I'm going to go back to her."

"Yes. I believe you will."

"Are you going to run?"

"No. Albert will be here soon. And if he doesn't come, I'll put the shadow on his son. They always loved each other. Either way, Albert dies."

"And everyone Charlwood has ever loved?"

"Yes."

"I won't let you."

"I know you'll try to stop me. Though you are less resolved on what you'll do should the father arrive. Interesting. Perhaps we are beginning to see the limits of your contradictions too, Sister Ellis; the lies you tell to be who you need to be."

I reached into my apron, and withdrew needle and bottle. As Abbey watched, I loaded the syringe to the brim, and perched, needle across my lap. "Enough morphine to kill a horse," I snapped. "I'll use it on you, and if I can't get to you, I'll use it on Charlwood. He can't run; he can't just . . . get on the next train. I will kill him before I let you curse him."

"All right."

"You believe me?"

"I'd be a poor truth-speaker if I didn't."

The relief of it hit me in a hot flood, along with a strange adulation. I was willing to kill to save a life; I hadn't known if I could, but Dr Abbey believed me; perhaps I was a murderer after all.

He shifted a little on his perch by the window, the light of battle flickering at his back. Was it a bit brighter, nearer? Was that the clunk of an engine on the road outside, the sound of voices raised in pain? I was so tired; just tired.

Then he asked, "Since we appear to be at a stalemate, what shall we do now?"

"How did you learn how to curse another poor bastard? The way you tell it, you didn't know shit. How'd you learn how to spread your poison?"

"Bitter experience."

"Seems right, for a bitter man."

"You have no idea what I've lost," he snapped, a sudden fury rising to his face, a lurch in his spine. "Margot is . . ." Slammed his hands over his mouth before he could finish the sentence, swallowed it down, turned away, as though to digest his own vomit, keep down the truth before saying it out loud.

"Dead? You might know the truth of people's hearts, Dr Abbey, but you surely don't know how to respect it. 'I really enjoy Wagner. I never betrayed my friends.' You tell lies to see if you can still lie, to test how far away your shadow is. I've listened to your . . . self-pitying confession. Sat here while you tried to work out what you actually think. Christ, you know what everyone else is thinking except yourself. 'Shall we be honest', Margot said – honestly dishonest, she meant. Lovers cos you both knew it was meaningless, lovers cos you both were incapable of love, easy sex, easy lies, knowing it was a lie made it so much easier, didn't it? *What did you do?*"

For a moment, he rolled between rage and shame like a coracle in the ocean. Shame won; it was obviously going to win. Didn't need a shadow to see that. He slumped back, curled over like a crow, suddenly an old man.

"I learnt a few hard lessons," he replied. "Then I killed them."

Chapter 45

It is as you have said: we were lovers because it was easy.

My history of relationships with the fairer sex has been, I would say, fairly catastrophic.

From my first infatuation with Isabella, to my entanglements with Margot, the truth has kept me from engaging in anything meaningful with anyone much at all. For a moment, I thought perhaps there could be a way in which Saira and I knew each other's hearts, without the burden of saying things that could be left unsaid. The same thought crossed her mind, but her truth met mine, and in each other's gazes we were forced to confront not what we believed in our hearts, but what we saw honestly in each other, and that can take the amorous wind out of anyone's sails.

I have, in my travels, visited brothels of the less contagious sort, but when Langa is close it is almost impossible to find a liaison that doesn't destroy itself with too much knowledge of a woman's life, truth, boredom or pain. You might think that knowing the truth of a woman's heart could make me a superb wooer, but what I mostly perceive is of how little interest I am to my conversational correspondent.

Margot was different. We went to great lengths to keep the truth away, so that we could believe whatever we wanted.

We would meet, sometimes in this city, sometimes another, and for a brief night we would forget ourselves and each other, and there was no place for infatuation, sentiment or meaning. We both knew far too much of each other to imagine that it was anything other than a brief flurry in the dark, and that was enough. That was extraordinary. The single most honest thing either of us could ever do; brutal in its honesty. Arousing in its honesty. The single greatest joy in my life.

It was a game. The shiver of betrayal, the excitement of finally making my own choices, being my own man – even if that man was a traitor. I had no illusions that Margot would ever leave Peadar Coman for me, though sometimes I dreamt of it. And whenever we met, she always made sure my shadow was far, far behind, and I understood why, and it was fine. She never trusted me. She just loved the game. The game made her feel ... alive.

Seven days after my first liaison with Margot in that Vienna winter, the baron died. He withered in front of the fire, a needle in a haystack of blankets and bedpans. Mrs Parr wrote to the Nineteen, informing them that he was too sick to travel.

    Return Cresswood England STOP Abbey
    proceed Istanbul STOP

Mrs Parr received the telegram, and pretended she hadn't. By the time we were spoon-feeding him he had a few days at most, swinging in and out of lucidity, so we took turns, sitting by his side, reading nonsense out loud to him as his breath whistled away. He had never wanted to die in his own bed, although now that death finally had him by the heart, he found his absolute certainty on this subject was in fact rather irrelevant. He was going to die; and for the first time this certainty scared him. Death does that; the truths of our hearts dissolve before that final, inescapable reality.

In the end, I stayed a little too long by his side. The truth was pressing hard against my lips, and he could see it, and was grateful that I ran the risk, and did not approve.

"What has Mrs Parr brought today – ah, the plays of Goethe. Lucky us. Are you ready? I'll try and do the voices ... "

211

Sometimes, when a man dies a slow and thoroughly unpleasant death, it is tempting to offer comfort. I looked in the truth of the baron's heart, and there was only the certainty of the darkness, and fear without comfort, and the fading-away of everything he had been. It is easy to want to remove another person's pain. You have seen it too, Sister Ellis. The young ones, the fresh-faced children, come to the front line, they sit with the dying men and they exclaim, "What can I do?"

"Nothing" is the reply they want to hear. "But don't you worry yourself, I am going to a better place."

In this way, the living ask the dying to comfort them, the ones who will go on. It is a very human act. It comes from a place of devotion, absolution. The nurses soon grow out of it.

"Dear God, I think this bit is in verse. Brace yourself, Baron ..."

I read to him as he died, and I was an appalling reader and dull company, and that was all there was to it. And Langa came. And with him, another truth, nestled in the deepest, most secret part of the baron's heart: that he believed I was a traitor.

This knowing came upon me slowly, a distraction that needled at the edge of my reading, skipping over lines. Then a creeping conviction, then an absolute certainty that made me put the book down and stare at nothing much, feeling the deepest corners of the baron's soul as if his blood pumped through the cavities of my chest.

He looked my way and thought for a moment that Langa was come, but seeing I was silent, knew it was not so. Then he knew what it might be instead that silenced me, but wasn't sure, and this was deeply disquieting for him. He had understood everything in his life with blazing certainty, but had, alas, allowed himself to grow almost fond of me in time. Fondness was a terrible curse. It reduced the clarity of the thing. Like many men who do not want to know the answer, he had never once asked the question, and knew in that act itself was truth.

And soon he would be dead.

These things are hard to judge, even for a doctor. A man might go in an instant, or linger for weeks.

"I am," I said at last, watching the open page in my lap. "You are right. You are right about me."

The words came, and that must mean Langa was near.

And yet again: "I think my father was a warm, friendly sort of chap, and my brothers have great depths of genial sentiment."

The words were hard, each syllable pushed through like a tired man trying to argue before a black-capped judge, but they came.

And then: "But I am. Also. What you think I am. I have never betrayed anything to agents of a foreign power, nor collaborated in violence, but in every other way, you are right about me. You are right."

The baron nodded once, and we sat in silence a while. Then I rose, and as I did, one hand brushed out, tickling the surface of my skin like the brush of a bottle fly. He tried to speak, and couldn't, sticky gum around his eyes, his lips.

I nodded, already half turned to the door. "I know it's a mistake. I know it is. I know there'll be a price. I just ... needed something that was mine. I'm sorry."

He wasn't angry. Disappointed, and pleased that he'd been right. Sad to see someone he accounted as near to a son making a terrible mistake. Resigned, knowing that there was nothing to be done. He had never experienced that sensation before. In a way, it brought him astonishing relief, and he was briefly annoyed that he hadn't been resigned to a few more things throughout the course of his life. It might have made things easier.

"Run," he whispered, and that was his last ever word to me.

That night, I stood alone on the platform of the station waiting for the train to Budapest, and rattled off the truth of every slumbering soul and dreary dream that shifted through the midnight air around me. I blurted the broken heart of

213

the porter and the injustices of the stationmaster, I wittered about the driver of the train and the engineer with his coal-baked skin, and when at last I boarded at an empty coach, I looked back over my shoulder and Langa was there, shuffling up the stairs, one hand held out to me, like a friend long lost, coming home.

I waved goodbye to him as the train pulled out of the platform, and received a telegram the next morning to inform me that the baron had died in the night.

Stop.

Dawn in Budapest.

I sat alone by the river that divided the city, and was briefly alone.

No one else's heart beat in my chest.

I dreamt no one's dreams but my own.

The sky was infinite, the last of the stars chased into the west. The birds stirred in the domes across the river, fluttered around the spires at my back. The cobbles beneath my feet were worn to smooth curves, the first smell of coffee and pastry was beginning to drift on the biting wind, but here, the banks were not yet open and only the maids of the wealthy were stirring, picking around the shuttered houses to stir embers back to life.

I felt entirely at peace, perfectly quiet and alone. I had a letter in my pocket from Margot, an appointment to meet that night. I had no other responsibilities in the day. I should be halfway to Istanbul, but no one would punish me for stopping a while as Langa shuffled after. I could not remember the last time I had not been drowning in the thoughts of other men. I had spent my coin of grief for the baron over the long months of his demise, and now felt free. I had seen too many people who loved powerfully for one who died a slow death turn to gratitude when the pain stopped, and had no guilt at the thing.

Naturally this state of affairs offered superb opportunity for the Austrians to swoop in and arrest me, which they did with a brutal efficiency and a hasty *"Entschuldigung*, you will now come with us, *danke."*

Well damn.

Being arrested by a foreign power had always been a possibility. Britain and Austria spied on each other with merry abandon all the time; it was just the way of things. Our interests were not entirely aligned, but we could all agree that no one wanted a powerful Russia or a frisky France, and if we stole from each other occasionally, who cared? That was just the game.

Damn.

I was handcuffed and bundled into the back of a heavy grey carriage, flanked on either side by gentlemen with thick brown coats, impressive moustaches and small bowler hats. I felt strangely detached from the procedure, noting without sentiment when the nature of the road beneath the cart began to change from cobble to mud, a rougher, ice-pooled track heading out of the city. The whole business seemed suddenly so absurdly irrelevant in the grand scheme of things. I was calm when, some few hours after my arrest, I was prodded politely into a frozen courtyard flanked on three sides by the cracked stucco of a grand hunting lodge, complete with stables and barking, eager dogs that spun and yapped around my legs, trying to work out if I was friend or foe. I was calm through a corridor lined with the severed heads and horns of a hundred slaughtered beasts, pinned up floor to ceiling, barely enough room for the ancient, wax-entombed stubs of candelabra to peek through. I was calm when led to a small servant's room in the highest floor of the house and padlocked by a length of chain to a bar across the window in a manner that smacked of hasty improvisation. A rope bed was pressed to one wall, and a fireplace of dirty ashes and unswept char was cold by the door, which was locked with a heavy clunk of bolt and key, leaving me alone.

For a while, alone I stayed, shivering in the cold, until at last this, more than anything else, made me uncurl from my huddled ball in a corner and stamp on the floor shouting, "Hello! It's freezing in here! Do you want me to fall ill?"

On reflection, it was such a monstrously stupid sentiment that I'm surprised my cries weren't answered with laughter. Rather, they were met with a silence so profound that for a moment I wondered if I'd just been abandoned here to starve, and the whole thing was a strange, barbaric murder attempt. Only the distant barking of dogs and the occasional strike of metal hooves on stone reassured me that life continued in this place.

One sense may quickly drown another. I was, within a very short time, extremely thirsty, and very hungry – but the cold was so much more profound than all of these that I could hardly spare the heat to think on them. As my fingers and lips turned blue, then white, the fear finally began to settle on me. What if there was something more to this affair than mere bombast between distant powers? Suddenly the abstract certainty in which I had invested my faith – that a place called Britain gave two figs for my well-being and would scour all of Hungary to find me – began to totter. My death might be an embarrassment for the Nineteen, but great men wouldn't be shaken a jot if I died in this place.

Now came the fear, so that when the door was unlocked and a woman came in to light the fire, eyes down and shoulders turned against me, I found myself babbling all sorts of imprecations and enquiries of her in English and ragged German, all of which she ignored absolutely. Her hands shook as she lit the fire, and the moment the kindling curled she was on her feet and out of there like I was a barking fox.

My chain would not permit me to huddle close to the flames, so I stretched myself as far towards them as I could, spinning my body so that now my face could get the benefit of their warmth, now my feet; yet no sooner was one part warm than another was cold again, and I cursed this damned room

and these damned people for keeping me in such an uncivi-
lised state.

A few hours after the sun had set, the door opened again,
and a man came in to leave me a bowl of chicken and potatoes,
just within arm's reach, and a jug of ale.

"What's going on?" I demanded in every language I could
muster. "I need to use the bathroom. Who are you? The fire is
getting low. I demand to speak to my embassy!"

He was less anxious about meeting my eyes than the fire-
starter, and clearly unimpressed. He said not a word, and left
me to my meal, though a few minutes later the woman came
back in to put more damp, mouldy logs into the flames, which
spat and smoked extraordinarily, and which I was immoder-
ately grateful for.

I tried sleeping that night on the bed, being mildly less
freezing than the floor, and it was profoundly uncomfortable
and I slept not a wink.

By the next morning, the confidence I'd possessed was
entirely smothered by cold, misery and ignorance. Two men
took me to the edge of what I took to be extensive forested
grounds, so that I might wash and relieve myself, and may as
well have been deaf for all they responded to my relentless
barrage of noise. They were not cruel, nor kind, nor any sort of
human that I could detect, and by the time the woman came
to relight the fire, I'd given up on asking anything.

"Thank you," I blurted, as she scrambled away from
the hearth.

She didn't look at me, but crossed herself as she
scuttled out.

The next night, I began to dream the dreams of the house.

In the stables, a man who dreams of . . .

. . . nailing on horseshoes, nailing on horseshoes, nailing
on horseshoes for ever but he can't ever quite get it right, tries
again, tries again, can't get it right.

In the servants' quarter, a woman who dreams of great black
demons sitting on her chest, come to eat her soul, and wakes

217

paralysed, and has woken paralysed a hundred nights before and still can't stop the terror.

Downstairs, a room of slaughtered animals comes alive, to chase the dreamer though crimson snow. He called out in German, and so did I, and the sound was enough to jerk me awake, and maybe him too, and the moon was full and peeking through the high barred window, and Langa was coming.

In the mid morning, the door was unlocked.

A man in black riding cloak, white leather gloves and tall grey fur hat stood in the door. He had a military bearing, and the truth of his heart was that he considered espionage and war to be precisely the same thing, and that it was a damned poor general who looked down on his spies, and a damn poor spy who didn't listen to his general.

He said, in thickly accented English, "How far is the shadow?"

It took me a while to answer, so he repeated the question, harder, impatient.

"I don't know what you mean."

"How far?"

"I don't understand. My name is William Bishop, I'm a doctor, your men – your *men* arrested me, I have been held here in these appalling conditions, I demand to speak to my—"

"You are Dr William Abbey, late of service to the deceased Baron Cresswood, of the Nineteen. You are cursed with a *lidérc* that follows you wherever you go. The nearer it is, the more you know the truth of men's hearts. Your presence has been noted."

"I don't know what you're talking about. My name is William Bishop, I'm—"

"Do you have people you love, Dr Abbey?"

I licked my lips. "I demand to speak to my embassy, I have no idea what you're talking about, I have no idea who—"

He sighed, and slammed the door.

*

Now is the time for terror.

I hauled and tugged at my damn chain until my wrists were swollen and bruised. I smacked the padlock against the stone wall, I cursed and stamped and sulked and fumed and almost dislocated my thumb trying to wiggle free, to no avail. I pretended to be dead, but no one came and I got bored of the pretence, and when someone did come they caught me off guard and I didn't have time to get into the character of a corpse, and I wasn't sure they'd care anyway.

All the time Langa comes.

He comes, he comes, the truth of the house begins to fill my soul, she believes in God which means she must believe in the Devil but why does the Devil seem so free to spread mischief whereas the angels hide their wings, why does evil run free and goodness never come when kind women beg for mercy? The priests answer but their words mean nothing, and now there is a devil in the house and she must pray, she must pray ...

He comes, Langa comes, and the truth of the man who brings me food is that it's a job, and it's a bad job, and he doesn't like his bosses, but he doesn't have any other job going, and he's got mouths to feed and that's all there is to it really. It's just a job. He doesn't think about it too much. He doesn't think about anything much, except the white pigeons he breeds; they are all the love and all the thought he has to give.

He comes, he comes, and on the morning of the fourth day the man in the fur hat returned to my door, and his name was Ritte, and he was the bastard son of a great man who was not so enamoured of his spawn as to ever acknowledge him, but who felt a degree of guilt over the whole affair enough to make sure he had a chance at promotion, even if it was in the dirty game of espionage, and Ritte respected that. Other bastard fathers of bastard sons were perfectly content to let the children starve, but his father had taught him the meaning of backbone.

And Ritte said, "You are Dr William Abbey, you are an agent for the British government ... "

"Yes, yes, I am, listen, you don't understand, he's coming – he's coming ... " But he understood perfectly, and before he could answer the certainty was on me and I bit my hand hard enough to leave semicircular dents in the flesh, riding the pain in search of some other answer. "I don't know anything. I just go where they tell me. I listen to people, and I write it down, but they don't tell me anything for precisely this reason. You understand, you know I need to keep moving, please, I'll do anything you need, just don't keep me locked up here."

Ritte watched without blinking, then, with a half-nod of his head, he gestured for his men to leave. The door closed behind him, a half-centimetre open, as he squatted down on his haunches just outside my reach, studying me as a hunter might study a wounded deer.

"Who am I?" he asked at last.

"You are Josef Ritte, you are military intelligence. You think a Russian woman called Polina ripped apart the truth of your soul and that's why your agents died, that's what we do, please – please! I only know what they tell me and they don't tell me anything, I know what the shadow knows, you don't want to be in the room with me when the shadow comes, no one wants to know the truth, no one does, they all say that they do but they don't, even you, I know you think you want to know now but you don't, I swear it, I swear."

"Incredible," he mused. "Tell me something else. My wife's name."

"Elke, you haven't seen her for seven months, it's harder to tell you about her because she is not in your heart, you married for politics, you respect her, that's all I know, I see what's in your heart, not what I want to see, you never really loved her but you admire her deeply. I'm not lying, I'm not lying ... "

"Can you lie?"

I twisted on the floor to shuffle a little closer to him, hands reaching out in prayer at the end of their chain. "He's coming, *he's coming*, please!"

"This is more effective than I thought. We had one such as

you in our service nearly a century ago, but the records were poorly kept."

"Please. I love her, I love ... You can't do this. You're killing them. *You're killing them.*"

"You will have to hope that I'm not," he mused, rising again to his feet.

"You can't do this!"

I'm never quite sure why anyone says that, and as quickly as I'd said it I knew he could do whatever he wanted, and I went back to begging again, not that it would make a difference. The truth was the truth, and it was absolute, and that was all there was to it.

Then the parade began.

The first man they brought to me had already been beaten to bacon, and had he wanted to talk I doubt he could have done through the tomato of his mouth. I blathered the truths of his heart out, of Magyar rebellion and assassins waiting in the streets of Belgrade and printers and bankers and men of quiet resistance, and when they had enough names dragged from the depths of his soul, Ritte said, "Enough!" and they took him outside, and I heard a gunshot five minutes later.

The next was a blindfolded Serbian, who kept on exclaiming that this was all a terrible mistake, and who didn't understand English but whose heart sang with terror, and who was innocent of all that they had accused him of, which was a little inconvenient, but he still owed the state a great deal of cash so it was probably worth, in Ritte's eyes, putting the fear of God in him.

"Pray, discourse with reason and pay your taxes!" was Ritte's sentence upon the gibbering wretch, a politician's answer to the physician's fresh air and walking.

The woman had killed a man, not for politics, but in revenge, and damn right too.

The Ottoman spy smiled constantly beneath his blindfold, hands folded in his lap, and nodded thoughtfully as I tore apart his network of spies and agents, as though to say, ah, they found another one, and as they led him away pronounced, "Until next time, sir; until the next."

They stopped after the first twenty hours, but by then I was too manic to sleep, voice run ragged from tumbling out the truths of these strangers' hearts. Ritte sat on a little stool by the door, watching me as he had done without a word throughout this festival of secrets, and a little before dawn, when nothing could interrupt the torrent, I howled the truth of his soul at his face, and he blinked a little, and did not flinch.

"Fascinating how little we know how little we understand this is such a useful tool so useful break him soon won't take much break the English doctor and once he's trained once you know he's safe, maybe then they'll be pleased with you maybe then they'll show you a little respect a little courtesy, not that it matters doesn't matter doesn't matter why want something you'll never get what matters is being right but a little glimmer of courtesy maybe they'll give it to you now maybe Father will look you in the eye he won't of course he never will perhaps he'll die soon and maybe death will make him pay you a little attention."

I laughed and that bought me a moment to breathe; only a moment.

"So invigorating! Better than a priest, better than confession; honesty, truth! Worried so long that you were deceiving yourself, you must know yourself before you know your enemies, worried for so long that you'd built yourself a house of lies but no, turns out you're exactly who you thought you were what a relief, what an absolute relief and not merely that, you're precisely the kind of brave, logical fellow you always wanted to be, excellent! It wasn't all for nothing, you didn't destroy them all for nothing, you are in fact where you want to be and honour and love would never have served you, not you, not love, honour or respect, just the job, just truth well done you!"

"I think it will be soon, no?" he enquired, arms folded, one foot balanced on the tip of the toes, other flat as he leant into the door frame. "You will have to tell me if you see it."

"Things would be so much easier if we couldn't lie. White lies they say white lies but it's all so goddam obvious and all that happens is we lose the respect of each other, don't respect, not equal, it's all just so stupid, so obvious. How much does the Englishman know well if you ask him he'll have to tell he'll have to answer the truth is on his lips I know everything I know everything I know what you want me to do and I know you'll never let me go but you need me to have a little hope maybe even learn to respect you it will be so much easier than the alternative you've heard rumours of course you've heard rumours, knives and chemicals, perhaps you even believe it too, perhaps the British do that to their prisoners after all *he's here he's here HE'S HERE!*"

And finally, Ritte nodded, and summoned his men, and they carried me screaming until my voice cracked downstairs, and dumped me unceremoniously on the back of a high-sprung carriage, and whipped the horses into motion and whistled brightly as they trotted towards the gate, and Ritte stood behind, watching. And as he watched, a hand of shadow, burnt and melted to nothing, reached through his throat. The arm that followed it shimmered black, caught in a perpetual blaze, then a shoulder, the tip of a chin, the hollowed end of a burnt-off nose, and by now I was out of voice to scream but pointed at Langa as he shambled after me, one hand raised as if he and I were children engaged in some playground game, before the carriage turned round a long stone wall, and galloped away.

We rode south for five days, never stopping, changing horses every five hours. Then we caught a train, slouched in the baggage trunk with two boys who smoked cheap cigarettes and spoke not a word of English except "frogs' legs", which they would say to me in response to any sound or sigh.

We rested for a day. Then caught a train again, and then horses. I tried to work out our direction by the turning of the sun, but quickly lost track of time and place. Not that I needed to pay much attention; it was obvious that we were luring Langa after me and then doubling back. I was not surprised when, on the tenth day, we returned to exactly where we had begun, a house in the middle of a forest of spruce and pine, Ritte waiting at the door, the dreams of its inhabitants pushing against the edge of my slumbering mind.

Then it all started again.

Chapter 46

One night to dream the truth.

Three more for the knowing to grow on my tongue.

Two nights after that of what I had always considered my most optimally productive time: the days of knowing, of looking into the hearts of men and plucking them out. After that, the truth would start to well on my lips, harder to hide, until at the last it would be a torrent and Langa would come, as he always came.

That was the way of the thing, and Ritte knew it, and sat with me for those first four nights like a nurse by the patient's side, watching and waiting for the truth to grow. I ignored him as much as I could, until loneliness and the desire for human companionship broke my sulk. Cooperation, however grudgingly given, had earned me a proper bed, a few books, some in English, some in German, and a Bible. I tried to read, but found myself running over the same paragraph again and again, until finally I switched to the German books, hoping that at least the challenge of the language would keep me occupied.

It didn't.

In the end, Ritte produced a pack of cards, shuffled it, played a hand of solitaire, silent, focused in a corner, won, shuffled again, dealt again, won again, said without raising his eyes, "You play?"

"Depends on the game."

"Do you know whist?"

"Everyone knows whist."

He dealt the cards without further questioning, pulled a red-bound notebook and a stub of pencil from his pocket, drew a score table between the confessions of men and notes of scandal. He did not force me to play; neither did he think I wouldn't.

I picked up my cards, hunched awkwardly on the side of the bed, and wasn't surprised at how easily he beat me.

"Are you a patriot?" he asked at last.

"No."

"Why not?"

"There are more important things to die for."

"Such as?"

I grunted, lost a trick, glowered into my hand. He pulled his lips in, but said nothing more, won, dealt again.

"How many do you kill?" I asked at last. "For your patriotism?"

"Fewer than my enemies would kill, if I did not get to them first."

"You can't know that."

"I can. It is my job to know the character of these things. If I sat down a hundred people from my country, and laid out clearly and in detail why certain men must die, I think not one of them would disagree when faced with the evidence I have. They might feel sick inside; they might hate themselves. But pragmatically, they would all agree. It is hypocrisy to pretend that you would follow a higher path; you want your government to do quietly all the deeds you bluster against."

"That's your choice. You haven't given me one."

"No, that is true. An assassin's bullet can start a war; a bomb may bring chaos. You are more discreet. Balance will be maintained, and the game will continue. This will not be for ever. We will keep you safe and comfortable. You will not be mistreated more than necessary."

I laughed at that, burying my gaze in the cards, unable to meet his eye. "You are going to cut up my brain the moment I cease to be useful. You think the British have done this before, to the sangomas and witch doctors of their empire, but when the old stories run out of new information, why not see what science can offer? Besides, you've spent too much time in my company, indulging in your introspections. I have to die to protect your secrets. As we are being honest with each other."

I felt no particular rancour towards him, even as I pronounced my own execution. In a strange way, I liked him more when Langa was near, and I could respect the integrity of his soul, find that depth of commitment that drove him, live it again in myself, rather than sit merely as a victim of his efforts.

He thought about this for a while, then simply replied: "Yes. Perhaps. Perhaps we will. When a soldier goes to war, he measures things differently. Before he was a soldier, he cared about money, what his neighbours said, whether a woman looked at him with affection, and would barter all manner of things to gain these commodities. When the first bullet is fired, this changes, and now he bargains with God: very well, you can shoot off my leg, but my left, not my right, and below the knee, please, not the hip. Or you can kill eight of the men of my company, but not my friend; or if you must kill me, please shoot me in the head rather than the belly, so that it's quick. This becomes the new marketplace of his existence, invested in so many pints of blood or missing limbs. It becomes normal. You, Dr Abbey, must ask yourself if you are not in much the same position. What will you barter for one more day of life?"

I found I had no answer, and knew that I would probably sell the world.

Locked in a room for even a little while, you become hypersensitive to every detail. One log more or less on the fire. The way the ash moves across the floor. The bed nudged a little off the perfect straight line. The cracks in the ceiling; the creaking of the floor; the turning of light through a high window.

When the woman came to light the fire, I was immediately aware of something different about her.

As always, she did not look at me, and ran away as quickly as she could, crossing herself.

But there was a truth in her heart, and it terrified me, or perhaps it terrified her and the line between our feelings was growing thin, and for a brief moment I wondered whether even one more day of life was worth the price that might have to be paid.

The next day, Ritte ordered the chains put back around my wrists and looped through the bar by the window, restricting my world back down to a miserable staggered half-circle. Then a boy, barely thirteen years old was brought in, blindfolded, and Ritte waited, eyebrows arched, to see what I might pronounce, and the truth of his heart was that he had dreamt of being a great man right up to the moment when they arrested him, and now his trousers smelt of piss and he wanted his mother and was afraid of his father, and if he survived this, he promised himself he would run away and learn a proper trade, and never learn to read because books were full of promises that broke people.

So I murmured, "He's just a child. He's no threat to you."

Ritte shook his head. "Not good enough, Dr Abbey. We'll come back when you're in a more talkative mood."

And Langa comes.

In the afternoon, the woman who tended the fire returned, and this time I knew with absolute certainty the truth of her heart, and nearly gasped with relief at it as she entered the room.

As always, she crouched by the still-warm embers to breathe a little life back into them, shuffle on another fork of coal, a log. The gun she drew from the bottom of her coal scuttle was a small revolver, barely large enough to dimple a Bible, but waved in the face it still made a notable impression. She held it in her right hand, bone popping through white skin, jaw locked and jutting, eyes wide and rippled with red, and when she looked at me she knew the truth of me as surely I as knew hers. I tried to apologise, to say something to make it right, but

228

my Magyar was non-existent and she barely spoke German, so all I could do was smile, nod, pray. A key came from her apron pocket, which she immediately dropped with shaking hands. Straining, I could just about reach it, pick it up slowly, studying her face, her heart, then turned and released the padlock on the chain. She jumped as the chain fell, gun shaking in her fist. I held out my right hand slowly, as you might to a nervous cat, and after a moment's hesitation, she dropped the pistol into my palm without a word.

I nodded, and she nodded in reply, and her name was Ljubica, and she did this shitty job with gratitude, grateful because it was a job, and her husband had died from the bite of a horsefly that had ruptured to a purple sepsis in his blood, and of her seven children three were nearly fully grown and one was ill, and she was terrified, and wished she was anywhere else, but the people who had come to her door promised more riches and threatened more pain than she could say no to, so here we were.

This practical truth punched through the rest. She was petrified. She did what needed to be done. These truths ran side by side in a screaming cacophony, so loud that thought had almost ceased entirely, leaving simply an automaton moving through necessary motions.

I tried to smile, tried to comfort her, to communicate some semblance of calm, and couldn't. I reached out to squeeze her hand, and she recoiled from me like the devil, so I let it go, and tried to breathe out the terror of her heart and only deal with the terror of mine. I shuffled to the door, my every step deafening, tongue twice the size it had been a moment ago, a gammon gag in my mouth.

The door was unlocked, the corridor lined with old grey floorboards that creaked and groaned as we slithered along them. Trying to be quiet was more laughable than simply moving, walking at a brisk pace as if my footsteps belonged, as if Ljubica and I were out for a brisk constitutional. A flight of stairs at the end twisted down, narrow, the servants' route to a discreet door set into wood panelling at the head of a far larger, grander stair for grander people. Here the carpet, worn and ragged, was orange and scarlet, vermilion and brown, a mismatched weave of geometric patterns, and the severed animal heads lining the walls watched us reprovingly from their perches with polished glass eyes.

We made it nearly to the bottom of the staircase before encountering the first guard. He wasn't even a real soldier; he just worked here, caring for the dogs and helping to drive game towards the shotguns of visiting guests. Having a prisoner in the house made him deeply uncomfortable, but like Ljubica he had a job to do. So when he saw us, for a mute second he tried to wrangle some logic – any logic – by which this situation was all right. And when he failed, and opened his mouth to call for help, I raised the gun and barked, "Don't!"

The threat silenced him for a second, and the hard calculations ran through his mind as they did through mine. Would I really shoot him? What would happen if I didn't? For a moment, the balance hung between us, and then he made a decision and yelled: "Help! Help me!"

With a curse I barrelled down the stairs towards him, knocking him to one side as I charged for the front door. He didn't try to grapple with me or resist, just sprawled at the bottom of the stairs shouting, "Help! He's escaping! Help!" with a thoroughly sensible attitude to the whole affair.

The door opened with agonising slowness, layers of ancient timber dragging, warped, on old stone. At the last moment, it sprang back, propelled by the weight of two men trying to shove through it from outside. I nearly lost my footing, was pushed back up by Ljubica, and in that moment the truth of her heart was that if I had to shoot someone so we both escaped, then I should damn well do it and she couldn't quite believe she'd given me the gun, since I was proving to be so wet! For a moment we balanced in a precarious tug of war, not quite sure who was coming and who was going, until I staggered backwards before their combined weight and the door slammed wide into the wall. Behind me, the man who had called for help contemplated getting involved, then decided to leave it to more qualified individuals.

One of these – whose name was Istvan and who really needed to piss, distractingly – caught me by the scruff of the neck. He had dealt with plenty of prisoners, prided himself on how quickly they learnt to obey him, couldn't quite believe that he hadn't been unleashed on me before and was going to enjoy pointing out to his superiors that this escape attempt would never have happened if *he'd* been given full authority over the situation. He wasn't planning on punching me too much, just a bit of bruising so I might learn my lesson, maybe suspending me by my ankles so I got the message without being damaged beyond use; but the woman he'd certainly make an example of, staff, fucking staff, told them not to trust her, kept on giving him dirty looks, kept on giving him the eye, he'd have to ...

He hadn't noticed the gun, of course. It was such a small thing and he was so preoccupied with his bladder and with being so much better at his job than anyone else that the question of whether the cowering English spy might have a weapon hadn't even crossed his mind. It was so absurd, and anyway, Istvan came from the streets, from knives and iron bars, from a world where a display of power was how you avoided the fight altogether.

I thought about pointing out his error, got halfway through a spluttered, "Um, I do have a ... "

But he wasn't interested, and his English was non-existent and his German was weak at best, and before I could engage him further in conversation he had lifted me up by my shirt, which tore against my armpits and made my arms flail like a chicken, and slammed me spine-first back against the wall. The panelling was not a single smooth surface; a small lintel protruded and cracked into my coccyx hard enough to make me nearly vomit; my skull smacked back, filling my eyes with blood.

By now, Istvan's companion, a man whose far less emotional

relationship with the situation made him harder to pick from the slew of truth beating against my senses, had grabbed Ljubica by the hair, and the only person who seemed to be aware that things were perhaps not quite what they seemed was the man at the bottom of the stairs who, much as I had done, was trying to point out through the woman's scream and my gasping that yes, no but yes, I really did have a gun.

There was no conscious decision to pull the trigger, and if I had been able to breathe I think I might have still tried to explain the situation to him, point out that, honestly, I had a weapon and this wasn't what you were supposed to do with people who had guns ...

I couldn't breathe.

I couldn't think.

The noise of other people's rushing hearts, of blood in the skull, my blood, her blood, their blood, drowned out all senses. I pulled the trigger.

The gun was small enough, and the retort muffled through the weight of Istvan's body against mine, that for a moment no one quite understood what had happened, least of all him. His mind was so alive with the excitement of the fight, with the roar of victory, that the actual pain as the bullet ruptured his belly registered only as a bite, perhaps a pinch of finger against folding flesh. He managed to smack my head back against the wall one more time, and hauling me bodily onto my tiptoes readied himself for another smash, and it was that effort that proved to be a step too far, and he dropped me, dizzy, confused. Now he looked down. Now he saw the blood spreading through his grubby shirt. Now he saw the gun in my hand, and the logical connection between these things permitted the pain to come in a sudden roar, a crippling, curling, nauseating rupture through his whole body that sent him to the ground with a howl.

I bent over double as the shock of his pain rocked through my own body, but Ljubica was already writhing her way free of the man who held her, and the guard by the staircase was also reconsidering his position. I had shot a man; I could shoot a man. This was new and unwelcome information in the sudden icy silence. Ljubica grabbed my arm and hissed something in a language I didn't speak, and as I kept the gun pointed at the two men still standing, she pulled me through the half-open door, and out into the dazzling winter day.

Truths I know: that there are three men who patrol the grounds, armed. They find their work incredibly boring, and I don't blame them, and they are all quite cold, except for one, who was raised in the Urals and thinks these idiots have no idea what real winter is like, and who fled abroad when he was thirteen years old and Tsar Alexander was killed and his father was caught whispering about rebellion and the legacy of Pugachev and the valiant Cossacks.

One of these men guards the front gate. He is an old man, a veteran of the Crimea, and the truth of his heart is that he killed only one man in that conflict, and the rest of the time he was just shot at by people he couldn't see, rifle fire and cannon coming from ... somewhere ... and people killed by ... someone ... and there was no order to it, no sense, it was just death from a place onto a place and none of it made any goddam sense, none of it at all.

I had no idea how we were going to get past him, of course, but this turned out to be a redundant problem, because as we approached, a woman dressed in green and black walked up to him from the dirt track on the other side of the high gate, asked him a question he couldn't hear, and as he leant in to hear her enquiry more closely, shot him in the chest.

Her gun was much bigger than mine, and echoed loud against stone. Then three more men were with her, and they had horses, and they were shouting, gesturing, come, come, come, so I came, and was thrown onto a beast far bigger and far stronger than me. I clung on with knees and arms and terror and hoped that he wouldn't work out that I was, when it came to battles of will, a gnat of this world, waiting to be crushed beneath his hooves. Commands were issued and I heard the truth of them, and looked down to my rescuer in green and saw

– not a spy from the Nineteen, a saviour sent by the British, but rather –

Margot, slipping the gun back into her great spinning skirt pockets.

Margot, come to save the day.

She waved with a little smile, a single cream glove in a ripple of fingers, then turned away, swung into the saddle of a grey mare, kicked her heels and was riding in the opposite direction before I could say a thing.

Chapter 47

Margot, a killer.

Margot, rescuer, come from nowhere to make things right.

A murderer.

My hero.

Butcher of men.

She hadn't flinched when she pulled the trigger, and it occurred to me that she had perhaps killed before, and the only reason I had not seen this truth in her heart was because it was largely inconsequential to her.

Or maybe I was wrong.

Maybe everything I knew was wrong.

Riding hard for the city, I had no idea, and no way to look and know the truth of her heart. Nor was she ever to permit me to see into her soul again, until the end.

There were consequences.

Ljubica fled Hungary, with her children.

Ritte caught her three weeks later, and she was shot, but the children were spared, for what little that meant. Peadar Coman, who had threatened and bribed her into action, knew that this was the most likely outcome. It was the truth of his heart, and he despised himself and me for making him do it. Women like Ljubica, he concluded, were worth fifty William Abbeys, and I was inclined to agree. But Margot had insisted, had been hysterical, and reluctantly the People's Society had agreed. A British traitor was worth keeping, in the balance of things. Good lives could be saved, though good people might die in saving them.

Coman and his men were all armed, rifles and revolvers paid for by blackmail, purchased from a Turkish gentleman who had been only too happy to arm Protestants, socialists and nationalists who resented the Habsburg rule.

Margot rode the other way. She killed a man, and she was gone. She had no desire for me to delve into the truth of her heart, and in that moment, blood splattered on my shirt and sleeves, neither did I. I couldn't imagine that either of us would be anything but disappointed by what we found.

Four miles' hard ride from the house where I'd been held, I was ordered to dismount and bundled into the back of a cart laden with preserved meats turned to stone by the cold. Coman didn't meet my eye as he barked, "Now you owe us."

I stared at my feet, and nodded, and didn't complain about the cold.

Some six hours later, sun down and horse shivering, crystals of ice forming in its lashes, I was dropped off outside the British consulate in Budapest. The driver didn't speak English; he waited until I was standing, bow-legged and frozen, before the front door, then whipped his cart into motion again without looking back.

For a moment I stood bewildered in a gently snowing street. Passers-by in fur hats and heavy boots glanced at me, found me a disturbing sight and looked away. A policeman in cape and flat hat found me suspicious, reached for whistle and baton. I turned away, the truth of his heart a buzzing, irritating ripple on the edge of my awareness, and hammered on the consulate door until it was answered by a man in woollen slippers and a fez.

"Good evening," I growled through gritted, rattling teeth. "I am a spy and it's all gone terribly wrong."

It took the British the best part of a day to work out how to get me out of Budapest. By then, Ritte had already set up watchers

236

across the street, not knowing for sure if I was in the consulate but unwilling to risk that I wasn't. Langa was coming, the truth preying on the edge of my lips. I stood and watched the watchers from behind the netted curtains of the consulate and on the tip of my tongue was:

It's the ones who write well they're the ones who get the attention oh yes he writes a nice report but he doesn't know what he's doing, no craft, no craft at all, I've got craft it's just that I can't write like that not fair, not right, craft should be its own reward ...

The consul was a man called Curran. He knew nothing. He was quite proud of knowing nothing; it made it easier for him to spread very affable, friendly lies while playing cards with his probable enemies. Ignorance took away the frisson of maliciousness, made him just a decent chap doing a decent job, and while the big guns might not respect him, he always felt it was more effective to be liked rather than feared.

"Rum old business, yes!" he chuckled as the telegrams flew. "Funny old affair!"

For a moment I missed Mrs Parr, and wondered where the baron had been buried, and if Albert thought I was dead.

Then three men arrived by riverboat, and gave their names as Smith, Jones and Williams, and two of them were in fact called Griffiths and he sang baritone and he sang tenor and had a lovely set of lungs on him, when they weren't conducting certain affairs abroad. "We are here to escort you to London, Dr Abbey," intoned the one who introduced himself as Smith.

"You like the Austrians, you like the way they do things properly," I blurted.

He raised one thin white eyebrow above a sky-blue eye glistening with the beginning of cataract. "Ah yes," he muttered. "They said you were a character."

"Characters are always trouble," I replied in a bright half-sing-song, trying to tame the truth about to burst from my lips. "It's a rich man's word for 'incompetent'."

"Couldn't agree more, sir. Shall we be going?"

"I'll be much better once we've got on a train," I whimpered gratefully, as they bundled me in scarf, hat and coat. "Much less eccentric."

We left the consulate in two groups of two. Griffiths and Griffiths went first, slipping out into the icy night. I watched from behind a darkened window with the man whose name absolutely was not Smith as a shadow detached itself from a doorway opposite and followed, and a moment after that, a bouncing cab pulled by a steaming grey horse trotted after too.

"Still one watcher, house to the left, top window," I chanted, swaying a little with the effort of keeping the words vaguely controlled, vaguely sane. "His name is Andras, he pretends he likes American cigars because he thinks it makes him seem cultivated, but no one believes it for a second and the habit is so costly that sometimes he won't even light the cigar, just roll it around between his fingers and lips as if he was going to but then decided against it. He has a runner he can send for help if we leave, the runner is fourteen years old and managed nearly four hours of incredibly intense watching of this consulate, proud, very proud, proud to be watching, until he got bored and is now asleep, but he doesn't snore otherwise Andras would have kicked him by now."

The eyebrow rose again, the lips drew in between pale, sprouting lips. Smith has seen some strange things in his time. This current assignment will definitely be on his list of unusual stories that he will tell his grandson, and which his grandson will not believe, smug little snot, beloved though he is.

"Anything else?" he asked.

"Andras hits his woman. They're not married but she's pregnant and he knows he has to marry her but he also doesn't like her and he doesn't know what to do about it so sometimes he hits her because he doesn't know what to do. It's a very stupid reason to hit a woman and he knows that, but he just gets angry and then he can't think, he knows he's a bad man but he can't stop it, so perhaps he should just be a bad man, perhaps that's just who he is."

"That is less helpful."

"I'm sorry, I know the truth of men's hearts, not their heads. Also you shouldn't know that – don't tell them that you know this otherwise they might hurt you, but you know that good, I'm so glad, I'm so pleased you understand."

I was clinging to his sleeve, on the verge of babbling, on the verge of tears. To my surprise, he patted me, three times, mechanical, palm flat on my shoulder.

"Don't you worry, Dr Abbey. We're all professionals here."

He was, and I was so grateful I nearly started sobbing into his great woolly coat right then and there. I realised that I trusted this man implicitly, and had complete confidence in him when, calm as a summer picnic, he murmured, "House to the left?"

I nodded, gnawing at the edge of my hand to stop any more words babbling out.

He patted me one more time on the shoulder, then went downstairs. A few moments later I heard the door open; saw him walk across the street as if he were strolling to visit a friend. He stopped beneath the door of the house where our watchers resided, and there was the flare of a match. He lit a cigarette, a horrid Egyptian stick he'd picked up a fondness for on the bank bond job, then pulled a flask of whisky from his jacket pocket, poured the contents over the front door of the house, and flicked the still-burning match into the pool.

Whisky burns blue when it ignites. The glow was unearthly, Smith a ghost shadow moving against it. For a moment I thought I saw Langa cross through his form, and turned away with a shudder, acid in my mouth. But it was no more than the play of light as he sauntered back towards the consulate, gesturing at my window for me to come down. I descended, bundled up tight, only eyes showing beneath hat and scarf, and as we walked away, trudging over slippery stone towards the river, Smith asked:

"They following?"

"They're trying to put out the fire at their front door."

"Think they'll use the windows?"

"They're too busy panicking."

"Good man."

"I need to get on a train."

"Boat first, then train."

"Is it a fast boat?"

"We'll travel with the current."

"Thank you."

"Just what we do, sir. Just what we do."

The boat was waiting for us beneath a bridge of scowling demons. It shone no lights, carried no flag. The captain had fought against the Prussians; he had known the bitter taste of losing for nothing, of pointless war, and now cared nothing for nation or creed; only coin.

As we pulled away from the wharf into the tugging currents of the river, I felt the beating heart of pursuers following us, pelting down the hill to the edge of the water. Ritte was with them. He was going to lose everything, and knew it, and for a moment I felt almost sorry for him.

For a moment.

Somewhere behind, Langa slunk through the shadows, following, following, and I turned my back to it all as we were pulled south, chugging and clunking our way towards the sea.

Chapter 48

It is hard to hate anyone when you know the truth of their hearts. I have, in my time, only hated one other man. He was made rich by coal, and used that wealth to purchase in order: a large house in Kensington, a larger estate in Hampshire, a wife, two mistresses, three music halls, five racehorses, an election, a steamer and, as they started to come into the fashionable realms of the rich, a car. He was, in fact, the first man I ever met who owned one, and, since there was no requirement other than wealth to have it, he was also the first man I met to crash one, which he did immediately, straight into the newly installed horse trough outside the village inn.

I was sent to investigate him by the Nineteen, on suspicion that he was selling British naval secrets to the Americans.

He was.

He was also selling them to the Japanese, Russians, Germans, French – anyone, really, with money to spend.

He did this with the gleeful willingness of a child who has discovered that he can lie and get away with it, and what's even better, someone else will be punished for his lying, and if he's lucky, he'll get to watch.

He always got away with it.

He was going to get away with it now. As I sat in the study of his repugnant faux-Tudor mansion beneath the old hammer ponds of the Weald, a fat ginger cat licking its nethers on the rug besides me, a parrot moulting gently in a cage to the side of his great mahogany and mother-of-pearl desk, my shadow followed and the heart of the man before me beat in my ears as he said:

"Prove it. Can't, can you? Can't prove a thing. Try and I'll take you to court. And I'll win. Yes indeed, so try it, please, I will enjoy the money. There's a workhouse in the village I fund, they're very grateful to me, I get the pick of the young ones, boys, girls. I have them whenever I want, and now I've told you, and you can't do anything about it. Never write anything down. Never hire people you can't destroy. Met a man once who said family was the strongest bond. Family! You can't choose family, they could be the most unreliable sort around. Fear is the strongest bond. It's an art. Too little, they'll talk; too much, they'll break. The perfect quantity, precisely measured, that is what you require. Everyone fears me. What's your name again?"

"Friar."

"I can destroy you, Friar. I really can. The only reason I won't is because you're small fry. A little man. It's the big men I like to hurt. I'm almost a socialist."

And his heart beat, and Langa came, and the truth of his soul was that he knew he was malign, and knew he hurt people, and he just didn't care. His was not an evil of deeply formed trauma, of suffering that shaped him into a beast of pain. He did not take pride in his actions, was not insane, nor particularly relished pulling the wings off flies. He hurt people to test the limits of his power, and found they were limitless, and that was satisfactory.

Nor was he unhappy or lonely. He had people whose company he found amusing. He had concerns about his health and age, which he shared with sympathetic ears. He wanted his son to do well at school, and had no qualms about sending servants to beat any man or boy he considered to be potentially standing in the way of the brat's advancement. He told his son when he did this. He wanted his son to understand the facts of life. The fact of life was that if you were strong, and rich, and could get away with it, then no harm would come to you. This

242

was the simplest truth. It was an act of love to make sure his child grew up aware of it.

And he would get away with it.

Which really rather proved his point.

This was the truth of his heart, and I suppose it would be fair to say that even then, I couldn't hate him for who he was. Rather, I hated him for everything that he stood for, and for the truth that nothing I might ever say could change his mind. He was the black wall that stood against the light; the ice that would remain at the end of the world. He was the tumour that the surgeon cannot excise, and which you will live with, watching it consume you, until the day you die.

He was fine with that. He was absolutely fine, and I'm sure his son is doing very well right now.

I didn't hate Ritte.

He believed he was doing the right thing. The necessary thing, to be good.

When I trained as a physician, we would give bread pills to patients who were sure to die. Several said it made them feel better. In the American Civil War, doctors reported that they could operate without anaesthesia on the wounds of soldiers without a single cry of agony, so long as they could convince the bleeding men that they had already given them something for the pain. My lecturers would take men and women from the workhouse to the surgical theatre and demonstrate their various maladies and afflictions to the students, including common errors in stitching and the fascinating ways in which sepsis might kill.

We learnt a lot, as our patients screamed and bit leather gags and writhed against their straps.

We were doctors, doing good.

I met a general once. He sends troops into battle in this endless, futile war. He represents his men with little lead figurines on a map. Each figurine is ten thousand men. At the end of each day of battle, he removes the appropriate number of figures from the table, and puts them on the mantelpiece above the fire. He did this for nearly a year at the start of the war, until he ran out of room in October 1916. Then he mentioned to his orderly that the figures were a clutter. Not to remove them; he is far too good a man to have them removed. Just ... that they were causing him exasperation.

I didn't hate Ritte. I wanted to; but frankly, if I had been in his position, might I not have done the same?

They smuggled me out of Budapest down the Danube, then west towards the sea. The journey took six days, crossing the Adriatic and wiggling up through Italy and France, pausing in one-train towns to swap papers and whispered understandings, watching our backs, waiting for retribution.

In the foothills of the Alps, not-Smith thought he saw some men following us, and we hid on the edge of a snowstorm, shivering and lost in a white blanket, lips turning blue, until they passed us by.

"Well?" he demanded, and it took me a moment to realise what he meant.

"I don't know who they are. It doesn't work like that."

"Worked pretty damn well in Hungary."

"It's a curse," I muttered through frost-wrapped misery. "Not a gift."

On the ferry to Dover, I watched the cliffs approach from the edge of the horizon, and felt only sickness and dread at returning to my masters, and wondered again who I had killed, and what on earth I was going to say.

Albert blurted, "Escaped!"

The colonel grumbled, "Escaped?"

Mrs Parr mused, "Escaped? Well."

In London, the Nineteen were waiting for me. I had rarely seen the colonel and the professor in the same room together, let alone the triad with Mrs Parr. They assembled in a white drawing room in Pimlico, sipped tea from porcelain cups and ate little biscuits, still hot from the oven, rich with butter. The colonel drank with his little finger out. Mrs Parr held her cup so tight I thought the fragile china might break. They assembled themselves three in a line, and I sat alone opposite them, tired, salt in my hair and barely three hours' sleep in my eyes, and hoped that the fatigue of travel would mask the scent of fear.

"I never would have thought – a daring escape!" chuckled Albert. "Breaking out by yourself in the middle of the night: a triumph!"

"I didn't think the Austrians would be so bold as to take one of ours in broad daylight," grunted the colonel.

Mrs Parr said nothing, and watched.

"We shall have to retaliate, of course," muttered the colonel. "Round a few of theirs up. Make it clear that this sort of thing isn't on."

"Your business, your business!" mused Albert, eyes bright and gleaming, the pupils open wide against the cold grey light of day. "What I want to hear about is how much they *know*. They've definitely had experience with this phenomenon before. But the fact they took you means they don't have one of their own. Did you get anything from them? Come come, you were there long enough, the shadow must have come, the timing of it ... "

Mrs Parr's fingers, even whiter around the cup, her face drained like the snow.

I took a long breath. "Are you asking if someone I love is dead?"

They had the decency to look briefly embarrassed. It was Albert who pushed on, softer now, tempering his interest with a modicum of humanity. "The mathematics, William, the mathematics of the thing ... "

"They moved me. Kept Langa close, but not too close. They knew what they were doing."

The colonel nodded, as if this scheme made perfect sense to him.

Albert leant forward, and I couldn't read the smile on his face.

Mrs Parr knew I was lying. Just like the baron, she knew, though she wasn't sure about what. After, I was sent to a house outside Canterbury and very politely and very thoroughly debriefed for four days. They didn't threaten me. At every stage the conversation focused on my heroic efforts and bravery. Someone said I should get a medal. Only their interest in the secrets of Ritte's heart kept them from pulling apart mine.

"But what about agents?" one interrogator demanded. "All this ... women's business ... about how Ritte *feels* and what he *cares* about doesn't give us much."

"It's what matters to him," I sighed, a repetition I couldn't quite believe my interrogators weren't bored of too. "I know what matters to the heart."

In the evening, they returned to my escape, phrasing their questions with an astonished, admiring, "But how *did* you get through the gate?"

When people lie, they tend to give fewer details, or they repeat the same details again and again, without much clarity. "Her dress was blue. Yes, it was blue. It was a blue colour."

Truth is much less clean.

"Her dress was blue, this sort of pale blue – no, maybe it was green. I think it was green. Well, it depended how you looked at it, and now I think about it, maybe she wasn't even wearing it that night."

I had spent so much time around truth and liars that even I knew some of these basic rules. Over those days in Canterbury, I lied, and knew that I was a very poor liar.

On the fifth day, they let me go.

Packed me back off to London, ready to receive orders for my next mission.

I had missed the baron's funeral. There was a lack of volunteers to take his place. Sheer headlong self-assurance of his flavour was a dying trait, even among the best English public schools, it seemed. With him dead, Mrs Parr, it was announced, could serve more usefully in a secretarial position. She was not invited to share her feelings on this matter.

The night before I departed, Albert and I drank port, stained lips and dirty glasses, and talked about almost nothing. Truth. Reality. Nothing. Finally he mused, the thing he'd actually wanted to say, "If the Austrians know something ... if they have information on the phenomenon ... We are coming from so far behind in the field, you see. Other countries, even Russia, have more experience of the thing. We are attempting to apply science to something that has always been considered magic, and if we can do that, if we can pick apart the mystery and find a force behind it ... Do you understand what I'm saying, William? If the Austrians know things about the shadow – even mystical mumbo-jumbo – that could be incredibly useful to us. To you. To curing you, even."

"They didn't say anything about a cure. They didn't care."

"No. No. Of course not. I just want to see us get ahead. It feels like we're coming from so far behind – you understand?"

"Yes."

"Well. Well then. Perhaps we can find ... something else."

"Perhaps."

By my maps, Langa was walking barefoot across the ocean as we spoke. The waves wouldn't disturb him. Foam passed through his burning form, the fish nibbled at darkness and tasted only ice. I wondered what I would see in Albert's heart if Langa was near, and felt I already knew the answer, and it was disappointing, and I hated myself more than anyone I had ever known for the things I had done.

I caught the Liverpool steamer to Dublin the next morning, shuffling across Ireland in a slow arc with Langa at my back, condemning men to die for their beliefs, ripping out their hearts and turning them into ink and paper, nothing more than a blot upon this earth.

Chapter 49

If I had been a casual traitor before, from then on I was Margot's most devoted servant. Travelling the world, there was no secret I would not reveal, no great scheme of powerful men I would not betray, if she willed it.

Let it all come down; let the whole thing burn.

And for the first time, I found myself a little of her mind: perhaps I was not cursed at all. Perhaps Langa's presence at my back was a duty, a blessing, and since that night in Baker he had been willing me on, urging me to finally stand up and do the right thing, work with him to tear it all down.

Let the whole world burn.

In the Sudan – the Mahdi's great war of independence and God is crushed by the redcoat and the Maxim gun.

Karl Landsteiner identifies different types of blood and the medical community becomes excited by what it can do with sharp needles and long tubes after so many years of failure.

The Cape descends into war again, Boer against British.

In America, unarmed miners are massacred; black men are lynched, their burnt bodies suspended from the long white branches of the trees like Spanish moss, as their killers thank the Lord and pass the whiskey.

And with a whimper, not a roar, the twentieth century dawns, and Langa comes, and I run.

Of course, things are never that simple.

In 1901, in San Francisco, I met a samurai.

Wanting to be a samurai had been Hideo's undoing.

"At the time, I didn't have any better idea!" he exclaimed. "It was the thing I had to do!"

Hideo was born to an old, respected family in Kyushu. When the Americans came and blasted open the hitherto-sealed Japanese ports, the brewing national crisis that had smouldered under the surface burst into flames. It was not merely a colonial crisis – how could a noble and martial empire respond to the sudden arrival of gunpowder and steam at its door? Rather, it was more deeply rooted, for centuries of samurai rule had been dented by that most deadly scourge: an excess of peace and contentment.

"It is hard to wear your ancestor's sword while running a fishing fleet," he confided. "Bickering over the price of tin – no good for the warrior spirit."

Hideo was sixteen years old when, in 1868, the Meiji emperor abolished the shogunate, hurled open the doors of Japan to the West and began to institute unprecedented change. When the samurai rebelled in 1877, Hideo's family split down the middle. His father, who had always been a stickler for the ancient ways and refused to admit that the vast majority of his income came from tuna, swore he would stand up for tradition and bring the emperor back to the true Japanese path. His mother and his sister, who had always had a good head for numbers, pointed out that this would do nothing for the family's burgeoning investment in the national telegraph project. Hideo, having spent the majority of his childhood being educated in sword, bow, horse-riding and the tea ceremony – matters of accountancy being considered beneath him – decided to join the revolution. When he informed his sister and her husband of this fact, his brother-in-law rose from the table, threw his cup to the ground and declared that Hideo was a spoilt little monster who spent so much time dressing up in his ancestors' borrowed armour that he couldn't find his own foot without some servant girl to tickle it for him.

Or words to that effect.

Years later, Hideo struggled to remember the gist of the thing.

Being a proud man of proud birth, and not inconsiderably into his cups, he couldn't let this insult go, and ran his brother-in-law through like a piece of knitting.

He'd never killed a man before.

That night, he ran away, and his sister cursed him. She had in her heart both the learning of this new world and the secrets of the old.

Hideo's wife died, his brother's shadow crawling out of her frozen chest, before he realised the error of his ways. He sought out the *yamabushi* of the mountains, killed a monk, contemplated suicide, realised that it would not save the lives of the ones he loved. Was surprised to find that he loved at all. He cut off his hair, threw away his swords, stowed away on a ship to Vietnam. It turned out his honour was of an entirely different sort from that he had imagined after all.

Nearly thirty years later, we met in America. He worked on the railways, shovelling coal. The job kept him constantly in motion, and every year he was astonished at how much further the railways had gone, reaching out to the Pacific in a tongue of iron. Sometimes he thought he saw his shadow through the smoke as he rattled across the continent; but then again, you could imagine things in the glare of the great white desert, or see strange patterns in the swirling dust.

I recognised him before he recognised me. He had not had the truth upon him for a very, very long time, whereas my shadow was five days behind, and the certainty of knowing was a nudging doubt that grew to a beating conviction as I watched him.

We met in San Francisco, before the earthquake, as the city scuttled up from the bay in a hammering of nail on wood, the creaking of iron and a thudding of fresh brick straight from the kiln. He was there at the end of a long journey, waiting to return east to collect more prospectors and dreamers come to supplant the old wagon pioneers and the lawless cowboys with their genteel urban ambitions.

I was there to listen to the naval men, to pick at the truth in the hearts of the sailors freshly come from the Pacific. I was alone, apart from the ever-constant check-ins and assignations I was required to meet as I wandered across the States, shadow at my back.

At least that was what I thought, back before the truth was known.

So it was that alone I approached Hideo at the railway bar, and bought him a whiskey. "Drink?" I grunted, pushing the dirty tumbler towards him across a bar slick with dry sugar.

No one else talked to the Japanese man. The Yellow Peril was in full swing, and though America was most keen on lynching black men and Chinese, they were not particularly discerning of one foreigner from another. The railway bar was one of the few places where a man of Hideo's complexion was safely permitted to drink, his place earned with a coat of oil. He had long ago resolved not to care. He had been in favour of lynching the white men who came to Japan when he was young, and he had been stupid too. At least, he mused, the men who wanted to murder him had the decency to be mostly hungry, mostly poor, mostly torn apart by broken dreams, their powerlessness turned easily into violence and bigotry with the enthusiasm of a starving man. The shadow of his dead brother-in-law gave him a glimmer of that truth, and in a strange way it comforted him.

He looked up slowly from contemplation of his shovel hands, which flopped across the counter in weary hooks. His shoulders were broad, tapering to a triangle of muscle that ran up to the back of his neck. His head seemed tiny in comparison, black hair cut to a fuzz beneath his hat. He wore faded blue overalls and a shirt whose colour could no longer be guessed at. A large gap between his two front teeth made him seem a little younger than he was. His age showed only in his eyes, in the frown lines that had embedded themselves

251

between his brows, and the crinkles that fanned out from the corners of his mouth.

"Sure. Why?" he grunted, neither accepting the glass nor pushing it away.

"I am followed by the shadow of a child who was murdered when I was in Africa," I explained, angling my body against the bar so I could better watch the room. "As he comes near, I learn the truth of men's hearts." I held out my hand as he raised one burnt eyebrow, a bare quiver above the deep, goggle-ringed socket. "William Abbey. I should be a doctor, but I ended up a spy."

Hideo, since coming to America, had made friends, fallen in love, fallen out of love, tried to find Jesus, failed, been paid a third of the wages of his white compatriots and seen the last of the Indians as they fled west across the plains. He had heard the sound of a hundred thousand buffalo running wild, before the men with guns came and blasted them into skin and blood for daring to roam; he had seen a comet strike the earth. Very little surprised him. I surprised him only a little bit.

"I prefer gin," he said, picking up the proffered cup and downing it in one. "But if you're buying, I'll take the good stuff."

That night we got phenomenally drunk.

"The ancient ways . . . the honour! The code! The . . . but actually, the price of fish, the price of fish was so important . . . "

We wandered, swaying on each other's arms, into the Chinese quarter of the city, the shacks of six-stool bars and two-table parlours, music, laughter, women berating inebriated customers, inebriated customers declaring their undying love for life, drink, women, opium, and the smell of sizzling meat heavy on the air. There was one Japanese family he knew, just one, who had access to sake – sake! The taste of his homeland! He could never afford it, of course, but as I was buying . . .

"Would you ever consider being a spy?" I mumbled in a hazy, slightly nauseous fugue as the sun rose across the ocean below.

"I mean ... if someone asked. Not me. Not the British, we're ... but if the Americans, maybe? Or your own people?"

A dismissive wave of his hands, a clicking of fingers. "I like the railways now," he exclaimed. "I have got used to them. I don't want to go back to dealing with people, even my own people. Besides, they don't want to hear the truth! You think the emperor wakes up every day and looks himself in the mirror and thinks, 'What if I'm not the descendant of Amaterasu and I'm just making this up as I go along?' You think the prime minister wants to hear that his ego has got in the way of a good decision, or that the people hate him, or the soldiers he sent to die did so for a stupid, old-fashioned idea? No one wants to know the truth! At least, not the true truth – not the truth of what everyone else thinks. They're quite happy with the truths of their own hearts, the ones that tell them that they're right, and that any doubts they might have about their own divinity are irrelevant and life is to be got on with regardless, thank you! You – you tell your people the truth?"

"When I have to."

"And does it change anything? Does it make a difference?"

I didn't answer.

"Of course not! Oh, maybe they'll adjust a naval plan or move a platoon somewhere, but if you tell them something they don't want to hear, they'll just assume it's because you're unreliable. No one wants the truth. The truth means they're not right. Being right is everything; it is freedom; it is suffering. Gin! Everyone wants gin! That's the truth, I swear it."

We had more gin, until finally I realised that walking into trees was a sign I might have had a touch too much, and we sat together in a contented, stinking haze until Hideo said, "I was raised to be Buddhist. And to worship the ancestors too, of course. We are very good at covering all the angles in Japan, and every decent Buddhist temple has a statue with a belly you can rub for fortune or lots of babies or luck with the harvest, and a fountain to purify your hands and mouth, and maybe a few demons or gods so you know it's not just about sitting still and listening to birds, that there's a divine intervention you can pay for with ready, honest cash. When I was young, I didn't have much time for it, though I preferred temple to visiting the shrine, because at least the Buddhists had benches and didn't shout so much. Then I came to America, and everyone keeps on talking about *truth*. The *truth* of Jesus, the *truth* of democracy, the *truth* of ... all that. God. God is true. And I thought, that's absurd. You can't see God. You can't touch God. There's no proof that God exists; all you've got is a lot of things you don't understand yet, and why would you say that some floating demon makes the things you can't understand happens?

"We live in ignorance most of the time. We make up stories to find sense, to make the thunder the wrath of a dancing devil, to make the sunrise about our lives, a gift to us, rather than just the turning of the world that turns regardless of whether we live and die. We tell ourselves stories to put ourselves at the centre of everything, and invent knowledge to prove this, and truths to justify why we are important, and one day I thought ... damn, maybe I am a great Buddhist after all! Because if I have learnt anything from my brother-in-law's ghost, it's that the world we see when we are trying to understand ourselves is nothing compared to the world we see when we simply let ourselves look. Truth ... is imperceptible to human eyes, because we are so caught up in being ourselves that we are never simply here, seeing, here, being, here. We desire truth, the story that makes us *right*, I think, more than anything we have ever known. It is nonsense. It is noise. Let it go."

At this, he let out a profound sigh, and turned his chin up to the growing light of day as if he might fly by its power. Then he rolled his head down to the ground, eyes closed, the breeze running across his crinkling, coal-cracked skin. Finally he twisted to one side and was profoundly sick in a fern.

Chapter 50

Say what you will for revolutionaries, they believe with great conviction. Since the shadow came upon me, I have been a magpie to the passions of other people, and Margot Halloran has always had a secret, blazing light.

After Vienna, we grew more reckless.

"I can't believe you got me out, that was the most . . . " I babbled through drink and fumbling lips.

"Oh for goodness' sake, you ridiculous man, of course I rescued you! When you didn't show, I just knew, I knew, and I told them, I told them that if William Abbey died they would never get another secret from me."

"You shot a man, Margot, you—"

"You have to live. William. William!" She caught my face in her fingers, held me tight, kissed me on the forehead, glowered into my eyes. "We have to live, you and I. We have to do the right thing by our shadows. Do you understand me?"

"Yes. I understand."

In Milan we met at the opera, and eyed each other across our separate boxes throughout the tedious, dire event on stage, and carefully avoided each other's gazes as we tramped out with the sore-backed audience after the performance and stumbled through chance into the same carriage as each other, where no sooner was the blind down than we were released from all decorum, freed for a few reckless hours from our duties and our curses to delight in simply being together, honest in our dishonesties, liberated from the masks that reasonable people wear.

"I want to burn it all," I whispered, as we lay together in the hotel in Paris, watching the sun drag across the ceiling. "I want people to see the truth."

Her shadow was near, and mine was not, so I don't know what she meant when she kissed me on the cheek and murmured, "Funny man."

In Istanbul, I thought I saw Coman leaving the hotel where they stayed, pounding furiously across the road, and felt for a moment anxious and ashamed, but she took me by the hand and breathed, "Truth-speakers cannot love. The ones we love the most we have to push away."

Then she kissed me, and I thought I understood everything, and had no idea what any of it could possibly mean.

Did I love her then? I love her, I don't love her, I love her, I don't love her. Even when Langa comes, I fumble at the words. Love is clean, it is a tangle, it is dazzling, it is self-deceit, I love her, I don't love her, I love her, and all these things are true, it is true, I love her – but it would have destroyed everything had I ever said it out loud.

Langa makes my love poison, but even that is just an excuse.

In Istanbul she fed me information on the secret police who were hounding the nascent revolutionaries and nationalists seeking freedom from the sultan's rule, and I gleefully passed it on to my masters, happy to enlist the British in destroying the enemies of my enemy.

In Singapore we huddled behind clouds of incense smoke as the mosquitoes gnawed at ankle and wrist, and she told me the secrets of pirates and smugglers, of great men who dealt in opium, silver and indentured workers for the American railways; and I betrayed British governors and their affairs, pox-ridden civil servants longing for a posting away from standing water, colonels and majors who prayed for a rebellion to put down, and the glory such a massacre might bring.

In Yokohama, we met beneath the red *mori* gate of a little shrine with paper streamers hanging from every post, and washed our hands and our mouths and stood silent together as the moon rose above grey curving roofs, and laughed at secrets shared and conspiracies hatched, and my shadow was never near, and hers sometimes was, and I thought I sensed it, and never asked.

In this way, she always knew my truth, and I never knew hers.

I was her agent, her lover and her confidant, and when she was finished with me, she went back to her husband, back to Coman and the revolutionaries, and I counted the minutes until we might meet again.

One winter's night at the dawn of the twentieth century, I sat in Albert's study, wet logs popping in the fire. Outside, London smoke had settled into choking, gas-smeared fog that blackened every inch of bare skin that waved through it. I stared into the bottom of my glass and found it empty. "Albert?" I mused at last. "Is there a cure?"

He let out a long breath before answering, considering all the amiable platitudes he might deploy again, and again, and again; the casual deflections and easy jokes that had been the baseline of his replies for so many years. Finally: "We've searched half the world."

"But if you found a cure. If you knew there was a way to ... to lift this. You'd tell me."

"In an instant, my God! My God, William!"

He seemed genuinely hurt.

Was he?

I didn't know. The sickness of not knowing, of having possibly overstepped the mark, of having doubted my friend, my not-friend, a man I betrayed, my friend – I didn't know. I didn't know how not to know. The trust built up between friends of shared action, of faith without proof of deed, of assumptions that when trouble came, so would help – this was meaningless to me. I had lived with only the truth for so long, with a definitive look into the hearts of men, and now to look at Albert, in whom I had chosen to trust, and to not know, horrified me.

I got to my feet, feeling suddenly dizzy, waved towards my glass in a half-hearted attempt to blame it on the alcohol.

"William?" Is that genuine concern? Is he my family? I would give it all to know. "Are you all right?"

"I have never met you when Langa is near," I blurted. "I ... I don't know how not to know. I don't know how to be ... what people are any more. I don't know ... what people are when they aren't stripped bare. You, the colonel, you put these people between you and me, all your agents, Mrs Parr, you make sure that I only ever know what they know, and they believe in you so much, I want to believe, I want to believe but I don't know how not to know. I'm ... sorry. I'm sorry. I can't ... I'm sorry, you don't deserve my doubts. It's not fair on you, you have never been anything other than ... I'm sorry."

For a moment I thought he would throw me out of the house, and that would have been fair. Instead, he put a hand on my shoulder, let out a little sigh, a breath I thought was more for himself, bringing his own, unknown temperament back under control, before guiding me back to a chair. "William," he sighed again, "there is nothing you need apologise for. I know you are used to knowing ... *truth*, and it must be challenging not knowing mine. We grow used to the rules we make for ourselves, however flawed. In truth, I am frightened of what you would see in me if your shadow was here. It is not just matters of state – if you were ever to fall into enemy hands, knowing what the colonel and I do – it would be a calamity. But it is also ... I am a good man. I believe that. I doubt it every day. I believe I am intelligent, more than most. I sometimes cannot believe what a buffoon I am. I think the world is understandable, but my own thoughts are sometimes such a muddle that ... Do you understand? I ... have my truth. But it cannot be my reality. I don't think anyone could live that way. All I can do is make the same promises to you and myself that other men do. If there is a cure for your condition, I swear that I will do everything I can to help you find it."

For a little while, I believed him, and was grateful, and I

never believed him, and I was full of rage, and these things were true too, and clouded my reality.

I run, and Langa follows.

I have met murderers who knew they were right when they did their deeds. Later, when asked, "Would you do it again?" they explain that they would not, because now they will hang, and they will tell their children never to follow in their path, and that they regret every action of their lives, but the truth in their hearts is that this story has no place in it for the ones they slaughtered. They were merely punctuation marks in their personal, quiet journey from cradle to the grave.

But then I met my sister, Anne, living happily in Mexico, long after Father was dead; and she believed in doing the best she could for her children, and loving her neighbours, and in a Christian heaven. She believed in heaven so much I could almost feel it, a divine light from a southern sky.

The man who ran into a burning building to save the child, because that's what you do. It's simply what you do. It is what needs to be done.

The lovers who fear nothing so much as the other being alone, or sad, or afraid, and find that they would compromise everything they ever thought they were, and face down every fear that has ever snarled from the darkest corners of nightmare, to keep the one they love safe and warm.

Children whose delight at the flight of birds is genuine and full of marvel.

A woman who found nothing so wonderful as the pleasure of the sea on her skin.

A man who swore his life to the service of his flock and would endure every insult under the sun, as long as it helped his tormentor find peace.

I have seen . . .

. . . so much love. Sometimes I forget that too. Sometimes, when I think about Albert, all I remember is the terror in the

259

hearts of men. But then I remember: Albert loves his son. And his son loves the father. And there too is my vengeance.

I don't know why the Nineteen took so long to destroy me. Perhaps they were ignorant; perhaps my treachery wasn't worth their time. Whatever the reason, in the autumn of 1902, they struck.

Chapter 51

I should have recognised the trap, but it was carefully laid.

Queen Victoria was dead, and the second Boer War was coming to an end. The pictures of slaughtered Boer women and children, of the camps in the veld and the brutalities of the British had tainted the victory; but with so many powers rising to challenge the rule of the Empire, it was considered satisfactory to finally have settled the matter by military might, and reaffirmed Britain's place on the world stage.

In Italy, a dead king joined a murdered tsar, and all things, it seemed, were in a spin.

In the USA, the president was shot by the anarchist son of an immigrant. During his tenure, America booted the Spanish out of Cuba, acquired Puerto Rico, Guam, Hawaii and the entire Philippines to boot. After his death, laws were passed permitting men to be arrested for their beliefs, and when the earthquake hit San Francisco the white potentates rubbed their hands together and wondered if finally, now, they could boot out the Chinese too and claim some prime real estate.

Meanwhile, miners were dying. At Rolling Hill, a hundred and twelve died when a methane gas mixture exploded. Eighty-four were immigrants, mainly from Eastern Europe. Those who didn't die instantly in the blast were asphyxiated. After years of striking for higher pay and better working conditions, the United Mine Workers of America called a strike in Pennsylvania. Of the hundred thousand men who walked out, nearly all wanted the same thing. Money to feed their families. Wages to increase as the owners hiked the price of coal to the big cities who depended on it. Tunnels that didn't collapse. Caverns that weren't full of explosive pockets of gas, or the corpses of their brothers still floating in the flood. Money to pay for doctors' visits when their coughing turned black. Recognition of their union.

These demands had worked before, in strikes across the Midwest. In Pennsylvania, the owners dug their heels in, and as the strike stretched from days into months and rumours grew of government intervention, the Nineteen diverted me from my usual trawl of admirals and senators to see what I might see.

And, of course, there was Margot.

Or rather, there was Coman. Standing on an overturned crate by the station door, he cried out against injustice, against the oppression of the people, against the brutality of Pinkerton's and strike-breakers, against the rich who valued the life of a miner less than a mule, for whom it was cheaper to let ten men die in the pit than to build the pumps to allow them to breathe. He spoke of justice, of the history of a proud American state that had fought so hard for the right of the working men. He called out in Russian to his brothers from the East, in Polish to his good sisters and friends, in Italian to revolutionaries, and in the language of liberty to the black men paid not half the wages of the barefoot white.

I had never seen Peadar Coman in action before, never stopped to appreciate him. He had just been a man in Margot's shadow, and yet here he was, a rabble-rouser and a leader of men, grown older as I suppose we all had, pronouncing an end to tyranny. He was, in his way, magnificent, but as I hid on the street corner, between liquor store and funeral home, and listened to his oratory, all I could think was that where Coman was, Margot was never far behind. I pictured her in the houses of the rich, picking apart their secrets and their desires. In that moment, any sense of my mission or my duty was secondary. Seeing her was everything.

Simply asking Coman was absurd. Instead, I followed the money, and found Margot in a smoking room in a hotel some three blocks from the station, where men in tall silk hats and expansive silk waistcoats sat in the blue fog of cigars and pronounced judgement on common sense and business, and gave orders that had room to be misunderstood.

"Handle things quietly," or perhaps, "See that he doesn't cause more trouble."

They were all good people too, these men of wealth and industry. They were not responsible for the interpretations of their underlings, and in a way, by never saying out loud what they desired, they could convince themselves that they didn't desire it at all. They went to church on Sundays, said grace at dinner, and only three of the five greatest there had been born to a silver-plated inheritance. They regretted that the working man didn't understand market forces. They regretted that the working man didn't understand how the real world worked.

And there was Margot, dressed in green with white lace gloves and a parasol against her chair, laughing and smiling with some ageing lady of the house in her corner, some well-meaning missionary sort who had, during the Civil War, often thought about helping the black man in his fight to escape slavery, oh yes indeed she had, she had most definitely thought about it.

For a little while Margot didn't notice me, and that was fine, and I sat behind my newspaper and listened to her soul. It was such a natural thing to me, second nature, that it didn't even occur to me until the moment she glanced up and saw the corner of my eye that this was a violation. I had spent so many years eavesdropping on the hearts of men that this blasphemy was nothing more than habit.

And the truth of her heart was that she had become a believer.

The woman I had met in Dublin, who laughed at her power and enjoyed the game – she was still there. But burning now beneath it all was a rage, an injustice, a passion that was if anything deeper and truer than Coman's, for it was fuelled by having tasted the pain of the poor man starving in the street as if it were her own, and having listened to the hearts of great men who would never, ever understand.

Margot Halloran believed in the battle she fought. And more than that, she had begun to believe that perhaps, in the manner in which she waged it now, it was unwinnable.

Here it is now, here is the niggling edge of my doubt, the shock kicking in like a mouthful of snow.

And the truth of her heart was that she had married Coman because it was convenient, and over time perhaps convenience had grown into something more.

And the truth of her heart was that she had killed a man in Austria, and forgotten about it, because it was needful, and there was work to be done, and that not all battles could be fought with words. Was this not war?

And the truth of her heart –

– here it is, here is the reason she has kept Langa away from me, from her, for all these years, here it comes –

– the truth of her heart is that she has a daughter, who has her husband's eyes, and her daughter is six years old, and her name is Vhairi, and she is everything.

She is everything.

She is Margot's world.

And if Margot has to burn down the old to make her daughter something new, why then, she will set hellfire to the roots of the earth.

Now, for the first time in almost ten years, Margot sat on the opposite side of the room as my shadow was drawing near, and I saw the truth of her heart, and she was fire.

I think it was my shock that caught her attention, a ripple of something unexpected on the edge of her awareness. She looked up, and knew me at once, and the laughing, childish joy of secrets shared that was our usual silent conversation passed over her face for just an instant, before vanishing again. Then she knew Langa was near, and for a moment saw herself through my eyes, and there was no room for who she believed herself to be, only the horror of clarity as she saw herself in the gaze of another.

Here we are, in that moment.

Frozen with the cruellest mirror that will ever be made.

And I see what Margot thinks of me, and she finds me amusing, and enjoys the thrill of illicit secrets and liaisons, and is perhaps even fond of me, and would be sad if I died, and hasn't given it much thought beyond that.

And she sees what I think of her, and knows that I love her, and knows that I can see the truth of her heart.

Being seen, breaks it.

Even now, I cannot precisely say whether her heart broke first, or mine; the truth melted together, like iron in the crucible.

She stands, making a sudden, mumbled excuse. She is halfway to the door before I have closed my newspaper, and every fibre of her screams indignity, rejection, fury. This violation that has been forced on her, this knowing, this seeing, it is an insult unlike any she has had to endure. She wonders if she hates me, and isn't sure whether she does, and knows as surely as I do that she most likely hates herself, almost as much as I hate myself, and that everything we do is a lie.

Following her would be futile, an insult, but I try. She flows from the hotel in a cloud of trailing smoke, marches into the street, heading straight for the station, a retinue of ever-present watchers and guards slipping into her wake, sent by Coman, he trusts her, he doesn't trust her, he loves her, he doesn't love her – she's given up on trying to make his choices simple. They block my way, funnel her on, leaving me behind, shaking, my world torn in two.

Most people believe many things, all at once.

It is simply the human way of things.

Margot fled, and was on the next train out of town.

I didn't follow.

265

Langa came, and for a little while I sat on the porch of the bootmaker's shop as the sun went down, and decided to look him in the eye once more, and tell him that there was no one I loved and nothing he could possibly do to me, and I drank some more rum, and the idea lost its appeal.

I moved on, outrunning the truth by locomotive train, reported back to my masters on the will of the mine owners and the miners, on their indiscretions, weaknesses, pains and truths. Told them that reason meant nothing to men who believed. That you could look at evidence until your eyes bled, but it was nothing next to a good story that tugged on the heart. That some things just needed to burn themselves out, and only pain could fix it.

Headed to New York, travelling fast enough to leave Langa merely on the edge of my awareness, rather than a blazing intrusion into my thoughts.

A ten-year-old boy drove the elevator up to my room on the sixth floor of the flashy hotel. His skin was the colour of winter earth; he wore a red cap, and had been trained to look no one in the eye, and not to ask for a tip. The money he was paid was not enough to live on, but he got two hot meals a day and by working six days a week he helped his mother pay for lodging, and that was all that mattered. Family was all that mattered. He would do anything to protect them, now that Pa was gone. So he stared ahead, and said yessir and nosir, and I tipped him a dollar, and he said thankyousir, and didn't meet my eye.

I slept in the roaring, barbarous city, listening to the trot of horses' hooves and the sometime blare of a car horn as a new automobile driven by men in white scarves and black frock coats creaked and farted and frightened the beasts crowding the cobbled streets. The zip-up skirt was the latest thing for the discerning woman; X-rays were the newest thing for the quack doctor, who promised that you could cure yourself of any disease simply by zapping yourself three times a day. On the far side of the river, wooden shacks and crumbling warehouses lived in another century, still waiting for the electricity wars to bring their gifts. In Manhattan, the city blazed, making of the newest thing the latest trend, whether it worked or not.

And at night, I slept, and dreamt the dreams of my neighbours. Another litany of shame, of tasks that could never be accomplished, of humiliation, of being lost, of being unable to fly, unable to walk, unable to swim, stuck, suffocating in invisible treacle. The odd dash of sexuality, the occasional flicker of ecstasy, broken by the cries of a woman who in her sleep has managed to kick out so hard she has pulled a muscle in her leg.

I wake too, curling up in agony around her cramp, and put my slippers on and try to find something to drink in this place, which isn't hard to do.

The telegram was delivered to my door by a man with a tightly shaven black beard, the visage of a carrion bird and the eyes of a Venetian beauty. He wanted a tip, and I was too drunk and bitter to care. He hoped to get me for that, one day, but probably wouldn't have the opportunity.

It said:

    Come at once M STOP

In all our years of secret liaisons and clandestine betrayals, Margot had never once telegrammed me. Perhaps if I hadn't seen her heart; perhaps if Langa was nearer, or if I had better common sense, I would have stayed away. But idiocy makes its own bed, and I had well and truly made mine.

I pulled on my coat and gloves, grabbed my medical bag, wondering if it might be some such emergency, thinking of her daughter, the unknown child, and went to find her.

She hadn't given an address, but there were a few places in New York we had met before, and it seemed certain I would find her in one of them. A drinking hole of Italian sailors; a woman who sold anything to anyone, and had in her upstairs attic nearly a hundred thousand dollars' worth of stolen goods that she might get round to fencing one day, when the winter

267

was hard; a hotel in Harlem: "No sir, we haven't seen Ms Halloran for nearly a year."

The sound of the city was iron on steel; new warehouses, new engines, new tracks, new girders, new bridges, new cables for the newest electric current, new roads for new vehicles, new nails in new boots prowling between the box markets and red-brick electricity houses. The speed of it all put crumbling tenements of wood and cracked glass against fine terraced houses where incandescent bulbs shone in the windows, pushed the new rich against the old poor, barefoot children running between governesses with lace umbrellas and high, bouncing prams. Old quarrels had split streets in two, as a Jewish family who once heard an Italian insult their religion whisper to their neighbours fresh come from the East that not a one of the Italians may be trusted, not a one; while an Italian grandfather remembered an insult given to him by a fellow from Sligo, and now has his children chant "Death to the Irish, death to the Irish!" even though not one of them has set eye on an Irish child.

The hard wall of division is written large on every block. Outside the hotel hangs the sign: *No dogs, no children, no blacks, no Jews* – while on the street corner opposite a boy from Cuba too young to realise his error dares to smile at a child from Krakow and is hastily barrelled away.

A flicker of drizzle turned into an on-off patter of uneasy, grubby rain.

Just before dawn, I stumbled into the last place left. I should perhaps have gone there first, but I could not believe that she would send a telegram with such flagrant urgency, and yet be somewhere so grand.

I found her in the Republic Metropolis Hotel, off 5th Avenue. It was her favourite haunt for grand dealings, a place of celebration after a successful blackmail, or when she had snatched a particularly juicy secret from a beating heart. The grand suite on the top floor was nearly eighteen dollars a night, and I had been invited to it only once, many years ago, when she had plucked the hidden treasures of a US cabinet secretary from his heart and spun such wealth from it that the unfortunate gentleman might have tried to sell Louisiana back to her to make her go away.

It was a place for triumph, comfort and ease – not for urgent telegrams sent in the small hours of the night. Yet stepping through the door, shoes squelching, coat dripping a circle of fat rainwater on the floor, I looked across the sofa-padded, crystal-hanging hall to the reception desk and recognised, lounging with a copy of the *New York Times*, one of Coman's endless bodyguards, dressed in custard-yellow corduroy and a blue blooming cravat.

If he'd wanted to blend in, he was making a terrible matter of it, and as a bodyguard he was so poor that he didn't even notice me as I marched across the lobby to the elevator, with the soaked-through swagger of one who owned both this place and every hotel south of Central Park.

A vase of dried lavender was perched on a high table outside the grand suite. The walls were panelled in a French style, pale blue and white. The door handle was polished on one side more than the other by the erosion of hands pressing against the knob. I knocked four times, and Margot replied, "Who is it?"

"William," I called back, muted, glancing over my shoulder to check that the elevator was descending, that no one watched this exchange.

A silence inside, then a shuffling of feet, a moving of body. The door opened, and there was Coman. His shirt was loose at the collar and sleeves, his braces hung down by his hips and he wore no socks. And the truth of his heart was that he knew precisely the nature of my relationship with his wife, and he despised me for it, but would never leave her, never let her go, never say out loud what he thought, because she must know it already. She must know that she was hurting him, and yet she did it anyway, and if she did it anyway knowing what she did, why then, she must need something from me that Coman

269

could not provide, and he loved her enough to let her take that, no matter how much it hurt him. He loved her that much. He loved her to the subsummation of all that he was. He loved her when she injured him. He loved her when she ignored his pain. He loved her even though he sometimes feared that what he loved was a fantasy, not Margot Halloran at all.

With so much love and so much pain, it was easy for him to loathe me. Standing not a foot away from him, his gaze fixed on mine, I knew it. He wouldn't hurt me, because that would hurt Margot, but he prayed with every fibre of my being that I could see his contempt, and was satisfied to note by the look in my eye that I could.

Then Margot was in the doorway behind him, wearing a purple evening gown, without jewellery or gloves, her hair hanging in a tangle of pins ready to be put up for the latest evening's adventure. Pushing the door open a little wider to see me, her eyes widened in surprise.

"William?"

On some occasions, truth hits like a jump through frozen water; on others it is a nausea of sickness. In that moment, it was both, and no sooner did I know it than she did too, and her head jerked upright with the force of sudden breath.

Then a third figure moved behind them. A child, still swaddled in puppy fat and the over-indulgence of her parents, with her father's basalt eyes and her mother's tilted chin. Vhairi, raised from the crib on her mother's stories, her father's revolution and the finest international travel that blackmail could buy. My eyes flickered from her to Margot, and for a long moment we waded in the truth of each other's souls, and found them wanting.

"You didn't send the telegram," I whispered, looking for words to deny the certainty I already knew.

She shook her head.

"What is this?" snapped Coman, all pretence of softness gone from him, pure old-country grumble.

"It's a trap," I breathed. "They're coming."

270

Margot was already moving, turning her back on me and striding into the room. Coman just stood in the door, not quite understanding, but his wife's bark – "Peadar!" – jumped him back to dumb life.

A child's voice, protesting, complaining as Margot, trying to sound a little gentler for the girl, commanded shoes, now; coat, now. I heard the rattle of the elevator gate behind me, the thump of feet on stairs from the other end of the corridor, and before Coman could protest, pushed into the room, forcing him out of my way, slamming the door shut and turning the lock. Margot was already halfway into a fold of coat, struggling with one sleeve while rummaging under the bed for a pair of shoes. Her handbag was open on the bed, a spill of coins and the gleam of a revolver glinting behind the catch. Coman grabbed a child's jacket from a hook by the door, urging the girl inside it, while I dragged a heavy chair along the thick carpet to wedge beneath the door handle as the hammering began. They didn't bother to call names or make threats; whoever was pounding foot and fist against the locked door knew precisely what they wanted, and negotiation changed nothing.

Margot had a window open, a blast of cold, wet air and the sudden sound of the street outside, the slosh of wheels through dancing water and the percussion of rain on metal. There was no fire ladder, but the front of the hotel had been built in the overblown, cod-Greek style that so many architects equated with classical grandeur, and between half-circle pillars of painted concrete, a lintel ran just about wide enough to get a foot on. She hopped out without hesitation, and as the bedroom door began to crack, panels breaking in long, jagged lines, she reached out a hand for her daughter.

Vhairi shook her head, urgent, begging.

"Sweetheart," murmured Margot. "Now."

She wasn't cruel or brisk. They had talked about this possibility before. The end of Vhairi's nose trembled, she snuffled back the beginning of tears, bowed her head and ducked out onto the lintel behind her mother, who caught her hand and

271

held so tight her child flinched. Coman followed, one hand on his daughter's shoulder, pressing her closer to the wall. I stuck my head out of the window, saw the street lamps below and the tumbling clouds above, and felt fairly certain that at least one of us was going to die in this escape. Then a voice called, "Abbey!" from the door, and a black-gloved hand had made it through the topmost broken panel and was flapping around, feeling out the shape of the chair I'd wedged against the handle. I slithered, graceful as a hernia, bum-first into the outside air, imagining feet giving out and clawing at nothing before falling to a six-floor splat below.

Margot had already rounded the first pillar, testing windows as she went and finding them all locked. Coman followed, chest pressed to the wall, hands sliding out either side of him like a clinging spider, cheek flat to stone, nodding and smiling encouragement at his child as if this was just the normal way of things. I mimicked his gait, fingers digging into grit, trying to slow my breathing as behind me the door gave another resounding crack and foot followed fist through the bending, breaking panels. The rain glued my hair to my face, pricked the tops of my eyes, but the idea of moving my hands from their insect scramble against the stone was absurd. Ahead I heard a sudden crack of glass as Margot, giving up on an open window, smashed the next one she found, sweeping broken shards with the rim of her bag in a crystal snowfall, and ducking in through the remains head-first, falling into a tangle of curtain, coffee table and potpourri. Vhairi, smaller, lighter, crawled in easily, caught by her mother's hands, then Coman, and by the time I tumbled like a clown through the shattered remains of glass and torn velvet, Margot was fumbling her way across the darkened room for the door.

We had come into another bedroom, less magnificently appointed than Margot's own, the smell of dry flowers just about overwhelming the stench of damp. I felt glass tear at my hands and trousers as I crawled upright, staggered after Margot and Coman as, carefully, she unlocked the bedroom door and eased it open a crack. The muggy yellow light of the corridor slithered through the gap, illuminating the thinnest line of her face, and for a moment she was a woman growing old; paler, more bones and less delight than I remembered, and none of us were as young as we had been. Her child stared at me in confusion, not understanding whether I was friend or foe, what she was meant to think.

Then, with a deep breath, Margot opened the door all the way, pulled herself straight as an umbrella and, with all the dignity of a busy woman not about to be disturbed, stepped out into the corridor, daughter in hand, marching for the stairs without a care in the world.

Not thirty feet away, our pursuers were barrelling through the broken remains of the grand suite's front door, and for a moment, as Coman and I stepped out after her, I thought we might almost get away with it. Then a man turned, saw the four of us and called out, "Hey!" not having the initiative to think of anything more exacting to say.

Margot burst into a run, and we followed, as the same men who'd climbed on to the hotel lintel to follow us turned round and now charged down the corridor in our wake. I didn't see if they had weapons. I just knew there were more of them than there were of us, and that they had orders, and intentions, and even if they carried nothing more dangerous than a fountain pen, they could hurt me a damn sight more than I could probably hurt them, so I ran.

The stairs down were hard, singing stone, grudgingly installed in the event that guests were too frightened of an elevator to dare catch a ride. A maid carrying a tray for delivery squeaked as we swept by, pressing herself flat into the wall; then screamed and cursed and dropped the tray spectacularly as our pursuers tumbled past her, swinging themselves round every curve with all the gusto gravity allowed. For a moment it was a question of sheer speed, of who was willing to hurl themselves more recklessly into the chase, or whose concentration broke first, causing them to trip over their own feet, miss their grip on the banister as they bent into a curve. Then Margot was at the bottom, Vhairi nearly falling over with the speed of her mother's run and chain-like grip, and as she yanked open the brass-padded door, a man came up before her, and she barely even broke momentum as she smacked her handbag up and into the soft plateau beneath his chin, staggering him backwards and squeezing past and into the warmer light of the lobby. Coman, moving like a cat, slammed both palms into the man's chest, knocking him against the wall. His head cracked, his eyes bulged, he slipped down as Coman danced by, and for a moment I was a doctor again and felt the instinct to stop, to check his skull, but Margot was halfway across the lobby, revelling now in her speed, people scattering, indignant and amazed, from her path, and at my back were men with some very specific instructions that beat through the rushing of my blood and into my brain, so I ignored the fallen man and kept on running. Margot's bodyguard, absurd in yellow and blue, leapt to his feet as we passed, and was the first man to die, tumbling without thought into our pursuers, buying us a few seconds of giddy, confident time, before a knife came down between his shoulder blades and he expired on the hotel floor, having never really given much thought to what he'd do if he actually had to do anything in this job of his.

Running into the street, into the pouring rain, slipping between carriages and the occasional creaking, popping, belching car with lanterns turned low to a glistening cobbled floor; running through the place where I was out of air and into a different body, where suddenly it seemed I had enough breath almost to laugh, and was flying. Ahead, Margot was sprinting, Vhairi at her side, skirts flapping wildly, laces loose and hair spun free of every pin and ladylike accoutrement; for a moment she was a girl again running along the cliffs, before her daughter's ghost followed her, before she had to run for ever.

Then a carriage swerved out into the street ahead of us, a long, low thing from which six men tumbled out, late to the business of the evening, determined to make their mark.

With men in front and men behind, Margot turned without a thought for the other side of the street, looking for an alley; couldn't find one, stopped for a moment, panting for breath, still smiling a strange, delighted smile, then made a choice and stepped out in front of a cart that sometimes carried tallow and is now returning from a delivery, the wood slick and slippery with congealed white animal fat turned to black slime by years of neglect, the whole thing glistening like hot ice. The driver pulled his plodding horse to a halt with a cry and a curse, and Margot had the gun out of her bag, and was still smiling, still bursting with the sheer exhilaration of being alive, until she felt her daughter's horror at her back, the dismay and terror of her child at the sight of her mother ready to kill a man, and hesitated. Coman did not, scrambled up into the driver's seat as the man hurled himself into the road, and then Margot was swinging Vhairi between them and clambering up behind to form a wall around their child. "Get in!" she hollered, as Coman snapped the reins and the cart begins to trot towards the bundle of men scrambling after us from the hotel door. I jogged along beside and managed to flop chest-down onto the back of the cart, slipping and sliding in grease, legs kicking out wildly behind me as I wriggled along like a worm, and then Coman slapped the reins again and the horse very reluctantly, whinnying and whimpering at the indignity of it, broke into the nearest thing it could muster to a gallop.

It was not much of a gallop. The horse was too old and too tired, too used to city traffic to muster any speed. But it was heavy, scared, and by the time it hit the first of our pursuers, a man too slow or too dumb to get out of its way, it had a great mass of momentum and the man went down beneath it with a crack of bones that doesn't even make the beast pause.

The others hurled themselves to the sides. One man, running full tilt, managed to grab my ankle, and I kicked out with my other foot, smacking him in the hand once, twice, before giving up on that idea and smacking him in the face. He let go, his weight half dragging me out as he fell, sliding on grease.

Another man managed to get one foot up on the driver's side of the cart, only to receive the full force of Margot's handbag, delivered in a great swooping circle to the side of his face. His grip weakened, and she hit him again, and as he fell, she pulled her bag close to her chest and brandished the revolver, this time holding it high and firing a shot into the sky as her daughter screamed at the retort. Coman snarled at the horse, whipped it into a spit-flecked spin at the corner of the street, swung it round into the wider avenue, and nearly fell off his perch as he hauled back to prevent us tunnelling straight into the back of a mule-dragged scrap wagon.

The stop was hard enough to send me spinning sideways into the low walls of the cart, groggy and confused, filthy and bleeding from a dozen tiny glass cuts across my arms and shins. Peeking up from my falling place, I saw the New York traffic, a locked-up mass of cargo, carriages, omnibuses and pedestrians, cursing and grumbling at each other as the rain washed away the piles of animal shit and the last vestiges of human civility. There was no pushing through it, and now our pursuers were on top of us again, hopping over their fallen comrades.

Hands grabbed at my ankles, dragging me towards the pavement. I caught a finger's grip around a handle at the back of the pallet and for a moment was suspended, legs one way, arms another, pulled like a tightrope between my pursuers and escape. Then my fingers gave way and I flopped, belly-first, onto the cobbles, breath smacked out, head ringing, hands a scraped and bloody mess as my pursuers continued to drag me backwards. Someone had caught Coman round the waist and was trying to lift him from his seat, throw him like a sack of flour to the earth. He punched at one man's head, wriggled and kicked like a suffocating squid as they clawed at him, and then a gunshot.

Margot, of course. I didn't feel the thoughts of the man she killed. He hadn't realised it would happen. In all the confusion, he had somehow not quite associated the woman with the gun,

276

nor ever imagined that a lady could pull the trigger. He did not see his death, and thus he did not fear it, and thus his heart was of little notice to me. But Vhairi's was. The child's heart shattered with the man's skull as her mother shot him point-blank in the face. She had never seen death, never thought of it as a concept, could not understand, but still faintly knew that only villains killed, and that her mother could not be a villain.

Margot must have felt it too. She loved her child; she saw her child's world break apart. She would defend Vhairi above all else, and so, tears pricking her eyes, she rose and turned, putting another bullet in the arm of a man grappling with Coman, who for an instant didn't realise what had happened until he suddenly couldn't hold on any more, at which point awareness came with waves of agony so potent they turned his stomach through his throat.

I have never been in a fight that wasn't defined by chaos. Smooth coordination is born of relentless drilling, and even then I have listened to the hearts of men who broke from the line when they thought they would be brave; who played dead in the grasslands of the veld, or turned their coat and begged to be fed by their enemies. I have met the proudest warriors of the Zulu bull who trained their whole lives with the stabbing spear, the cowhide shield and the Martini–Henry rifle and who, at the moment of truth, realised that they didn't want to die the slow death of their bleeding kin. I have met proud soldiers of the Mahdi, fallen samurai and warrior monks from the cloud-lost mountains, and in my experience, nothing pre-pares you for an unexpected fight quite as much as experience of wildfire and a stiff shot of brandy.

Like the running beast, this final gunshot at last sent the street into panic. Bewildered passers-by, drivers, herders, amblers and fine folks out for the night who had watched our little brawl now scattered in every direction, their sudden terror sweeping over me hard enough to knock out the breath that I had barely begun to regain. Cabbies hurled themselves from their seats; horses bucked and pushed and staggered against each other, trying to break free; a dog barked and heaved at its leash, a man fell to the ground dead, another screamed in agony as Coman kicked him in his wounded arm and leapt free, and all things broke apart.

For my part, fallen to the floor, groggy and bewildered, I was suddenly of far less note to my would-be assailants, who variously ducked for cover behind car and carriage, pressed their backs into doorways and red-brick walls. Margot leapt down from her perch, fired another shot into the air, entirely oblivious to the corpse cooling by her ankles, hollered, "Vhairi!" and gestured towards the rapidly emptying street ahead. Coman nodded, scooping his child round the waist and carrying her like a rolled-up canvas; broke into a run, sprinting for the throng of scattering people and braying animals, the crisscross pattern of turned-again vehicles wedged tight together. Margot saw me as I crawled to my feet, snapped, "Run!" and without waiting to see if I obeyed her command, hitched her skirts in one hand and set off.

I followed, every second expecting someone to grab me from behind. No one did. Leaping over the crawling shape of a passing gentleman who'd been too befuddled by the noise and confusion to work out which way was safety and which was danger, I swung round the side of a stalled brewer's cart, ducked past a screaming, kicking horse the bucking, twisting mess of stalled vehicles that lined the street. Margot was ahead, gun glinting in one hand; Coman close behind. I skidded in a splatter of filthy puddle past an elderly woman in a fox hat, who screamed and beat at me with her umbrella as I passed; then turned sharply as Margot did, heading now up a sideways street lined with drugstore, grocery, milliner, barber and purveyor of suspicious bloody meats, heading west. In a moment I realised her destination, saw the flash of sparks from beneath the high tracks of the elevated train, heard metal on metal, and a second later, heard the gunshot.

It didn't come from Margot; that was the surprising thing.

It took me a moment to process this fact, but having

understood it, the conclusion seemed fairly banal and inevitable.

Another shot, and this time the lamp post to my left rang like a cathedral bell as the bullet slammed into metal, a fresh crater in the black iron. I kept running, then slithered to the ground in a sheet of rainwater as Margot turned and shot back, firing quickly, twice, three times from her little revolver, blindly towards our pursuers.

On the third shot, the gun clicked, and with a curse and a snarl she dropped it into her handbag and now, bent double, charged like a bull down the middle of the street, swerving between the confused, rattling traffic, heading for the train. I scampered after, flinched as another bullet smacked into the wooden side of a cab at my right, nearly fell as a second shot bounced in a busy wave just behind my feet. I could hear the jingle-jingle-jingle of the police bell in the distance, saw faces peering out of windows, felt the momentary panic of a father cradling his son in the shadow of a doorway, heard the scream of a woman ahead as she realised what was coming straight for her, saw her freeze like a startled owl as we passed, too locked in her own dread to think, to move, to get to shelter.

Another shot, and I thought perhaps a splinter of something had caught me in the waist, because an angry bee stung me. I kept running. Four steps, five steps, and perhaps I realised I had been hit with something more than a splinter, because the pain was a sudden tearing up into the hollows of my ears and down to the soft skin between my toes. Six steps, seven steps, and I became aware of the heat of the blood running out of my side, the soft warmth of it soothing through the cold of the rain and the sticky panting of exertion.

On the eighth step I fell, and that was confusing, because I hadn't planned on falling and couldn't see the reason for it.

I tried to stand, and my legs kicked loosely, and wanted to obey, and didn't, and seemed as confused by this as I was.

I heard Margot calling my name, but from the wet ground all I could see were feet moving between wheels and stamping horses' hooves. I think Coman caught her by the arm and pulled her away. I think she was still calling my name as he did, but it was unclear. Langa was coming, he was coming, but still too far away that I couldn't be sure if she loved me, or if she cared that I was down. There was too much noise to get a clear sense of it, though I stretched out a hand towards her and willed her to hear my love more clearly than I could sniff out hers.

Maybe she heard it. Maybe not. I can't imagine the ghost of her dead daughter was any nearer than the boy I had let burn.

Only one truth mattered, and I couldn't really resent it, even then. Margot loved her daughter far more than she loved me, and that was entirely fair, all things considered.

Then another shot rang, and she staggered. She didn't fall, Coman caught her before she could, but her face was grey and her daughter screamed. She hadn't screamed all this time, a good girl, a quiet child. Margot hobbled a pace, and her left leg buckled, then she hobbled a step more, and Coman held her round the waist and slung her over his shoulder like an old carpet, and took his daughter by the hand, and they ran.

They ran into the rain, still pursued by men firing, clattering through water and stone, and I couldn't see if they got away. Couldn't taste the truth of it. I lay on my back and looked into the gently growing dawn sky, a wet slosh of yellows and greys pushing back against the purple of the night, and heard footsteps moving around me, and couldn't judge whether they were close or far, and didn't really care.

It occurred to me that dying would be convenient, at this juncture. As long as the bullet had missed my stomach and hit something usefully rich with blood, such as liver or spleen, I could bleed out in a matter of minutes. I wouldn't be able to betray anyone more than I already had, and need not suffer a slow, lingering demise. The thought was almost comforting, and I was briefly astonished at how quickly my priorities had shifted from the desire to live to the urge to die hastily. Perhaps Ritte had been right all along: at the end, we barter with what little we have to give.

Then a man was standing above me, and tutting, and he said, "Someone get the doctor," and for a laughable moment I tried to explain that I was a doctor, and really all this wasn't necessary at all, before the blood loss hit me and the darkness took my sight.

Chapter 52

If you think medicine is poor now, Sister Ellis, fifteen years ago it was mediocre. Oh, we had the confidence of gods – our microscopes and our mercury pills, our tinctures of opium and our exciting, newly sterilised tools! But this war has given us so many tens of thousands of men to practise our craft on; an opportunity to hone our butchery. It is perhaps ironic that it is still so much easier to invent poisoned gas than it is to treat it. Our capacity for destruction always runs ahead of our willingness to invest in the well-being of others.

In a way I suppose I should be grateful to whoever it was who pulled the bullet out of my chest and stitched me back together again. The scar is truly magnificent – I think he must have used sailor's rope to do the stitching – and the pain when I move in certain ways is remarkable. However, I think he sterilised his instruments and the environment, adopting what was for then a somewhat new-fangled approach to these things, because I neither died of sepsis within a week, nor woke a dribbling wreck, my mind obliterated by the surgeon's fever.

Instead, I surfaced some three or four days later on a ship.

At first, I assumed that the rocking of my world was simply the consequence of having been shot, and perhaps of having died in the process. The urge to vomit somewhat decreased my conviction that I was dead, but even then I couldn't be sure that this wasn't a side effect of massive quantities of opium or ether, to numb the pain.

When I did vomit, into a bowl that had been helpfully left

beneath my bed, it was the single most extraordinarily painful thing I have ever experienced, nearly ripping out my stitches and leaving me a howling, sobbing wreck on the cabin floor.

This provoked some attention. A door, which I now noted with some interest had a porthole in it, was opened, and in with the stench of salt came a man dressed in waxed coat and leather shoes. He looked at me for a moment without much in the way of sympathy, then turned back to the gloom whence he'd come and called out some words in French, which I was too befuddled to catch.

Only now did it occur to me that perhaps I was neither dead nor on land, but had been captured at last by the French authorities, finally indulging their long-held desire for a truth-speaker, and that as Ritte had done before, I was to be chained up in some forgotten room and made to pronounce upon the enemies of the Republic. Then another man entered, wearing a cream smoking jacket and sporting a flat straw hat held beneath his chin with a length of string. His shoulders were too big for his chest, his legs too small for his torso, his eyes small in an almost spherical face, his lips drooping and generous, his skin the colour of a winter moon. He looked at me, tutted once, nodded once, and said in a clipped, English accent, "Ah yes well yes hum better feed him yes," and walked away.

Thought slows.

It slows down.

During the terror of the chase, I had no time to deal with the pros and cons of being alive, dead, captured or free. Every second was its own explosion of certainty. Every moment was a negotiation with eternity.

Alone, locked in a cabin on a boat in what I presumed was the middle of the Atlantic, I had time to contemplate my predicament, and the only conclusion I could reach was that it was a disaster.

Sometimes I slept.

Sometimes I called out for drugs to take away the pain.

Sometimes they came.

Sometimes they didn't.

Sometimes I fed myself.

Sometimes they fed me.

One night, the sea was so rough I thought we would drown. Rolling from one wall of the cabin to another in a wretched tangle of sheet and cot, I wondered what had happened to Colette Maury, my travel companion on that return voyage to Liverpool, and if she'd found love and comfort in America. I wondered where Margot was, and hammered my fist against the door on those few occasions when the tossing of the ship brought me to easy hammering distance; but no one else seemed concerned, and the next morning even I was grateful to be alive as the fresh breeze billowed in through the open slats of the window.

I played a hundred possibilities through my mind, a thousand scenarios, trying to pick apart any outcome from this situation that wasn't a calamity, and found none. I invented and discarded stratagems and ruses, and they were all so quickly and apparently useless that I was in fact a very quiet patient, having nothing to say to my captors that I hadn't already said a thousand times to myself. They didn't need to be cruel or violent to subdue me. My own dread was perfectly up to the task of making me, by the time we reached Liverpool, an entirely docile and dreary customer.

Only one thought, one hope stuck with me: perhaps Margot had escaped.

I wished Langa was near, knew that this Atlantic voyage put him weeks behind me, longed to know the truth of my captor's hearts. More than ever, his absence felt like a sense cut off, a blindness when I most needed to see. How poor I was at dealing with people on their own terms.

In Liverpool I was carried by stretcher off the boat to a train by four silent, busy guards. There was no attempt to hide me, no effort to restrain me or commands to keep my mouth shut. The tear in my side made running an impossibility; putting up a fuss seemed only an invitation to greater pain. At the station, kindly women smiled and wished me a speedy recovery, and men with neat ties nodded a gesture of mutual support and goodwill as they scurried past, grateful that they were not suffering from whatever malady assailed me. I didn't respond to any of it, but sometimes my guards would tip a hat in acknowledgement, concerned kin.

We travelled first class, which had never happened when I was in the government's favour. At the station we were met by four more men, who crowded into a space barely fit for three at the back of a carriage that crawled its way through the low smoke of London to a house, not near Whitehall as I had thought, but on the edge of what I took to be Hammersmith. I could smell the sewage of the Thames and the detritus of thin, diluted shit it left behind when it flooded, see the green and yellow lines of algae the floodwaters had left at the highest marks when it burst its banks. Yet the suburb also boasted cleaner air than the centre of the city, grand terraces of white houses set in a line, from which children played in bright-buckled shoes and where the maids always had a clean apron to wear. High elm trees bent over the roads and railway tracks, and the grocer's shop proudly displayed posters in the window of the pleasant day trips you might take from London to the flowery delights of Sydenham, Acton, Kew Gardens and leafy, breezy Epping.

I was put in a pale pink room containing a dovetail dresser, a gold-framed mirror, a wardrobe containing a single, stinking tweed coat and an old yellow pillow; a bed, a table to put water on, and a bucket to pee or puke in, depending which situation caught me out first. On the dresser was a pile of books, mostly creaking tomes of Dickens's least loved works, or tales of misery in Manchester, where a single cough from a beloved character's lips foretold nearly two hundred pages of inevitable, tedious decline.

Once a day, a doctor came to inspect my wound, a man younger than me, who was trying to cultivate a pair of old-fashioned whiskers and could manage little more than a spike of faded yellow hair on the tip of his chin. I recognised in him something of Albert's way of things, for he was all for carbolic acid and wonderful new ways of stitching flesh together, and when I hoarsely muttered during his ministrations that I too was a physician, he burst into an ecstatic ramble on the wonders of toxins and the buzz around an element called radium and the wonderful properties of metals that glowed.

If he knew I was a prisoner, it was entirely secondary to him, though he never once gave his name, and the hearts of men were closed to me.

After five days, the doctor's visits stopped, and he was replaced by a nurse who said nothing except "roll over" or "lift" or "sit", and puppy-like I obeyed. Under her observation, I began to walk round the autumn garden, shivering and hobbling like a grey old man. I took dinner downstairs with two guards, instead of spoon-fed in my room; I was permitted very weak tea at breakfast and another cup at three in the afternoon, and ordered to inhale foul-smelling vapours from a steaming bowl every night, which I was assured was good for my healing and which I snappily replied was good for nothing except rousing my temper.

Only once did I attempt to explain to this woman, ice made flesh, that I was a doctor, which was met with the stiff reply, "And you've been very naughty too."

That seemed to settle the matter. Men were doctors; children were naughty. I was definitely in the latter category.

For two and a half weeks this was my ritual, and I began to wonder what they were waiting for. Yet fear can only be at the forefront of your mind for so long, and while every bump in the night was enough to rouse me with a gasping start, the routine, however tedious, began to dominate my day.

All that ended just before the third week, when Albert came.

He arrived a little after dinner, and I was brought to him in the parlour, where he was already enjoying a cigar and a tumbler of whisky. The sight of him brought all the terrors of what was to come back to full, glorious life; his presence could only be the beginning of change, of the waited-for retribution that had been my promise.

Nevertheless, the scene was familiar – warm and welcoming – so I settled without complaint in the thickly padded chair opposite him, and took the whisky that was passed to me, and was not offered a cigar.

For a while we sat in this manner, he studying a landscape painting above the cold fireplace as if he had never before seen romanticised mist off badly painted fields. He smiled all this time, but didn't meet my eye, and I studied him and waited like the child the nurse thought I was, for all that had to follow.

At last he said, as one who has already run through a conversation in his mind and sees now no point retreading it with another, "When they ask, answer simply and to the point. There is nothing they do not already know."

I held the tumbler tight between both my hands, and waited for him to look at me.

He did not.

"When it is over, there will be a brief period of adjustment. I cannot promise it will be without pain. But I want you to know that it is for the best, and you will be well looked after."

I do not know if he meant to terrify me with these words, or to comfort. When I feel kind, I sometimes think the latter. I do not feel kind very often, these days.

Then he said, "I have missed our conversations. I have brought you some papers to read. There is interesting work being done. We live in exciting times."

I thought for a moment he might say something more.

His lips thinned, his fingers tapped once along the edge of the glass. Then he drained his glass down, stood in a single swoop, nodded once with his head towards me, his eyes towards the wall, and walked away without another sound.

The next day, the soldiers came for me.

Chapter 53

I didn't know where they took me. I was blindfolded, and knew only that we walked a little, then rode in a carriage for a while, then walked a little more on smooth stone through a place that smelt of cold and damp. In the distance I heard a factory bell, and a man calling out what I thought were commands to a crew; but I couldn't be sure. Sounds faded the further we walked, the colder the air became. I thought we were underground, or deep inside sealed tunnels that had not seen sunlight for a very long time.

Then they sat me down, and removed my blindfold, and the colonel was there, and Mrs Parr, and a man with thin grey hair and a beaked nose above an ocean pier of a chin, who watched everything and sometimes daubed at his neck with a handkerchief, though the room was cold, and sometimes checked his fob watch for the time, and contributed nothing else.

Langa, where are you? I need your truth now.

The colonel didn't bother with accusations, or demand that I tell him everything.

Instead, he laid out my crimes clearly and concisely before me.

My relationship with Margot.

My relationship with the People's Society.

My betrayals.

He put down names, places and dates, stretching back over three years. I was relieved that he had nothing from earlier.

He asked, "When did it begin?"

I said nothing.

He snapped, "Who are her confederates?"

I said nothing.

He barked, "How much does she know?"

I said nothing.

Mrs Parr stood, hands folded in front of her, no seat offered or asked for as she shivered inside her onion skirts, and for a moment I thought she might cry, and found the idea incredibly strange. She was the only person who met my eye apart from the colonel, and his gaze was not a conversation so much as a battering ram into my soul.

The interview can't have taken more than an hour. At the end of it, the colonel slunk back into his chair, shaking his head, a disappointed parent who cannot believe the foolish, naïve truculence of a spoilt child.

"Very well," he snapped. "We will move on."

So saying, he left the room.

Mrs Parr remained, watching me. She watched as one of my captors came up behind me and, hauling me up by the scruff of the neck, proceeded to clamp on handcuffs. They hadn't felt any need to before, and now every fantasy of physical pain I had ever imagined surfaced in a single, bowel-twisting surge of reality. Mrs Parr licked her lips, reading something of this perhaps in my face, and as the guards pulled me towards the door, she stepped forward suddenly, her shoulder nearly knocking against mine, and whispered in my ear: "*I didn't know.*"

They pulled me away from her, and dragged me down another arctic, wet corridor of crudely carved stone.

We were not underground. Apart from the oil lanterns my captors carried, thin, high bolts of daylight were permitted to intrude, carrying with them the occasional squawk of a seagull, crash of wood on metal. I tried to count steps, paces, couldn't work out why I bothered, and then I was in front of a long metal door like the gates to a factory, which were with great labour unbolted and slid back on a shriek of rust.

The sound of a man's voice struck just before the smell.

The smell was an instant memory – the operating theatre at the London Hospital, ammonia, steel, leather and the thin, clear fluids that seep into a half-healing wound once the blood has stopped, forming crystal yellow scabs around broken skin.

The voice took a moment longer to place. A softness to the vowels through the babble, a bluntness to some of the consonants, a slight American roll to an R. Then the door was opened all the way, and I was pushed into the tall, round room where the man waited, and I knew him, and he was Hideo.

The ancient ways ... the honour! The code! The ... but actually the price of fish, the price of fish was so important ...

Sometime would-be samurai, who was cursed for his arrogance and found his way to the railway lines of America, I recognised him by his left eye and something around the jaw. His right eye had been removed when they cut into his brain, leaving a hollowed-out, healed-over socket of smooth, shiny skin. The surgeon who had carved into his skull had used a metal plate to replace parts of the bone he had removed, riveting it in place with fat, gleaming bolts that stuck up around the rim like silver blisters. The rush of fluids into the rest of his facial cavities had distorted his jaw and cheeks, first extending them like the belching throat of a toad before draining away to leave collapsed wrinkles of cockerel flesh. He muttered and whispered incoherent sounds and words, sometimes in Japanese, sometimes in English. Sometimes a phrase burst through the nonsense, before vanishing again into gibberish.

"Came home late last night came home late ... "

Then without warning his voice would curl up into a shriek, like a frightened animal, before dropping back down into that relentless conspiratorial whisper, before falling silent without a warning, before starting back up again in a sudden rush.

Straps across his chest and legs held him upright in the wheelchair in the middle of the room, but months of inactivity had caused his neck to reduce to a tendon-laced arch drooping against the piping of his collar. Where his arms protruded from beneath his shirt, they were merely a surgeon's skeleton draped in spider's silk, not the limbs of a living, moving thing at all. His mouth rolled open and on a tray around him were pipes and tubes for pushing drink and liquid food between his twitching lips.

"Don't like it don't like it but have to do what you don't like ..."

And there it was.

Look a little closer, and even with Langa still crossing the Atlantic, even with my shadow so far away, I could catch a glimpse of it, the thing that everyone in the room had perhaps thought they'd seen out of the corner of their eye, but couldn't quite name.

A shadow. The shape of a man, decapitated, flowing in and out of Hideo, darting, his movement broken and confused, into his body, then out of his body, flung back as if repulsed by magnetism, then trying again, and again, and again, pushing and tearing into his flesh. His shadow, in the room with him right now, clawing at him, pushing the truth onto his tongue, relentless, as trapped as he.

I looked at him in horror, too stunned to pay much attention as I was lowered onto a stool a foot in front of his chair. Having pushed me into my seat, my guards backed away quickly, pressing themselves to the edge of the room, as a man in an open lab coat revealing a gaudy red waistcoat beneath edged up behind Hideo and pushed a needle into the pockmarked, syringe-torn crook of his arm.

This done, he stepped back briskly, passing straight through Hideo's dancing, twisting, writhing shadow without seeing what he did, but perhaps feeling it, for he too seemed to want to put as much distance between himself and the man in the chair as possible. He crossed the room to a table by the wall, and inserted a fresh wax cylinder into a phonograph. The long brass horn was swung towards me, the cylinder started turning, the man in the white coat bending down to blow away little trails of wax as the knife cut its recording.

Hideo's head rolled to the left, rolled to the right, and finally, still at a listless, drooping angle, his one remaining eye focused on me.

"Scared," he whispered. "Had too much time to think thinking hurt all the things all the things had to happen one day had to happen couldn't run Margot where is Margot do they have her do they have her should have thought about her more selfish just thinking about me my pain pain so scared of pain so scared of being hurt know I'll talk humiliating it'll be humiliating how quickly they'll hurt me how easily I'll talk probably going to cry when they shoot me probably gonna piss myself Jesus what have they done what have they done what have they done to Hideo?"

I couldn't speak.

Not that there was any point in speaking.

In a relentless, gibbering, dribbling drawl, Hideo unpacked the truth of my heart.

"Love her love her? What is love hard to say hard to measure these things so easy to see in others saw a woman once saw her love so scared of love of the power of it only fear only years of fear did such things betrayed everyone betrayed everything just a shadow followed by a shadow Langa where are you where are you I need you now do they have Margot no they can't have Margot they'd have told me by now used it to laugh to gloat she got away she got away thank God she got away but how do I know know nothing that's their power that's their ... "

The phonograph scratched his monologue into the cylinder, pouring out the secrets of my heart. Sometimes the man in the red looked up and asked a specific question – who was Coman, what was the nature of Margot's shadow, how did we communicate, what were her intentions?

I didn't answer, and didn't need to. Every truth I know was immediately on Hideo's lips.

"Justice peace freedom she didn't used to believe used to laugh laughable ideas so funny loves the money the victory the power but sometimes you have to believe learnt to believe they were in Marseille there was a man called ... "

"Please stop," I whimpered, and Hideo did not.

" ... we write to each other there is a code it is ... "

"Please. Stop."

"Sex is power too we never let our shadows come near no need for truth truth will destroy everything did destroy everything the game the power we love the power love knowing that we can lie to each other love knowing ... "

I tried to get up, and immediately a guard stepped across the room, pushing me down. Hideo's eye flickered to him and for a moment there was a cry of:

"Devil devil devil devil devil get out get out get out get out oh Jesus this place this place is this place ... !"

I tried to stand again, and the guard kicked me across the back of my knees, pushed me to the floor, held my head down with the palm of one meaty hand, scowled, shoved me harder, then, satisfied I wasn't moving, nearly ran for his position by the wall, as Hideo's cry of "Fuck don't let them see don't let them see don't let them see what I took!" echoed after him.

"Hideo," barked the man in the red waistcoat. "How many other truth-speakers does William know?"

Hideo's eye snapped back to me, a compass swinging north. "Polina Russians had her told me to be careful told me to run, Nashja beautiful likes to laugh terrible breath, Khanyiswa who lies, Saira please not Saira please don't tell them about her who knew the truth of my heart and I know hers and her truth is beautiful her soul is beautiful we never kissed because it was not honest please not her not Saira oh Jesus they're going to do this to me too they're going to cut out my brain."

"What happened in Austria? How did you escape?"

"Stop," I whimpered. "I'll tell you. You don't have to do this."

"Margot Margot saved me," Hideo declared, oblivious to everything but the truth and the shadow. "She killed a man Margot came and killed Margot rescued Margot where is

293

Margot they can't find out can't do this cut out her brain cut out my brain please just make it stop."

After a while, the phonograph stopped. Hideo burbled on merrily, and I thought maybe that was it as the man in the waistcoat slipped the cylinder into a cardboard tube, passed it to his assistant. Then he loaded up another, cranked the phonograph handle, and set the knife to the wax.

"Again," he barked, as the machine began to record. "Tell us everything."

I'm not sure how long they kept me there.

I tried to keep count of how many cylinders they cut, recording Hideo's relentless, soulless babble. I gave up begging. Gave up offering to tell them anything at all. Stopped caring after a while about the litany of terrors that Hideo pronounced from the pit of my soul. He waltzed into my heart and pulled it out for anatomical display, every secret, every lie and every childish doubt I'd ever held, and I supposed there was a kind of justice in that, and thought that Ritte had been right, and it was catharsis of a sort, and Margot had been right too, and it was violation beyond all naming, and no more than I had done to others for decades.

When they were done, they took me back to the house in Hammersmith. Mrs Parr watched me from the door as they led me away, and the man in the red waistcoat put Hideo back to sleep with a needle in the arm, his shadow still dancing, dancing, dancing through his flesh.

In my prison, I slept like a stone, fully dressed, stretched out sideways along the edge of the bed.

Somewhere, Albert and the colonel would be listening to the essence of my soul, scratched into wax. I wondered who else they'd share it with, how many others would sit around and have a good old laugh at the truth of my heart, before the sound quality degraded from too many plays.

I wondered where Margot was, and if she was smart enough to escape, and was grateful at last that she had never let me near her when Langa was close, except that once, when I made a mistake. There was only so much of her in me to betray.

I wondered where Saira was, and whether they had already telegrammed to India with her description and a warrant for her arrest, ready to lock her up and cut out her brain.

The next day, they had more questions. I gave them everything, betraying everyone I had ever been traitor for before.

Then I went back to bed, and waited.

That night, I dreamt the dreams of the sleepers in the house, and they were peaceful, and without regret.

Three days later, they took me to Albert.

Chapter 54

There are caves in the desert in northern India, where the widows go.

Saira never strayed too far from them, waiting, perhaps, for the day when she could walk no further, and would take that last journey into the sand, and pray that there was no one left who she loved.

I always looked for her, whenever I could, following the stories of the truth-speakers, listening to the hearts of men. I found her once, through the throng of the marketplace, infant hands clawing at our clothes below, monkey paws snatching at wares from above. A while we stood, as the hawkers pressed fancy articles of carved coral and bone, of yellow gold and hammered lead into our hands, offered up sticky sweets and dripping fruits, sacks of grain and paper fans. We bathed in the truth of each other's natures, and she disapproved of everything I did and had become, but understood why it had happened, and I was grateful – so very, very grateful – that she had the kindness to know me, all of me, through to the very bottom of my heart, and forgive me.

The relief of it, the sheer gasp of relief to stand in honesty before another person's gaze and let them see to the bottom of me, to the very heart, and to find in their truth the revelation that I was, in fact, entirely ordinary in my inadequacies nearly floored me. I found myself gasping for breath, like one suffocating in the press of bodies and midday heat, and at once she was marching towards me, tutting, and people cleared from before her like the cursed one she was, and she snapped, "Not here! They'll think you're mad and rob you blind!"

Instead, she led me to a wooden bench beneath a crooked palm tree, a nest of wasps busy above, a stray dog eyeing us nervously from below. We sat in its shade, the sounds of the city broken down for a little while against the white walls of the enclosure, a fountain in the centre of the yard long since run dry, cracked bleached lichen clinging to old stone, And there, we rested a while in silence, as she picked through the essence of my heart, listening, learning, feeling, judging and saying not a word.

The years had not been kind. Time had put dents in her faith. Not a sacred calling, not the noble mask of truth-speaker now; rather, an ageing woman shunned by people who should be grateful to her, her feet turned to stone, her stomach a sunken curve beneath spiky ribs. Where was the divinity in her cause, she wondered, when men would beat her from their villages for telling the truth they asked her to pronounce? Where was the justice when girls who were raped and beaten by their own kin were cast out into the dust, shunned for being victims of another man's crime? Their only redemption was in the road, the dust, the truth. Not that it gave any particular kind of relief.

"Let it burn," I whispered, but she tutted and shook her head, and fire was never her way.

Sometimes Saira stood on the lip of the road as the sun came up, and waited for her shadow. She would let the truth burst from her lips, shout it to the skies, and people would run from her, terrified of her knowledge, and she would let it happen as her fate came closer, and closer, and closer, shuffling hob-legged through the dust, a blip against the glory of the rising sun. She would face it down, look it in the eye, dare it to touch her, dare it to find someone, anyone she might possibly love. One time, it had come so close that she had felt the cold of it burn through her skin; but at the last minute, she always fled.

Perhaps there was a piece of humanity left in her too, she

mused. Perhaps one day she might love again. She doubted it. But hope was a persistent canker.

Please don't. Please don't do that again. Please don't face the shadow.

This is the truth of my heart, and she knows it in an instant.

She is, in a way, glad I came.

She hasn't seen many of her sisters for a while. The roads have grown thin. There are rumours that some were taken away by the British, but she doesn't know where.

It is good, is it not, to communicate like this.

To be honest with each other.

To see each other for who we really are, rather than the truth we believe ourselves to be.

I wonder if she has found a cure, a way to lift the curse.

She no longer finds the idea sacrilegious.

She heard of a woman in Ceylon ... but that was not to be. And another woman in Myanmar, but she couldn't make the journey, and anyway, the reports were dubious at best.

She thinks we will die this way, she and I.

We sit together a while in silence, until the shadows come.

Then we part, and run our separate ways.

Chapter 55

The operating room was scrubbed white tile, floor to ceiling. Shutters were thrown back from high, clean windows, letting in floods of sunlight, and mirrors were positioned around the edges of the room to redirect the beams to the centre, aided by smoky carbon lamps.

The operating table was covered with a white sheet.

I screamed and kicked and fought with all my might when I saw it, and managed to break one man's nose and kick another in the groin before five men manhandled me down, strapping me tight with belts and leather. Shaving my head was a hard, bloody affair, as they were forced to remove and reattach straps to get at my scalp, and every opportunity they gave me to twist or wriggle I was thrashing like a drowning fish. They got it done in the end, and a boy in braces swept up the bloody clumps from the floor.

I heard Albert arrive, rubber boots and commanding voice, sending away all but his assistants – the boy and the man in the red waistcoat. He wanted privacy for his work. One mistake could ruin everything, and he didn't want to waste this opportunity, or make me suffer needlessly.

This truth I knew, the moment I heard his voice. Langa was nearer now, Langa was coming, and with my shadow came also the truth of the heart of the man in red, whose name was Griswold and who was so grateful to be Albert's protégé, so honoured to have this chance to learn, so excited that today he would finally get to assist in this, Albert's most profoundly important and dangerous operation.

As for the boy who swept up my hair and mopped blood from the floor, the truth of his heart was only that he cared for his two sisters and his brother, and Albert's money had bought his loyalty absolutely, and he had not blinked when put in front of the mad Japanese man who knew the truth, and was therefore very brave.

Albert pulled a stool up behind my head, and I flinched as his hands pressed against the bleeding surface of my skull.

"It's near now, is it?" he asked, and didn't need to hear my answer to know the truth of it. "We need to test the procedure as it goes. I know there are people you love. I want to keep them safe. Do you understand that?"

I did. He meant it. He was going to cut into my brain, turn me into another Hideo, screaming and gibbering for the rest of my days – and he was going to do it with compassion, and love, and an absolute conviction in the necessity of his work. He respected me. He liked me. He regarded me as a friend. My betrayal had broken his heart, and he had been the very last to believe it, even when the colonel presented the evidence. If he hadn't heard Hideo blabbering my confession on the phonograph, he still might not believe it, but he was a man of truth.

Truth above all things.

And the truth was that I had betrayed them all, and that the best thing he could do, as a good man, was see that my suffering was minimal.

So he said, "It will take several procedures. If you can report on your experiences throughout as much as you can, that will enable the most accurate and quickest operation. Our experiments demonstrate that the phenomenon cannot make its leap to a target individual – to someone you love – when certain areas of your brain are no longer intact. By careful lobotomy we can reduce your overall emotional faculty, your personality if you will, to a series of automotive functions. This permits the shadow to remain in your proximity, without risk to others.

Do you understand? William? The more cooperative you are, the more functions we can preserve."

Functions such as pissing, speaking, drinking, breathing and the beating of my heart. These were of most relevance to Albert now.

"How many times?" I asked, and felt the probing of his fingers around my skull pause.

"How many times . . . what?"

"Have you done this?"

"Eleven."

"Eleven like me?"

"None like you!" None he considered human; none he would have called friend. Even now, he wanted me to understand how much he valued that. "We found truth-speakers, yes. Primitive peoples in the deserts of Australia, or the jungles of central Africa. People who barely understood elementary concepts, and could not cooperate fully with our aims. We could not send a bare-chested barbarian into diplomatic circles or ask them to infiltrate foreign governments, so we had to come up with another solution. When a white man, an educated, civilised man, turned up, it was an extraordinary opportunity. But the science of this . . . has always been more than the colonel can really understand."

The sharp smell of disinfectant, and a sudden touch of something cold and liquid against my scalp, mopping away tenderly, preparing the skin for cutting.

"The colonel is very happy to call it magic. Mysticism. This does not challenge his world view. The unexplainable is very easily explained – it is the unexplainable. That tautology is simple; it is his truth. It is the same rationale that every psychic and mystic has held down the centuries, but now we are in an age of science, and can begin to peel away this truth in search of a thing that is *actually* real. No longer do we accept the limits of our ignorance. Ignorance is to be pushed at, torn down, and behind it we find answers and more questions, more and more, as we expand the powers of our understanding

301

into a waiting void. Such things frighten the colonel, of course. The beauty of the unexplained is that it can be codified and categorised without ever needing to look truth in the eye. Why do men die? Because God made it so. Why is there wickedness? Because Satan walks the earth. To find an actual answer to these questions, and worse, for that answer to be that men die because we are nothing more than puny manifestations of dust, shambling across the globe, and that men are wicked because it pleases them – this is a truth he cannot accept. It destroys his world. It breaks his heart. He would far rather believe in magic than in truth, and there he and I have always been at some disagreement."

The motion of cotton on my skull stopped. There was a soft flutter of falling fabric as he set his swab aside. The knife would be next, and I tensed against it – but instead, there was the daub of a brush. He was marking out where he would cut, measuring precisely and carefully a line that began a few inches above my right eye and extended round to the tip of my ear.

"I experimented on others of your kind. The first six died. The seventh died after a year, while we were still perfecting her care. Thankfully, from the eighth onwards, we have had far greater success. I hope you understand the implications, William. We can operate on your brain, and it alters the behaviour of the shadow. The creature cannot strike those you love. It is tamed by reason; by science. It is not some mystical, incomprehensible phenomenon. It obeys laws, it can be controlled by reason. Think what this means. For every unknown, there *is* an answer. For every prayer we have wasted on a Creator, there is a truth, waiting to be unlocked. If we can control the inexplicable, what other 'truths' that we have taken for granted for so long might crumble before us? Is it true that men are wicked? Is it true that they must die? How much bigger the world appears when you discover that all the truths you have ever known are nothing but stories you were told as children, collapsing beneath the force of that primary, observed truth

302

of things as they *actually are*, not as they appear to be in the hearts of men."

The brush stopped moving. I heard wood against metal, then metal on metal as he picked up the first of his cutting blades. A laugh rose unbidden from the back of my throat, and died in the same breath. He hesitated, murmured, "Something funny?"

"Hideo once said pretty much the same thing you just did. If you hadn't cut his brain out, maybe you could have talked more on the subject."

"I don't enjoy hurting people, William – you know that, I think. Langa should be near enough for you to know it."

"Neither do you regret it," I replied. "I'm not sure what that makes you." I thought I felt him shrug, then the tip of the blade pressed against skin. I blurted, "Did you catch her? Did you find Margot?"

He didn't answer, and didn't need to. This time, I laughed so hard I shook, tears running down the side of my face and dripping onto the sheet below. Albert tutted, pulling back an inch. "Please don't do that," he chided. "I don't want to have to paralyse you."

"Why not?" He didn't answer, leaning back in with the blade. "Give me something for the pain."

"Unfortunately, I require you fully conscious to track the progress of the procedure. I did warn you that there would be some discomfort, but it will pass."

"Is there a cure?" I blurted. "Is there a way to cure it?"

He hesitated, and I knew the truth of his heart in an instant.

"No," he replied, and pressed forward, a light, easy slice, just enough pressure to fold back a flap of skin. Compared to being shot, it was an unremarkable pain, a precise gasp rather than a shock of horror, but somewhere between the terror, the laughter and the tears I decided to try a bit of howling, if I could get the breath, just to see what it did for him.

I had opened my mouth to give it my all when a voice calmly said from the door, "Kindly step away, Professor."

I couldn't turn my head, but I would know her anywhere.

"Mrs Parr," murmured Albert, frozen, knife in hand. His fear rippled through me, a shadow to his incredulity. "What are you doing?"

A footstep, sharp heel on cold tile.

"Kindly step away, Professor," she repeated. "As you know, I am entirely capable."

A snap of metal on metal, a shuffling of chair as Albert leant away.

Another step, and another, Mrs Parr coming closer. I strained to see her, and couldn't, but the truth of Albert's heart was that he was astonished, and he was now rebuking himself, and he was building towards fury too, not that it would do any good – fury at her, fury at himself. And the truth of the man called Griswold is he also can't believe this is happening, that the stupid old woman is going to spoil everything, and he is surprised to find that he is too terrified to look at her, too terrified to look at the gun in her hand, though he keeps on telling himself to be brave and gaze at her like a man.

"If you wouldn't mind," Mrs Parr commanded, and reluctantly the man in red obeyed. Straps loosened, and as soon as I could move a hand, I scrambled and tugged at my restraints, half falling from the operating table in my haste to get away, a thin line of blood following the curve of eyebrow from the beginnings of Albert's first incision, slithering to my temple.

Mrs Parr stood before me, an oversized revolver in one hand – an absurd tool with a black iron handle – and a portmanteau in the other.

"Dr Abbey," she breathed, "you will walk behind me."

And the truth was that she was salvation, rescue, and she was angry, and she was ashamed, and all of this came with such potency that it was hard to really know any truth in her thoughts, other than that they burnt like a blizzard across her soul.

Obedient, I moved behind her, and with a sharp nod she began to reverse towards the heavy doors of the operating theatre, keeping the gun still pointed at Albert and his man. The corridor outside was deserted, and as Mrs Parr stepped into it, she gestured at me to pull the door shut behind her, an iron key that weighed nearly as much as the gun emerging from her pocket to turn in the lock. This done, she put the revolver in the portmanteau and with a single sharp nod turned on her heel and began to march down the corridor.

"We will only have a few minutes," she barked as we walked. "I need you to listen with both ears and that other sense too, so that we don't have to deal with any stupid questions. There are six men guarding this building. Two of them I have sent to deal with a broken gas pipe; it will not be long before they begin to wonder how the damage was done. One of them is an indolent wretch and is sleeping. That leaves three. There is a pantry at the side of the building, and a fig tree growing by it up a wall. You will need to climb. You should make the drop on the other side without injury. I will walk out through the front door; at my age I am not climbing fig trees. You will not wait for me. You will turn right immediately on leaving these grounds and proceed to the end of the lane. There you will turn left and walk for approximately five hundred yards until you reach a small passage between yew hedges. Walk down that for fifty yards until you see a gap on your right. You will be able to push through to come into the rear of a churchyard. A rhododendron grows by the grave of a man called Schroeder Croll. Beneath it you will find a bag with papers and money. I have not left any further instructions. If they catch either of us, they will put us in front of the Japanese man with only one eye, and ignorance is our best defence. I will not look for you, and you will not look for me. If you hear gunfire, or think something has happened to me, you will not turn around. You will proceed to the churchyard. Do you understand?"

As she talked, she had walked, and now we stood at the end of a passage devoid of pictures, ornament, carpet or life, by a red wooden door to I knew not where. Here she turned, looked me in the eye at my silence and snapped, "William! Do you understand?"

"Yes. I understand."

"And do you see the truth of my heart?"

"Yes, Mrs Parr. I do."

"Good. They used me too, William. They made me ignorant, a foolish little woman. That was my job. That was all I was good for. Do you understand?"

"Yes, Mrs Parr."

A long intake of breath, a little nod. "I am going to step outside now. You will count to twenty, then follow me. You will turn right to head along the wall towards the pantry. You will not look back. Am I clear?"

"Yes, Mrs Parr."

"Count now."

She pushed open the door, sudden, dazzling sunlight knocking me back as she stepped briskly onto gravel framed by grass. She turned sharply to her left, and marched away, out of sight.

I counted to twenty, forcing myself to go slow, heart running in my head, then stepped into the light.

There was a small, neat garden, vegetable patches set out in square boxes between the soft green grass. A bulging, squat oak tree leant over a small mound of tools, the highest leaves reaching out to bump against the windows of the house. To my left, Mrs Parr's voice drifted on the breeze, a gentle chatter, "Are you sure I can't get you anything? Tobacco, cold meats?"

Another voice answering, perfectly well-meaning but a little bored by this old woman's pestering. I turned right, hand pressing to the yellow brick, following until I came to a small outhouse butting up against the main property, a dark window framing gloomy shelves of eggs and paper bags. A pale fig tree stood by, leaves thick and soft, the soil not quite rich enough to produce sweet purple fruit. Mrs Parr had left a stepladder against its base, as if some gardener had been planning on pruning and never got round to the task. I unfolded it, used it to boost me up to the first branch, started to climb.

The sound of Griswold shouting came just as my foot

306

touched the top of the tall brick wall. Then another voice joined it, and feet ran on gravel.

I swung out precariously onto the wall, began to edge my bottom down, feet dangling over the edge.

Somewhere, muffled by the sharp edges of the house, a gun fired.

It fired twice, and then once more.

The final shot was not a revolver.

I listened, heard the wind moving in the trees and the distant whistle of a train. A pair of crows bickered on the other side of the lane, startling three pigeons into the sky.

Feet tore against the earth, and I closed my eyes and dropped down to the other side of the wall.

I landed awkwardly, sliding down mossy verges to the harder mud of the lane. I thought I heard a voice shout, but it was hard to tell. I turned right, and walked away.

I was in suburban south London. Behind the wall to my right was a generous yellow-brick house with blue shutters and a weathervane. On the other side of the lane, framed in elm and oak, was a vicarage painted black and white, ready to partake in Sunday tea and a little light supplication. The path sloped downwards towards a line of trees dotted with cottages and the beginning of newer, terraced roads. A funnel of smoke from behind the treeline spoke of a train heading for the distant splat of the city, smeared in brown and soot. I walked, and did not run, and turned left and strode for five hundred yards until I came to a child-wide passage between two competing yew hedges grown by men who knew where their boundaries were and were damn sure that other people should learn to respect them. I shuffled fifty yards until I found the arching gap in the right-hand side where needled leaves had given way to a hollowed-out cave of wood, a child's doll left in the dirt beneath the bower of green. Crawling on hands and knees, I pushed to the other side, bursting into a churchyard of clean white tombstones only just beginning to bloom with coal dust and lichen. Beneath the dark leaves of a rhododendron I found the grave of Schroeder Croll; behind it, nestled between tomb and wall, I found my medical bag.

I didn't know how Mrs Parr had found it. That had not been a truth that beat clearly in her heart. All that mattered was that I understood and obeyed; this had been her truth, her certainty and her demand, and there was no fighting it. And if I knew the other truths of her heart? If I knew that she blazed at having been kept in the dark for so many years, having been lied to and manipulated so that she could lie to and manipulate me? A stupid little woman, patronised and ignored and finally ordered to send her ...

... to send one she respected and valued ...

... to the operating table in chains?

Well, that would only serve to make me get a move on, wouldn't it?

Mrs Parr had never had children, and did not permit herself to feel love. Such things were fancies for fools. She would have made a far better truth-speaker than me.

Mixed into my instruments was a clean shirt, clean socks and a fistful of money. I did a quick count, and it must have been her life's savings. I closed the bag, hugged it close to my chest, marched to the edge of the churchyard and let out the breath I didn't know I'd been holding.

Somewhere at my back, men were running, shouting, hunting.

I could hear the edges of their hearts, the truth of their souls.

I could not hear hers.

I turned my face from them, and ran.

Chapter 56

The sun was rising at the truth-speaker's back as he paused, grey light creeping in around the curtains.

Lieutenant Charlwood lay sleeping between us, more of a boy than I'd ever seen him. I could hear the creaking of the pipes labouring against ice, ready to burst. I could hear the babble of my sisters' voices, raised high, anxious. There was a big push nearby, right on top of us, a big battle to win. There was always some big battle to win, somewhere along the line.

Finally, with a sigh, Dr Abbey closed his eyes, and murmured, "Charlwood dreams of saving his men. In his dream, he never quite gets to them. Something always holds him back, the air turned to stone. He never knew the names of all the privates in his company. Truth be told, they all looked the same to him. Just another Tommy. He felt bad about that. He always wanted to like the common man more than he did. He always thought it was a bit rough to assume that the rich man and the poor man are so far apart. Obviously different, of course. Culture. Learning. Maybe even breeding, to a degree. But that's no reason to put a good chap down, is it?"

His voice had slipped into mockery, disdain. Was that the truth of him? When everything was gone, was the only truth left in him that he was a bitter, twisted old man?

As I thought it, I saw him flinch, look away.

"We never know the truth of ourselves," he mused. "Not really. Not until we see it reflected in someone else's eyes. Saira had a sense of it. There is the truth we tell ourselves, she'd say, and then there is the reality of the world as it is, and that is always harder to see."

"You were someone better, once," I replied. "If you're telling the truth."

He smiled, ran his fingers through his hair. This time I looked for it; saw the long streak of white rising up from a thin, faded silver scar that ran above his right eye to the tip of his ear, a calculated scalpel cut. Then his hair fell around his face again, and putting his head on one side he said:

"I despise who I am." Thought about it a moment longer, and added, "Most of us would have cause for regret, if we ever truly looked at ourselves in the mirror. You can live with yourself after that revelation. You can even find redemption. But looking is terrifying. Looking is sometimes too hard."

He gazed down, and then almost immediately back up, eyes bright. "Albert is here."

I heard the sound of the car a moment later, listening for it now, wheels through pebbles, and looking round saw Abbey pull the folding knife from his pocket, knuckles white. I lunged forward, syringe pressing against Charlwood's neck before the doctor was halfway to his feet. "I'll do it," I snapped, astonished at my ferocity. "I'll kill the boy before you can curse him."

Frozen for a moment before me, I watched Abbey read the essence of my soul, and I was happy to let him look. He raised his hands a little, placating. At the end of the corridor, the front door bell rang, jangling on its rope. Slowly Abbey sank down against the window frame, knife slipping back into his pocket, hand closed tight around the handle.

A voice in the distance, the sound of the chain being pulled back from the door.

The cannon paused, then gave another thunderous encore, then returned to a more regular, rhythmic thump-thump-thump.

The door closed, a woman's voice mingling with a man's.

You shouldn't have come, you shouldn't have come, there's a battle nearby, there's been a push, you shouldn't have come ...

I didn't know if that was what Matron said, anxiety pushing

through her stone skin, but the hospital dripped with the fear of it.

Couldn't hear the man's answer, just a voice, low and insistent against the popping of gunfire outside.

"All right, Sister Ellis," murmured Abbey. "What do you want to do now?"

Footsteps on tile, the crack of the loose one three rooms down, then an uneasy knocking on the door. People never know how to visit the sick, whether to burst in all merriment or shuffle in full of concern; to pretend that life goes on or wallow in pain. When neither of us answered, the door was pushed back uncertainly, and a man stood framed in it.

He was smaller than I had expected, and older, his dark brown hair already a deep charcoal grey. He had a pinched face, tight around forehead, cheeks and lips, squeezing dark, sunken eyes. His beard had expanded out and down to form a bib beneath his jaw, and he had the beginning of a stoop and walked with his feet turned out to the side. For a moment I wondered if this could possibly be the fearsome professor, the hated Albert that Abbey had described, but then the two men saw each other, and there was only truth left.

Whatever went through the professor's mind, it took a while to sink in. He had a lot to look at. Abbey, by the window; his son, broken and sleeping before him. Me, ready to stick a needle in his boy, kill him rather than let him be cursed. Fair dos to the old man, he took to it all well enough, clearing his throat after a moment and pushing the door shut behind him, before turning to me and saying:

"Do you work here?"

The question, given everything, weren't what I expected. I felt suddenly absurd, needle in hand, so straightened up a little, finger still on the plunger of the syringe, and looking him in the eye said, "Yes. My name is Ellis."

"How is my son, Sister Ellis?"

My eyes flickered to Abbey, but the professor was still staring straight at me, as if the doctor didn't exist. "Sleeping, sir," I replied.

"And his condition? His letters were unclear, and the kind lady who answered the door appeared preoccupied. However, as we are here ... " When I didn't answer, his lips thinned, and straightening he added, "I would appreciate the truth. I think that will be ... very pertinent, don't you?"

"His legs were blown off." Abbey spoke, simple, reporting facts. "There was damage to his pelvis, lower abdomen. It's a miracle he's alive. Not necessarily luck. He's doing well, but the chances of complications are high. He doesn't really understand what's happened to him yet. He doesn't want to know. He thinks he would be better dead, but it isn't brave to believe that, so he sits in a cycle of flickering courage and deepest despair. I sedated him, so Sister Ellis and I could talk."

"What complications?"

"Apart from the psychological?"

"Yes, if you please."

"Infection, of course. He's already had one severe fever, and in the short term he won't survive another. The damage to his pelvis has changed the layout of his internal organs; fundamentally the support for his intestines and stomach has been removed, and it's likely that he'll suffer digestive problems for the rest of his life, if they don't just fail of their own accord. Of course urination will be extremely painful and difficult from here on in, and he'll never have children. I would also predict respiratory difficulties long term, especially if he remains bed-bound. Morphine addiction is inevitable too, and it will eventually lose its efficacy as a pain medication."

"Are there alternatives?"

"Heroin, perhaps. But all the information I have suggests that it will suffer much the same progression as morphine over time."

The professor nodded once, still watching his son. Then he took in a long, hard breath, and turned sharply on the spot to look Abbey in the eye. "And have you done it yet?" he asked. "Have you put the shadow on him?"

For a moment I thought Abbey would try to lie, but the truth was too close to his lips now, and he couldn't hold back the answer. "Not yet. Sister Ellis seems to think there is no justice in it. She believes this very strongly, which is highly frustrating when one is trying to have a clear state of mind. She is less convinced as to whether I should kill you."

The professor nodded again, head turning to me. "Thank you for protecting my son, Sister Ellis. I did not think that William would find him. Nor did I think him so far gone that he would use a father's child to murder him. I see I was mistaken, otherwise I never would have let this happen. I am ... very sorry for that. I apologise that you have found yourself caught up in this business between us. I take it William has been talking? There is a point, if he stays still for too long, where he really can't resist the urge. How close is Langa now?"

Abbey's lips curled in tight, so hard I thought I saw him flinch with the pain of holding back an answer.

"Close," I answered. "I think."

"So you are compelled to tell the truth, yes?" Abbey looked away, but even that gesture was twisted in a nod. "Well then." The professor perched on the edge of his son's bed, near where the boy's feet would have been, an old habit from a different day. "You are here to kill me, of course."

"Yes," Abbey replied.

"I suppose you've tried for long enough."

"Had to try harder."

"Do you intend to simply slit my throat, or were you planning a more ... complicated procedure?"

"Until you walked through that door, I really wasn't sure. I'm moving towards stabbing you in the heart and being done with the whole thing."

"In front of the sister?"

"Yes."

"Will she try to prevent you?"

"She doesn't know. She hopes she will, when the moment comes, but genuinely isn't sure. You should have brought a gun."

"That thought occurs to me – now. How much does the sister know?"

"Plenty," I snapped, at these cold, busy men.

"All ... nearly all of it." A stumble, a forced rattle of breath, a thing that had nearly been a lie and that the shadow would not permit.

"Well then." Albert adjusted his position, hands folded in his lap, hat still on his head. "You'd better tell her the rest."

Chapter 57

I ran, said the doctor, eyes fixed on his enemy, as the battle sputtered outside. What else was there? Running from the British Empire ... it is not so easy. Not a corner of Africa where the Nineteen hadn't extended a tendril, not a port in Asia where they didn't have prying eyes. A telegram could be flashed to India, Canada, Australia, the Cape, Malaysia, Egypt, and the authorities would be waiting for me weeks before I arrived. And would the pashas in Palestine really protect me against my former masters? Was it in the interest of the Meiji emperor to anger the most powerful nation on earth? Of course not. Perhaps I could run to my former adversaries? The French would be only too happy to have a truth-speaker, or the Austrians could cheerfully lock me up again. None of these options appealed, so in the end I sailed for Lisbon, and then took the first ship for South America. The United States had already decided that continent was an area of special interest to them, and their growing power and belligerence would, I hoped, keep British interference at bay. I had learnt enough of my craft that I could pass for German or French if I had to, and Mrs Parr's dwindling gift of money was enough to get me to a place where my medical bag could bring a little income.

Mrs Parr did not make it, if you are wondering. Albert saw her body. He felt deep regret that these things had come to pass, and didn't attend her funeral. That's his truth. He still doesn't understand why she did it; why the batty old woman helped me. He's very bad with people.

I did not mourn her in any way that society would find acceptable. There was no time, and she would not have approved of wailing and ashes. Hideo died too, in the end. While pouring liquid food down his oesophagus, they ruptured it, flooding his lungs with pea soup, on which he suffocated. But then, Hideo was still a work in progress for Albert. In time he'd do much, much better.

It took just over a month to reach Panama, still then little more than a graveyard for the thousands of men who had tried to build the canal, and fallen to yellow fever. From there I hopped south, until I came to Peru. The country was still teetering from years of war, from bitter violence and devastation, but there was hope in the air too, a new government promising great progress from behind its palatial walls. Ambitious men of class and privilege were determined to forge a new nation state, equal to any in the world, and though they had very few of the resources needed to do this and even less will for this state to serve the whole people, rather than those who owned the most land, doctors and men of foreign currency were welcomed. Though rusty, my ministrations were still superior to those of the quacks selling patent medicines and deceit. The country had its traditional healers, the *curanderos* and witch doctors of the mountains, who ranged from hideous, wailing predators who sucked on the hopes and fears of dying men, through to individuals who actually had some interesting things to offer, and who knew the best leaves to chew for sickness at height, when to offer a diuretic and when to walk away, and which flowers kept the mosquitoes at bay. All were suspicious of me and my foreign ways, and I did not blame them. Some were actively hostile, and I fled many a place before they could set my bedding alight; others sat with me and talked long and earnestly of vaccination and smallpox, naming the gift of immunity as perhaps the single greatest advancement science could offer.

In this way, wandering the mountains, I hid from my enemies until Langa came, as he always does, shambling across ocean and mountain peak, bringing the dreams of my neighbours and the truth of their hearts to my lips.

He would always come, and South America, though well hidden from the British, lacked that one major resource that I most earnestly needed for my well-being – reliable trains. I needed to sleep, needed to rest. Langa did not. Only by travelling fast could I ever outrun him, and the high mountains wrapped in cloud were no place to be a sprinter.

I headed for the coast, and in Lima secured myself a position as a ship's doctor on a vessel carrying copper from the mines of South America to the hungry new shipyards of Yokohama. From there I took passage on a ship carrying rice, silk and students to Hong Kong; where Chinese silver and workers fleeing the growing chaos in the south were loaded for transportation to Calcutta; where opium, hungry labourers and cotton was loaded for the East and beyond. In British ports, I barely left the ship. Instead, I asked my crewmates for newspapers and journals, for reports of every nature, which I pored over on the hot, chugging voyage back to Hong Kong for any clues as to the fate of my friends – for the fate of Margot.

I found no mention of her in the press. Nor of the People's Society. Whatever their fate, they were of no interest to the reporters of *The Times* or the *Gazette*.

In this way I lived for over a year, bobbing across the Pacific, ministering almost entirely to inflamed sailor's genitals on the way. Oh, sometimes there was an outbreak of dysentery, a flurry of fever or a broken limb to liven things up, but for the most part I tended to crabs, pox and various forms of discharge. In time I found myself positions on the larger passenger vessels, where my quarters were upgraded from a hammock in the cloying below-decks heat to a room with a window I could open when the seas were calm, and my clientele to first-class travellers who were evenly split between venereal disease and seasickness, with the occasional boil in need of lancing. My security grew – not quite enough to accept the offer of employment on the New York–Liverpool line, but enough that I was happy to be hired as ship's doctor on the great vessels that sailed through the Azores and the Caribbean, or carried hopeful migrants to the colonies of Africa and the southern hills of Kerala. Travelling as much as I did, Langa had no chance of catching me, and for months on end my dreams were free of his shadow, and I knew only the truths that men deigned to speak, and found this to be a revelation.

It wasn't until the middle of 1904, the year the Russians and the Japanese went to war, that I finally learnt what had happened to the People's Society. Coming into Charleston one sticky, blazing summer's day, I took the chance to stretch my legs and see the pleasures of the town. The Civil War had devastated the city, and black hands had helped rebuild it in all its timbered elegance. Industry had come with smoke and iron, then the city had been shattered by an earthquake and rebuilt again by the hands of black men, adding courthouse and post office, white verandas and flower-coated balconies to the genteel houses of the finer sort, and plumbing and the beginnings of electricity to the harder, block houses for the rest. In thanks for their labour, the government of South Carolina disenfranchised the black man, and the white man settled back into a city that felt every bit as polite, ordered and pious as if it had never been burnt to the ground.

It was in Charleston that I saw the hanging of five men and two women of the People's Society. They had preached the gospel of liberty and equality, of a woman's right to vote and equal pay for all people. They were dangerous and had been judged, and their execution was needful for the law. The man who pulled the gallows trigger was drunk, visibly swaying on the stage as the nooses were put round the condemned necks. The sheriff had to shout to get his attention, to the booing of the crowd, and he half fell onto the lever rather than pulling it in an orderly manner. Six of the seven trapdoors opened. Three of those who dropped were lucky, and their necks were broken. Three suffocated slowly, gasping, writhing, twitching, eyes popping and tongues licking the air. The last — a

318

woman – stayed where she was, the mechanism beneath the door on which she stood jammed. The sheriff walked over and kicked it three, four, five times with his boot as the crowd hissed and surged and snapped its displeasure, until finally it gave way and she dropped. Someone screamed, and I was grateful that Langa was not there, that I did not know the truth in the hearts of these onlookers, in those who jeered, those who leered, those who laughed at the demise of their fellow man; or those who wept, who curled up inside in horror, those who had never before seen a person die.

I knew three of them by sight: hangers-on in Margot's People's Society. I do not think they saw me in the crowd, when they died.

In America, it was easier to find out about the fate of the People's Society. Sedition would not be tolerated. Anarchists, socialists, revolutionary immigrants with un-American ideas: all were for punishment. Good God, railed the press, was it not a mere three years since the president had been gunned down on this sacred soil? Three years since the blood of patriots had been shed? And for what? For a fantasy? For the delusions of a madman?

We may die, said one woman of the Society as they led her to the electric chair, but our ideas have already changed the world.

If that is so, the judge replied, then it is the duty of every American to change it back.

Chapter 58

The Nineteen caught up with me, of course. It was only fluke that let me escape for so long. I was the doctor on a vessel loaded with families from Guangdong, tired clusters of Irish, Cape British, Jewish and American all drawn to the promise of gold in Australia, when we came into the port that would be called Darwin. Gold had transformed it from a place barely worth consideration to a scrambling destination for eager travellers, shovels in their satchels, reminding me of Kimberley in my long-past youth; and in doing so it had acquired, without my taking note, a telegram line.

The policemen who were waiting when we docked must have received their orders weeks before we arrived. They wore clobbered-together dusty uniform of blue tunic with silver shoulder knots, black buttons and dark blue riding trousers designed to guarantee heatstroke in an Australian winter. Half the police force of the Northern Territories had turned up for my arrival, numbering all of five, the oldest a man in his mid-sixties who had perhaps been assured that this would be an easy retirement, the youngest a boy of seventeen with the beginning of a frail ginger beard beginning to spout beneath his burnt face.

In the rush of gold diggers and immigrants tumbling out of the ship into the half-chaos of the barely functional port of this juddering, stumbling place, I nearly walked straight into my would-be captors' arms. But I was in no rush to set foot in this provincial outpost, or lose the comfort of the sea air for the blistering dust of Darwin's unpaved streets, and this reticence saved my life, for the policemen, not quite sure how to manage anything resembling a significant crowd, started shouting and tugging at the off-loading passengers, calling for William Abbey and waving a somewhat unflattering picture that the Nineteen had clearly taken while I was shot and drugged in their care. No one paid the officers any particular attention, and my expression when bleeding out is perhaps less animated than when discussing the treatment of ulcers in unwelcome places.

So it was that, as I prepared to disembark without a care in the world, Lumaban, our disastrous ship's cook and notably more successful gambler, came to the open door of my little cabin, leant against the frame, watched me scoop up my bag and hat and mused:

"Have you ever heard of a man called William Abbey?"

Lumaban was short, a bullet head on square shoulders, with remarkably soft hands that he secretly rubbed with animal fat from the stove to keep tender. To people he disliked, he pretended not to speak anything but Tagalog and a few colourfully specific words of English. When he won at cards, he crowed in Spanish; when he bullied his crew he could do so in Hindi, Cantonese, Portuguese or Malay, and he had once sailed with a Dutch captain who talked entirely in Christian aphorisms and gruesome curses, which he threw in occasionally because he enjoyed the sound. I had never considered myself close to the man, and always gambled conservatively at his table; yet here he was, saving my life.

I took a moment to close my bag, consider his question. "Abbey?" I repeated, tasting the word for the first time in many, many years. "Can't say I have. Why?"

A half-shrug, unblinking from the door. "There are some people here looking for him. Policemen."

"Really? I wonder what he could have done."

"Not my business."

"I suppose you're right. Well. Thank you. I'll certainly keep an eye out."

Lumaban nodded once, his job done, and turned away from the door. I counted to ten, then picked up my few belongings, followed him down the hall and stowed away in the captain's secret stash below decks, where he hid jewellery to bribe bandits, smuggled booze and stolen art.

When, nearly eleven hours later, I felt that the policemen might have given up, I unlocked my cramped limbs and committed myself to the Darwin dusk, cursing my own arrogance and wondering what on earth I was going to do now.

Chapter 59

In Australia, walking the dusty roads from Darwin to Perth, I met Jarli.

The dreams began when I was a week or so out of the city, shuffling with a caravan along a dirt road of rutted dust at an excruciatingly slow, hard pace. The flies clung to every part of us, swarmed in black cloaks across our backs, shimmered in the horses' eyes, too thick to part. Sometimes the land broke out into beautiful vales of sea-kissed green and stubby trees sagging with fruit; two miles further, blasted animals of bone and balding hide blinked at you from grassland the colour of floorboards.

Jarli was short, walking alone with a metal flask at his hip, a long, straight stick in his hand, a cloth around his waist and a bowler hat on his head. He carried no other provisions, and along his chin erupted a beard of curling dark hair flecked with grey, tangled as tumbleweed. His skin was the colour of sunset and desert shadow, his teeth were dazzling white, and he went without fear where white men would not go.

This was not a remarkable thing. White men were, in his experience, bizarrely ill-equipped to life in this place, knowing neither the water signs nor the easiest and safest ways to travel.

His mother's shadow followed him. This was no bad thing either. Her mother's shadow had followed her, and her grandmother had spent her life with the shadow of her father before. As she lay dying, Jarli's mother had talked him through the rite he would need to perform to bind her shadow to him for ever, so that he might become the truth-speaker, the master of the corroboree, wandering the songlines until finally he had a child, who he would raise and protect until he died and passed on his mantle.

In this way, he wandered the desert, and spoke the truth in thirteen languages of his people, and a little bit of English too, not that the English were remotely interested in listening to him.

This lack of interest, and the frequent hostility of white men, made him turn away from our shuffling caravan. But his shadow was never more than a day behind, and mine was perhaps four days and closing, and even at fifty yards' distance there was a calling between us that made him stop, and turn, and seek me out from between the faceless, yellow-dust travellers, and see.

I also looked, and, slower than he, understood.

His astonishment at seeing an Englishman with his condition was palpable even through the distance between us. Of the many remarkable things he had known, this was a thing close even to heresy – but then a truth-speaker has little time for ignoring the obvious that is before our eyes, so with a gesture, he waved me over.

"I'll catch up," I told the leader of our convoy, and as people tutted at my recklessness and warned that I would catch a nasty disease, I stepped into the chittering, slithering grass, and walked towards Jarli.

He waited for me, studying the intricacies of my soul, and when I was a metre from him, gestured at me to sit.

I sat, first on my haunches, then cross-legged as he did, and for a while we remained there, studying the nuances of each other's soul. Sometimes he spoke, the easy truth on his lips, a thing that might have been compulsion or might simply have been the habit of his trade. But his native speech was not English, and he had no particular interest in my language, so he poured out the truth of my nature in a chatty, impenetrable tongue as I listened to the truth of his heart beneath the sounds.

The truth of his heart was much like the truth of any man. There were things he regretted, prides he clung to, resentments he harboured and that did him no good. He had been lonely for a while, after his mother died, and then he had decided that human company was overrated anyway, and was now almost entirely incapable of meaningful human interaction, other than speaking the truth. He offended many people greatly when he spoke, and didn't care. Truth had no need for tact. He sometimes ate poorly, sometimes ate well, had stolen in the past to survive, wasn't sure if he believed in the power of the Rainbow Serpent, thought that many *ngangkari* were bumbling idiots out to have a comfortable life, though he'd met a few who definitely had a certain something about them he had to respect. Truth had worn away most absolutes from him like sand grazing down skin, leaving only the walking, the rising and setting of the sun, new experiences and old paths, and the choices he made today.

He was not impressed by me; he was not unimpressed either. His initial fascination at meeting me was quickly tempered by the realisation that I too was human, with a human beating heart, and now there was only the truth of who we were, sitting in this place, watching each other's souls. Anything more – like or dislike, fear or hatred – struck him as a monumental waste of time. Only this moment, and this truth, mattered.

And then it was done.

He stood with a nod, having gleaned from me all he desired, and I stood too, and half bowed awkwardly, not sure what thanks I could give to a man whose language and culture I did not know, and he understood the gesture, and smiled a dazzling grin, and turned away, and kept on walking.

Four days later, I reached Perth, and looked at the wide sea and the iron ships of the great white men, and remembered a thing in my soul that I thought had been lost when Margot fell in New York: let it burn.

Let the world burn, so that the truth may come.

Let it all burn.

Jarli had seen that in me, and through him I had seen it reflected in myself. And it was good.

I had just enough savings from my medical work to pay for passage to Singapore, and by the time the creaking timbered vessel set out, a relic of a bygone day crewed by rogues and smugglers, Langa was only a few hours behind, and I stood with my face to the wind and sang out the truth of men's hearts, and found it, for a few moments, glorious, sacred and free.

Chapter 60

From Australia I headed north, and for the first time in a long while I did not fear my shadow.

I travelled at a leisurely pace, and everywhere we made harbour I proffered up my medical services for a reasonable fee, and found plenty of patients willing to be told the truth of their condition. Not that they had been sinful, and that was why their husband died; not that the blood of a cow or the scales of a fish or a dip in sacred salts might cure them, but that this was their predicament and perhaps they might die, and perhaps they might live, and that was the truth of the matter. In places where the young ate the powdered skulls of their ancestors served with pig and fish; in grand mansions where crystals could heal you of the blackening of your blood; in the bazaars where nothing was so special as cinnamon bark and the blood of a crocodile, I spoke truth, and even where it was not well received, for the most part it was believed. Some, of course, some always run from the truth, to opium and quackery, to a promise of an impossible cure at the cost of all they have. But now that I was remembering how it felt to be a truth-speaker again, my words rang in the hearts of men, a welcome and familiar song, even if it was a lament.

And for the first time in a long while, I found myself with a destination.

I forged new papers, new names. I became the Frenchman I met in Guangdong, stealing his name and story to bluff my way into the parlours of wealthy men. I was the American arms dealer come to Tokyo to offer the latest in high-calibre rifles; the British diplomat stricken with malaria, yearning for quinine, whose brow I wiped at the height of his fever in Rangoon. I dined them, treated them, listened to the truth of their hearts, stole their names and through this means bluffed and bartered my way into courthouse, palace and colonial manor. Theft came easily to me, and there was not a trick I could not call, not a gambler I could not outmanoeuvre with Langa at my back. But most of all, I travelled to gather information, picking at the secrets that I had not been able to pull apart when I simply ran away.

I headed west, sweeping through northern India in a haze of lies, double-dealing and quiet, cordial larceny, changing my identity every other day. It was a gamble, but if the Nineteen were coming for me then I would give them a chase worth the name. Langa gave me the truth men wanted to hear, let me play the drunken fool or the wily politician without a blink, drawing the hearts of others into my own. For a little while I loved my shadow, and whispered to him in the night that finally I was working in his service.

In India, I had my first real success.

Chapter 61

Sights seen through a stranger's eyes.

In Delhi, what British architecture there was had been put in piecemeal, as if unsure of its own footing; yet every palace abutted onto a rookery of crooked buildings that leant on each other like a line of dominoes about to fall. In some streets, brilliant colour burst out in greens, reds, purples, yellows and oranges, in sacks of saffron, turmeric and indigo brought to trade; fruits of every size and shape, tough shining skins and rich, dripping juices that crystallised in the hairs of thieving monkeys. In others, the only colour was dusty bark-grey. Grey dust beneath the grey toes of the grey old men who watched and tutted and found nothing that pleased them. Grey walls of grey houses; grey seeping into the rags that passed for clothes for the children who grew old there. Grey that had not seen rain for a very long time.

A Parsi businessman in a quiet hotel stands before the mirror every night and recites, "She stood upon the balustraded balcony, inexplicably mimicking him hiccuping, while amicably welcoming him in."

He's edging a little closer to sounding like he went to Eton. When he does, perhaps then he'll be treated with respect.

A mission school where the children sat in blue sailor uniforms and recited the names of Tudor kings and the odes of Shakespeare; a widowed wife sees through the open window a devout Hindu man, who can contract and expand each muscle across his abdomen like he's shaking out a bedsheet. She recites a quick prayer, and does not look away.

Endless plains of unbroken yellow; forests vanishing into busy, howling, chittering darkness, where at night the elephants played and the monkeys fought for yellow fruits. Buffalo bored of cracked fields; a stone bearing ancient laws of wise kings, which even the British hadn't dared tear down.

Wise men, sitting naked on a rock, hair and beard become their new clothes, who the people tolerated and occasionally revered, despite the fact that their wisdom was rarely to the point on matters of the monsoon, animal husbandry, the price of tea or the cultivation of jute. One man, who has loved both men and women, declares that love is the key, and the British tell him to wear clothes and be civilised, the fool!

"I know the truth of all men's hearts," I explained. "I am followed by a shadow that kills the ones I love. Do you know anything about this?"

The wise men upon their stones considered this a while, conferred among each other, nodded at some ideas, rejected others, then one delivered their verdict.

"Have you tried fresh air and vigorous walking?"

And finally, at the end of it all, Saira, one last time.

Chapter 62

I ... Langa is ... there are things that are ...

Sister Ellis, you have been ... kind. The truth of your heart is nothing to be ashamed of. It is not the job of a truth-speaker to pass judgement, but you have judged yourself and found yourself wanting. Please know that you are ... you are normal. Normal in your fears, your shame, your anxiety, your goodness and your pain. You are wholly yourself, wholly true, you are ...

So I ask you, do not let Albert speak for a little while. There are questions he could ask that I would be compelled to answer, Langa is so near now it is hard to ... to keep the truth from being ... If he asks I will answer, and if he does, I will kill him.

I will kill him.

Do you understand?

Well then.

I knew where to find Saira. I had spent enough time looking into the truth of her heart to know where she would be. On the edge of the Thar Desert there is a range of red-rock caves where the widows go. Please don't ask me where, it is ... it is hard to ... As they near the end of their lives, the widows who have grown too tired to outrun their shadow set out into the dunes of the desert, walking from cave to cave, oasis to oasis, until finally they are too weak to walk any more. There they fall; there their shadow comes. They think that by ending their days in this place, the shadow will take pity on them and spare any they might still love, having neither life, love

331

nor death to catch in its darkness as it approaches, only the endless dust.

Saira had gone to the caves, not for death, but for wisdom. The secrets of her order were scratched with nail and daubed in blood in the furthest shadows of the darkest places, ancient tales from the oldest times. Here the women learnt the intricacies of their curse, but now, of course, there were almost no women left. This new century was taking them away, binding them in new laws and new ways, just as readily as Albert was pulling out their brains.

She had escaped his reach only through the grace of her shadow. It had finally become a blessing, the friend she had been told for so long it was meant to be; a gift of the gods. I had betrayed her at Hideo's feet, but she was smarter than the British, and knew how to hide. It was only a day away from her when I found her, sitting on a yellow rock beneath the thorny marwar tree, wrapped in rags and bone. I took a long time to reach her across the cracked, rocky earth. She watched me all the way, now smiling, now frowning, until finally I stood before her in a tiny sliver of barely-shade beneath the burning sky.

She had grown old beyond her years. Time had stripped hope from her heart, and left with it merely duty and the winding road.

For a while she regarded me, as I watched her, and our shadows came towards us across the baking sand. She knew all that I had done, and in her heart I saw the faces of the truths she had told and the shadows she had thrown, and knew that she despised herself too, despised everything she had become, and in this regard we were peculiarly united.

Then she held out a hand, and I took it, and without a word she led me into the shadows of the cave.

I think there will be no more truth-speakers in India now.

Too many fell, and the world changed.

The widows are gone, but their secrets live. In the caves on the edge of the desert, in the deepest, darkest corners where only the shadows remain, scratched into stone are the written truths of their order. The secret stories of the temples; the hidden histories of the women who died. The names of the shadows that followed them, and the journeys they travelled. Equations to track how long you have until the shadow touches you; precepts to learn how to keep your heart true in the face of the truths of other men. Stories of when the shadow came too near, and how a woman ran. Instructions. How to run. How to speak. How to protect a loved one. How to die in the desert. How to cast the curse upon another.

Saira taught me, knowing precisely what it was I would do with this knowing.

I thanked her with my heart, and we walked a while beneath the stars until the truth was on the edge of our lips, trying to break free. We climbed to the highest ridge and squinted across the desert, and she thought she saw her child moving through the blackness, but she imagined it, for it was far too dark to see, and I thought I saw Langa against the horizon, and this was also most probably a lie.

And finally, when the truth was unbearable against my lips, I asked my question and she replied.

Sometimes you need someone you love to tell you the truth of your heart.

When it was done, I held her close for a little while more, before she turned her face into the desert, and walked until the darkness consumed her.

Chapter 63

There will be no more truth-speakers in India.

Of Saira's order, she knew of three who had been taken by the British. One had died on the operating table. Two were still living. I found the first in Delhi, following Saira's suspicions. She was chained to a clean white mattress in a well-ventilated room in a house without ornament or flourish, guarded by men in civilian dress and a housekeeper with no tongue. The widow was unconscious, which was a blessing, drugged, a hollow in her skull. I planned my approach for three days, letting Langa drift nearer all the time. I listened to the hearts of her guards, the secret desires of her warders and keepers. I watched as they dragged shackled men to the door of the prison where they kept her, and waited the few hours it took for them to be pulled outside again, weeping and broken, their hearts plucked out, their confessions wrapped in wax cylinders beneath a warden's arm.

A local outbreak of cholera gave me my excuse to knock on the door, all business and professionalism. I had the right papers and the right knowledge, passed myself off as a military doctor, knowing precisely what part I needed to play to appeal to the hearts of these men, knowing when they doubted me and when they believed that I spoke the truth, letting Langa guide my tongue, letting Saira's knowledge guide my heart.

"It's when your faeces become liquid, with an integrity that is not dissimilar from saliva – that's when you know you're really in for it!" I chirruped, and there questions about my business ceased.

334

I was watched by four men as I examined this broken woman, her shadow spinning in and out of her sleeping form. Her shadow was a teenage girl, head cracked and twisted to one side, and I felt for a while as if she watched me while I worked, this blackened ghost, knowing what I intended. I took the widow's pulse, examined her one good eye, cleaned the weeping sores on her back, tested the reflexes in her knees and arms, and at last administered what I assured them was a vaccine, and was in fact a lethal dose of heroin, and on my way out ordered her keepers to boil everything twice and eat no raw vegetables until the epidemic was over.

Chapter 64

I am a murderer.

That is the truth of it.

Sister Ellis has seen this, many times. The man who lies screaming, screaming, screaming. The gas took his sight, but he can still feel the blisters, big as an orange, full of yellow pus, rupturing across his body. The poison will kill him, not in a day, not in two, but in a week perhaps, and the only thing that will stop his pain is if his heart gives out. This is truth. This is the inescapable truth that we all know, and the doctors turn their faces away and wonder which of their number will do what needs to be done and end this man's torment. Someone else, of course. It must be someone else. We are not murderers. Nor are we kind.

The lieutenant lies dumb in his bed. He will never walk again. For the rest of his life he will constantly dribble a slow flow of pee out of what is left of his groin into cotton sheets, the acid turning the blasted skin to a red, raw flame. The loss of his sexual organs will change his body, his voice, his relationship with his fellows in ways that are both predictable and entirely unique. On some days he wishes he was dead; on others he resolves to live. He switches between these two states as fast as a butterfly's wings. Perhaps now it is merciful to kill him. Perhaps now it is murder. Tomorrow he may beg to die. The day after he may rejoice in his loved ones. Each second is a new universe; each minute is a new truth.

The doctor's code is not perfect. Sometimes the harms you

336

choose between are so damnable as to be indistinguishable from torment.

I travelled the world, looking for and murdering Albert's truth-speakers wherever they were chained. It was harder after India, of course. There are only so many times a doctor with my features can bluff his way into a station of the Nineteen. After I killed the second widow, the Nineteen responded with a full-scale manhunt across the city and surrounding states, but the telegrams were too slow to beat the trains, and I was on the boat for Aden within a day.

I had to be careful.

I made money at the poker tables when Langa was near, reading every hand of my opponent like it was my own. Sometimes, when waiting for him to catch up, I played at doctor. I wandered the slums on the edges of the cities, and for a few shillings or a pennyworth of rice bandaged the sores on an old woman's feet, or set the broken bone of a child who fell while running to the factory, avoiding high society and the claws of the Nineteen until my shadow was near again. It felt good. It felt like the right kind of fire.

Then, when Langa arrived, I trimmed my beard and scrubbed my shoes, and sat behind my newspaper at the clubs where the British went to lament their burdens, and listened to their hearts, and followed the interesting ones home, and listened to their dreams, until there was no shadow that I could not unpick. I came close to calamity many times, and did things I am ashamed of to survive. I did things that were ... that are ...

I am a murderer. That is also true.

In Cairo, following the heart of a man come to Egypt to escape an unhappy marriage and an even more unhappy mother – who still had no qualms about making her displeasure known with five letters a week, to which he only occasionally replied – I found my way to another of the Nineteen's truth stations. The woman chained inside it was called Patigul, but her guards didn't know that. They called her missus — "Missus wants feeding missus wants cleaning missus wants wants wants!" I spent a little too long gathering information, and Langa came too near too fast, a burble of truth spluttering from my lips, which I dispelled with a train ride to Suez. There I waited until he was almost on top of me, before rushing back to Cairo by the last train across a black desert squashed by an infinity of stars, dust and rock encasing the train as it squeaked and rattled towards the glow of the city.

That night, I broke into the truth station. I was not a very effective burglar, but had at least taken time to learn the patterns and habits of my enemies, when they rose and when they slept. With my shoes tied together around my neck, I slithered in socks across the warm wooden floors, tasting the last traces of a late supper on the air, heard the snoring of the keepers upstairs, the slow, gentle muttering of the woman chained in her chair as she dreamt the dreams of the city sleeping. In a study where my picture hung in full glory on the wall with a command to apprehend and sedate, I rummaged through files and folders by the half-light of a hurricane lamp. A man slept in the same room as the woman. The man was deaf, infection having taken all sound from him when he was twelve. He did not mind that the woman screamed out the truth of his heart for all the world to hear; he did not know what she said, and so slumbered on his cot in peaceful quiet. I crept softly by, shutter down on the lamp, moving by moonlight through the high latticed windows. Patigul dreamt in her own tongue, but as I drew near, her eyes opened and she stared right at me, and her voice began to rise, babbling out the truth of who I was, of what I intended, of my murderous heart.

I would like to say that there was some acknowledgement of what I did, when I put the needle into the scarred crook of her arm. I would like to say that she said thank you, or yes, or no, or showed any sign of human response to her murder. She did not. She burbled the truth of all things at me in a language I did not speak until the drugs began to take her, loud enough that I thought the house would wake. It did not. The shadow

338

of a young man darted in and out of her like a wild, starting thing, faster and faster as the poison took. A few hours behind me, Langa came, and through his knowing I looked into her eyes and saw only myself reflected back in them, and was glad that even that truth was growing faint.

She was already dying by the time I reached the door, the first muscle contraction seizing her against her bonds. She was dead by the time I climbed out of the window into the street below, startling a pair of stray cats that hissed and snarled and skittered away.

In all, I murdered five people chained to the stations of the Nineteen.

Rather, Albert murdered them first. I killed them, he killed them, I killed them, he ... You see, the truth is never so simple; all these things are true all at once. He cut out who they were, turned them into automata, gibbering shadows pinned to the floor. He sliced out their souls and left just enough behind that they could live in perpetual, blathering torment, the shadow breaking across their lips without end. As a scientist, I suppose I could admire what he did. His mastery of the butcher's art was supreme. I have no qualms about what I did. I travelled the world, put an end to Albert's cruelty, and my nearest and dearest companion for all that time was Langa.

I still looked for Margot, of course. I scoured the news for any sign of her. For the longest time, I found nothing. I knew in my heart that she was alive, that she and Coman had escaped from New York; I had seen as much in the truth of Albert's heart. But what more did that mean? The People's Society was dead, gunned down as surely as the men who marched on the Winter Palace in 1905, as surely as the ever-growing list of kings and prime ministers dead by their own people's hands – Carlos I of Portugal, Ito Hirobumi, George I of Greece, Mahmud Sevket Pasha. It may have been the killing of Franz Ferdinand that tipped us into this bloody war, but it has been coming such a long time, such a long, bloody road.

I couldn't find her. By 1909 I was almost coming to terms with this, telling myself, as the widows did, that to love someone was the greatest cruelty a truth-speaker could commit.

Yet even though she was gone, there were different stories beginning to filter into the press, which set my nerves on edge. In America, a great cotton man who had for forty years simply ignored the abolition of slavery, beaten and chained the black men and women on his land, kept their children as chattels, and not a word murmured against it. He died without a sigh, and then his wife, and then his youngest son, and then his daughter, all without cause, all within a few days of each other. Only one child was left alive, and that child insane.

In Russia, a duke, his wife, their two children, dropping like flies; the sole survivor a girl of seven who blabbered and blathered words that the alienists dubbed the sign of a disturbed mind. That duke, they said, loved to visit the prisons where the women who had marched for bread were waiting for their Siberian exile, and pick the prettiest of the lot, and when he had his way, he would send them to the taiga with a flower in their hair and no boots on their feet, as befitted revolutionaries.

It was familiar, a pattern that I felt I knew and could name. But I was a coward, and full of fire, so I ignored it, and kept about my murderous course.

Chapter 65

I killed my last victim in 1909, in Hong Kong. An infant boy was emperor of China, the Guangxu emperor rumoured poisoned by his own adopted mother. The winds were blowing from Beijing towards the sea, and had blown this truth-speaker straight into the hands of the British. The truth-speaker's shadow was his mother, murdered in a fit of fury. She had spoken the truth at the Daoist temples, stabbing herself with needles and sitting on thrones of spikes so that the demons might possess her; sometimes shrieking lies to make a bit of money, sometimes speaking truth when the shadow came. Her son had been far less savvy in his practices.

Hong Kong had been beset with plagues in the past, from which the British had created the illusory need for the city to be fragmented into racial quarters. On their high hills, the Europeans escaped the worst of the disease and crime that riddled the lower slopes of the island, while from the mainland trickled an ever-growing number of migrants fleeing the inevitable, imminent collapse of a dynasty of nearly three hundred years' imperial rule.

The truth station was guarded round the clock, pictures of my face nailed up behind every door. I would not get inside. Instead, I dumped the body of a young man stolen from the morgue by the foot of the Nineteen's house, to be discovered in horror at dawn. When that merely provoked outrage and suspicion, I added a strategically spilt pool of pig's blood the following day, turning the gutters crimson, as well as a whispered note to a journalist of the seedier sort that the authorities were covering up a recent surge in cases of bubonic plague. The neighbours did the rest, reporting that they had seen inauspicious signs, heard strange noises and terrible screams from the truth station. I was prepared to tell people that I too had witnessed men, weeping and broken, being led from the premises, but thankfully more than enough locals were ready to resent the stamp of authority and suspect great evil that I didn't need to get involved.

A small crowd gathered on a Tuesday, demanding to be let in and see the house. By the Wednesday, an armed guard of British soldiers in white pith helmets were guarding the door, uneasy against the mob that only grew in the face of this provocation. By the Thursday, one British soldier, with the coloniser's usual fear of overdue retribution, pulled his pistol and fired into the crowd, wounding a girl, who would never walk again. He was beaten to death when the mob broke in. What they found inside confirmed their greatest fears – torture, experimentation, barbarism – and they carried aloft the still-blathering body of the man with a hollow in his skull, paraded him through the streets as a sign of British perfidy, until they were faced with a line of troopers, rifles raised. A stand-off ensued, broken only when a few people began to realise that some of the truth the shattered man was howling struck a little too close to the realities of their hearts. He was lowered to the ground. The crowd began to shuffle a little away from him; then, at a command from the British captain to fix bayonets, as one they turned and ran, scattering like earth from a meteor strike, leaving the truth-speaker babbling on the street as the soldiers charged.

I was prepared to step in and slip him enough curare to kill a tiger, but a British soldier saved me the trouble. Finally given the command to charge, he let go of all his terror of the roaring crowd by launching himself like a rocket down the street, shooting at anything that moved, whimpered or sneezed, and stabbed my man in the chest as he passed without even noticing what he did. So died the last living of Albert's experiments, proclaiming as the life went from him that his murderer knew not what he did, lost in a cloud of blood and fear.

There things might have ended. There it might all have come to rest, except that there was one face in the crowd of spinning, terrified people that showed no fear, and that watched not the murder of the man in the street, but me.

Langa was four days away, walking patiently across the sea, so it took me a while to recognise the truth in his heart. When I finally met my follower's eye, it was on the Peak Tram. He stood out as one of the few white men queuing for third class – reserved for "others and animals" – rather than the first- or second-class seats for British civil servants, soldiers and residents of Victoria Peak. He was taller than almost everyone around him, though hunched in a beige cape buttoned tight across his goose throat. He wore a wide, low hat and short trousers that stopped just below his knees and one inch above his high white socks. He had button shoes and carried a parasol with a bamboo handle, and his hair was white-blond, his beard growing tatty at the edges where it bumped his collarbone, and he was Josef Ritte, thousands of miles from home, looking for me.

As the tram cracked and clattered up the hill, my immediate tug of terror evolved to curiosity. The Austrian watched me from above the head of a Chinese woman sent shopping by her British masters, the weight of goods under her arms and balanced on her back nearly twice as wide and twice as broad as she was. At the front of the tram were two seats reserved for the governor and now surrounded by men with fob watches and striped trousers; ladies dressed in white and taffeta, as far from the blood of the streets below as angels from hell. Beneath us, the city folded in steaming green, wild animals scattering and scrambling into the undergrowth as we ascended towards the white manors, cooler breezes and colonial estates of Victoria Peak. A kite circled overhead on a high, hot thermal, while below, a thousand tiny boats bumped and pressed against the fat sides of the iron ships and grumbling clippers come fresh to port. Ritte watched me, and when I got out in a flood of human heat and moisture to the chittering summit of the hill, he followed.

He followed as I walked, heading not further up, but a little down again, finding the winding paths that had until very recently been the only means of access for the wealthy to this temperate paradise. The sedan chairs no longer beat a path up this route, but still came the delivery men, with grand pianos, wicker chairs, boxes of eggs, barrels of beer and news of the finer things of life.

Beneath the rustling, whispering leaves of the acacia tree I paused to check the time, and Ritte approached, leaning against the trunk beside me as if he were catching his breath. For a while we stood there, he looking up towards the peak of the mountain, and I down to the waters below, as I listened to the truth of his heart.

Then he said, "I was waiting."

"Are you armed?" I asked.

"No," he replied, and it was the truth.

"Why were you waiting?"

"I was told the British had a truth-speaker here. My source said the truth-speakers have been dying, but there was still one left in Hong Kong. I was sent to kidnap him, so we might study what your professor does to their minds, perhaps replicate it. Then I saw you. So I waited."

"For what?"

"For whatever you were going to do next."

"Why?"

He gave a little shrug. "A living truth-speaker is more interesting than a talking corpse."

I bit my lip, tasted blood. "I am armed," I growled. "I carry poison and a pistol. Why would I not use them on you?"

He sighed, disappointed; annoyed, even. "Because you haven't. Your shadow is near, I think. You see that I mean you no harm."

"I see that now. I can't help but remember when that was not the case. I remember . . . most particularly."

"Dr Abbey," he tutted, "do you think I would wait all this time in this hellish, stinking place, surrounded by your British and their ways, without good reason? You will hear me out, I think. You are curious enough for that."

"You don't know that."

"No, I don't. I lack your . . . unique qualification. I have often regretted that. But we are still talking, and the last truth-speaker is dead, so I don't see why we can't celebrate with a nice cup of tea."

"I'm going to walk away now. I hope you understand that this is for your safety."

I turned to go, shaking with fury and dread, acid in my throat. He shrugged again, infuriating, and let me walk a few paces before landing his final blow. "I know where your woman is. Halloran. Or rather . . . I know where she has been. Would you like to know too?"

If Ritte had a shadow, perhaps he would have laughed, because of course, in a single moment, in a few short words, he had me.

Chapter 66

We dined in a hotel overlooking the sea. The menu was roast pork, apple sauce, potatoes and cabbage. The walls were hung with images of family life in Surrey; the newspapers, a few weeks out of date, were the London *Times* and *Gazette*.

Ritte drank white wine. I drank nothing, the shuddering of anger and fear now mixed with unstoppable interest, creating such a cocktail of sentiment that I barely knew where one feeling ended and another began.

He said, "There is a pepper grown in these parts, I cannot remember its name; the taste is quite extraordinary, and they say it is an aphrodisiac to boot ... "

"Langa is four days away," I snapped. "Say your piece and be done with it."

A sigh, a rolling-back in his chair. He smoked thin cigarettes scammed from American sailors, and coughed thick brown phlegm, and hated this city, and hated what his life had come to, and showed not a jot of malice as he spoke.

"I have done," he mused, "certain despicable things."

Silence a while. I caught my fingers drumming on the table, clenched them into fists.

"After you and I last met, I was dishonourably discharged. My methods had always been considered controversial. Maybe heretical. People won't invoke religion until it is useful to them, and it was useful then to have something to get rid of me."

"I really don't care."

A tut, a puffing of cheeks; it is exasperating for him to have

346

to deal with one as irrational as I. "My conversations with you during your brief sojourn at the estate put me in jeopardy. Certainly I had proved the efficacy of a truth-speaker as a valuable tool – but what had the British spy plucked from my soul in the process? Well, everything. I marvel at my recklessness now, but then, when you are a man alone with secrets, there is something invigorating about having the truth of your heart laid out before you. It is an icy bath for one's self-esteem, an excellent rebuke to ego. It was also, of course, a terrible, vain, self-important error.

"Since being expelled from my position, my life has been remarkably boring. I hunt, acted for a while as magistrate, resolving endless petty squabbles. I took up painting, but found it excessively dull. Finally my vanity was quenched, by monotony and small-minded boredom. Have you ever tried whittling your own spoons? Dear God, how I prayed for a war or rebellion to keep me occupied."

"I could shoot you; that would be diverting."

Another tut, another huff of exasperated breath. "The Halloran woman; yes, I am coming to her. Intelligence reached my masters that your Nineteen had started building little prisons in some of their key cities. Safe places into which people were brought full of secrets, and from which a few hours later they departed, their deepest truth suddenly known. At first we assumed this was something to do with you, but no! The Nineteen may keep their secrets close, but the People's Society, as it was rounded up and burnt to the ground, were persuadable, by one means or another. And what stories they told – of this woman, Halloran, and her secret British lover, of shadows and betrayals and a gunfight in New York! My my, I thought, when my masters came to me with all of this – my my, but William Abbey has been busy. Of course, I was still the expert in such matters. It is embarrassing for my superiors to admit this fact, but in certain areas I am ... invaluable."

Few words pleased him so much; few things satisfied him as much as rolling this sound round his lips.

"They put me back on an embarrassingly small salary, sent me into the world. Find out what is happening here; learn about the British truth stations. No sooner did I start investigating these little dens of truth and blood than you started destroying them. How many have you killed? Five? Six? You and your masters really do disagree on certain points, do you not?"

"Margot," I snapped. "Tell me about Margot."

He leant back in his chair, licked his lips, enjoying the aftertaste of sauce, the feel of a wine glass rolling in his hands. "Are you familiar with Margrave Otto von Durlach?"

"No."

"Your state is the better for it. He is – or rather was – a vile, pompous little man, but wise in investments. He foresaw before many of his type that the middling sort of classes were potentially growing more profitable than families of breeding, so quietly invested in tin, steel and chemicals. He made a great deal of money, and when his workers died in the mines or suffocated in the chemical laboratories, corpses already mummified by the acids in the air, he said it was just business, and what was one to expect?

"He died of a sudden heart problem twelve months ago. We would have thought nothing of it, but then his wife died too, his youngest daughter, then three friends of the family, all aged twelve or younger, and finally his son. His son, who was eleven, killed himself by jumping from a cliff into a low river. The press wrote of it as a terrible tragedy, and of course the duke was of such a nature that these things lend themselves easily to drama.

"The death of Monsieur Blanchard of the Blue Cross shipping line four months later attracted similar note, for he had famously proclaimed when two of his vessels went down within weeks of each other that the captains were to blame, and the fifty-seven sailors who drowned, and that any accusation that his ships were not seaworthy was to be taken up with the insurance companies, and he would sue any man who dared repeat such claims. His wife died first, of an unexplained heart condition. Then his son, and his daughter, and a friend of his still-living child, and finally him. I can only conclude, for him to have died fifth in this sequence, that he was as poor a father as he was an employer.

"He left one heir, a boy of fifteen. We cannot find him; he has disappeared from the institution to which his parents sought to confine him after a series of lunatic episodes. From the fact that many of his former friends are still living, I would say the child has done well, so far.

"The American railway magnate who ordered his Chinese workers to dig deeper with their nitroglycerine slung around their necks, because their lives were cheaper than explosives. The British politician who bought his seat in the Manchester election, and used his power to destroy the homes of ninety families so he might finally build his glorious new tennis courts. The Belgian general in the Congo who ordered two hundred African men stripped, suspended from the trees of the forest and their bodies maimed, and drank gin beneath them as they slowly bled to death, until finally he decided the flies were a bit too much, and set fires burning beneath his living victims to help purify the air, and to remind others of the nature of their working relationship ... I'm sure you see the pattern here. A sudden, unexpected death that sends them to the ground without a whisper. Then another, and another, and another, every person their lives have ever touched – dying.

"We recognise this, of course. We know how the *lidérc* kills. I assumed you did it. The British have been so eager to catch you, and a man who has killed before will perhaps find it easier to kill again. But as I followed your trail of blood, it was not what I expected. You did not appear in the same place as the victims I was supposed to connect you to. Your actions did not correspond with the death of the margrave, or the industrialist, or his wife. You were simply killing British agents. That thought led me to a different line of enquiry: who else, I wondered, might be performing these crimes?

"The investigation has been most invigorating. Such a relief after so many tedious years. My breakthrough was finding the daughter of a British tea manufacturer in India. He had ordered the ringleaders of a pickers' strike to be cut into four, the various pieces of their bodies sent by night to their kin and fellow conspirators as a reminder of what he could do to them, and how little they could do in reply.

"The father was dead, of course, by the time I found the child. The girl is eight years old, and loved her father very much. He was kind, gentle, affectionate – some might say overly sentimental. He would carry her on his back and play at galloping up and down while she charged at invisible dragons or was swept away on the back of a giant flying eagle. He would caw and croak the noises of the monstrous beasts she tamed and slew, and so, of course, he died first, when the child was cursed.

"Do you know how to put the shadow on another, Dr Abbey?

"Your friend Margot – she knows. She knows.

"The girl was in a hospital when I found her, and I would say her curse was just a few hours away. I rescued her. She is on her way to Vienna now. She will be safe, for a while."

He finished speaking, and sipped his wine.

I sat a while.

Then stood, marched to the window, looked down across the city below.

Then returned to my chair, but could not sit.

Then marched to the bar and ordered something to drink – I forget what. And didn't drink it. And paid too much, and forgot the change.

Then returned to my chair, but could not sit.

Then went out to the balcony to breathe some fresh air, and to shudder and shake and listen to the buzzing of the insects clinging fat-bellied to the dark green leaves, and the trilling of birds in hidden branches.

After a while, Ritte joined me.

I said, "You should understand that I despise you. It is a very childish, very deep and passionate thing. There is nothing that is not spiteful in it. I just want that to be clear."

"I understand."

"And I don't believe you."

He shrugged, and though he had no shadow, he knew that I was lying. I believed him, I did not, I believed him, I did not – the mind holds many truths all at once, until at last it is forced to see.

"The child ... the girl ... what will you do with her?"

A pause, a little roll back on his heels, roll forward onto the balls of his feet, suddenly uncomfortable in his shoes. "I don't know. She is half-Indian, and thus cannot pass in civilised society as you did. We will probably just keep her in a travelling cage, like the Russians do. Like your British did. It is—"

"If you say that it is just business, I cannot guarantee the placidity of my reaction."

He sighed, leaning with arms folded across the balcony railing. "I have done ... despicable things," he repeated, seeing through the city as if it weren't there. "It turns out that all I needed was to be bored."

"You're going to operate on her. On the child."

"Not me. But my masters, they are very impressed by your professor's techniques, they have been trying to study—"

"I think I left my gun by the dinner table, if you wouldn't mind waiting here just a second so I can shoot you?"

"Dr Abbey," he snapped, before I could move, "if I was otherwise inclined I could have anaesthetised you by now, locked you in a crate and put you on the first ship to Pula. Your actions have made you predictable."

"Why haven't you?"

"Because I'm growing old. No. That is not it. This girl, this *child*, I took her from the hospital and promised I would send her somewhere safe, and she looked in my heart and ... well. She saw it clearly, knew as an adult knows, because I knew it.

What we intended for her. What we would do. It has been ... I never had a child. Elke and I were never ... and she died, my wife, I mean, she died, and I never really had much interest, not since my own father was so ... I am growing old. I wish I had been ignorant, when I looked the girl in the eye. I do wish that."

He straightened, let out another puff of breath, shook himself like a dog spinning water from its fur, and finally met my eye.

"It is my experience that the truth has very little effect on policy. People will believe what they want to believe. They hear what they want to hear. We will cut out a child's brain, and for what? So we can misinterpret according to our egos. And you: we will kidnap you and perhaps do the same, and it will all be, fundamentally ... a rather silly little exercise. Meanwhile your Halloran, she will travel the world and curse the children of great men, and many people will die. Many, many people. Children. That is also the truth of it. Now, perhaps I can find her on my own, and stop her, since she clearly needs to be stopped. But I think my chances of doing so are much higher if I have an ally who knows her well. So here I am ... *reinterpreting* my orders. What do you say?" When I didn't answer, he straightened up, bristling, and in a voice that snapped a mote too loud for this quiet place, barked, "Come, I do not know the truth of your heart, and here I am. Come! She is cursing the children, using a child's love for a parent to kill them. Will you let that stand?"

"I don't believe you. I ... can't believe you."

"Then allow me to prove it."

And this is the truth of Ritte's heart: that he is still looking for truth. Many years ago he sat in a room with me as I blathered out his deepest secrets, and even then found himself noting some of the things I said with a sense of ah yes, how true; or no, not at all, he's missed the mark entirely. He has never believed anything anyone told him about himself, nor truly known what he values. He hopes that perhaps, now that he is growing old, he will find out. He hopes that maybe, in the murder of children, he has found a line he will not cross, and perhaps at last a mirror he is happy to look in.

I closed my eyes against the brightness of the sun. "What exactly do you propose?"

Chapter 67

Langa comes, and I wait for him. I have turned my face towards the shadow and reached out my hands, in search of truth, or blood, or sometimes just a familiar, comforting thing. He has been more constant in my life than any family or friend; we have been together for so many years.

In 1909, I struck a devil's bargain with Josef Ritte. It is of immense satisfaction to me that Albert is hearing this for the very first time; the Nineteen is not as far-reaching as it likes to think. Did I believe then what he claimed: that Margot was cursing the children of great men?

I believed it, I did not. The mind holds many contradictions.

He had money, connections. I still knew something of the People's Society that he did not, and could see into the hearts of men. Perhaps even into Margot's heart, if we could find her.

Unlike the baron, Ritte was fascinated by the secrets of his unravelled soul. I have never spent so much time with one who both dreaded and hungered for the truth. His relationship with the shadow had evolved over the years to an almost religious experience. Like a self-flogging priest, he feared the pain and yearned for the bleeding, a combination of sentiments I found thoroughly unappealing.

But he could keep me safe from the Nineteen. I don't know what lies he had to spin to his own masters to do it, but for a little while, I could close my eyes at night and not fear the darkness.

We sailed west, heading for Italy.

I avoided Ritte as much as possible. The Austrian stayed in the second-class lounge, smoking and making idle chatter with a widow of a certain age, who found the idea of reckless dalliance far more interesting than the reality of the man with whom she dallied. A day from Ceylon, we were struck by a storm that sent all scurrying below decks, and the aroma of puke and alcohol rose up through the floorboards with the hot sun of the following morning. I made myself mildly useful, assuring passengers in first class that a little seasickness did not justify medicinal electric shocks or the licking of crystals of radium chloride. If man can make a substance that sizzles or sparkles, he will surely try to use it to cure his gout.

In third class I was more useful, diagnosing not so much conditions brought about by the voyage, but long-standing maladies that the travellers could not afford to cure on dry land, and that convenience now lent to my inspection. In this manner I passed the remainder of the voyage happily avoiding Ritte until we reached Suez, where intelligence was waiting for him from his contacts and commanders.

"So much to work through!" he tutted, leaning over a great map of the world spread out on the small table in his airless little room. "So many possibilities!"

A packet of newspaper cuttings and reports, well over a hundred and fifty unexplained deaths, was laid out on the cabin floor. One stood out to him – the death of a father, his wife and his daughter in Bordeaux; the sole survivor – a girl of seven – committed to an asylum for her gibbering madness.

"Unfortunate," he muttered. "By now the French will have worked it out, and will be picking her up. My masters will be exasperated."

"I wonder if the French will wait for her to grow up before scooping out her brains."

"Oh no – she is a nice girl from a wealthy family! It would be a terrible waste. With appropriate training in languages and deportment, they can have her seducing the greatest men in Europe by the time she's fifteen."

He spoke without sentiment. Just the truth; just the God-gifted, praise-heavens truth of the thing. I stood in mute, seething silence and Ritte muttered and drew lines from Bordeaux in pencil across his map, calculating the speed at which Margot's shadow would travel, the likely radius within which she was still moving, the places she might be.

"It doesn't have to be Margot," I muttered. "It could be a madwoman. It could be ... anyone at all."

He puckered his lips, clicked his tongue, said nothing. My stumbling words were not truths poured down from heaven, and thus didn't interest him. "By now, she could be in Moscow, or halfway across the Atlantic Ocean. But it is probable that she is moving across Europe. Berlin, Vienna, Dublin or Naples are most likely. By the time we reach Italy, we should have a sense of the thing!"

I didn't argue, and stared at the map of murders he was drawing across the cabin floor, and wondered how we had come to this.

We made port in Taranto a few days later, and within an hour were ensconced in a decaying old hotel lined with wilting vines that never bore grapes, whose chief attraction appeared to be its proximity to the post office.

There, more letters and packages were waiting for my companion, reports of blood and whispers of madness. Within two days we were on the last train from Taranto, hugging the eastern coast through Ancona to the north, falling asleep to moonlight over water and waking to the first signs of snow and the grey, flat plains that hug the foothills of the Alps. Our crossing to Innsbruck was delayed at the border by filthy sideways rain that verged into snow; our papers were examined and examined again, our bags torn open and put back together three or four times by various officials of different nations. Ritte barked and snapped in his highest, most imperial German until finally the black-coated inspectors permitted us through to the other side of the blasted, shivering valley.

By then thicker snow and an overflowing river down the line confined us for eight hours to the border hotel, which had run out of all beverages save a brutal wine made by the proprietor's uncle and infused with the aroma of that man's sweating feet.

We neither ate nor slept that night, and by the time we were on the road again on a crystal-clear morning that belied the settling cold, Ritte was back at his maps, muttering to himself: Prague or Vienna, Prague or Vienna? A baron was rumoured dead in Munich, another piece to the puzzle, but by now Margot – not Margot, some demon with her face – would have moved on, the damage done, and our delay had put us eight days behind. That would give her shadow time to travel nearly two hundred and eighty miles, landing her either in or just beyond a circle of travel that included at its edges Prague, Vienna, Parma, Trier, Bratislava and Turin.

"She will choose a big city; a city she knows well," he muttered. "You know her – where will she go?"

"I knew her," I replied. "If it's her at all."

He gave a sniff of indignation, and chose Vienna.

"No," I murmured. "She prefers Prague." I couldn't meet his eyes, felt like a child again, wished Langa were near.

A smile at the corner of his mouth, his finger drifting over the map. "Prague, then."

We arrived in time for a sodden downpour that left the Danube raging against its banks, inches away from inundating the ancient stones and the newer, imperial bastions of culture and prestige. We were only there for four hours before a telegram reported a woman matching Margot's description crossing the same Innsbruck border we had slaved across not a day before, heading in the opposite direction. I laughed at the fury on Ritte's face as we turned south again. I wondered if we had passed each other in the night, two trains heading in opposite directions, faces half glimpsed through dirty, coal-streaked glass.

I slept with my feet up on the couch, hat over my eyebrows, and laughed again at Ritte's even more fervent rage at being questioned at the border again by inferior men, and wondered where Langa was, and decided he was probably somewhere on the northern edge of the Hindu Kush, about to descend to the jagged hills of central Asia, or to the flatlands that clung to mighty rivers and the dusty places of hidden sacred tombs. What sights would he see, my shadow, as he crossed through the lands swept over by Alexander and Genghis Khan, by Tamurlane and the great Persian kings? What dreams would he hear as he passed by the sleeping towns of the Tigris, or through the rattling markets of Istanbul? I wished for a moment that we could just sit and talk, he and I, and share in the wonders we had beheld.

"Where now?" Ritte barked, as we disembarked into wet sideways snow below the Alps.

I looked at his map for a long moment, the criss-crossing rings of distances travelled and times taken. "Milan," I said at last. "She always liked the opera."

A sharp nod, a yap of "Come, come!"

The landscape around Milan was a blasted torment of the modern world: mountains gouged open for metal and stone; flat fields of endless wilting stalks ploughed into earth, and finally, ahead, the belching chimneys and grinding endless roads of factories, freshly sprung up around the railway lines, ringing the older city and its mosquito-buzzing nights with fire.

A woman met us at the railway station, and I instantly wished Langa was there to tell me who she was, for she gave her name merely as Madame Rossi, and held out one gloved hand for Ritte to kiss, and spun on her heel once this formality was done to march us through the churning streets of stone and timber, old and new. Her hair was the colour of lead, her eyes algae; her walk was the march of a triumphant army, her hands clenched into fists around the handle of her swinging black bag. She wore the tight, high collar of a mourning queen and the sharp-toed boots of a fashionable young lady, and watched everything from the corner of her eyes, and never once turned her head unless her whole body spun with it.

"I was surprised at your telegram," she informed Ritte in brisk German, laced with a flavour of something I supposed might be Italian. The spy scrambled to keep up with her as she ploughed past men in huddling coats and shuffling steps, walking from one place they didn't want to be to another they didn't want to go. "Of course my resources are limited, times being as they are. I have not had any official word on my situation for several years, so yes, I was surprised – very surprised."

"Madame," he replied with a courtesy and obsequious bobbing of the head that he'd never graced me with. "You are as always ingenious, splendid and thoroughly underappreciated by your lessers."

She snorted her distaste at the absurdity of his words, puffing up simultaneously with a peacock pride. "Well," she muttered, whole form swaying from side to side now with the momentum of her march, "we shall see."

We lodged in a grubby hotel a few streets from the squat castle, and for two days nothing happened. Madame Rossi and Ritte did whatever it was that Austrian spies do when looking for a needle in a foreign haystack, and I visited those places where sometimes I had met Margot for our secret assignations, for stolen nights and laughing days, and found them full of people and empty of soul, and wondered what on earth I was doing.

On the third day, Madame Rossi broke into our rooms with a cry of triumph that years of stern education could not suppress. "Josef, I have it! I *have* it! One man dead, no more than twelve hours ago, matching your description! He sided with the general in 1898, told the army to shoot and just keep shooting when the protesters marched for jobs and bread. His wife died an hour and a half before he did; twenty-eight years old, dropped dead in the middle of the street, trying to comfort her child. The child was screaming nonsense, and her mother had to hold onto her to stop her running away, and that is how she died. They don't know where the girl is now; I imagine the family has her hidden away."

My eyes locked with Ritte's across the room. "We need to find the child. It is very, very important."

"I will take you to the man's house. You can join the louts who are waiting there, much good it will do you."

The house was a tasteless modern beast slammed into too-tight streets to the south of the cathedral, all columns and great double doors, stables to the side and the smell of sluggish, river-stained sewage seeping from the nearby alleys and drains. A small crowd of the curious and the professionally nosy had gathered by the front door, some in black, others making no pretence of mourning. The cobbles were powdered with the spilt residue of a dozen flashes from the eager cameramen, the air thick with the smell of oxidisation.

Much as Albert had, Ritte considered me largely useless without Langa's presence, and ordered me to wait across the street from the abode as he and Madame Rossi bustled and hustled, seeking servants with low morals and empty pockets, gathering whispers from the assembled there and wondering which lie might most effectively gain them access to the house. This left me standing for nearly two hours, beating my hands against a settling, damp cold. When the rain came, it was a thick, hammering downpour that sent all but the most determined photographers scurrying for shelter, and I grumbled and harrumphed and waited for my minders to return, and finally, in a fit of pique that had been growing upon me from the first cry of "Wait here, we will do the work!" to the latest drop of icy rain down my spine, marched across the sodden street and up to the front door of the house.

Hammering on the door provoked no answer, which was hardly a surprise, so instead I called out, "The child says she sees a shadow. It comes slowly towards her, reaching out for her, and the nearer it comes the more she speaks the truth until the words are unbearable. Then it touches her; she faints. At that moment, someone she loves dies. From the corpse of that individual the shadow rises again, and walks without rest towards the girl. It's terribly cold and unpleasant out here; may I come in?"

The woman who let me in wore a veil. Her black skirt and peaked sleeves made her seem far wider than she was; somewhere beneath all that shadow, a frame of skin and skeleton shivered against the seams. A hook nose and flat chin sloped off beneath the gauze about her face, and her hands were adorned with a mixture of rings studded with semi-precious stones, which knocked dully against each other as she fiddled with the lock. A man in red stood behind her, watching me, ready to throw me out at the slightest sign of charlatanism. I shivered and stamped my feet by the door and pulled off my coat and, with no one to take it, slung it over my arm where water could seep into my jacket and skin.

The woman and the man watched me, unmoving, a tableau frozen in the hall, half illuminated by the light of a paraffin lamp. No other lights shone in the house, and only the shadow of the rain running down dirty windows spoke of the outside world.

I looked at the woman, and did not need Langa to tell me that she would be next to die, when the shadow caught up with the child again. "Where is she?" I asked.

They didn't answer. I wondered for a second if they spoke any English, and tried again in feeble Italian, which came out nearer to Spanish. "I have a shadow that follows me," I explained, swinging back to English with diminishing hope. "The nearer the shadow comes, the more the child cannot help but say things that she should not know. The hidden, deepest secrets of your heart. People will come for her. They will take her away. I cannot cure her. There is no cure. Take me to her, and she will tell you the truth of it. But I can help you. Please."

The two figures frozen in the hall stared at me a moment

longer, then the woman half turned to the man and said something at speed in Italian, which I could not follow, and he nodded, and said something back, and marched away. She shuffled towards me, laid one gloved hand on mine, nodded once, said in heavy English, "You follow, now, please."

I followed.

They led me to a carriage pulled by a grumpy, tired mare. The man in red drove; the woman and I sat together at the back in silence. She pulled the blinds down, daring me with a look to defy her will, and I sat with hands folded in my lap as we bounced and rattled over uneven streets at a resentful trot. We didn't say a word for the near-hour in which we travelled. When we came to a halt, it was on a muddy track lined with stiff, regimented cypress trees. From there we walked down a narrow path to a single house set back from the road, where a lantern shone in the highest window. A man guarded the door, a dog slumbering at his feet. He rose at once as we approached, looked at me with suspicion, at the woman with deference. Let us in.

Up a staircase of stone, ducking through the low doorway at the top, into a corridor that smelt of old wood and fresh bees-wax candles, to a room with a white wooden door bolted shut. I could hear the child before I opened the door; her Italian was too fast, too frightened for me to make any sense of it, but the rhythm of it was an old, old friend. The woman went in first, grabbed the child in an embrace that pulled her close, as if she could somehow muffle the babble of noise in sheer love and fear. I followed, and the girl's eyes as they turned to me were red with crying and fear. At once she pointed at me and the rush of her words rose. I stood and let her talk, grateful that I couldn't understand the truths she pulled out from my heart. The woman listened, her face unreadable in the low gloom, nothing but a shroud. After a minute I said, "Have you heard enough? Does she tell you that I speak the truth?"

The woman nodded.

"We need to get her moving right now. Is there somewhere you can send her, far from here? A relative, perhaps?"

"My daughter, in Napoli."

"That will do for now. I need horses, one for me, one for you and the girl. You ride?"

"Yes."

"Good. Her shadow is very near now. Does she say I'm honest?"

The woman listened a moment, then nodded. "Yes."

"And you believe her?"

Another moment, a settling-in of dread as she decided between two truths – the truth of what had been before, of an ordered world with heaven above and hell below, and the truth of what her world must be now.

She nodded, reaching her decision, and bundling the child up in her arms shooed her from the room, and towards the sodden night.

We started walking before the horses came. I carried the child on my back for a little while, marching east, away from the city, away from the place where her mother had died, as she gibbered out the secrets of my heart, arms wrapped around my chest. Dawn was a spider's thread on the horizon when I paused to rest, legs burning, back a bent, aching weight. The man in red had run before, hired the fastest horses he could. He threw himself on one, plucking the girl from my arms, and was cantering east before I could say another word. I crawled, aching and yearning for sleep, onto the back of the other, and followed.

The girl stopped babbling the truth a little before ten a.m., and was asleep almost moments later. The man in red stopped the moment she did, fearful perhaps that she was simply dead, then looked at me for answers, but I didn't have any Italian, or he any English, so I simply smiled and nodded and hoped that conveyed enough, and on we rode.

We drew a long, wide loop around Milan, swinging south and finally north again at the end of the day, trusting to guesswork and a little maths that we had pulled her shadow far enough away that we could make a dash for the railway station. The girl sometimes stirred and sometimes slept, and I watched her constantly for the burble of truth that could not be denied, and was grateful that she said nothing. She was no more than seven years old, still dressed in the blue and white frock she had been wearing when her mother died, perhaps less than ten hours ago. Her father had died an hour and a half after that; it had only taken so long for the shadow to crawl from one parent to the other.

On the edge of the city, we paused to eat, and I telegrammed Ritte.

Station STOP

The woman in black was waiting for us in the ticket hall, buried beneath a great volume of luggage, far more than anyone could ever conceivably need. She had already purchased tickets for the last train to the south, and was swaying from side to side like bamboo in the wind, crying out as we approached and reaching up to grab the half-unconscious child and bundle her close again.

"We go now," she barked, as our ragged group tried to work out how best to transport the absurd number of cases she had provided. "We go now!"

I grabbed as many belongings as I could, and followed her, groaning a bit at the weight of the things, towards the platform below. Even on this cold evening, with the last train pumping smoke and steam through the billowing narrow corridors, the station was crammed with travellers, too many for the building, a volume of humanity that its tight brick walls and old, sloping platforms couldn't contain. The woman in black ploughed through them all, head down like a bull, girl clutched to her side, while I jostled and muttered half apologies, and ached and wanted nothing so much as sleep.

For all that the Italian state had made great steps forward in seizing control of its railway lines, the state of the trains and the passenger cars was still deplorable. Ancient rolling stock, splintered, creaking, cracked and rusted orange, squatted with the allure of a dying millipede. Men shouted and hurled insults at each other as train doors slammed open and shut, bouncing on crooked hinges and failing to sit properly in their locks. Our second-class compartment was a hurried mess of padded seats devolved to cracked wood, and fittings hanging off the walls and ceiling, barely lit by a single oil lantern dangling overhead. Nevertheless, it was a train out of the city, so the man in red scrambled on board, and he and I passed luggage between us to form a little avalanche of over-packing in the corner, before handing up the girl as tenderly as a broken flower. The woman in black boarded immediately after, and as she settled, I caught her arm.

"Who did this?" I asked. "Who did this to her?"

She struggled for a moment with the words, moving through French on her way to English. "A woman. Hair like winter wood. Smiling eyes. Spoke English, like you. Walk with limp."

"Did she have a name?"

A single nod, exhausted, the child held close to her side. "Her name is Margot."

The whistle blew, and the door slammed shut behind them as the train pulled away.

Chapter 68

Margot – what have you done?

What have you done?

What have you done?

I staggered like a drunk man through the crowds at Milan station. Stopped now, oblivious now. Then walked a few more steps. Then stopped again.

If I had been a better spy, I would perhaps have known that someone was watching me, and in more than the distracted way of strangers alarmed by the strange.

I was always a terrible spy. I depended too much on Langa, used him to do my dirty work for me.

Consequently, as I shambled in a daze towards the city streets, I neither spotted the knife coming nor, when it pressed suddenly into my back, really registered that this new presence was a blade at all, until the man who held it hissed in my ear, "Go left, now."

"What?"

This was not the reaction he was expecting. A knife should make people immediately obey, but I was too stupid to really connect what was happening, even though he spoke English with a familiar lilt in my ear. So he cut me. It wasn't deep, or a clean little slice; he simply pushed the tip of the blade into the back of my shoulder blade hard enough to make me nearly choke on my own tongue, and then, his point made, grabbed me by the other arm and dragged me across the street.

I thought of shouting for help, of explaining I was being

kidnapped, but in that moment the Italian for "excuse me, I am in mortal danger" vanished from my tongue and all I could think of was how stupid it would be to have my throat cut at this exact point in time. So meek as a kicked puppy, I permitted myself to be pulled into the shadow of a crooked, tumbledown building slated for destruction when the new station finally arose, pushed up against the wall and spun round a hundred and eighty degrees, the knife now laid across my throat, pricking at beads of blood, and my attacker finally visible to me.

"It's your fault," hissed Peadar Coman, as he pressed the blade in a little deeper. *"It's your fault."*

"Coman," I gasped, "Please, wait, it's—"

His lips curled with hate, and he hit me. There was no reason for it, no plan, he just wanted to with every fibre of his being and so he did, and with a knife in his hand I neither fought back nor begged for him to stop. When I dropped, he picked me up, slammed my head back against old timber, and hit me again until the blood ran freely down my face, salt in my mouth, crimson at my neck. In that moment I knew as surely as the shadow had come that he was going to kill me. The certainty of it nearly made me laugh; finally, finally a truth that I could know for myself without Langa's help, the last, most important truth of my whole life.

Then a gun clicked behind Coman's head, and Ritte said, "Is he a British spy? Should I kill him?"

Coman froze, but the knife didn't move from my neck. I closed my eyes, trying to find some clarity in the dead, nauseous pain of my own body, trying not to giggle at the absurdity of it all, clutching my ribs as the pain of laughter pushed up regardless. "He's Margot's husband," I breathed, perhaps the last breath I'd ever take. "And I have no idea if he's willing to die to kill me."

By the weight of the blade against my throat and the fire in Coman's gaze, for a moment neither did he. Only Ritte seemed calm, collected, confident of his course. "Really. Why does he want to kill you?"

"It's my fault," I replied, staring straight into Coman's eyes, trying to read something of the man in them I had never bothered to know. "It's all my fault."

For a moment, the weight of the knife against my neck eased a little, but Coman's body was still pressed to mine, the gun still lodged against his skull. I wanted to wipe blood from my face, the strange itching of it as it began to dry more distracting than the solid thrum of pain where he'd hit me, and didn't dare move.

Then Ritte mused, "Of course, there is always another—"

He didn't finish his own sentence before smashing Coman as hard as he could across the back of the head with the butt of his gun.

Chapter 69

There are two types of head injuries – those that leave you permanently crippled, and those that daze you for a few seconds. For a few seconds, Coman was dazed, and I shoved him back as hard as I could, palms to chest, trying to buy myself an inch of clearance from the blade in his hand. His feet tangled, so Ritte hit him again, and one more time, and this time the knife fell from his grasp and I caught it with a gasp and scrambled back on all fours like a drunken sloth, waving it half-heartedly.

Ritte, however, had little patience for threats, and hit Coman one more time to drop him to the ground, before kicking him in the belly and proclaiming as the other man crumpled, "Nothing like seeing old friends, yes?"

In the end, we managed to drag him into the back of a cab, me slumped bleeding on one side, Ritte in the middle, Coman curled at the end of Ritte's gun on the other. No one felt much need to chat as we clattered the few streets to our destination, tipping the driver a month's salary, and when Madame Rossi answered the door she exclaimed, "No blood on the upholstery, *please!*"

"Fear not, much of the blood is already dry," Ritte chirruped.

Coman was guided to a seat by the window, the shutters drawn. I washed away the worst of the blood in a pewter bowl as Ritte sat, gun in lap, eyeing up the would-be revolutionary.

The water brought a little clarity, a moment to think. Madame Rossi put another log on the small fire in the corner of the room, and folding herself down on the armchair nearest it produced from her bag a plush blue velvet box containing her own tiny revolver, which she set to cleaning in a click of chamber and swish of metal brush.

Finally, when I didn't think it likely that I'd throw up embarrassingly, I sat on a suitcase opposite Coman, there being nothing else left to perch on, and said, "Hello, Peadar."

His curling hair was flecked with grey; his beard had grown almost spherical around his weather-worn face. He had lost weight, his eyes sinking deeper into their sockets, the mischievous light of adventure long since replaced by a different flame; but there was still enough of him there, beneath the dirt and braces. A panel showing the crucified Christ was above his head, but he looked neither at it nor me.

For a while, we just sat there, to the click click click of Madame Rossi's gun.

Then: "Is it true?" I asked. "Is it Margot?"

His eyes flickered to me, studying my face. He leant a little closer, then drew a little back, then smiled. "Oh. You don't know."

"Tell me."

"Where's your shadow, Abbey?"

"Far behind. I'm asking, not knowing. Is it true?"

"Then you'll have to wonder for yourself, and do without knowing, won't you?"

I sighed, and now that I wasn't moving, dragging myself through Milan's streets, the aches and settled indignities of the day were beginning to grow into something brutally sore and stiff across my whole body. Coman watched me, hunched and crooked, a man still counting up avenues of escape, waiting for his chance. Finally: "Thought you were dead. Thought the Nineteen shot you."

"They didn't. They decided to scoop my brains out and turn me into a gibbering automaton to spout the truth. My colleague

370

over there chained me to a wall for a while too. Water under the bridge, as they say. *Is it true?*"

He drew back, and said not a word. "It's her," I sighed. "You wouldn't be here, following her path, if it wasn't. Margot is doing this. Margot is cursing the children. Why? What happened, Coman? What in God's name is happening?"

A half-shrug, and even that was too much like cooperation for Coman, as he turned his face away.

Langa comes, he comes, and the truth of my heart is … is that I believed many things all at once. I still do not know what I believe. That is the truth of the thing.

"When he told me," a nod towards Ritte, "what Margot was doing, I didn't believe it. I still can't believe it. You lived with her for all those years. Had a daughter with her. Loved her. I know you didn't fear the truth of your soul, but that was before she started *murdering children*. I wonder what the truth will be now, when my shadow comes?"

He was silent for a while, staring into nothing.

When he finally spoke, it was at first too quiet for me to hear it.

"What?"

Again, a whisper, staring at the wall. Then almost a shout, a sudden fury, snapped across the table loudly enough that I nearly jumped. "It's your fault! *It's your fault!*" For a moment I thought he'd try and hit me again, and across the room, Madame Rossi paused in her ministrations, little pistol held close to her chest. Ritte's index finger bounced along the barrel of his own gun. "It's your fault, you led them to us, you destroyed everything, *she is my wife* it's your fault!"

He was out of breath, so I let him breathe a moment. "Yes," I replied simply. "It is." And finally, the question that has been lurking just behind it all, driving the knife in his hand and the fire in his eyes. "Where's Vhairi?" Langa is not here, but he recoils like a man punched in the gut, and I know. But some truths have to be said, to be real. "Where's Vhairi?"

He shook his head, but that wasn't enough.

"Where's Vhairi?"

For the longest time, I didn't think he'd answer. Perhaps a minute. Perhaps five. When at last he did, he spoke to no one except himself.

Chapter 70

"She was hurt," he said, "In New York. Not Vhairi – Margot. The night you betrayed us, they chased us through New York, and Margot was shot. She said it wasn't bad; the pistol was fired from a long way behind, the bullet caught her in the calf. For a while she could even walk, run. We ran so far that night. By the end it was like we had only one person's courage left between the two of us, passed round like a ball. Sometimes I had it, and I was brave enough that we could slow down, stop, see that she was bleeding. Then I'd hear a door slam or a man shout, and I'd drop what courage I had and just run, and we'd run until finally Margot was brave enough to tell us to stop, and then we'd stop a little, by the Hudson or below the railway tracks, until the sun came up. That was when Vhairi started crying. She'd been such a good girl, all night such a good girl, but she started crying then and that made it all real, and that was when Margot collapsed.

"The bullet wasn't deep, but she'd been bleeding all night, and we'd just made it worse, much worse, by running. I didn't know where to go, or who to trust. I told her that bastard Abbey had betrayed us, betrayed us all, but Margot said no, you were as surprised as us, she knew the truth of your heart, knew every part of you, it made me sick, our daughter was crying and she was defending this ...

"There was a smith in Brooklyn, shoed horses, who was sympathetic to the Society. He knew how to pull stones from hooves and a bit about setting an animal's leg, and he was the best we had. He gave Margot a bottle of rye and pulled the bullet out on the pantry table. There was so much blood, I didn't think such a little thing could bleed so much, and he dug around so deep to get to it, but we didn't know where else to go. Vhairi had stopped crying. I didn't understand then that she'd seen her mam shoot a man in the face, didn't know what that meant; but I never saw her cry again, or smile, or laugh.

"Margot was too weak to move after we pulled the bullet out, but her shadow was coming. She'd left the picket lines too soon, doubled back to New York before her time, there wasn't enough distance between her and Doireann. She started speaking the truth, saying it out loud, the next night. The smith was a good man, but he didn't need that. He wanted us gone, and she said it, and that made it real, but she wasn't walking anywhere. It wasn't just the pain; she couldn't bend her leg properly, it didn't hold her. I fashioned her some crutches but she was only doing a step at a time, a little step at a time. I knew we needed to get her on a train, get her far away from her shadow, but the station was being watched, the docks too. They were everywhere.

"I hired a carriage to take us north, towards Bridgeport, just me and Margot and Vhairi, but it was so slow. So slow. Margot lay across the seat and stared at us and just . . . ranted. Ranted and raved, but all of it was true. How I'd never forgive her for all the men she'd been with who weren't me, how I didn't know for sure if Vhairi was even mine, how her daughter could never forgive her either, wanted to run away. In the end I made Vhairi ride outside with the driver, her lips going blue in the cold, and she didn't say a word, never complained.

"By the time we got to Fairfield I knew we weren't moving fast enough. The roads were wet and bad, and we kept on getting bogged in mud. Our driver wasn't one of the Society, just a greedy man, and the more urgent I said it was, the longer he seemed to want for his break, to relax and have a cigar, or the longer he said the horses needed to rest. At the end of the first day, he called a stop at seven p.m., and said we'd start again at dawn the next day and it wasn't safe to ride by dark. Margot was half-delirious now, the hole in her leg this big, purple, veiny thing, hissing secrets at the dark. That was when I stole the carriage. I didn't know what else to do. I just knew we needed to get to a boat, a train, somewhere they weren't looking for us, but they were looking everywhere. They were just … everywhere, men who knew our faces, our descriptions, hunting for the People's Society. The telegram travelled faster than any shadow, waiting for us wherever we went.

"I suppose it was inevitable that the horses would get hurt. I drove them too fast in the night. We didn't hit anything, but it only takes a bad road, a hole, and one of the beasts fell badly and broke its leg. That was when we were in the middle of nothing, just the three of us in broken mud and turned fields far as the eye could see. We waited in the coach for dawn, and by the time help came Margot was burning up, stammering truth through chattering teeth. A farmer came by, helped us into his cart, but no sooner were we on our way again than she was telling him the state of his soul, pouring out his secrets, and he threw us out again. That's when I drew her gun, threatened him, stole his cart. I knew he'd run to get help, but what else could I do? Doireann was coming and we were moving so slow, so slow, every step we took was so, so slow, and she was coming.

"All the time Vhairi watched, and listened, and didn't smile, and didn't cry and didn't say a word. Not even when her mam looked her in the eye and said, 'Yes, yes, it'll be you, you'll die first, you'll be the one that dies.' Vhairi already knew that was true, of course. She'd never doubted but that her mother loved her.

"I think that was what broke Margot's heart, breaking just when her daughter's did. I think maybe they broke together. She caught my hand in hers, and her skin was ice and slippy with sweat. 'Kill me first,' she hissed. 'Kill me first you'll do it thank you thank you you'll do it … '

"She was right. I would. If killing Margot would save our

child, I'd do it. God help me, God forgive me, I'd do whatever it took and she knew it, and she understood and smiled at me like she was grateful, before the truth came again. But first, I had to try to save them both. Whatever it took, I had to try.

"The law was waiting for us in Bridgeport. They'd been sent our descriptions, the three of us travelling together. They didn't know what we'd done, just that we needed to be arrested, locked up. There wasn't any fighting it; nowhere left to run. Margot was in and out of sleep by then, so when I saw the bobbies closing in I told Vhairi to run. I didn't want her to see what I might have to do to her mother; didn't want her to see how Margot died. But she shook her head, didn't smile, didn't cry, just sat there, shook her head.

"'Run, for God's sake, run!'

"She didn't. She just sat there and Doireann was coming, she was coming, and I had to kill her mother to save Vhairi's life, it was the only way, but she was just watching me and she wouldn't goddam run!

"That was when I failed. It's ... my fault.

"The bobbies grabbed us and I should have killed Margot first, I should have put a stop to it all, but Vhairi just stared at me and I couldn't do it. Not in front of my child. I couldn't do it, I just ...

"They took us to the gaol, just a few cages in a red-brick building where the law drank rye and counted dollars from the local protection rackets. Put me in one cage, Margot in another. Sat Vhairi down by the detectives' desk and gave her a cup of hot cocoa and asked her if she wanted something to eat, nice girl like her, shouldn't go hungry, and what she knew about what her mammy and pappy had done. Vhairi didn't say a word. She didn't touch the drink they gave her, or the food, just stared at me and her mam as Margot blabbered the truth of men's hearts, until finally the bobbies couldn't take it no more and they gagged her, and she just kept on talking through the rag in her face.

"The doctor came to look at her leg, and thought it might

have to be amputated. He needed to take her to the infirmary, and reluctantly the bobbies agreed and carried her out like an old bunch of flowers, still rattling the truth of their hearts through spit and cotton.

"Vhairi just sat, and waited.

"It was quiet, with her mam gone. Just the clock ticking, and men talking outside.

"Finally she got up from her stool and walked to my cell. It was all one big room, so the law could watch the law-breakers from the comfort of their desks, feet up and coffee in hand. No one stopped her; no one paid a child much of any attention. She sat down by the door and put her hands through the bars, and I sat down on the other side of it and held her close, pressing her into me as much as ever I could through the cold metal cage.

"I held her there, don't know how long.

"The clock ticked and ticked and ticked and she held me and I held her and I couldn't let go and we waited. I held her so tight that when it came, when Doireann crawled out of her frozen heart, almost nothing else changed. She didn't slump in my arms, cos I was holding her so close. She didn't gasp in pain or let go of my hands; just grew cold and a little loose in her fingers, which then grew stiff again. I'd never seen Doireann before, couldn't see much of Margot's dead daughter in the face of this shadow as it pulled itself hand over hand out of the heart of my child, and she faded almost as quickly as she'd come, turning like a lost traveller before finding her magnetic north and walking on her way. Didn't let go. Didn't let go. Didn't let go.

"It was only when the policeman asked Vhairi if she wanted to sit by the fire, and she didn't answer; only then that they came over; only then that they asked what was happening, only then that they pulled her from my arms, tiny, limp, skin already grey and lips purple, only then.

"Just then.

"Just the breaking.

"Just that."

377

He stopped talking.

Sat a while.

Watched nothing.

Heard nothing, except perhaps memories.

Then, a turn of his head, a change in the depth of his gaze, remembering perhaps for a second where he was, where he was not. "After," he muttered, and stopped, and tried again. "After. The infirmary was four miles from the gaol. That was good. That meant I'd be dead soon. Margot loved me, and now that Vhairi was dead, I'd be next. That was good. It would be quick, and it would be soon, and it was better than living without my daughter. But I was wrong. You hadn't betrayed the Society – not yet. Ever since New York, the survivors had been looking for us, tracking us first by Brooklyn, then by the road we travelled and the things we did. Before the doctor could cut off Margot's leg, they were there, bustling into the infirmary like they owned the place, grabbing her from under the law's nose and putting her on the back of the fastest carriage they could find. Me they broke out at gunpoint, and I told them to leave me, to let Doireann come, to let it end, and they told me I was special. Important. That the revolution needed me. I never hated them until that moment. Revolution. What self-important, arrogant little monsters we were. But I was still a vain man, and in that moment, I did not want to die.

"We left Vhairi in Bridgeport. We left her to be buried by men who never knew her name. I left her.

"Let it burn. All of it. Revolution, freedom, the Society, it can all burn. All of it, burn, just ...

"I don't remember much of the next three months. The Society moved us from safe house to safe house, but the law was all over us. Arrest after arrest, there was nowhere we could go where we weren't being hunted. They kept me and Margot together, as if I wanted to ever see her again, as if I could look her in the eye. I thought she'd die, but she didn't. The fever broke. She slept, and didn't scream the truth. Then

378

she'd wake, and say nothing, and then sleep again, and sometimes have nightmares, but I think they were all her own. It wasn't until Boston that she woke properly, looked at me, and knew. It wasn't Doireann that told her. It wasn't a shadow. She just knew. She didn't scream, at least not on that first day. It was near a month later when I found her shouting at the wall, bent over double as though she was about to pull her own belly out. I couldn't hold her, didn't have any comfort to give. Then she was quiet again. We were both just quiet.

"In Charleston, we realised the game was up. The law was waiting for us at the house of a friend, someone who should have been able to give us shelter. We barely got out alive, the last of our friends in America gunned down trying to protect us. They didn't stop to ask questions; we were anarchists, blackmailers, we deserved everything that was coming for us. The Society was dead. Now we were on our own.

"We stole, lied and robbed our way to Mexico. I had a friend there, not one of the Society, just a friend. He gave us shelter for a week, said we could stay longer, but I knew we couldn't. Doireann would come. She would always come.

"Margot said, 'Does it matter?' and I knew she didn't love me, and perhaps would never love again, and thought maybe that was fine, and we could sit here, together, her and me, and wait for the shadow to kill someone, and hope that someone was me.

"But running was habit, so I packed our bags instead, and took the boat to Caracas, and I got some work labouring in the docks of La Guaira, and she sat indoors and stared at the wall, and one night I told her we needed to talk, we had to speak to each other, and she looked right through me like I wasn't even there and said, 'Why?'

"And I didn't have an answer.

"What could we possibly say that wasn't already known and true?

"I hadn't counted the days properly; every day was the same, working and waiting, that time just grey, coming, passing, nothing. I didn't realise how close Doireann was until Margot left her room one ordinary day, and looking our landlady in the eye simply proclaimed, 'It is a sin. And you'll do it anyway,' and spun on her heel and walked away.

"Even then, I didn't drag her to the docks. In a way I was daring Margot to do it, to look me in the eye and tell me that her shadow wouldn't kill her, that I wasn't still her husband, the father of our child. I wanted her to scream at me, to beg me to run, to tell me that my life mattered, but she just sat at the end of the bed, hands in her lap, and waited. She knew what I wanted, and it didn't matter. None of it mattered.

"The day before the truth became unstoppable, a babble on her lips, I asked her to walk with me by the sea. She looked at me, then looked away, then rose and without a word walked by my side.

"We didn't talk.

"The truth was enough between us.

"I would head south in the morning, without her, and maybe she would stay and maybe she would run, and maybe Doireann would come and I would be dead within the week, and maybe she had never loved me at all. Who was to say? I was no truth-speaker. I would not know, until the end, but I hoped she loved me, and I wanted to live.

"All this I knew, so she knew it too.

"In the end, as the sun set, she held my hand, and we watched the crimson water.

"'Let it burn,' she breathed. These were the first words she had spoken for days. Then a little louder: 'Let it all burn.'

"I left her the next morning, and either she never loved me, or she also ran. I want to believe that Doireann never caught her. I have always been a self-important man.

"That was ... many years ago.

"I settled in Portugal. New name, new everything. Stayed away from revolution, said little, talked to no one about the past, and lived. A good life, in its way. The People's Society burnt. All across the world, it was burnt to the ground, but you can't stop the change. Everywhere, it's coming, the guns, the revolution, the war to end all wars – you can feel it in the air. We were only ever a tiny part of this picture.

"Then the great men started dying. And their wives. And their children. And it wasn't just how they died – I knew them. I *knew* them. These names in the newspaper, how long had the Society talked about them? The enemies of freedom, the great oppressors, they started dying all across the world, not with a flash, but with a whimper. It was her. It couldn't be her. It had to be her. I ... I had to know. I packed what I had, sold everything else I'd worked to make, and followed the blood. I suppose you did the same thing. It couldn't be her, it can't be her, but the names of the dead – the Society's enemies, there was a list of the most dangerous, the cruellest men, 'the little black book', Margot called it, God help us I had put names in it myself, she always said it was ridiculous, nonsense, but every death followed that list, I knew it, I knew it was her, can't be her – then I came to Milan and there you were. William fucking Abbey. There you fucking were, and I knew. It's your fault. It's my fault. It's ... I just knew. That is all. That's the truth."

Chapter 71

The guns are coming, Sister Ellis.

Can you hear them?

Great men have played their games. They meant it for the best. Their best was whatever was best for their big ideas. For nation. For honour. For glory. For profit. For God. For empire. These were the things that were for the best, and so they pursued them, and now the guns are coming. This war will tear the century to pieces, and in her way, Margot was right. She was right. Nothing changes, unless you make it change. Do I believe that? Langa comes and I believe it and I do not believe it and I know the truth and the truth is such a complicated, messy thing, he tries to make me speak all of it all at once to deny myself in a single breath, the guns are coming and so is he and ...

... and in that place in Milan I lied to Coman. Langa was far away then, so I could do it. I looked him in the eye and I said, "There's a cure."

He tried to hide his hope, and couldn't.

"This list she's following – this black book of the Society's. Do you have a copy?" He didn't answer, and though Langa was far, I knew what was in his heart, and what was in mine, so I pushed on. "There's a cure. I can remove her shadow. I know how."

"You're lying."

"No. I learnt it from the widows in India. They took me to their secret caves; I can save Margot."

"If you could do this, you'd have done it to yourself already."

"No. I can only do it to another. But if I find Margot, I can teach her how to save me. We can end this. All of it. Doireann, Langa – all of it."

"I don't believe you."

I shrugged. "Then make that choice. We'll keep looking for her, and more children will die. That man there," a nod towards Ritte, "is a spy for the Austrians. I'm sure he'll have no compulsion about putting you in a cage. However, if you would like to save Margot's life, help me. I have a cure."

For a moment, Coman wishes he has a shadow.

I watch it on his face. I've seen it on Ritte's face too, on Albert's and the colonel's. They yearn to have a clean, simple answer, to be gods among men, knowing all.

Without, he simply has to trust.

"If you hurt her ... "

"I won't."

"If your friends ... "

"They won't. I met Ritte when the shadow was on me. He is racked with a sense of failure and despair. He wants to feel valuable again. He wants to be redeemed for despicable things."

"I despise you, Abbey."

"I know. It's fair. Think about it."

I stood up, nodded to him once, drifted to the door. Ritte rose without a word, following. Madame Rossi stayed behind, unarmed, smiling patiently, watching Coman, who stared at the wall and barely blinked.

He said yes, of course.

I didn't need Langa to know he would, and felt disgusted at myself. There was no reproach from Ritte for what I had done, nor did he say the obvious, waiting truths about the path we were on. Merely: "You did well."

Coman gave us the book. Decades of names compiled by the Society, for the day they finally tipped their hand into murder. It was neither little nor black; he had scratched the names together from memory and half-heard conversations, dawdled on hotel stationery. Dozens of the names were crossed through already, dead by gunman's hand, or Margot's.

Margot, who had become a murderer.

There was no denying the truth of it now.

Ritte stared at the names, sent telegrams, conferred with Madame Rossi, drew lines and calculated times, and at last proclaimed our destination.

Chapter 72

Chasing Margot.

Do you know we're coming?

Maybe Doireann does.

Maybe, as we criss-cross Europe, Doireann and Langa will meet on an empty road, and their fingers will tangle as they pass each other by, and they will share an understanding, a truth, that only the dead can.

Milan, Rome, Munich, Cologne, Brussels, Berlin, Langa is coming now, he's coming, marching up through the mountains as we chase Margot and her names, gathering information, hunting, until at last –

– at the end of the road –

– we came to Paris.

Paris in winter. Tight, treeless streets of too-tall houses with lights burning dim behind locked shutters; pools of ice by the sluggish Seine, the stain of the factory fires on the mid-afternoon sunset. The summer wine does not warm; the kitchens smell of duck fat and pork grease and the already fractious tempers of people, stuffed and hungry, begin to fray.

Not so, perhaps, the inclination of Monsieur Guillot of the 2nd arrondissement. He was all mirth and merriment, and why would he not be? A respectable manufacturer of ether, he had grown as the chemical sciences had into a respectable importer of morphine, then heroin, the latest medicinal wonder-drug to cure all addictions. With a perfect conscience and the adulation of his business partners and the tax authorities, he plied his goods to the poorest corners of the city, offering heroin for babies, heroin for dentistry, heroin for an aching back, heroin for a bad day. He personally didn't touch the stuff, for he had a suspicion that long term it might not do any good, but the gentler pleasures of a swig of ether served on a bed of absinthe with a fine cigar were an acceptable balm to a stressful day.

The People's Society had tried and failed to blackmail him before. "Do whatever the hell you want!" had been his cheery reply. "Everything I do is legal, fair and above board. You try and shame me and I'll laugh you out of the papers!"

In the winter of 1909, blackmail was the last thing on Margot's mind.

Guillot had two children.

The elder, a boy of twelve, was destined for great things. His Latin, Greek, maths, philosophy, German and English tutors all said the same. He liked to leave caustic soda in his governess's bed and nails in her shoes, and had once urinated in her bonnet. When she tried to discipline the boy, she was locked in the basement for an hour by Madame Guillot, who screamed that she was a moment away from calling the police. When she tried to leave her job, her father hit her and told her the family couldn't survive without it, and what was she doing, foolish, stupid girl?

The younger child, a girl of eight, existed to be neither seen nor heard. She was, by all accounts, a very stupid, dim-witted creature, but at least she had good teeth and hair; she needed to be married off as soon as she reached a reasonable age. Her music teacher reported that the girl had a melancholy temperament; the governess suspected that beneath the sorrow was a highly sensitive, intelligent child – but no one listened to her.

Even in winter, this child preferred hiding in the garden to her parents' house. No one looked for her there, which must have made it quite a surprise when, sitting alone on the wooden bench beneath an awning of dark ivy, she heard a woman's voice.

386

"Mademoiselle? Mademoiselle?"

Behind the iron gate, always bolted and locked, that guarded the back wall of this green place, a woman. Joy, when it becomes cruel, does something strange to a human face. The smile is bright, wide, filled with teeth, and entirely unnatural. The eyes do not move with the lips; the voice is a little too high, the spine is taut even as the fingers, open and beckoning, are loose and easy. Margot was once full of life, but in that winter in Paris, she was a crooked wax sculpture of herself, melted and crudely reset in fire.

But perhaps to a child's eyes, she was simply a woman, wrapped in fur, a heavy cylinder of a hat on her head, smiling. She approached.

"Mademoiselle, can you help me? I am looking for Mademoiselle Guillot; are you her?"

The child nods.

Margot's smile grows wider as she squats down to the girl's height, only iron between them now. She reaches into a pocket, then extends one gloved hand through, a boiled sweet wrapped in sticky paper in her hand. "You are Mademoiselle Guillot? I hadn't realised how pretty and clever you were. My name is Margot. I was sent by your aunt, Leonie, she said I should stop by this house and say hello to her beautiful niece."

"You know Aunt Leonie?"

"Oh yes. We are very good friends. Has she never mentioned me? We travel together, I went with her this summer to Venice and Rome, she must have told you about that."

The child nods again; all this is true. This woman is a speaker of truth. She edges closer, reaching for the sweet in Margot's hand. Takes it. Margot's grip turns in an instant, catching her by the wrist, hard, the smile never faltering, and now perhaps the fear that the girl had, the sense of a thing uneasy, flares, because she flinches and tries to pull away.

"You're hurting me!"

"I'm sorry. I just wanted to see your face better. There's nothing to be frightened of. Nothing at all."

387

Now, with her other hand, she draws a pocket knife from her voluminous coat, and the girl is too frightened to scream. "This isn't to hurt you, child. You don't have to be afraid."

"Let go, please let go!"

Margot does not let go, but unclipping the knife nudges her sleeve back from her wrist, to reveal dozens of simple, straight scars, the newest one still clotting, running up her skin like sleepers from the railway tracks. She finds a clear line of skin nestled between two old, ridged white scars, and cuts. The blood curls instantly round her arm, quick and red. The girl opens her mouth to scream, but Margot looks up and there is a thing in her eyes, a thing like the fire of the boab tree, that silences the girl.

The words she begins to speak are not the words I know. Every place casts the curse in a different way. Margot called on different powers from the widows of India or the sangoma of the Cape. But their purpose was the same, as was the blood that fuelled the curse.

"Margot!"

For a moment, I thought she wouldn't stop, so I shouted, louder, running down the street, pulling her back from the gate: "*Margot!*" Four days and nights of watching this place, of waiting, and here we were, about to fail in all things. "Let her go!"

Her grip on the girl's wrist broke, as did the thrall she held on the child, who now, at last, screamed.

The blood dripping crimson from her sleeve onto thin snow, Margot blinked up at us for a moment, bewildered. Ritte, Coman, panting down the street behind me; she took in each, lingering for a moment more on Coman before returning her gaze to me. Then, without a flicker in her expression, she turned and ran.

We had all grown old. The chase was not one of sprints and bounds. She hobbled a little while, one leg limping and stiff behind the other, and in a tumble of half-run, half-shuffle, we followed. Coman reached her first, barrelling past me, calling her name. She turned, saw him following, knew he would catch her up. With a scowl, she marched beneath a cross to which dried flowers had been tied with grubby string, into a church of low wooden pews and hot candlelight.

Here, in this place of incense and a golden Jesus, of echoing feet on bare, cold stone and the muted light of day fading through narrow windows, she stood before the altar. Coman reached her in a moment, caught her by the sleeve, and she turned instantly, one hand on his shoulder, another at the back of his head, pulling his face close to hers, whispering, as if they were husband and wife still, young lovers, keepers of terrible secrets brought together after a long road apart. Slowing, leaning on the edge of a pew, I watched them, wished that Langa was near, thought I tasted something of Doireann on the wind, and saw a hint of her in the darting of Margot's tongue as she swallowed back the truth that her shadow would speak. Ritte arrived last, pistol in hand, face framed in candlelight, snow melting on his boots, drawing in ragged, excited breath.

For a moment, the four of us stood there, frozen in that hollow stone place, before at last Coman moved half a pace back, caught Margot by the hands and, shaking his head, breathed, "It wasn't you."

Not quite begging. Not far from it either. He stared into Margot's eyes, imploring, and I heard Ritte sigh behind me, and felt suddenly very old, and tired, and wondered if it would be inappropriate if I put my feet up for a moment.

She met his gaze without fear, blinking and saying not a word. His hands tightened on hers. "Why did you do it? To the children? Why the children?" Her head turned a little to one side, and for a moment she smiled, old and sad, and half nodded, urging him to understand. He shook her now by the shoulders, nearly shouting. "*Why the children?*"

"It was the only way," she replied, a little surprised, hurt almost by his indignation. "I thought you understood. You did once. It was the only way. Everything, burning. All of it, burning down."

His hands fell away from her, and finally, he had the knowing of it too, and there were tears in his eyes. She smiled, nodded, squeezed his shoulder again, pressed her forehead against his. "I'm sorry," she whispered. "It was the only thing left. I had nothing else worth doing."

He shook his head, pushed her back a pace. She stumbled, nearly lost her balance, her bad leg twisting before she caught herself with a sharp in-breath on the altar. Ritte edged a step closer, waiting. Slowly, Margot straightened up, and now, looking past Coman, turned her attention to me.

"Hello, William," she said. "Thought you might be dead."

"Brain surgery," I replied. "Evils of empire and all that."

A twitch of an eyebrow, turned to steel. Her head tilted towards Ritte. "And who is this? A failed Austrian spy, yes? A man so unsure of who he is that he needs a shadow to tell him. The truth is irrelevant to you, old man. You are still only capable of hearing the parts of it that please you. Why are you here? Ah – the spy is here to kill me."

A finger stabbed towards Ritte, but her eyes flickered to Coman, searching his face, looking for something beneath his confusion.

"If I must," Ritte replied. "To end these things."

"Revolution is coming," she answered with an easy sweep of her hand. "Fire and war. You cannot stop either."

"We can stop one despicable thing, ma'am. Maybe not the rest."

"Margot . . . " Coman began, but she waved him into silence.

"How far is Langa?" she demanded. "A little too far. Then you will be left to wonder, to ask yourself, why this?"

"I don't wonder," I replied. "I don't need a shadow to know. What is the use of you – of us – if the truth changes nothing? What is the point of truth when your daughter dies? Let it burn. Let all of it burn. The world did not weep for Vhairi, or Doireann. Let it weep."

"*Margot* . . . " Coman again, reaching for her, waved into silence again as she stared into the truth of my heart.

"Oh William," she tutted. "What lies have you told to bring him here?"

A flicker across Coman's face; a moment, perhaps, of understanding. "No," he spluttered. "No: Abbey has a cure."

Her eyes danced to me as I eased myself a little more upright, breath slow, fingers gripping tight into wood. Coman didn't flinch; didn't look away from his study of her face, put one hand on hers, barely touching. Asked: "Did he lie? Is there no cure?"

Her eyes locked in mine, and they were not the same eyes I had known before. "William," she mused. "You have grown old, haven't you?"

"So have you."

"Do you think you can persuade me to stop? When Langa comes, you and I will sit in the truths of each other's hearts, and when you know me as the truth-speaker must, then you can leave your daughters behind too, and you can be the one who kills them, and you can have nothing left but the road and blood. Will you join me then? Will you see? No. You are too much of a coward. You love, you do not love. You forgive, you do not understand, you hate, you pity, you forget, you remember – you are very ordinary in your confusions, aren't you?"

"Yes. As ordinary as everyone else."

Her head tipped a little on one side now, her eyebrows twitching down, and now she held out her bloody arm, the fresh knife cut seeping from cold flesh. "Are you still a doctor?"

I shambled slowly towards her, tore a strip from the altar cloth, wrapped it tight around her limb, pressing it over the wound and knotting it firm as the crimson slowly conquered white.

Ritte watched without a sound. Coman swayed like a drunk man, not sure whether to fight or fall down. Margot read my soul as I worked, and finally, without warning, put a hand to my cheek.

"You ridiculous, regrettable man. How long have you been alone? You should have tried harder to find me; I would have understood." Then her forehead crinkled and her lips curled down. Her fingers tightened around my jaw, pulling me close, brow to brow, touching, as if we could pour our thoughts into the other's skull. "What did Albert do to you? William? What did he do to our brothers and sisters?"

I shook my head, tasting bile. Her teeth flared behind her lips, and tighter now, a hunting animal, a woman with nothing left but to kill, she whispered, urgent, "Did you get them all?" A glimmer of something in her that was, for a moment, nearly human. "Did you get all the hollow ones?"

It took me a moment to realise what she meant. Then I nodded, once. "Yes. They're all dead. I killed them all."

"Did you get *him*? Did you get their maker?"

"No. I . . . I am a doctor. I don't kill the living."

Half-dead words on my lips. The feeblest excuse a killer had ever used.

Her face hardened. "Then you have done nothing with your gift. *Nothing*. You should be grateful that I am here to finish your work."

Her fingers brushed my lips, and in the same moment that my soul cracked, hers stiffened, and stepping back quickly she looked Coman in the eye. "William lied to you," she barked. "He can't cure me. He doesn't know how."

Behind me, I felt Ritte straighten up, Coman grow still. I sighed, tied the last knot in the bandage on Margot's arm, stepped away, let her read the truth of my heart. She smiled, nodded once, touched her bloody fingers to her lips.

"I know I am a monster," she mused in the ringing silence of the church. "William doesn't believe in God, but last night he got down on his knees and prayed. Like most people who seek intervention from the divine, he knows it is impossible. I have cursed children with Doireann just moments behind me, I have looked into their hearts, I have felt their terror. I stood by the coffins as their parents and brothers and sisters were taken to the grave, looked in the eyes of the children I have damned and I know their horror. I know that I am a monster;

I have seen that too. I became a monster when I killed my daughter."

Doireann, buried in an unmarked grave.

Vhairi, dead in America.

"This has been coming; this has always been coming," she whispered, catching at Coman's hand as he snatched it away. "There has always been a black book, there has always been a list of the dead, I just did it, I did what had to be done, this is why monsters exist, this is why we live, this is what is necessary, this is the only thing left, it's what Doireann wants, it's what she wants, it's what Vhairi wants ... "

He spun away, pressing his hands over his eyes as if he would be blind, neck twisting side to side.

"I punish the vile. I put the oldest, blackest curse on their children that their very line, their seed, may be wiped from this earth. Truth has no need for shame. Truth exists merely in reality as it is; all the rest – love, guilt, regret – are just words we put on it. I am become a monster. I am truth. I will never stop. There is no cure. Saira knew it, William – there was never a cure. We don't *need* curing. That isn't the point of us at all."

Coman shouted, no words, just a cry that brushed back the candlelight, and for a moment I thought he might hit her. His hand flew wide, he caught himself on the side of the altar, hauling down breath, shaking, straightened up again, turned to her, eyes burning, tears dripping now down his cheeks, rolling off the end of his chin. Ritte took a step nearer, old spymaster straight and stiff, shoulder angled towards Margot like a duellist. Coman followed Margot's gaze, saw the gun, looked to me, back to Margot.

"William won't kill me," Margot breathed, unblinking. "But if it will stop me, he won't get in Ritte's way. He didn't know it until now, but now it is true."

"I spoke to Saira, before she went into the desert," I said, before Coman could speak or move a muscle. "I asked her a question. Do you know what I asked?"

Margot smiled, and for a moment her eyes drifted to me, and

393

there she was. Just for an instant, there she was again, living, laughing, clothed in light. "Yes."

"And do you agree with her answer?"

"Yes. I do. But it's not enough."

Coman's hands were turned out to hers, like a dancing partner waiting on the edge of the floor at the end of a long night, the last candles burning out. She looked at them as if seeing hands for the first time, marvelling at the construction of finger and bone, the bend of knuckle and the bulge of flesh, of soft sense and ageing skin, of the hairs that laced the back of his hands and the lines that swept across his palms. One hand slipped into his, turning it this way and that. Ritte shifted, watching, waiting. Her eyes turned up, meeting her husband's gaze. "I ran," she whispered. "I let her come so close I could have held her for ever, and then I ran. I always loved you."

Coman smiled, kissed her on the cheek. I knew an instant before he moved what he intended, but Langa was too far behind, my warning too late. He spun, ran straight for Ritte, arms out and chest flaring, and the spy raised his gun and without hesitation, fired. He put one bullet in Coman's thigh, another in his ribcage, but Coman was already moving too fast, and the tumbling of his fall took him straight into Ritte's throat, scrabbling with open hands for his windpipe. The two toppled backwards, the Austrian smacking his head against a pillar as he fell, and for a moment they wriggled on the floor.

I grabbed for Margot as she ran, caught the back of her coat, which slipped from my grasp, then lunged and grabbed again, tangled in a fistful of collar, pulled her back. She spun, face entirely calm, kicking out with one leather-pointed toe for my knees, scratching at my eyes. I raised a hand to shield myself as she drew her arms out from their sleeves, leaving me clinging to fur and air, then she was hobbling for daylight. I followed, and two gunshots smacked out behind me. The first was muffled, little more than a door slamming in a distant corridor. The second was deafening, a ringing, bouncing retort round the church as the pistol fired into air, not flesh.

I ducked instinctively, looked back at the two struggling men, saw Coman roll to one side. The gun was in his hand, Ritte's fists locked tight around Coman's own as they struggled for control. Coman's skin was already blanching, the blood a black slick around him in the candlelight. Ritte's eyes were open and he was gasping, surprised, one hand at his belly. Coman raised the gun, pointing it straight at me, and I half ducked, half tripped down behind a pew, wriggling on my elbows beneath the wooden bench as he sent a bullet flying wild. Looking back, I saw Margot, framed in the door, wavering, neither coming nor going, winter light turning her into shadow against the outside world. She looked at me, at Coman, bleeding out on the floor, at Ritte, and I could not see her face as she made her decision, and turned, and ran.

I peeked my head up above the pews and Coman emptied another bullet in my direction, missing by a mile, picking a hole in stone. I ducked down, crawled to the edge of the aisle, peeked out again. He fired instantly, and the pin clicked on nothing. He let his arm fall, and stared up into space. I crawled on hands and knees to the two men, hissed, "Ritte! *Ritte!*"

Slowly his head turned to blink at me, and lifting one hand away from his belly he said, in a reasonable voice, "I believe he got me."

The bullet wound had burnt a charred pattern into his shirt and waistcoat, obscuring the round indent in his flesh. I cursed and slipping in blood, scampered back to the altar and ripped the whole cloth off, scattering gold and wax in an arc. Bundling the sheet into a fist, I pressed it hard into Ritte's belly, and now, at last, he groaned with agony. Beside him, Coman watched, empty gun still in one hand. I leant over to him, ripped back his shirt, tore his trouser leg, cursed and cursed again, ran, skidded in blood to the open door of the church and, cupping my hands around my mouth, called at the top of my lungs, "Police, doctor, anyone – help!"

*

It took thirty minutes for the cart to arrive to carry Ritte and Coman to the hospital.

By then, Coman was dead.

I held his hand as he died. He didn't seem to mind that it was me. I thought perhaps he would tell me not to hurt Margot. I thought he might say that she was kind, or misjudged, or that there was still hope for her. I thought he might die with his daughter's name on his lips, dead and buried in an unknown tomb. Perhaps he thought of all these things too, but he said none of them. In my experience, when death comes it takes away all lies, all self-deception and cries for meaningless, pointless hope. The only truth I have ever seen the dying say that has mattered a damn is "I love you" to those they leave behind; and Coman's love was as dead and buried as he.

Ritte's wound smelt of faeces, and I told him he'd be fine.

He said, "You're a liar, William Abbey," and I believe it was a compliment.

I stayed with him through the night, and in the morning he was still alive, and I wasn't sure if that was a mercy.

I walked through the Paris dawn, covered in other men's blood, and people steered clear of me and avoided my glare, and in the hotel room I washed, and put my bloodied clothes in the fireplace, and wrote to the Austrian embassy to inform them of Ritte's location and condition, and packed a light bag of everything I might need, and went to the telegram office.

I sent a single message, to Professor Albert Wilson, care of Her Majesty's Government.

```
Margot knows coming for you for your
child STOP
```

That done, I got on the fast train for Calais.

Chapter 73

"You saved his life?"

I couldn't stop myself asking the question, it seemed so ridiculous.

Abbey's head tilted to one side, watching me like a cat. The professor stared at the end of the bed, at the flat sheets where his son's legs should have been. Something tore open the earth outside, made glass tinkle in windows, the floorboards creak.

"You think I should have let him die, Sister Ellis?" A gesture to sleeping Richard Charlwood, dreaming an ether dream between us. "He was just a child. Not yet ten years old. I saw it in Margot's eyes, as she picked apart the truth of my soul. I saw her understand, *know* about the truth stations, about Albert's experiments and all he had done. I knew what she'd do next. 'You should be grateful that I am here to finish your work.' So yes. I telegrammed London. Murdering Albert's victims was easy. They were not living people any more, they were trapped in hellish torment, doomed to pain. But killing Albert in cold blood? Cursing his child to do it? That was a very different proposition. Besides, I have always been a coward."

The professor didn't look up as Abbey spoke. Wetted his lips like he was going to speak, then didn't. I didn't know if he was angry, or ashamed, or anything else.

A thump of shell shook the room, a rattling through the floor, a swaying of shutter and a sloshing of water in the glass by the bed. I held tight to the bedside table, half closed my eyes and thought I

397

heard a rifle crack, or maybe a branch break in the garden outside, and snapped, "What happened to Ritte?"

"He lived. For a few years more. He never ate properly again, and the Austrians were if anything even more displeased with the outcome of his exploits than they had been before. But he was not. He had, at last, I think, found a little truth about himself. I don't know whether it was the shadow, or the face of death, that gave him the peace he was looking for. Perhaps a bit of both."

Another shudder as a shell fell, a little nearer. Smoke drifted by the window, footsteps ran in the corridor outside, voices raised in brisk, busy command, trying to disguise fear. The professor finally looked up, glancing past Abbey to the world outside, and murmured, "Perhaps . . . ?" and stopped, gesturing at his son.

"They won't evacuate us," Abbey replied, eyes half closed. "We're not important enough to send trucks for, not right now. We have to sit it out."

"How did you know she'd go after Richard?" I demanded, anger spinning inside me, though I didn't know why. "How could you be sure?"

"I wasn't sure *when*. It might take her years. But I knew she would. She had looked into my heart and seen Albert sitting there with scalpel and drill. And she meant what she said about our shadows – that they were a blessing, not a curse. Albert made them a curse. It was only a matter of time before she destroyed him. I thought of letting it happen. It would have been easy, it would have been . . . a kind of justice, but a child – a child – I kept on thinking – a child. Coman was dead and I am disgusted by what I am, but on those few occasions when I am at peace with myself, it is when I am a doctor. Do no harm. Do not let a child die. I assumed that on receiving my message Albert would send his son into hiding. He was a brilliant man; he would deduce the meaning of my warning. However, when I reached London, imagine my surprise to find that not only was Richard not in hiding, he was being flaunted in plain sight."

"Not flaunted, it wasn't—"

"I am compelled to speak the truth," Abbey snapped, cutting

off the professor with a scowl. "Albert, as you can see, is not. He knows that 'flaunted' is a perfectly good word for it. 'Paraded' might also be another way of putting it. He paraded his son, turned him into bait. It was a trap, of course – one set for me as much as for her. I didn't need Langa to recognise the danger. From the first moment I set foot in Dover I could feel the claws of my former masters closing in, every policeman and railway porter across England alerted to my – and her – presence."

"Tell the truth," snapped Albert. "If he is near, tell the goddam truth!"

Abbey sighed, closed his eyes, too tired to fight the compulsion on his tongue. "The Nineteen made him do it. Catching us was considered worth the risk."

"I wanted to hide him. I tried to send him to Scotland, get him away, but they stopped me, *my own people*, they stopped me," snapped Albert, eyes blazing, not at me or Abbey, but at his sleeping child. "They made us prisoners in our own house, prisoners in a golden cage, they said . . ." He caught himself, and I wondered what words he might have uttered, if his shadow made him speak. But he turned away, stared at his hands. Finally: "He is my son. Margot lost her daughter, and it made her mad. He is my son."

Abbey watched him a long moment, and there was a flicker of something on his face, a rounding in the eyes, a pushing-out of breath, that I thought might have been . . . a thing that fools called compassion. Then it was gone, and there was just tiredness, and the truth.

"I had been on the road for so long, and learnt many tricks. Truth and deception were second nature then, and so I watched Richard and his father as they went to church, walked together across Richmond Hill; visited tutors and colleges, friends of the family, the opera, the music hall, public lectures and events. The child was barely old enough to chant his nine times table, and there he was, every night, being dangled in public, while a ring of men waited for me; for Margot. Whatever the . . . the circumstances of the thing . . . Albert baited a trap for us with

399

his own child. And you think our current predicament isn't a kind of justice?"

"Not for him it isn't," I barked, tilting my chin towards the sleeping lieutenant. "You two play your games, but not for him."

A shrug from Abbey, forced, a struggle. Silence from the professor. Then: "Finish it, William. Let her have the truth."

So he did.

Chapter 74

Waiting, in London.

December 1909 gave way to New Year 1910, and still Margot didn't come. Once I had seen that Richard was a trap, not just her next victim, everything changed. I should have run; should have just let the jaws close. Every minute I spent in that city was an old terror, waiting for the things that come in the dark. The knock on the door; hooded men; chains and the surgical table, the knife in my skull. Every stranger was watching me, every other street carried a picture of my face. But I couldn't leave. I had thought I was saving a child's life by warning Albert, but all I had done was put Margot in danger of the surgeon's blade. I could not cure her, or make her stop; neither could I let another child die. What else could I do? What else was there?

I waited and she did not come. January gave way to February, and I began to dream the dreams of my neighbours. By day I lodged in Whitechapel in a room with seven others, rubbed dust into my skin, dined on eel and boiled potato. By night I stalked Albert's son, circling the ever-moving perimeter of guards set upon him until I knew the faces of every man. They nearly caught me a half-dozen times, and a half-dozen times more than that I lost my nerve, until Langa came.

He's coming, he came, he comes, truth is not reality, we filter all things through our hearts, the truth of our hearts, Richard is waking Albert is so scared more scared than he's ever been nothing matters except now, this moment, he would lose it all for his son and didn't know until this instant that this was what love was, he comes, he comes, she is coming, he is *coming*!

At night, I waited for the Nineteen to come and pluck me to my death, and instead, Langa came.

My old friend. Returning to me at last.

Everything was easier. Everything simpler. I looked down upon my prey and knew the truth of men's hearts, and I rejoiced in the knowing. God-like, this is how Margot feels as she tears into the souls of men, their every sin washed through me, their every thought my balm. How many must die for her new world, let it all burn, let everything burn, this war will wash away the old world in blood, a new world, there is no place for us in it but let it burn, let us burn, all of us burnt as the tree, Langa comes, my sweet, blessed boy, he comes at last and with him comes the answer, all the answers, the truth drenched in darkness, thank you, thank you Langa, thank you!

It was with Langa at my back, that I finally saw her.

Like me, she had taken pains to affect a disguise. Gone was the beautiful woman I had known. Gone was her pride, her haughty manner, her joy and her delight. Instead, a beggar stood crooked outside the music hall on a Thursday night as the wind bit in sideways down the bustling street, hustling for coins, stooped and shrouded in a shawl, head down and knees knocking, and she was Margot, come for Albert's child, as she always would. Descending from the evening's pantomime, from the painted revelry and the shrill mockery of the year's events, from the parody of the costermonger's warbling and the high kicks of the petticoat girls, came Albert, Flora, their child and their silent entourage sweeping the crowd for the danger that they want to come and the truth of their hearts is . . .

Complicated. Love, fear, guilt, excitement, dread, hope, hate — Flora hopes that her husband will remember what it is to love again; Richard is bored, things simple as only a child can be; and in Albert, such a maelstrom. To look at it, for a moment

I thought it might break my heart, the lines between his heart, my heart, her hearts, all our hearts are breaking.

Their guards ... their captors, if you will ... have only one thought in mind: find the woman, find the man. It is a pity they cannot kill us on sight, but their orders are to shoot us in the knees before they aim for the chest.

Margot knows all this too, as surely as I, watching this huddle as they descend the steps. Their passage sweeps them across the street towards the wider thoroughfares of High Holborn and Kingsway, and as they pass, her eyes follow, and our eyes meet, and here we are.

Langa is here, and I cannot lie. I cannot lie but I do not know how to tell you this in words. We stood apart, she and I, in the middle of the London street, in the city where it had all begun. Coman, the Nineteen, and at her back was the shadow of the daughter who died, and at mine came the boy who burnt by the boab tree, and between us spun the hearts of men, oblivious to our communion, and their truths were ...

Cold but hand warm in the touch of the one I love and

hungry but filled to the brim with a thousand other feelings, swept up in the brush of snow the sound of laughter the taste of winter's air the brush of wool the weight of feet upon stone

frightened, angry to be alone.

For a little moment, when the shadows come, there are no people walking through the world from the cradle to the grave. There are no men or women, no young or old. We exist in an instant balanced in togetherness, sharing the heat, the cold, the air and the earth of this moment, the songs of every heart, our songs; their sorrows, our sorrows. The bitter stories that make up the heart of men strive always for some clean repose, some simple solution, and make of their needs realities that melt as quick as snow. Now this is truth, and now it is not. Now we must believe, and now we have forgotten all that we were, and in every moment our lives dissolve into something new and who we were yesterday is vanished as quickly as who we were in this instant when we breathed out, and only in the eyes of strangers do we see ourselves, and only in the hearts of men do we know the meaning of the words we utter as if they were truth. Man's mind swirls in contradiction, striving for ever to settle on truth, truth, truth, to find an absolute that it may sit in for perpetuity, blessed at last with a stone that stands constant against the turning of the tide, and never finds it, for in man's heart there is no truth at all, only seeking, picking, wondering, and on a very rare occasion, the meeting of another's eyes.

So we looked.

And our shadows came.

And for a moment, we were one.

And I knew at last what I had wanted to know since I had met her: that there was no such thing as simple as the storyteller's love in her, that love was a tangled measure of a thousand different things, and that sometimes there was a word called love that she knew and understood, and then sometimes it was gone, and she could not master it, and being unmastered, she longed to let it go, and then thinking of it, it came again.

Perhaps, when Doireann came, her shadow would kill me.

Perhaps she would at that.

For a while, in coming to London, Margot had toyed with it, and at the last moment shied away from taking her daughter's blackened hand.

And in that way too, perhaps she loved me. Perhaps that mercy was enough.

And finally, we were out of time, for she knew my heart as surely as I knew hers, and knew how things had to end.

So seeing, she reached the only conclusion left, and pulled a pistol from her pocket, and marched into the street.

No time for curses, no place for dark ritual or the death of children.

She had eyes only for Albert, her gun levelled at the back of his head, and God help me, I stood by and would let her do it. Her hate was mine; she had caught it from me, and in a way she was being kind too, killing the father that the son might live. I didn't want it, I wanted it, I was horrified, I couldn't look, *I wanted it,* forgive me God, forgive me, forgive me my heart, a man stood by the boab tree as an innocent boy burnt, and all these years later, these many, many years later, an old man would watch the woman he loved shoot another in the back of the head, and nothing had changed, and nothing had changed, and nothing had changed, and the world burnt.

She didn't get close enough to pull the trigger.

The jaws of the Nineteen snapped shut around her as soon as the pistol was drawn from the folds of her tattered, muddy skirt. One man cried "Gun!" and another barrelled Richard to the ground, thinking the child the target of the attack. Albert began to turn, and in credit to what little humanity he had left, the realisation of what he had done nearly floored him. After all that scheming, all that fantasy and dreaming of what he would do with Margot in his hands, the reality now stood before him – that a woman was coming to kill his son. It didn't even occur to him that she would kill him, so fixated was he upon his child. It was as if he had never seen his boy before. Certainly, he had a son, and that son was beautiful, and clever, and talented, and he loved him inasmuch as any father must. But he had not been a living creature of free mind and independent feeling, a breathing soul as beauteous as any angel, until the moment that his life was in danger of being extinguished. Then, for that second of revelation, Albert saw just what a lacklustre father he had been, just how far from the path of righteousness he had strayed; but all too late, it's all too late you came too late Albert came too late and you know it coming going coming going he's coming and *you came too late*!

When Albert realised the pistol was aimed for him, he was so surprised he didn't move.

Which was why he barely blinked when his nearest guard, a man by the name of Young, who had served some time in the military and had ceased to be alarmed ever since a man with a knife had nearly taken his ear off in Burma over a business with some chickens, shot Margot in the leg, and then, as she stumbled, hit her round the side of the head with the butt of his gun, breaking her jaw and two of her teeth, before stamping on her wrist and snatching the weapon away from her as she fell.

Now the street got about the business of running. Most ran away, a busy, chaotic affair of crowds unsure which way to go, of steaming breath and slipping, slithering feet on cracked black ice. Flora had Richard round the waist and was half carrying him with remarkable speed any direction but that of her husband, while Albert was knocked to the ground by his own escort for fear of a second assailant. I ran for Margot. It was not an intelligent decision, nor was there a plan. It is perhaps one of the stupidest choices of my life, and yet one of the very few I am even remotely proud of it, for all that it achieved nothing.

I had to push and shove and stumble my way through a tide of humanity that flowed the opposite way, elbowing and cursing, so that by the time I reached the scene, Albert was half recovering, crawling back to his feet. The tumult of people gave me a little cover, and I caught the military man square in the back with a kick that made my hips creak in the cold, sending him sprawling face-down into the ground. Another man, who looked like he might be vaguely involved in proceedings, received an elbow in the face, followed by a remarkably successful punch to the throat, both of which floored him, wheezing and bloodied, long enough for me to reach down and hook one of Margot's arms across my shoulders, dragging her halfway to her feet. She nearly made it all the way up before her weight gave beneath her again, and I sagged, off balance and panting, only for a hand to reach out from behind me and grab me by the hair. Cursing, I tried to catch hold of the arm that pulled me from her, managed to fumble my way to what felt like someone's eye, tried to dig a finger in, felt the face at my back lurch away and the grip on my skull briefly slacken, before something hit me in the ribs hard enough for blue powder to burst into flame across my eyes, and a pistol was pressed into the side of my neck.

"Calmly, William, calmly," panted Albert, though he was as calm as a steam engine about to burst. "Calmly!"

I half shrieked some animal noise, I don't entirely know what, buckled against him, felt an arm slither across my throat, nearly choking me, kicked and scrambled and half fell in the grip that held me, dragging whoever was at my back down too, felt another arm grab for my flapping limbs, another for my feet.

In the end, three men pulled me down, largely through the exercise of sitting on my limbs and back until I finally understood that I couldn't shift them. That, more than any pistol, silenced me, as much as a loss of breath, and cheek to stone I lay beneath them, not three inches from Margot's gaze as she regarded me.

And the truth of her heart was that I was an idiot, and she was glad, and she was glad that she would die this way, and she was glad that there would be an end, and she wished she had killed Alfred, and she hoped that Doireann killed me soon, so that I need not be afraid any more, and she loved me, and she had never really loved me, and things were never simple in the hearts of men.

She knew the truth of my heart too, and knew what would be done, and smiled a little as they picked her up and carried her away.

At least, she thought, this way she would be a different kind of monster.

Then Albert's face was where hers had been. He squatted on all fours opposite me, and gazed into my eyes, so that I might see the truth of his soul. He tried very hard in that moment to imagine what it would be like when he cut off her hair. He yearned for me to feel, as he had felt, the sudden wet release of the drill as it popped through skull; the satisfaction as he prised away bone, the texture of brain beneath knife. He wanted me to know the texture of little pieces of it in your fingers, how it stuck to your skin, before you wiped it away into the glass dish at your side.

This was his intention, but the heart feels more clearly than it thinks, and all I really knew was that he was more angry

407

than he had ever been, not at me, but at himself, and ashamed to have called himself a father, and being as he was angry and ashamed, he could not begin to look himself in the eye or think clearly, and so turned his hatred onto the world, as an easier target for his self-loathing. In time, that would become a habit for him, filling his soul with hate. Only when Richard lost his legs did Albert remember again that he was the villain, and he was ashamed.

Luckily for him, Langa was near enough that I knew the rest, and he saw it in my face and the way I struggled against his men, and heard it in my screaming, and this done, stood up quickly, and went to follow Margot's stretcher to her end.

Chapter 75

For a while, they kept me in a locked room in I knew not where, and I was grateful for that, because Langa was coming. As long as he reached me before they could drill a hole in my head, I was grateful.

Then they moved me, and I screamed until they hit me enough to stop me screaming.

The Nineteen had a Model T.

I had never been in a car before. I found the whole experience incredibly uncomfortable and unnerving. For a moment I understood the baron's distrust of all this new-fangled machinery.

The car stopped and started many times, and they blindfolded me and threw me in the back like a piece of luggage, and we drove for a little over an hour in teeth-rattling discomfort. There was some sort of gap in the floor of the boot, so that whenever we bounced over a puddle or melted pool of snow, I was splashed in the shoulder and side of the face with filthy frozen water, and several times the engine just stopped altogether and the driver got out to shout at the contraption.

When at last we stopped for good, it was on a muddy path in the middle of a ploughed, blackened field. I was hauled out by a man dressed in grey, flat cap upon his brow, long, white scar across his right hand, and deposited by the steaming, smoking front of the vehicle.

I waited, as grey clouds rushed overhead and the carrion pecked over the last stems of winter grass. Then another car pulled up, protesting at every bounce and rattle, moving no faster than a walking pace, the driver cursing every inch. Albert was swathed in coat and scarf, a bowler hat on his head. He opened the door and stepped out into soggy ankle-deep mud, scowled, cursed the car again, tried to compose himself, and walked towards me.

I waited, shivering, watching, listening to his heart. His eyes tracked me as he walked round to my side, then stayed on mine as he stood before me. Then lowered for a moment, then came back to my face. Then he knelt down in front of me, and held out his right hand, palm up.

"Is he near?" he asked. "Is he coming?"

His hand floated before me, fingers open, slightly bent by their own construction. I found myself listing muscles of the hand, flexor pollicis brevis, opponens pollicis, but the distraction wasn't enough, and I nodded, peeling my lips back against my teeth.

He nodded too, flexed his hand towards me again, inviting.

I don't know why I took it.

His heart, my heart; the lines were thin as the shadows drew long.

He smiled, relief flickering like a candle when our skin touched, his fingers nearly as cold as the winter wind against my neck. He clasped my hand tight in his, looked away again, looked back.

"Am I good man?" he asked, and there were tears on the edge of his eyes, and he had grown old. "Did I do the right thing?"

"No," I replied, for that was the truth of his heart, and he already knew it, but needed it said out loud. "You did not."

He nodded again, and this time when he looked away, it took him a long time to look back. "What are we like?" he asked.

I tried to tell him. I tried to speak of hatred and cruelty, of self-important little men in our self-important little stories, from which we had created nothing but worlds of pain. Instead, all I could manage was "I love her." It seemed the only truth that mattered.

He nodded, said nothing.

"Please don't. Please don't. Albert – please don't. We can find another way."

"Did you find a cure? William? Did you find a cure for it?"

I shook my head.

"Then there's nothing else to be done." He pulled his hand from mine. I tried to hold on, and couldn't. He stood, awkward, creaking, thought about trying to brush the mud off his trousers, saw the futility of the motion. Nodded once at the man behind me, then, addressing the air above my head and nothing else, said, "You'll have an eight-hour head start. After that, the Nineteen will come for you. I can't hide it any longer than that. Thank you – for Richard. For trying to ... Thank you for the truth."

He walked away. I shuffled on the spot, craning to see him, and the man at my back gently held me down.

"Don't do this," I called. "Don't make me do this. Albert! Please, let her go and do whatever you want to me, please!"

He didn't look back, struggled with the heavy door of the car, folded into it awkwardly, unused to the shape of things, muttered as the engine struggled to start.

"I will come for you!" I snarled as it spluttered into life. "I swear I will come for you!"

He didn't look at me, focused on laboriously turning the car, which took far too long, and rattled away into the dark. I watched with the man with the gun until it was out of sight. Then the weapon was removed from my head, and the man cranked the handle of the car until it finally belched into submission, and after several false starts at a creaking turn, managed to point his vehicle the other way, and drove off into the midnight mist.

I stayed where I was until they were gone, then rose to my feet, and began to walk.

Chapter 76

Beneath the red Australian sun, the truth-speaker walks barefoot along the songlines, and talks to fire, and listens to the hissing of the serpent in the bush.

The woman who taught Margot how to curse is dead, her bones buried by the side of the land that was no longer hers.

Saira closed her eyes as the shadow came, and it dissolved before it could reach her, hands outstretched, failing at last with the final beating of her heart.

In the temples of Hunan, the priestess spears her tongue with a burning needle and calls on the spirits to bring her the knowing, and the people pay gold for good fortune, and comfort themselves with rice and meat when she tells them the truth, and quickly find a new way to interpret bad news.

The sangoma is shot in the savannah as she runs into the dark, because a black woman was seen stealing grain. All black women look the same, the white man says; maybe it was this one. Maybe another. She would have been a thief anyway.

On the operating table, Albert prepares to cut into the skull of the woman I love. He does it for his country. He does it for humanity. He does it for knowledge. He does it for truth. He does it so that one day he might know God.

He does it because, like the rest of us, he doesn't know how to do anything else any more.

I love her, I love her not.

Coman is buried in an unmarked grave.

Ritte has never cared much for friends.

And in a muddy field in England, I turned, and turned again, tasting the cold winter breeze, licking in the scent of a home I would never see again, and whispered, "I love her, I love her not, I love her, I love her not" until finally I found the point of the compass where the whispering was true.

I turned towards it, walking by moonlight, skirting the edge of the old wildwood where the badgers snuffled beneath frozen trees. I clambered through a foot of untouched snow, stumbled through the churchyard of cracked stone, beneath icicles hanging from the old wooden gate. I followed the railway tracks, letting the whisper become a chant – "I love her, I love her not, I love her, I love her not."

And finally, in the rising light of dawn, I saw him, heading towards me, dead ahead, shimmering tiny against the horizon. I nearly laughed to see him, my old friend, but the sound caught on the words that now rushed from my lips, unstoppable in their joy. "I love her, *I love her*!" I broke into a run, though he never changed his pace, reaching out for him, throat breaking in the frozen air, the sun a nail of white spilling at his back.

"I love her *I love her I love her* I LOVE HER I LOVE HER!"

Langa raised his hands to me as I ran to him, fingers outstretched, the fire still tumbling black from his broken flesh.

The tears spilt down my face as I reached out to greet him.

413

Chapter 77

Abbey was humming, a drifting, warbling note that he half held back with jaw clamped and mouth thin. It took me a moment to realise that his story was done, but that the truth was breaking up from within him, pushing and pressing against his soul, and that somewhere behind the noise were words that he could barely hold back.

I could hear my sisters running in the corridor, the thump of cannon too close, and rifles too, a snap-bang knocking against the night. Not night, I realised – not night. Just a day turned dark by the smoke tumbling across the window, a thick, greasy black that blotted out the sun. I looked at the professor, who was leaning over his son, pressing a hand to his sticky face, and I thought that maybe Charlwood – Richard – might not wake up, that he'd slept too deep, too long, and that the professor had come to watch his boy die.

Then Abbey blurted, because he had to speak, "She died instantly she died she died the shadow came and she died and Albert saw it too, he saw just for a moment the shadow rise from her chest and knew it was Langa, he knew it was Langa and he thought it was beautiful the most beautiful thing he'd ever seen God why would you forsake us why would you make these things teach us how to see how to learn what is our truth what is truth truth is all truth we look for truth for I hunted him I hunted him I wanted him to pay but he ran now he runs now he runs and hides hid in America for a while I looked for him there hid in Singapore I hunted him ran to India that's where the trail went dead but his son! Oh his son was so brave wanted to be a brave little soldier ran away to war stupid stupid boy I would have kept you safe I would have spared you stupid so stupid so proud so brave so stupid look where you are now and that's how I found him found his son found him just like Margot did . . . "

He stopped, sudden as he'd begun, gasping down the breath, pressing both hands over his lips, groaning, rocking, tears in his eyes. "Killed her killed her killed her loved her killed her he's here *he's here he's* . . . "

The professor lunged forward so sudden, I hadn't known he had it in him, flung himself round the bed and reached for the knife in Abbey's hand. I stood frozen a moment, not knowing what to do as the two men swayed and struggled, but it were over before I could make a choice, Abbey shoving the professor back hard enough that he tripped and fell, then diving for Richard's throat with the blade out.

I shouted something, maybe *stop*, tried to grab his hand, reached up with the morphine needle, and in the scuffle of hand and steel, found myself pressing it against Abbey's neck. He froze, eyes meeting mine, lips trembling in a tangle, and there we were, I wish you'd seen it, Matilda, the four of us, such a bleeding mess. I didn't know how we'd got here, didn't understand what I was doing, but maybe like the man had said, it were both the stupidest thing I'd ever done, and that I was most proud of.

"Not this not this please not this if you can see please not this," hissed Abbey, and it took me a moment to realise that he was speaking the truth of my heart, babbling out the terror of my soul that I were too busy to think on. Then his eyes darted to the professor and he hissed, "Not my son not my son not my son there's so much I did wrong so much I failed at not my son please mercy mercy mercy I'll do anything me instead not my son mercy — *where was your mercy!?*"

He screamed the question, screaming the only way he could get it out of his lungs, a blabbering, jabbered thing through the truth, and then was back again to his gallop, "Must get out leave the patients leave the patients must get out they were only going to die anyway they agreed to die I didn't agree to die oh God forgive me I thought when tested I would be someone else . . . "

I stared into his eyes, trying to fathom whose truth this was now, and at the moment the door clicked and began to open had it solved, because I was standing stiff to attention, needle hidden in my apron, and Abbey had spun to face the window, shaking with the effort of keeping still, knife turned away and pressed against his body.

Matron burst in, and the terror that Abbey muttered was hers, and looking at this scene she saw at once the professor on the floor and barked, "Sir, you need to leave now! Sister Ellis, the kitchen, immediately!"

"Yes, Matron."

She waited for us to obey, and when we didn't, for the first time in her life she didn't enforce her command. The earth shook and there was darkness at midday and Abbey whispered, forgive me, forgive me, forgive me, as Matron snapped, "Well – move!" and ran away before she could see her bidding done.

The door bounced back on its hinges as she scampered into the hall, the gunfire snapping now so near outside I thought I could feel the weight of the trigger on my own finger, feel the heaviness of it on my shoulder, feel the hearts of the men fighting they beat so close to mine.

I put the needle down, stood up straight by the soldier's bed. "I have to evacuate the patients now, Dr Abbey," I said, stiff as starch. "I am going to ask a sister to help me."

Abbey turned slowly back from the window, and looked me in the eye, and smiled. There were tears in his eyes. "Asked Saira, at the end went to her asked her do I love her do I love Margot and she said 'stupid man, stupid foolish man, I walked to keep you safe, you know I did that' and she said 'yes, yes you love her, you love her, you love her', I loved her even at the end but she loved the fire more well it's burning now, Margot, it's all burning down."

And his eyes went to the professor and he stammered, "Love my child love my child love my child we are all good men until we know the truths of ourselves God knows the truth I never believed in God but if there is no God how can we ever know the truth of anything at all except I love my child I love him I love him I love him."

Slammed his hands over his lips, swallowing down the sounds, a half-howl, an animal cry. For a moment I thought he might cut himself, attack the professor, the child, me, and I snapped, "Abbey! Look at me!"

He did. "Matilda I wish you could see me now I think you'd be proud of me so proud of me doing the right thing someone has to do the right thing I'm brave for you brave for you so much easier to be brave for you simple now simple so simple now see? See how easy love could be?"

The words tumbled and his tears fell, and he smiled at me, and though I don't know the truth of his heart, I think perhaps in that moment, he was grateful. I can't pick at why, I don't have a shadow that knows the truth, I don't follow the songlines or know the secrets of the widows' caves, but I do think he was grateful. Perhaps he were grateful cos in that moment, all I could think was how much I love you, Matilda. That was my truth. And it was simple. Finally, at the end, the simplest thing was true.

Then he turned to the professor, and raised his knife, point out towards the old man.

"Run," he said.

For a moment, I thought the professor wouldn't.

Abbey's lips shivered with the effort of speech, his whole body quivering like the forest beneath the shelling.

"Langa comes, the road is long, where is your mercy, Margot dead on the floor, so many children, where is your mercy, this is the only mercy I know – *run!*"

Sometimes we don't need a shadow to know the truth.

The professor looked at the doctor, and nodded, and turned, and ran.

Abbey swayed for a moment like a drunk man, then followed, shuffling like a shadow across the earth.

417

Chapter 78

The battle never broke through the walls of the Jardin du Pansee that day. The Germans made it across a trench, and overran the triage hospital, killing some, sparing some – there didn't seem any order to it, any reason, whether you lived or died just depended on what soldier found you, how bright the blood burnt in their eyes.

They came to within a mile of our walls, and the shelling hit the garden, blowing apart the bench where sometimes I'd sit with Sister Helene, and blasting out all the windows on the east side. Matron was gone, evacuated with three others what were just the three she found near her when she bolted. The rest of us stayed, not because we weren't scared, but because we were as scared of leaving as of going, and besides, the soldiers couldn't leave. They couldn't run away, and what kind of sisters were we if we left them to their fate? Life isn't much worth living when you can't live with yourself.

We dragged as many as we could from the windows, and the walking wounded from their beds, and piled them against the walls, thinking perhaps that might protect them when the shelling came. I don't know if it would have. Within an hour, the counter-attack was under way, French troops from the Algerian corps, what were usually set only to digging and burying the dead, running into the machine-gun lines in torn coats and ragged shoes. They kept on shooting until night came – real night – and then finally they stopped, to count the dead. Everyone was back in their trenches, Germans on one side, our lot on the other, some seven hundred dead in between. Matron reappeared as if she had never been gone, with new orders and a little speech about keeping our nerve, as all around us the world burnt down.

I didn't need no shadow to know the truth of Matron's heart, and didn't blame her for being human.

Of Dr Abbey, he were nowhere to be seen. Everyone assumed he'd just done a bunk.

But I heard later the story that I know was the truth, sure as I know any truths in this strange, spinning heart of mine.

I heard that at the very height of the fighting, as men cowered and blasted at each other through the trees, crawled on bellies through broken walls and cowered in the holes burnt by fire from the sky, two men were seen passing through the battle, as blind to it as if they had been hit by gas dropped from heaven.

The first man, old and dressed like a banker, far, far from his accounts and pen, scrambled and slithered through broken forest and over bloodied earth, now running, now gasping for breath; now stumbling into a creek where the dead were piled four deep, now crawling up untouched forest where still the blackbird hopped between the trees. A muddy, dishevelled shape, he paused sometimes to look back over his shoulder, as if fearful of the setting sun, and then ran on, and responded to neither German nor French, nor would he stop when the planes rattled overhead or the machine gun turned the spinning air to splinters.

And at his back, another figure moving through the smoke. He wore a doctor's coat, but those who saw him said he was more akin to the figure of death, striding ever onwards, eyes set only towards his prey. He did not run; he did not stop. He had learnt long ago how the chase was done. He never slowed, never looked back, and it was said that all who saw him felt a darkness pass over their hearts, and that he shouted out in German, English and French to all who met his eye, and called them brothers, fellow travellers, heart's kin, and knew their secrets, and forgave them all.

If you look down on the battlefield, you can see them now, I think, one running into the darkness, the other following. I do not know what will become of them; I do not know whether death is mercy, or love is easy, or vengeance is peace, or if all these things are lies, or truth, or if it is the truest thing of all to say that life is all of these, all of these truths together, in perfect contradiction, blinding us to a greater truth that lies beneath.

All I know is what I see.

Two men, running through battle, lost to any truth but their own, hunter and hunted, looking for a little mercy, a little knowing, as it has always been and will always be until the last fire burns away the hearts of men.

And behind them, the shadow.

extras

about the author

Claire North is a pseudonym for Catherine Webb, a Carnegie Medal-nominated author whose debut novel was written when she was just fourteen years old. She has fast established herself as one of the most powerful and imaginative voices in modern fiction. Her first book published under the Claire North pen name was *The First Fifteen Lives of Harry August*, which became a word-of-mouth bestseller and was shortlisted for the Arthur C. Clarke Award. The follow-up, *Touch*, was described by the *Independent* as "little short of a masterpiece". Her next novel, *The Sudden Appearance of Hope*, won the 2017 World Fantasy Award for Best Novel, and *The End of the Day* was shortlisted for the 2017 *Sunday Times*/PFD Young Writer of the Year Award. Her novel *84K* received widespread critical acclaim and was described by bestselling author Emily St John Mandel as "an eerily plausible dystopian masterpiece". She lives in London.

Find out more about Claire North and other Orbit authors by registering online for the free monthly newsletter at www.orbitbooks.net.

if you enjoyed

THE PURSUIT OF WILLIAM ABBEY

look out for

THE SISTERS OF THE WINTER WOOD

by

Rena Rossner

Every family has a secret ... and every secret tells a story.

In a remote village surrounded by forests on the border of Moldova and Ukraine, sisters Liba and Laya have been raised on the honeyed scent of their Mami's babka and the low rumble of their Tati's prayers. But when a troupe of mysterious men arrives, Laya falls under their spell — despite their mother's warning to be wary of strangers. And this is not the only danger lurking in the woods.

As dark forces close in on their small village, Liba and Laya discover a family secret passed down through generations. Faced with a magical heritage they never knew existed, the sisters realise the old fairy tales are true ... and could save them all.

1

Liba

If you want to know the history of a town, read the gravestones in its cemetery. That's what my Tati always says. Instead of praying in the synagogue like all the other men of our town, my father goes to the cemetery to pray. I like to go there with him every morning.

The oldest gravestone in our cemetery dates back to 1666. It's the grave I like to visit most. The names on the stone have long since been eroded by time. It is said in our *shtetl* that it marks the final resting place of a bride and a groom who died together on their wedding day. We don't know anything else about them, but we know that they were buried, arms embracing, in one grave. I like to put a stone on their grave when I go there, to make sure their souls stay down where they belong, and when I do, I say a prayer that I too will someday find a love like that.

That grave is the reason we know that there were Jews in Dubossary as far back as 1666. Mami always said that this town was founded in love and that's why my parents chose to live here. I think it means something else—that our town was founded in tragedy. The death of those young lovers has been a pall hanging over Dubossary since its inception. Death lives here. Death will always live here.

2

Laya

I see Liba going
to the cemetery with Tati.
I don't know
what she sees
in all those cold stones.
But I watch,
and wonder,
why he never takes me.

When we were little,
Liba and I went to
the Talmud Torah.
For Liba, the black letters
were like something
only she could decipher.
I never understood
what she searched for,
in those black
scratches of ink.
I would watch
the window,
study the forest
and the sky.

When we walked home,
Liba would watch the boys
come out of the *cheder*
down the road.
I know that when she looked
at Dovid, Lazer and Nachman,
she wondered
what was taught
behind the walls
the girls were not
allowed to enter.

After her Bat Mitzvah,
Tati taught her Torah.
He tried to teach me too,
when my turn came,
but all I felt was
distraction,
disinterest.
Chanoch l'naar al pi darko,
Tati would say,
teach every child
in his own way,
and sigh,
and get up
and open the door.
Gey, gezinte heit—
I accept that you're different, go.
And while I was grateful,
I always wondered
why he gave up
without a fight.

3

Liba

As I follow the large steps my father's boots make in the snow, I revel in the solitude. This is why I cherish our morning walks. They give me time to talk to Tati, but also time to think. "In silence you can hear God," Tati says to me as we walk. But I don't hear God in the silence—I hear myself. I come here to get away from the noises of the town and the chatter of the townsfolk. It's where I can be fully me.

"What does God sound like?" I ask him. When I walk with Tati, I feel like I'm supposed to think about important things, like prayer and faith.

"Sometimes the voice of God is referred to as a *bat kol*," he says.

I translate the Hebrew out loud: "The daughter of a voice? That doesn't make any sense."

He chuckles. "Some say that *bat kol* means an echo, but others say it means a hum or a reverberation, something you sense in the air that's caused by the motion of the universe—part of the human voice, but also part of every other sound in the world, even the sounds that our ears can't hear. It means that sometimes even the smallest voice can have a big opinion." He grins, and I know that he means me, his daughter; that my opinion matters. I wish it were true. Not everybody in our town sees things the way my father does. Most women and girls do not study Torah; they don't learn or ask questions like I do. For the most part, our voices don't matter. I know I'm lucky that Tati is my father.

Although I love Tati's stories and his answers, I wonder why a small voice is a daughter's voice. Sometimes I wish my voice could be loud—like a roar. But that is not a modest way to think. The older I get, the more immodest my thoughts become.

I feel my cheeks flush as my mind wanders to all the things I shouldn't be thinking about—what it would feel like to hold the hand of a man, what it might feel like to kiss someone, what it's like when you finally find the man you're meant to marry and you get to be alone together, in bed . . . I swallow and shake my head to clear my thoughts.

If I shared the fact that this is all I think about lately, Mami and Tati would say it means it's time for me to get married. But I'm not sure I want to get married yet. I want to marry for love, not convenience. These thoughts feel like sacrilege. I know that I will marry a man my father chooses. That's the way it's done in our town and among Tati's people. Mami and Tati married for love, and it has not been an easy path for them.

I take a deep breath and shake my head from all my thoughts. This morning, everything looks clean from the snow that fell last night and I imagine the icy frost coating the insides of my lungs and mind, making my thoughts white and pure. I love being outside in our forest more than anything at times like these, because the white feels like it hides all our flaws.

Perhaps that's why I often see Tati in the dark forest that surrounds our home praying to God or—as he would say—the *Ribbono Shel Oylam*, the Master of the Universe, by himself, eyes shut, arms outstretched to the sky. Maybe he comes out here to feel new again too.

Tati comes from the town of Kupel, a few days' walk from here. He came here and joined a small group of Chassidim in the town—the followers of the late Reb Mendele, who was a disciple of the great and holy Ba'al Shem Tov. There is a small *shtiebl* where the men pray, in what used to be the home of Urka the Coachman. It is said that the Ba'al Shem Tov himself used to sit under the tree in Urka's courtyard. The Chassidim here accepted my father with open arms, but nobody accepted my mother.

Sometimes I wonder if Reb Mendele and the Ba'al Shem Tov (*zichrono livracha*) were still with us, would the community treat Mami differently? Would they see how hard she tries to be a good Jew, and how wrong the other Jews in town are for not treating her with love and respect. It makes me angry how quickly rumors spread, that Mami's kitchen isn't kosher (it is!) just because she doesn't cover her hair like the other married Jewish women in our town.

That's why Tati built our home, sturdy and warm like he is, outside our town in the forest. It's what Mami wanted: not to be under constant scrutiny, and to have plenty of room to plant fruit trees and make honey and keep chickens and goats. We have a small barn with a cow and a goat, and a bee glade out back and an orchard that leads all the way down to the river. Tati works in town as a builder and a laborer in the fields. But he is also a scholar, worthy of the title Rebbe, though none of the men in town call him that.

Sometimes I think my father knows more than the other Chassidim in our town, even more than Rabbi Borowitz who leads our tiny *kehilla*, and the bare bones prayer *minyan* of ten men that Tati sometimes helps complete. There are many things my father likes to keep secret, like his morning dips in the Dniester River that I never see, but know about, his prayer at the graveside of Reb Mendele, and our library. Our walls are covered in holy books—his *sforim*, and I often fall asleep to the sound of him reading from the Talmud, the Midrash, and the many mystical books of the Chassidim. The stories he reads sound like fairy tales to me, about magical places like Babel and Jerusalem.

In these places, there are scholarly men. Father would be respected there, a king among men. And there are learned boys of marriageable age—the kind of boys Tati would like me to marry someday. In my daydreams, they line up at the door, waiting to get a glimpse of me—the learned, pious daughter of the Rebbe. And my Tati would only pick the wisest and kindest for me.

I shake my head. In my heart of hearts, that's not really what I want. When Laya and I sleep in our loft, I look out the skylight above our heads and pretend that someone will someday find his way to our cabin, climb up onto the roof, and look in from above. He will see me and fall instantly in love.

Because lately I feel like time is running out. The older I get, the harder it will be to find someone. And when I think about that, I wonder why Tati insists that Laya and I wait until we are at least eighteen.

I would ask Mami, but she isn't a scholar like Tati, and she doesn't like to talk about these things. She worries about what people say and how they see us. It makes her angry, but she wrings dough instead of her hands. Tati says her hands are baker's hands, that she makes magic with dough. Mami can make something out of nothing. She makes cheese and gathers honey; she mixes bits of bark and roots and leaves for tea. She bakes the tastiest *challahs* and cakes, *rugelach* and *mandelbrot*, but it's her *babka* she's famous for. She sells her baked goods in town.

When she's not in the kitchen, Mami likes to go out through the skylight above our bed and onto the little deck on our roof to soak up the sun. Laya likes to sit up there with her. From the roof, you can see down to the village and the forest all around. I wonder if it's not just the sun that Mami seeks up there. While Tati's head is always in a book, Mami's eyes are always looking at the sky. Laya says she dreams of somewhere other than here. Somewhere far away, like America.

4

Laya

I always thought
that if I worshipped God,
dressed modestly,
and walked in His path,
that nothing bad
would happen
to my family.
We would find
our path to Zion,
our own piece of heaven
on the banks
of the Dniester River.

But now that I'm fifteen
I see what a life
of pious devotion
has brought Mami,
who converted
to our faith—
disapproval.
The life we lead
out here is a life apart.

I wish I could go to Onyshkivtsi.
Mami always tells me stories
about her town
and Saint Anna of the Swans
who lived there.

Saint Anna
didn't walk with God—
she knew she wasn't made
for perfection;
she never tried
to fit a pattern
that didn't fit her.
She didn't waste her time
trying to smooth herself
into something
she wasn't.
She was powerful
because she forged
her own path.

The Christians
in Onyshkivtsi
built a shrine
to honor her.
The shrine marks a spring
whose temperature
is forty-three degrees
all year,
rain or shine.
Even in the snow.

It is said
that it was once home
to hundreds of swans.
Righteous Anna used to
feed and care for them.
But Mami says the swans
don't go there anymore.

There is rot
in the old growth—
the Kodari forest
senses these things.
I sense things too.
The rot in our community.
Sometimes it's not enough
to be good,
if you treat others
with disdain.
Sometimes there's nothing
you can do
but fly away,
like Anna did.

5

Liba

When we get back from our morning walk, Mami is in the kitchen making breakfast and starting the doughs for the day. Tati shakes the snow off his boots as he walks in. "*Gut morgen*," he says gruffly as he pecks a kiss on Mami's cheek. She pins her white-gold hair up and says, "*Dubroho ranku*. Liba, close the door quickly—you're letting all the cold in."

I let the hood of my coat drop down. "Where's Laya?"

"Getting some eggs from the coop," Mami sings. She and Laya love mornings, not like me, but I'd wake up early every morning if it meant I got time alone with Tati.

I shrug my coat off and hang it on a hook by the door as Mami pours tea at the table. "*Nu?* Come in, warm up," she says to me.

I shake the chill off and start braiding my hair, which is the color of river rocks. Long and thick. I can't pin it up at all. "Your hair is beautiful like moonstone, *dochka*," Mami says. "Leave it down."

"More like oil on fur," I say, because it's sleek and shiny and I never feel like I can tame it. It will never be white and light like hers and Laya's.

"Do you want me to braid it for you?" Mami asks.

I shake my head.

"Come here, my *zaftig* one," Tati says. "Your hair is fine; leave it be."

I cringe: I don't like it when he calls me plump, even though it's a term of endearment, and anyway, I know what comes next. Laya walks in and he says, "Oh, the *shayna meidel* has decided to join us." The pretty one. I concentrate on braiding my hair.

Laya grins. "*Gut morgen.* How was your walk?" She looks at me.

I shrug my shoulders and finish braiding my hair, then sit at the table and lift a cup of tea to my mouth. "*Baruch atah Adonai eloheinu melech haolam, shehakol nih'ye bidvaro—Blessed are you, Lord our God, king of the universe, by whose word all things came to be.*" I make sure to say every word of the blessing with meaning.

"*Oymen!*" Tati says with a smile.

Instead of trying to be something I will never be, I do everything I can to be a good Jew.

6

Laya

When I was outside
gathering eggs,
I searched the sky,
hoping to see something—
anything.
One night I heard
feathers rustling
and turned around
and looked up—
a swan had landed
on our rooftop.
It was watching me.
I didn't breathe
the whole time
it was there.
Until it spread
its wings
and took off
into the sky.

Every night I pray
that it will happen again
because if I ever see
another swan,

I won't hold my breath—
I will open the window
and go outside.

That's why I rake my gaze
over every flake of bark
and every teardrop leaf,
hoping. I see that
every finger-branch
is reaching for something.
I am reaching too.
Up up up.

At night I feel
the weight
of the house
upon my chest.
It's warm
and safe inside,
but the wooden planks
above my head
are nothing like
the dark boughs
of the forest.
Sometimes I wish
I could sleep outside.
The Kodari is
the only place
I feel truly at home.

But this morning
I'm restless

and that usually means
something is about to change.
That's what the forest
teaches you—
change can come
in the blink of an eye—
the fall of one spark
can mean total destruction.

There is a fever
that burns in me.
It prickles every pore.
I'm not happy with
the simple life we lead.
A life ruled
by prayer and holy days,
times for dusk and dawn,
the sacred and the profane.
A life of devotion,
Tati would say.
*The glory
of a king's daughter
is within.*

But I long for what is
just outside my window.
Far beyond
the reaches of the Dniester,
and the boundaries
of our small *shtetl*.

It hurts,
this thing I feel,
how unsettled
I've become.
I want to fit
in this home,
in this town.
To be the daughter
that Tati wants me to be.
To be more
like Liba.
Prayer comes
so easily to her.

Mami understands
what I feel
but I also think
it scares her.
She is always sending me
outside, and I'm grateful
but I also wonder
why she doesn't
teach me how to bake,
or how to pray.
It's almost like she knows
that one day
I will leave her.

Sometimes I wish
she'd teach me
how to stay.

I close my eyes
and take deep breaths.
It helps me
resist the urge
to scratch my back.
I want to crawl out
of this skin I wear
when these thoughts come
and threaten to overwhelm
the little peace I have,
staring at the sky,
praying in my own way
for something else.

Something is definitely
inside me.
It is not glory,
or devotion.
It is something
that wants to burst free.

Help us make the next generation of readers

We – both author and publisher – hope you enjoyed this book.
We believe that you can become a reader at any time in your life,
but we'd love your help to give the next generation a head start.

Did you know that 9% of children don't have a book of their
own in their home, rising to 12% in disadvantaged families*?
We'd like to try to change that by asking you to consider the role
you could play in helping to build readers of the future.

We'd love you to think of sharing, borrowing, reading, buying or talking
about a book with a child in your life and spreading the love of reading.
We want to make sure the next generation continue to have access
to books, wherever they come from.

And if you would like to consider donating to charities that help
fund literacy projects, find out more at www.literacytrust.org.uk
and www.booktrust.org.uk.

Thank you.

hachette
CHILDREN'S GROUP

little, brown
BOOK GROUP

*As reported by the National Literacy Trust